THE ANTS OF GOD

THE ANTS OF GOD

W. T. TYLER

Copyright © 1981 by W. T. Tyler

ISBN: 978-1-4976-9715-7

Distributed by Open Road Distribution
345 Hudson Street
New York, NY 10014
www.openroadmedia.com

To my daughter, Ann

THE ANTS OF GOD

ONE

1

It was nearly three o'clock in the afternoon when the train reached Awash station in the fierce African heat. The plain was white with dust. In the distance a few antelope and gazelle grazed on the dun-colored grass growing along the volcanic rock that littered the ballast bed. The steel rails shone like knives in the sunlight and bisected the plain as straight and true as a plumb line. In the distance lumps of rose and purple mountains lifted their peaks through the shimmering heat to the east. Behind the train to the west lay the sheer brown face of the Ethiopian escarpment, towering to eight thousand feet along the serpentine track the train had just descended. Its facets and fault lines were already cracked with evening shadow as the sun fell from its zenith.

McDermott looked out the train window and saw only the sky and the animals. The sky was like scalded milk—a pale blue without clouds beyond the high haze. The animals were sluggish and undernourished.

"Do you know the Yemen?" asked a small Frenchwoman with bobbed hair as she shared his coach window to watch a camel caravan leave a dusty village at the foot of the escarpment. In the coach every seat except the one beside him was occupied by middle-aged French tourists on their way to Harar, Djibouti, and the Yemen. Some carried overcoats; others, scarves and sweaters. Their faces, like hers, were as gray as boiled pork from the Parisian winter they'd just fled.

McDermott told her he'd been to the Yemen several years ago. It was her recognition that he was somehow identified with the waste-

3

land the tourists were watching through the dusty coach windows that had drawn her attention, just as it was the face itself that had finally provoked her question. His face was burned by the sun, and his arms were even darker. He was wearing a short-sleeved khaki shirt and khaki trousers, like an agronome or *ingénieur*. She knew he was an American. His hair was dark and short, the brown eyes sympathetic without being intrusive. The smile came easily.

She took a picture through the coach window, rewound her camera, and said she'd wanted to visit the Yemen since her student days in Paris decades earlier. Then she brought an old French guidebook from her shoulder bag across the aisle and showed it to him.

"I think San'a has not changed very much in all these years, isn't that true?" she asked.

"I think so," McDermott said.

"You are going to San'a?"

"To Djibouti."

Looking at the rocky plain afterward, McDermott thought of the Yemen. The monotony of the wheels recalled a bit of drunken doggerel an Irish aviation mechanic once sang at the military mess in Oman during the Friday night dart games. He'd forgotten the Irishman's name, but he had worked in the Yemen for a UN survey team. McDermott remembered something about *rose mountains* and *suqs dark and narrow*. He sat studying the mountains to the east, and finally the Irishman's drunken voice came into his mind and he remembered the first lines of the refrain:

> *In Yemen's rose mountains*
> *Among mossy fountains*
> *I met a young maiden*
> *Samira Rah'man*

That was all McDermott could remember. The French tourists were already on their feet, and he watched through the train window as the coaches drifted noisily to a stop at Awash station. He followed them down the steps and across the blinding glare to the railroad restaurant. The concrete block walls were overgrown with green vines and shaded by a few tabid ash and laurel trees powdered with white dust. The restaurant beyond was cool, shadowed with green sunlight. The concrete floor had been doused with water and swept down in preparation for the train's arrival. Under the high asbestos roof on open trusses were a dozen tables spread with red checkered tablecloths where a few Ethiopian and half-caste waiters were bringing dishes. The French tourists were served a common bill of fare.

McDermott resisted the waiter who attempted to seat him with the Frenchmen and sat alone against the back wall. When the waiter brought the spaghetti and salad, he ate without relish, returned the warm bottle of beer to the tray, and ordered a bottle of mineral water instead. After he'd finished, he smoked a cigarette, picked up his briefcase, and went back out into the hot sunlight. The train from Dire Dawa to the west had arrived on the far track, an hour late, and the hungry passengers hurried across the railbed to the restaurant. McDermott moved down the tracks and away from the black vendors hawking their wares near the empty coaches.

"*Well, I'm goddamned fed up with it,*" complained a young American voice from nearby. "I'm just goddamned tired of it and so's everyone else. You've had your way so long we don't know what the fuck we're doing anymore. We don't care about the frigging ocean. We've already got our tickets back to Addis, even if you haven't. So we just don't wanna hear any more about that saltwater shit—"

"Why don't you go fry your head," said a long-legged blond girl. She wore faded blue jeans, open leather sandals, and a blue tennis shirt. "You can change your tickets like I did."

"The hell with that noise!" another young girl cried. "We're not changing anything! If you don't dig it, then buzz off."

Six young Americans in blue jeans, denim, and tie-dyed shirts were squatting in the shadows of the restaurant wall, their backpacks, guitar cases, and sleeping bags at their feet. They were arguing with the blond girl standing in the sunlight. Her face was turned away, her eyes fastened to the distant mountains that showed as pale as smoke through the glare to the east.

"I'll tell you how stupid it is," a bearded young man continued, getting to his feet. "I'll tell you, only you don't wanna listen. Ask someone else then. Hey, mister!" he called.

McDermott stopped and looked back. "Are you talking to me?"

"Yeah, if you don't mind." The blond girl was still looking toward the mountains. "Is that train going straight to Djibouti tonight or Dire Dawa?" asked the bearded young American.

"Dire Dawa," McDermott said. "You have to transfer at Dire Dawa to get to Djibouti." The blond girl turned and looked at him angrily. He went on anyway: "There's an overnight sleeper to Djibouti at eight. Sometimes it makes it; sometimes it doesn't."

"That's what I figured," said the youth. "Thanks." He turned to the girl. "You heard what the man said. I told you that train wouldn't get us there tonight. It'll miss the frigging connection, and we'll be stuck again. Tomorrow night we could be in Nairobi, not another goddamned fleabag hole like this one."

The blond girl picked up her backpack and shouldered it. Another young man said, "If you're gonna split, then like do it, and stop all the time rapping about it. You've had your way too long, that's your problem. We'd be in Nairobi right now except you had to go see Rimbaud's house."

"Yeah," a dark-haired girl joined in from the shadows of the wall. "Only we never got there. Now it's the crummy Indian Ocean, and we'll never get there either."

McDermott walked along the track away from the train. The heat breathed against his face like the gases from a furnace. Plumes of white dust lifted into the windless sky behind two Land-Rovers moving across the open plain away from Awash station. Hawks stirred on the warm currents of rising air south of the escarpment; below them soared a few black buzzards. Behind him on the track Ethiopian village women hawked their wares to the passengers in the second-and third-class coaches, selling oranges and bananas through the open windows.

The French tourists returned to their seats in the first-class car. McDermott was the last to board. Sitting in his seat next to the window was the blond American girl who'd been arguing with her friends outside. On the seat next to her was the nylon backpack. He lifted the pack to the overhead rack and sat down. The girl was looking through the sun-glazed window, watching her friends boarding the other train westbound for Addis Ababa. The train slipped forward and gained speed as it moved out across the open plain. She didn't look back.

McDermott sat beside her, swaying silently with the idle drift of the coach over the uneven ballast bed. A few miles beyond, she put her head down and pulled a handkerchief from her pocket. He saw her wipe her eyes and knew that she'd been crying. He sat uncomfortably in his seat and finally reached forward and brought a copy of *Aviation Age* from the briefcase at his feet.

As the sun dropped to the west, the scrubland beyond the windows began to reclaim its color from the bleaching of the midday sun— browns, sables, and roses appeared where only an alkaline ash had been. Camel trains plodded through the dry wadis and sent curtains of dust aloft, as sheer as silk. Wild pig and dik-dik galloped from the scrub as the train rocketed across the iron trestles and sent thunder echoing up the dry streambeds. Baboons loped away from the commotion, disappearing across the shoulders of the gorges, or climbed higher in the trees to stare back, vexed, at the speeding iron.

At the solitary stations along the track black vendors jostled beneath the windows with their lifted wares. The dirt streets otherwise were silent and empty. A few Arab, Greek, or Italian shops were visible, their doors open to the afternoon sun, their interiors in shadow. On the foot-worn earth banks near the tracks, Galla and Afar nomads in rough chammas stained sable-brown by the wind of the desert studied the coaches silently, arms draped across the barrels and stocks of the old British and Italian muskets they carried like sticks across their shoulders.

The American girl called for two oranges through the coach window from a barefooted young girl who was blind in one eye. She leaned from the window to summon the girl from the rear, gesturing to the older women to make way for her. As the young Ethiopian girl lifted her face into the sunlight to hand up the oranges, her bad eye gleamed like a boiled egg under her smooth forehead.

The blond girl peeled the oranges as the train slid forward. Both were rotten under the soft, greenish skin.

"That little bastard," she said. "No wonder she was shoved to the back."

She threw both oranges out the window, stepped over McDermott's feet, and went forward to the washroom. When she returned, her face and hands were clean, and she'd combed the snarls from her lank blond hair. But her clothes were no fresher, and as McDermott lifted his magazine to let her pass, he caught the odor of stale laundry and dried perspiration now mixed with the pomade from the liquid-soap dispenser in the washroom.

She sat back in her seat, lit a cigarette with a sigh, and looked out the window, like an ingénue who'd just given a stage cue. McDermott ignored her, and she sighed again. A few minutes later she'd grown tired of waiting. "Don't you speak any language known to man, or what," she complained. "What's your problem, anyway?"

McDermott put down his magazine. Her forehead was broad, her eyebrows darker than her blond hair, which had been bleached in flaxen streaks by the African sun, and her face was attractive. But he thought she knew that. Her mouth was wide, the upper lip a little petulant, like a woman accustomed to having her own way and ready to pout her way to victory when she didn't. "Nothing I can think of," he said, looking at the bold green eyes that were confronting him coolly. "What's yours?"

"You don't think very fast then. Like maybe it takes you a couple of months to make up your mind. If you're on this train, you gotta have problems, man. No one in his right mind would be out here in the middle of Turkeyville flats if he didn't. Unless you're one of the misfit types—macho and all that shit."

McDermott couldn't think of anything to say. She slumped deeper in her seat, as if she'd already written him off and was now waiting for him to tell her why she shouldn't. "*God*," she sighed theatrically as he lifted the magazine again, her knees thrust against the seat in front of her. "You've got problems all right."

"What kind of problems?" He put the magazine back in his briefcase.

"Alienation. What else? Like watching people and not even trying to communicate. What's the matter—afraid you'd get involved or something?"

"Some people like to be left alone."

"Sure—like when you're dead, man. You're not dead—you're not even a tourist, like the rest of these grunts. No camera, no guidebook—none of that Disneyland shit. How come you're so far out of place?"

"Maybe I got on the wrong train."

She laughed. "Maybe we all got on the wrong train," she said, but when McDermott smiled, she resented it. "Maybe it's not so funny either, being on the wrong train. Is that the way you put people down, laughing like that?" She leaned forward to scratch her ankle, but McDermott thought the effort as phony as her sigh a few minutes earlier. "It's not so funny when you think about it. What's your problem, anyway? You still haven't told me. Ashamed I'm an American, and maybe you'll have to give me mouth-to-mouth resuscitation in front of all these Frenchy schoolteachers or something? What are you going to Djibouti for?"

McDermott thought about it. "Business," he said.

"That figures." She dropped her eyes to the briefcase, and looked back up at him, her head still back. "Sure. Business. With a big-deal briefcase and a barbershop head, what else could it be? What are you—a government guy or something?"

"No—"

"What kind of business?"

"The airplane business."

"No kidding. You mean a travel agent type? What'd you do—get this geriatric weenie roast together to come look at the wild animals? Is that how you bring in the bread—hauling around a planeful of old dudes that are too weepy-eyed to tell a cow from a camel?"

"Not quite."

"So what are you going to Djibouti for?"

"I'm a pilot and I'm going to Djibouti to pick up a plane."

"A jock! Why didn't you say so. *Good God.*" She rolled her eyes and sat back. "I shoulda known. I knew it had to be something like that—something a little weird, a little out of date. No one's a pilot anymore, man. You're either an astronaut or a hang-glider freak.

There's no in-between, it's all dead space." Her head was back against the seat as she studied the short trim above his ears and the back of his neck. "Is that what keeps you in the barber chair for so long—afraid long hair'll goof up the headphones, like in the World War Two movies?"

"Maybe that's it."

Beyond the window the light was changing. The villages were fewer, their mud and adobe walls glowing in the fading light. The dust sent up by the herds of cattle were mists of boiling brass; the acacia and thorn trees were dwarfed by their shadows. The dust was in the golden air outside and in the coach itself—on damp cheeks, necks, arms; on parched lips and in dry throats. The passengers sat among the lengthening shadows of the coach like spectators in a darkening theater, watching the proscenium awaken.

"That must be pretty neat," she resumed absentmindedly after a long silence. Her voice was far away. "Going where you wanna go. Just picking up your feet and going. No problems, no hassle. Is that the way it is?" She turned.

"Sometimes." In her momentary lack of self-consciousness Mc-Dermott had discovered another girl sitting there beside him.

"Like, you can go to Nairobi or Cairo anytime you feel like it?" In her lifted eyes he found her age for the first time—twenty or twenty-one, but still just a schoolgirl.

"Sometimes."

"Who do you fly for?"

"Myself sometimes. Other people other times."

"What kind of people?"

"I used to fly for the Desert Locust Service."

"In Ethiopia?"

"Ethiopia. Saudi Arabia. The Yemen once."

"You like Ethiopia?"

"I like the flying."

"You could fly someplace else if it were just the flying, couldn't you?" His nod told her what she wanted to know, and she put her head back against the seat, looking out the window again. "I think this country is gross. I don't mind the villages and the boonies. The people are okay, but it's the government that gets me down. It's rotten. The poverty is what gets to you. It's like Calcutta, and I've never even been there. Lepers, beggars, people living like goats back in Addis. Now I'm going to go swim in the Indian Ocean and wash it out of my mind. All of it. I'm from California. If I can't swim in the ocean when I want to, I get freaked out. Anyway, that's where I'm going." She touched the glass of the window. "Those guys hassling me at Awash were from all over. Landlocked types. St. Louis, Ann Arbor. Rye, New York, preppies. Maybe that's why they've got problems. Academic drudges, locked up in their skulls. I'll bet a couple of them don't even know how to swim either. Big talkers, that's all. . . ." Her voice wound down.

"You're in college?"

She roused herself. "I finished last year. No—wait a sec. Two years ago. It doesn't seem that long, which is why I forget. I went to Cal at Berkeley. Now it's like I'm on my way to nowhere. Do you know where that is?"

"I think so," McDermott said. "It's halfway between East Chicago and Gary, Indiana."

She laughed. "That's just Endsville, straight-up. Nowhere is the Santa Fe yards in Oakland at three o'clock in the morning." She stood up and tried to pull her backpack from the overhead rack, but couldn't move it. McDermott stood and lifted it down for her. She settled it on her knees, untied a side pocket, and withdrew a cotton tobacco pouch. She slid the backpack to the floor and began to roll a cigarette. Her hands were slim and well shaped, but her fingernails were dirty and discolored. The underside of her arms was marbled with dirt.

McDermott stood up again. "Thirsty?"

She looked up in surprise. "Sure. Are you?"

At the back of the coach was a refreshment bar and opposite it a blue leather lounge seat where two Ethiopian train employees were sitting and drinking beer. A thin Ethiopian woman in a blue smock sold stale sandwiches, Coca-Cola, and beer across the linoleum counter. She was small, bony, and brown-skinned, with a child's small hands, and

11

eyes as black as bitter coffee. The two Ethiopian men were teasing her in Amharic. They sometimes drew a smile from her lips but, to the French tourists she served, her face was as lifeless as a sack of sorghum.

McDermott and the blond girl stood at the counter, drinking beer and swaying with the motion of the coach. One of the Ethiopian men said something to the woman, who looked at the American girl, clicked her tongue disapprovingly, and replied in Amharic. Following her eyes, McDermott discovered the reason for her complaint. The girl wasn't wearing a brassiere under her blue tennis shirt.

"Why don't we get some air," he suggested, and they went out through the rear door and stood on the platform between coaches, leaning over the half-door of the vestibule, watching the scrubland sweep past. The sun was down and the air had grown cooler.

"*Flying beats the train*," she shouted above the roar of the wheels, her hair flying across her face. McDermott couldn't understand her, and she brought her head closer: "I said it beats the train—flying, I mean." McDermott nodded, and she laughed. "*Smile*," she shouted above the iron clatter of the undercarriage.

McDermott thought she looked happy, but he felt sorry for her. A few minutes ago he had felt her despondency and isolation as acutely as his own. He studied the rim of mountains to the west where the sun had disappeared. She nudged him and he held her beer bottle as she lit another cigarette. It was misshapen and loosely packed—marijuana. As she touched the match to it, her head turned back into the vestibule; the twisted end flared like old newspaper before the tobacco took the flame.

"Where are you going after Djibouti?" she asked.

"Addis probably," he said.

"And after that?"

"Someplace else."

She seemed pleased. She leaned out into the windstream, her blond hair blowing as she hung out over the half door, her eyes narrowed to slits by the sand-laden wind, but still she was smiling.

When they reached Dire Dawa the station platform was crowded with scurrying passengers, policemen, taxi drivers, Ethiopian soldiers, and tattered urchins cadging coins. The smell of boiled coffee mixed with the fragrance of woodsmoke and the metallic fumes from the old diesel trucks waiting along the freight dock. The train was an hour late. On a second track at the far end of the platform the Djibouti train was waiting. The conductors hurried the Djibouti-bound passengers from the incoming train toward the already crowded coaches.

The windows were open. Ethiopian and Somali families sat inside on the hard wooden benches, carrying pasteboard boxes, baskets of fruit and vegetables, tin Thermos bottles, and fiber milk jugs. The aisles were piled with suitcases, wooden lockers, and squalling children. Two bearded French priests in dirty white soutanes sat huddled, reading French paperbacks in the anemic yellow light, oblivious to the tumult about them.

"God, I don't even have my Djibouti ticket," the girl remembered in panic halfway down the platform. "They told me at Awash I'd have to buy it here." She thrust her backpack to McDermott. "I'll just be a sec. Don't let them leave, okay?" She ran back along the platform toward the ticket windows.

McDermott climbed aboard the coach behind the engine and found his compartment at the front of the car. At one window was a leather-covered chaise longue which converted into a bed; at the window opposite was a small reading chair. The compartment was paneled, like a nineteenth-century smoking car, in dark mahogany. At the rear was a private WC with a brass plate on the door: *toilette*. He put his bags on the carpeted floor, lowered the window, and looked out over the crowd, searching for the girl. He waited until he felt the train lurch under his feet, and went out into the aisle, looking for the porter. The coach contained four other compartments, but they were all second class. All were occupied. In the last cabin the door was open and two worried Ethiopian businessmen in suits and ties were sitting together on a lower bunk, talking conspiratorially, the way Ethiopians do among strangers. The stranger was a fat Italian who sat on the top bunk opposite, pulling off his trousers. Under the trousers he wore a pair of striped pajama bottoms. "*Ecco!*" he called to McDermott, pointing to the unoccupied lower bunk beneath. "*Ça va?*"

Still searching for the conductor, McDermott climbed down the steps as the train began to inch forward.

"*Hey. Hey wait!*"

He heard her voice before he found her running figure, dodging through the crowd, and followed by a dozen barefooted street urchins, all excited by the chase, all screaming *Baksheesh, baksheesh!* at the top of their lungs. She sprinted forward and sprang aboard just as the coach left the platform. She slumped against the iron bulkhead, still holding on to the handbar, her face damp, her shoulders heaving. "Jesus, I thought I was a goner," she gasped.

The station lights vanished and they were suddenly back in the darkness of the scrubland again.

The French conductor took her ticket, looked at it dubiously, then leaned forward under the coach lamp to read it again. He studied her face disapprovingly, but then shrugged and pushed open the cabin door to his right: "*Deuxième classe, mademoiselle.*"

The fat Italian trader was stretched out on the top bunk in his striped pajamas, reading an Italian newspaper as he chewed the meat sandwich in which it had been wrapped. The two Ethiopians were still in conversation on the bottom bunk opposite, but they too were now in pajamas.

"Are you kidding?" she protested immediately, looking at the empty bunk and then at the conductor. "Forget it, man." She turned to McDermott: "Is this guy for real? You mean he expects me to sack out under that rhinoceros? What in? My hard hat and combat boots! Come on, tell him he's gotta do better than that! What about the other cabins." She went out into the aisle and knocked at the door of the next cabin.

"Occupied," the conductor said. "All occupied." He took off his hat and wiped his damp, plump face. Without the hat he suddenly looked weak and irresolute.

"Can't I swap around or something? Isn't there someone I can trade with? What are they, vestal virgins or something?" She knocked at the door again.

"*Ce n'est pas possible,*" the conductor muttered, putting his cap back on. "*Pas possible.*" He tore her ticket in two, returned half of it, and went back the passageway.

"A lotta help you are!" she yelled after him.

"Maybe we can work something out," McDermott said.

"I can sleep in the aisle, can't I?"

"Maybe you won't have to. Come on." She followed him down the passageway to his compartment. "If we can't work something out, you can stay here. I can take your second-class bunk."

"You mean this is all yours? All this? This whole compartment? It's half the train."

"It's first class—the only way you can get any sleep on this train."

"No one has to take any bunk down the hall. There's enough room for both of us." She found her backpack, and began untying her sleeping bag, kneeling on the carpet under the window. "Who needs a bunk anyway? Who wants a crummy broom closet when the Hilton is next door? This is groovy, man. At least we've got privacy. If I'd known about this, I wouldn't have had to screw around buying that stupid ticket, would I?"

"I don't think so."

"What's wrong?" She lifted her head. "I'm not crowding you, am I?"

"No, there's plenty of room." He saw the sudden look in her eyes, the sudden vulnerability in her face.

"What's the trouble then? Something's bugging you. I can tell."

"I just remembered there's no snack bar on the train," he said, hanging up his two-suiter. "I forgot to get some beer in Dire Dawa."

In the lights of the compartment McDermott couldn't see the desert they were crossing, so he turned off the cabin lights and lay back on the bunk, looking out at the ghostly landscape illuminated by the crust of moon above the western mountains. The room was partially lit by the WC as the door banged open and shut, open and shut in the gentle rocking motion of the coach. It had grown chilly, the room colder as they crossed the wasteland. He thought she'd fallen asleep on her sleeping bag, her head against her nylon backpack. But finally she stirred again and pulled on her denim jacket, sitting up to look out the window. "You're not sleeping, are you?" she called.

"Not yet."

"You know what?"

"What?" he asked.

"I don't even know your name."

"It's McDermott. What's yours?"

"Penny. Penny Palmer." She waited for his reaction, and when he didn't say anything, she said: "That's a pretty shitty name, don't you think?"

"Penny? It's an easy name," he answered sleepily, his head back against the cushion.

"It's a little trite, don't you think? I'd use Penelope, like my mother, only guys would think I'm trying to hide from my past or maybe challenging peer-group pressures. Penny's so insipid it isn't even funny. Even in high school the kids would say 'You'd better stop screwing around; here comes Penny Palmer.' In the second grade they even made up a song: *'Penny Palmer, teacher's pet. Tells Miz Stone when your pants are wet.'* What can you do about names, anyway?"

"Get used to them."

"Yeah, but McDermott's not a bad name to get used to. What's your first name?"

"Scott."

"Sure. That's easy too. But a crummy name saddles you with a lifestyle, too, don't you think? When I was a freshman at Cal, I finally beat the rap. *'Penny Palmer, she's okay. Makes out, flakes out, balls all day.'* Only that was worse. God, was I sensitive. Did you ever feel that way about your name? I'll bet you didn't."

Her face was hidden in the shadows. He'd been flying for two days in western Ethiopia before he'd caught the train from Addis that morning. He fell asleep.

He awoke at the frontier and sat up as she shook his shoulder.

The overhead lights were on.

"Someone's trying to knock the door down," she whispered. "Jesus, I thought you'd taken a sleeping pill or something. Who do you think it is?"

"It's the frontier," he said, getting stiffly to his feet. His mouth was dry and rusty. There was no drinking water on the train and he remembered again the beer he'd forgotten to bring. "Where's your passport?"

"Passport?" She looked at him blankly. "I dunno." The knocking came louder.

"When did you last have it?"

"In Addis, but that was a week ago."

"What about the visa for Djibouti?"

"They said they'd take care of it—some Peace Corps creeps we met there. They said they'd get it. God, I didn't even look."

"Why don't you see if you can find it."

She rummaged through her backpack, and McDermott opened the compartment door. By the time the three Ethiopian soldiers had finished looking at McDermott's papers, she'd found the passport. The Ethiopians wore heavy military overcoats, olive-drab helmet liners, and dusty combat boots. Two carried carbines. McDermott took her passport, found the Ethiopian and Djibouti visas, and passed the passport to the corporal.

"What about the ott-pay?" she asked suddenly. "What about the ass-gray."

"The what?"

"You know," she whispered, her head turned away from the soldiers. "The *ottpay. Ott-pay*, man. What are you, a functional illiterate or something? Don't you know pig Latin? The *grass*."

"These guys don't know grass from Uncle Ben's alfalfa."

"Excuse me?" the Ethiopian corporal said.

"She was wondering about the customs fee," McDermott said. He followed the three Ethiopian soldiers to the end of the corridor where the customs officer was stamping passports. When he returned, Penny took back her passport and slumped down on her sleeping bag.

"Jesus. I was scared shitless. All I could think of was the pot and getting thrown off this crummy train. It's a wilderness out there, man. It's nowhere." She looked out the window at the cold desert under the moonlight. When she turned, McDermott had taken a nylon jacket from his two-suiter and was pulling it on. "Where are you going?"

"To see if I can get something to drink."

"And leave me here." She scrambled to her feet and pulled her denim jacket over her shoulders, but McDermott was already out the door. She ran down the corridor after him. "Hey, wait for me! *Hey, McDermott!*" He was already on the ballast bed, and she jumped after him, nearly falling over a switchman's lantern. McDermott caught her arm and steadied her. "You sure don't waste time, do you? Where are we going?"

"I won't know until I get there," McDermott said.

They went past the single light in front of the adobe frontier post and back a narrow rutted road that divided the miserable cluster of mud houses and huts. There were no lights. It was cold in the mud road. McDermott led her deeper into the darkness, searching for the flicker of an oil lamp or a kerosene lantern that marked an open shop. The road smelled of cattle and camel dung. A few white shapes lay along the verges of the road in front of the mud buildings—nomads wrapped in thin cotton sheets, sleeping with their heads into the wind. "Do you know where we're going yet?" she whispered at his elbow.

"I think so."

"You've been here before?"

"A year ago."

"You better do more than think so. This is the *Planet of the Apes*, man—it's nowhere." She was afraid that the train would leave without them. She stopped, searching the darkness behind her, but couldn't see the coach lights. "You miss a connection and *zap*—you're back in the tenth century again. Who needs it?" She discovered herself alone when she turned: "*Hey.* Where are you?"

He was standing in the darkness ahead of her, looking into the doorway of a mud hut where a light flickered. The low doorway was half-covered with a strip of cloth. A small flame glimmered in a bowl of oil on the mud floor. A few Somali cattle buyers sat on stools among bags of charcoal, unsalted hides, pots of rancid butter and oil. They were smoking and drinking glasses of sweet tea. An old Galla woman found four bottles of warm Ethiopian beer among the crates stacked behind the counter. Penny stood behind McDermott, looking at the men squatting on the stools, unable to make out their faces. "Don't you think it's gonna leave?" she whispered as the old woman was slow to make change. "Didn't you hear the wheels creaking or something?"

"Americans," a voice spoke from the shadows. A few figures stirred.

"Yeah, thirsty Americans," McDermott said easily without turning. He took the dirty bills from the old woman, turned and looked at the cattle buyers, and said something in Arabic. A few of the old men grunted in recognition. One laughed as they left.

"What'd you say that for?" Penny asked in the street outside. "Did you see the knives in their belts? God, they could have zapped us. Do you know what an American passport is worth these days? Why didn't you say we were Swedish. That's neutral territory, man. The US isn't these days, not with all the PLO freaks running around Africa."

"Maybe I don't speak Swedish."

"Maybe they don't either."

"Are you always as logical as you sound?"

"Who's being logical? If I were logical, I'd be in bed in San Francisco. I just want to get my ass back on that train."

The wind blew dust and chaff in their faces as they walked back. Ghostly clumps of rootless grass and thorn rolled across the road like wagonless wheels, vanishing into the wasteland.

"I guess you're pretty used to wandering around alone," she said after they'd returned to the compartment. The train began to move forward.

"Sometimes."

"Did you ever come here with the Locust Service?"

He opened a bottle of warm beer and gave it to her. "There's nothing here the locusts want."

"You can say that again." She sank back against her sleeping bag. "What's here anyone wants?" She watched him uncap the second beer bottle and stretch out on the bunk. "Take you, for example. What's in it for you?"

"I like the flying."

The train lurched to a stop again at the French customs post. The French officials who came aboard were accompanied by Legionnaires. After they'd inspected the first- and second-class car, they moved back through the third-class coaches. Penny brought out her tobacco pouch and rolled a cigarette as she watched them through the open door of the compartment. The Legionnaires searched for contraband

and *kat* among the rolls of bedding, the vegetable baskets, and the rope-bound suitcases. The green switches of *kat* were thrown out the open windows where they were collected by other Legionnaires. Occasionally a passenger was ejected, too, most often a woman or young girl. They were herded aboard army trucks waiting by the roadside to be driven back to the Ethiopian frontier.

"Hey, they're throwing people off the train," Penny discovered. "They're just kicking them off. No crap. How come?"

McDermott looked out the window. "Prostitutes."

"Prostitutes! Out here? Are you kidding?"

"Djibouti's an army town."

"I think I'll take a look." She got to her feet and pulled on her jacket.

She didn't return until the train had started to move again. "You're right—prostitutes. They just dumped them in the truck like old laundry and took off." She opened another bottle of beer and handed it to him.

"No thanks."

"C'mon. You're not pissed or anything, are you?"

He took the beer and turned on his side. "About what?"

"I dunno. About my crowding you, maybe. Everything's worked out okay, hasn't it?"

"Sure. Don't you ever relax?"

"I'm relaxed. Only you always look like you're deep into something, something heavy."

"I was thinking."

"About what?" When he didn't answer, she said: "C'mon. What were you thinking about? Don't be so mysterious."

"I was thinking about a drunken Irish aviation mechanic I used to know. He used to sing a crazy song about the Yemen, and now I can't remember it."

She opened the last bottle of beer and sank down on the sleeping bag. "How come you wanna remember it?"

"I don't. I just can't stop trying."

"How about a joint then. That'll help you remember. Either that or help you forget trying." He looked at the tobacco pouch she'd taken from her pocket.

"No thanks."

She rolled the cigarette carefully. "What's the trouble? You hung up on health foods or something?"

"No."

"Trying to keep your body pure?" She lit the cigarette.

He watched the smoke drift away from her face. "Habit, maybe. Maybe just discipline. I don't need it, that's all."

"No kidding." She smiled. "What kind of discipline? The Los Angeles cops?"

"Like any discipline. First there's the beer, then the whiskey, then something else." He settled the pillow under his head. "Anyway, I'm not twenty-one anymore. I'm too old to start."

"Is that right." She sat against the bulkhead, still smiling.

"That's right. You get all those goofballs inside, and pretty soon you don't do anything but sit. Not move, not think, not fly. Just sit."

"No kidding—just sit. Are you serious?"

"Sure I'm serious."

She took the cigarette from her mouth. "Sometimes you really are a jarhead. When I get a headful, I fly. As much as you, I'll bet. That's what it's all about. Like the hang-glider guys, like surfing, like going with the wind. Like what you do, I bet. So what's wrong with that. I go where it takes me. At least I'm not polluting the atmosphere when I fly. You do. You take maybe a thousand gallons of gas to get your lift. I can go on the lint in my pockets, so why knock it? It's not hurting anybody."

"You're not flying at all," McDermott said. "You're just polluting your own skull. You're sitting on your ditty bag on a train that's maybe doing thirty knots not counting what it loses on the curves. You may think you're flying but you're not. Even if any foreign substances make you think you are."

She laughed in surprise. "*Foreign substances!* Are you kidding? What's foreign about this? That's the whole point. This is me, man." She stripped off her jeans jacket and stood up, still laughing. She kicked off her sandals and swayed slowly with the motion of the coach. "Foreign substances!" She drifted around the compartment, her eyes half-closed, swaying from side to side. The desert passed beyond the window—gray anvils of rock, salt pan, clumps of thorn, honeycombed lava beds; and inside, under the compartment lights, she moved to her own music, oblivious to it all.

She finally collapsed across the foot of the bunk where McDermott lay, holding out the damp, pinched butt of the cigarette.

"Try it," she urged. "Go ahead. Take a drag. Get your bio in gear. Try something new. It's not gonna bite you." She lay across his shins, her nose and temples damp with perspiration.

"No thanks."

She brushed the strands of hair from her forehead. "You're pretty weird. You really are." She lifted herself and turned back across the room, dropping morosely to her sleeping bag, knees first, before she sprawled forward, facedown, her head turned away from him.

She didn't move. After a while McDermott turned off the overhead light. Stretched out on the bunk, he watched the landscape sweep past. He got up finally and went into the bathroom, washed his hands and face, brushed his teeth, and went back to the bed. She hadn't moved. He took off his shoes, pulled off his shirt, and put on a gray sweat shirt. He lay back against the pillow. Ten minutes passed before he heard her stir. She went into the washroom and looked back at him from the door. She turned on the overhead lights suddenly, and McDermott sat up, blinking painfully. "*God!* Aren't you even gonna put your striped pajamas on, like your greaser friend down the hall?" she jeered. Then she snapped off the light and slammed the WC door behind her. She was gone a long time. She finally left the washroom and stood in the open door, the light behind her limning her silhouette. "Hey, McDermott."

"Hey yourself." She was wearing a long-sleeved cotton shirt that reached her thighs, and her legs and feet were bare. Silhouetted against the light, the body within the cotton shift was as lovely and graceful as he knew it would be.

"I was wondering if you wanted to sleep with me or anything," she said tonelessly. "I thought I'd ask now and maybe save some grief later. Some guys ask; some don't. I don't wanna get scared shitless in the middle of the night when funny hands start grab-assing. They may not be yours, you know."

"How do you feel about it?" McDermott asked. He knew he wasn't being propositioned. He was conscious of the desert rolling past the window, her body in the door, the pale patches of moonlight lying across the bunk, and the artificiality of their predicament. He knew he'd like to sleep with her, but there was nothing between them but a common destination, and to pretend that there was seemed beyond his own ingenuity. Maybe it was his pride. He was too old to lie to her and too honest to tell her she meant anything to him. And even if he weren't, she was too sly to be convinced, and too young to pretend.

"It doesn't make much difference to me one way or the other," she said halfheartedly, a reply McDermott thought honest enough. "I'm kinda tired, though, and I've got a headache."

"Why don't we just forget it then," he said. Her tone had convinced him. She turned off the WC light and he lay uneasily in the darkness, wondering if he'd reached the age where desire had given way to pride, self-respect, and the fear of failure—the ultimate pretenses of his approaching middle years. Ten minutes later he heard her rouse herself and drag the sleeping bag across the floor. She unrolled it next to the bunk, and he heard the zipper being closed, followed by her voice:

"Hey, McDermott." Her hand groped along the side of the bunk, her ring rattling along the wood. Her fingers brushed his arm and just as quickly went away. Had his hand found hers, he knew what would follow, but now it was too late. "Okay," she sighed, reassured, snuggling back into her sleeping bag again. "I just wanted to see if you were there. People disappear, you know."

He didn't go to sleep right away, remembering other nights, other opportunities—some missed, some not. She lay within reach of his arm, but then he heard the sound of her breathing, as rhythmic and steady as the sound of the wheels under him. The moment had been lost to him. Had his self-respect grown, his pride prospered? No. He wanted her even more. What were the compensations for opportunities missed, revelations passed in the night, time moving past him? There were none. He could see the moon through the window. It painted the rectangle of pane silver and the cold desert lying under the stars. He could see the heavens, the nearer constellations: Venus, the Great Bear. The coach wound through the scrubland and he drifted toward sleep, listening to the wheels and looking at the stars. And then the forgotten words came into his mind, unbidden, and he remembered the drunken refrain:

> In Yemen's rose mountains
> Among mossy fountains
> I met a young maiden—
> > Samira Rah'man;
> She drove a small burro
> Through suqs dark and narrow
> Singing 'Cloves and sweet almonds—
> > Alo a long dong'

He had remembered the words, but their recollection brought another mystery, as stubborn as the first. He didn't know what had made him remember them.

2

McDermott awoke to the crash of iron couplings as the train moved into Djibouti in the early morning. Penny was sitting on the floor next to the window, his open briefcase on the carpet beside her, reading a leather-covered flight manual. Nearby were aerial navigation maps of Ethiopia, Kenya, and the Sudan.

"I guess you're a pilot all right," she said as he sat up. "I was kinda checking you out. You hear so much B.S. on the road you don't know who to believe." Her hair was damp, as if she'd just washed it. The compartment smelled of shampoo and herbal soap. The wet cords framed her slim face and fell down across her shoulders and back. She was wearing a clean blue T-shirt and jeans. Soapy water lay over the floor of the WC. "I couldn't sleep," she told him as he washed his face at the basin. "Didn't you hear all of that racket in the next coach? Two Ethiopian broads were fighting tooth and nail. One had a knife. God, there was blood all over the place."

"Is that right," McDermott said, eyes shut, searching for a towel. There weren't any. They were all on the floor, soaking up the spilled water. After less than twenty-four hours in her company he knew her talent for exaggeration. If she'd seen as much blood as she wanted him to believe, she'd have been in the sack with him, yelling her head off.

They found a taxi outside the train station and drove into the city. The laurel trees shading the boulevards were motionless in the morning heat. Except for a few schoolchildren on their way to the French *lycée*, the streets were deserted. Between the white buildings, they could see the ocean, gray and torpid in the distance. Even the sunny square in front of the old hotel was empty and listless. A few Somali taxi drivers were washing down their dusty vehicles with sponges dipped from buckets of dirty water. The first dry wind of the morning stirred through the etiolate growth of Indian laurel trees along the square. The shadowy arches of the Moorish arcades were empty, the iron shop shutters still closed.

"This place is dead, man," Penny complained. McDermott reminded her that it was only seven o'clock in the morning. On the pavement in front of the hotel a young Somali was mopping the sidewalk. Two dark-skinned busboys in white jackets were moving tables and chairs onto the pavement of the sidewalk cafe next to the hotel. An old Frenchman in walking shorts and white knee hose sat alone at a table, reading a newspaper and drinking coffee. Penny lifted her backpack from the trunk of the taxi to the curb. "Maybe some of the kids are around somewhere," she mused, looking around without enthusiasm.

"Sure," McDermott said. He paid the driver. "You'll find something."

"They're probably flaked out on the beach already," she muttered disconsolately. "Where is it, anyway? Hey, where's the beach?" she asked the Somali taxi driver.

"Beach?" He smiled and held open the rear door. "Come, we go."

"Yeah, I'll bet," she said mistrustfully. She looked back at the hotel, at the empty square, and the bright sky overhead. McDermott picked up his briefcase and slung his two-suiter over his shoulder.

"Hey, are you in a hurry or something?"

"I've got a few things to do, that's all."

"Is this where you're gonna stay?" She looked up at the old hotel, painted in pale lemon. The windows on the second and third floors were concealed by heavy wooden shutters. Flowers grew in wooden boxes on the small wrought-iron balconies in front of the windows.

"Until tomorrow."

"You don't screw around, do you." She put her backpack down again, looking back out over the square. "Jesus. This is *Djibouti?*"

"Don't you know anyone here?"

"Who would I know?"

"Maybe there's a hostel someplace—a youth hostel."

"Yeah, and maybe there's a YWCA and fat women in sneakers playing volleyball. Who needs it?"

"You'll find something," McDermott said.

"Yeah? Where?"

"I thought you were used to traveling alone."

"Who's alone!" she protested. "That's a bummer—being alone. There was always a bunch of us before, not this solo crap. It sucks. Who wants to spend all the time worrying about being alone." A few of the taxi drivers were watching her as they washed their cars. Some were smiling. "Look, don't you have time for a swim? Just a quick skinny-dip or something? I mean you're so freaked out on being clean under the skin, being free and all. Being in the ocean is free. It's like flying. No foreign substances. That's as free as you can get—"

"I don't have time."

"Don't you wanna swim in the Indian Ocean, for God's sake? I mean here we've come all this way, through all that moonrock and lava and stuff, just to swim in the Indian Ocean. Can't you feel that? There it is—right over there—and here we are! Try something new for once, can't you! I mean you've got to pull up your socks, McDermott. What are you, some kinda weirdo J. Alfred Prufrock or something, just walking around on the beach all day singing mermaid songs to yourself and not even getting your toes wet?"

"That's not the Indian Ocean," said McDermott. He didn't know who J. Alfred Prufrock was, but from the sound of the name and the derisive edge to her voice, he thought he must have been some college professor who'd called her down in front of three hundred other Berkeley freshmen when she'd smarted off once too often.

"Are you kidding! Not the Indian Ocean? You're putting me on!"

"That's the Bay of Tadjoura," McDermott said. "The Indian Ocean begins to the south of here."

"The south? *The south!* Oh, Christ, why didn't you say so!" She wiped her damp face across her sleeve, picked up her backpack, and moved despondently across the sidewalk, collapsing in one of the chairs in front of the restaurant. "Now I'm really screwed up. I really am." McDermott thought she was going to cry. "I thought I had it all together. I really did. Everything was together and now you come along and mess it all up. God, McDermott—you've fouled up my homing gear. You've screwed up my karma. I'm fogged in, man. I'm a wasted bird."

"You sure are, kid," McDermott said sympathetically. "Maybe we could talk about it, but I've got things to do."

"And I'm wasting your time, is that it?"

"You'll be okay. You can find some kids your own age and you'll get untracked again. Try the beach."

"I'm not a kid," she said coolly. "I'm twenty-three."

"Then pick up your chin and act like it."

She pushed her hair away from her face. "Okay, then. Let's go swimming. I want very much to go swimming, okay? I don't care whether it's the Bay of Tadjoura or the Bay of Bengal. I don't care if it's full of tin cans, crabs, crocodiles, or condoms. I haven't had a bath for a week. I'm sweaty, crappy, kinky, frazzled, and freaked out. Satisfied? But I still wanna go swimming." Her face was cool again, her hair completely dry and even lighter in the morning sunlight.

"Is that all you want—just a bath?"

"I want to go swimming in the ocean. Not just a bath. Jesus, you're about the most prosaic guy I ever met. A psychic bath, if it's all the same to you. I thought you were a pilot. I thought you knew about those things."

"I've got things to do. Maybe later, but not now."

"*Now!*" she insisted, her green eyes suddenly alive in her slim face.

27

"Now. Not this afternoon, and not tomorrow. Tomorrow may never happen. Now."

McDermott recognized the determination in her face. He picked up his briefcase. "Go ahead then, kid," he said. "Don't let me stop you. It's all there, yours for the asking."

He went across the pavement and into the hotel lobby. His room was on the second floor, cool, high-ceilinged, with an old rotary fan above the bed. He opened the inner shutters and turned off the air-conditioning unit. Thin strokes of sunlight fell across the tile floor. He pushed open the outside shutters and stepped out onto a small, wrought-iron balcony, its scrolled filigree corrupted by a hide of ugly yellow paint.

He took a warm shower and was standing at the washbowl, his face covered with shaving lather, when a knock came at the door. He thought it was the bellboy, bringing the coffee and croissant he had ordered, but it wasn't. It was Penny. She leaned in the doorway, her backpack at her feet. She didn't look up at him, but was looking down at her sandal instead, lifting it off and on with her toes.

"It's not such a hot idea after all," she said. "So maybe you're right. Maybe later's better. Anyway, it's no big deal. We can go later." She tossed her head, moving her hair down her back again, and looked up at him. Her eyes were still cool. "What are you doing, anyway?"

"Shaving."

"No kidding. I thought maybe you were having breakfast. What is it, banana cream pie?" She touched his jaw with her finger, and brought it to her lips. "Hmmm. Peppermint meringue. Aren't you gonna ask me in?"

"Come on in." She followed him into the bedroom and dumped her backpack on the floor next to the bed.

"One thing I like about you, McDermott, is that you're always so enthusiastic. How'd you get to be a pilot, anyway—a couple of Episcopal aunts push you out of the choir loft to see if your little wings could fly?"

"It was a barn roof."

"I should have figured. You all alone?"

"I haven't looked under the bed," he said. "I haven't looked in the closet either. Go ahead. Maybe you'll find some of your bushy-haired friends in there." He went back into the bathroom and began to shave again. She leaned against the door, watching him.

"You know, sometimes it's hard to figure out whether you're serious or not. Sometimes I think you're just trying to put people down."

"Fat chance," he said. When the bellboy came with the breakfast tray, she met him at the door, and carried the tray to the table near the bed. He heard her lifting the covers from the warming dishes, and then her voice:

"Hey, you only ordered two rolls. Is that enough? Hey, wow. Coffee."

"Help yourself." She reappeared in the doorway and put a cup on the shelf above the washbasin.

"I'll bet you never figured on maid service, did you?" She broke the croissant in two and held out a piece. "Go ahead, take a bite."

"I'm shaving."

"So what?" She put the piece in her mouth. "I used to know a guy at Cal who chewed cookies while he shaved. He was kinda skinny, and he said it helped him shave. Oreos and Fig Newtons. That was his breakfast. He was always about three hours late to his classes. That was at Cal my junior year."

McDermott scraped his jaw with the razor. "Was he your roommate at Cal or just a sorority brother?"

"*Fun-ny*. Don't be so hostile. Are you mad or something?"

"I'm shaving."

"You still haven't answered my question, which is the only reason I'm not flaked out on the beach right now. It'd be okay if we went swimming after you finished your business, wouldn't it? I mean you're not gonna be all day, are you? Couldn't we go later?"

"Sure."

"You're not uptight about last night, are you? My sacking out like that. I had a headache—"

"No."

"God, you are opaque sometimes." He wiped his face on the towel.

"Do you always get your own way?" he asked as he went past her into the bedroom.

She followed him. "Are you kidding? Get my own way? If I always got my own way I'd be someplace else, doing something, not hung up in a dump town like this one, waiting for things to happen. I'd be swimming, surfing . . . sailing maybe. Do you know how long it's been since I've been swimming in the ocean? Do you? If you did, you wouldn't worry about this rinky-dink appointment you've got, or whatever big deal it is you're cooking up. We'd be at the beach, not this crummy, two-bit hotel room." She collapsed full length across the bed, bounced twice, and lay sprawled across the counterpane.

"You think it's a dump?" He rubbed his head with a towel.

"Sure I think it's a dump, don't you?" She moved her head from the pillow to watch him, one eye hidden. "It's just the way I feel. It is," she repeated stubbornly when he didn't reply. "Don't personalize. It doesn't have anything to do with you." She shut her eyes. "It's just this town, this place. It's like a dead end, almost."

McDermott looked at her silent figure. His was an average face, without any striking features; the overall impression it conveyed was determination. The nose was straight, the jaw firm, the eyes distant without being cool. It was an interesting face, but McDermott knew it had no attraction for wandering college girls, confused groupies, alienated debutantes, or suburban housewives in overpowered station wagons. If he wasn't vain, he was stubborn and proud. He thought Penny was trying to take advantage of him—his plane, his pilot license, or maybe his freedom. He wasn't sure which.

She turned on the bed to watch as he brushed his short, dark hair at the dresser mirror. He used two silver-backed military brushes, one in each hand, moved with the same short, vigorous strokes he'd developed as a crew-cut Air Force officer years earlier. Penny was intrigued. She sat up. "I guess you have to brush it a lot, don't you?" she asked. "I mean the way it stays in place like that."

"It helps."

She continued to watch. "Why don't you get some barber to razor in a part—you know, with a straight razor. Like the black guys used to do before all this Afro jazz. That'd be cool. That way you wouldn't have all that fuss. Doesn't it hurt your scalp?"

"Why don't you mind your own business for a while," McDermott told her, putting the silver brushes away.

She collapsed back against the pillow. "*God!* I was just trying to be helpful. Do you resent advice or something? I thought everything was okay, and now you're hacked off again. Do you want me to split? If you do, just say so." She stared at the ceiling, waiting, her eyes open.

"I'm not hacked off about anything," McDermott said. "I've just got things on my mind, that's all."

It was the sort of oblique concession that six years of married life had taught him—the clash of strong wills with clumsy weapons on murky issues, ending neither in victory nor defeat, but in withdrawal: a retreat to professional solitude on McDermott's part; some silent assertion of superior taste on the part of his ex-wife. The larger problem went unresolved. She was the daughter of an Omaha dental surgeon; McDermott was an Air Force pilot. She was well educated, self-indulged, with ambitions appropriate to the wives of those station wagon squires of suburban Omaha, but not to McDermott. Until he met her, McDermott's Air Force flying career was all that mattered to him. Once married, he was willing to compromise, but not surrender. She wanted him, but she also wanted the comforts and surety of the suburban life in the Midwest. She remained with him for six years, accompanying him to Air Force bases in Europe, England, and Japan, a prisoner of the PX economy she despised, of overheated government quarters, officers' club cuisine, and the patronization of generals' and colonels' wives she thought her inferiors, if not social imposters. It ended on a snowy holiday evening in Omaha during their annual leave when she told him he would have to choose between the Air Force or her. She wouldn't return to England with him. They'd been to a Junior League Christmas dance that night. It was three o'clock in the morning and snowing outside. She not only confronted him with the choice, but described what she expected of him if he were to leave the Air Force. She'd spoken to her uncle about a position in his brokerage firm, and the uncle had been agreeable. McDermott said he might give up the Air Force, but not for the Omaha bond business, selling securities to her relatives and friends. She filed for a divorce two days later. There were no children.

When McDermott returned alone to the American air base in England a week later, he recognized his mistake in taking her back to her family in Omaha for the holidays. It was midmorning as he climbed the steps to the base apartment where they'd lived for six months. He was usually flying at this hour. The drafty halls were full of squalling children, the smell of wet diapers and frying bacon. Pregnant women in rubber boots and plastic hair curlers were dragging in tubs of damp laundry from the January mud outside. *No wonder*, McDermott thought, and moved to the base BOQ the same day. The divorce was completed the following March.

"Don't think I'm trying to change your life-style," Penny announced as McDermott pulled on his shirt, "because I'm not. I mean it was just a suggestion, that's all."

In the hot Djibouti sunlight outside the hotel that morning McDermott had recognized the same stubbornness he'd known in his wife, if not a half-dozen women remembered and then forgotten along the way. Although he'd beaten Penny then by simply ignoring her, the victory had proved no more decisive than the other odd battles he'd won during those earlier campaigns.

"What about swimming," she continued, rolling over on her side. "You don't resent that now, too, do you?"

"Swimming's fine. Sure, we can go swimming."

"Thank God." He went into the bathroom, and she sat up, peeling off her T-shirt, slumped bare-breasted on the side of the bed. "What time will you be back?" she called.

"About three."

"I think I'll sack out then, okay? Maybe take a shower, and then take a nap. I've still got a headache."

He brought out his dop kit and gave it to her. "There's some aspirin in there."

She covered her chest with her shirt. "Thanks. Where are you going anyway?"

"To the airport to look at a plane."

"Flying?"

"Probably." He picked up his briefcase and opened the door.

"How come you didn't tell me?" she moaned. "That's not fair."

"How come you didn't ask?" he said. "Think about that for a while."

3

The plane was a twin-engined Beechcraft with two 550-horsepower Pratt & Whitney turboprop engines. It was painted a dull gray, like the sandpaper skin of a mako shark, standing silent and squat under the hangar roof at the edge of the airfield. Beyond the open doors the sea shimmered in the distance; dhows and *sanjoks* under full sail dipped in the swell of the bay. McDermott circled the plane, carrying the maintenance record in an aluminum binder, followed by the mechanic and the plane's former pilot, both Frenchmen. The pilot's name was Bouchet; he was small and dark, with mossy sideburns and black hair, wearing a pair of chrome-rimmed sunglasses. He'd flown the plane up from Madagascar a week earlier, where it had been used to provision a French oil company drilling off the East African coast. The mechanic was older, wearing loose coveralls and a straw hat whose brim was cut away so that nothing remained but the sweat-stained crown, which fitted his gray hair like a skullcap.

They spoke in French, but McDermott's French was frugal, almost monosyllabic. Like most military men who'd learned a foreign language long after his mental habits had been established, it was a social intrusion, as awkward as a finger bowl. But silence was also natural for McDermott. He could lock himself in a cockpit for hours without feeling the compulsion to utter a single word, could stand at a cocktail party or sit at a dinner table without advancing the conversation by a single syllable, and not show the slightest uneasiness in his silence. When he flew a night interceptor out of a NATO base in Germany, his squadron leader wrote in his fitness report that McDermott was the most uncommunicative man he'd ever met. An Air Force psychiatrist working on a space medicine study concluded after three hours of clinical conversation that McDermott was probably antisocial. His ex-wife thought him merely socially awkward, the consequence of a deprived childhood spent in a Methodist orphanage in western Pennsylvania while she herself, at thirteen, was already entertaining her peers at afternoon tea dances at the Omaha Country Club. A middle-aged English pilot with whom McDermott had flown following the locust swarms out of Saudi Arabia and across the Red Sea thought him unusually taciturn, especially for an American, but a marvelously keen pilot. In a letter of recommendation he'd prepared for the American oil firm in the Persian Gulf that subsequently hired McDermott, he wrote, "*He is simply the best bloody pilot I have ever flown with, war and peace together; and why in God's name he is flying out here in this howling waste of dry-sucked thorn, sand, fleas, flies, and raging fever simply defies my besotted faculties.*"

As they circled the Beechcraft that morning, McDermott occasionally asked the mechanic a question. When he hesitated over a few of the French technical terms, Bouchet translated. "*Ça va?*" he would ask McDermott, following one of the mechanic's interminable explanations in French, and McDermott would nod. The nod was sufficient, for French or anything else, and McDermott wasn't one to suggest by the reflex of a few French words that he understood more than he did. This was important. Whatever the opacities of his personal life, McDermott was a scrupulously honest man. He lived within his own intellectual capital, and he lived modestly, never presuming that there was more to his life than he understood. His existence depended upon preserving that balance. Words, ideas, or attitudes that implied that he knew more than he understood might one day prove his downfall. Those who claimed to understand fluid mechanics, celestial navigation, or center-of-gravity computations in an overloaded aircraft might be secure in their own ignorance, but dangerous to McDermott. Fate would pluck them from the cockpit and smash them against the earth as indifferently as a farmer plucks a grub from a stalk. So, like many pilots, McDermott had a healthy respect for his own ignorance, skepticism about the infallibility of belief, and contempt for those taught by the more manipulative trades that survival could be prolonged by concealing their ignorance from others or from themselves.

Politicians made these mistakes McDermott thought, so did lawyers, bureaucrats, Air Force intelligence analysts, geopolitical gurus, weapons salesmen, and dollar-a-word journalists. So did college kids in unwashed denims sitting in candlelit coffeehouses, plucking guitars as they sang of the misery and sorrow down on the bayou or out in the California lettuce fields where they'd never done a day's work in their lives.

"*Ça va?*" Bouchet asked.

McDermott shook his head.

"No. *Encore une fois.*"

The mechanic began again, this time more slowly.

A little before noon Mr. Picot appeared. He was the manager of the French maintenance firm that had serviced the aircraft—a gray, secretive little man with thinning hair and eyes as restless as a fox. He wore white walking shorts and white hose on his thin, bandy legs. He'd been awaiting word that McDermott had taken delivery of the plane, and had driven impatiently to the hangar when the word hadn't come. He found his chief mechanic squatting with McDermott under the starboard engine, probing a balky fuel line. The French pilot had disappeared. Picot was irritated because further delay would cost him money. He was an accountant and looked at the world as a function of his ledger figures. Individual character meant less to him than the fixed sums of national or racial behavior: blacks were stupid and lazy; Arabs were sly and treacherous; Americans were a superficial people, a race in headlong pursuit of the dollar, belonging to no certain past, and speeding toward a chaotic future, perhaps carrying the West with them. Picot expected an American pilot to be locked in the Beechcraft cockpit by now, and six thousand feet above the Bay of Tadjoura. But watching McDermott's face peering up into the engine, Picot knew that there was nothing he could do or say to deflect the man's attention from the plane. His mind was fastened to the machine the way the aluminum panels were riveted to the airframe, and Picot knew, too, that he would have to pay for the additional maintenance repairs. But McDermott's insistence upon technical perfection also increased Picot's suspicions.

The Beechcraft's new owner was an East African trading company with headquarters in Tel Aviv. The firm's local agent had told Picot that McDermott had leased the plane to fly hides and skins from the firm's concessions on the Omo River in Ethiopia to processing plants in Addis and Nairobi. McDermott had also signed a contract for certain charter services for the UN.

Picot was no fool. He knew that hides and skins were no more transported by air than salt or coal was. The agent was lying to him.

Among the French Legionnaires at Djibouti were a few Belgian, German, and Spanish mercenaries who were veterans of the Congo rebellions and who still gossiped of hidden diamond mines in the Kivu and Oriental, of plundered treasuries, and rusty strongboxes filled with gemstones which they might one day claim from the caches deep in the interior. They talked, too, of how some of the stones had already been found, and of how the illegal traffic trickled into Uganda, the Sudan, and Ethiopia from the Congo, where they were purchased by the buyers from the diamond cutting and polishing factories of Israel. But the same monotony of life that makes Legionnaires of bored grocery clerks and hod carriers of the metropoles also infects the dreariness of tropical barracks life. Legionnaires who spend their days on irksome work details live out at night the same fantasies that once promised to deliver them from their European imprisonment, transforming mica-rich streams slumbering beneath a tropical rain forest into rivers of bullion; transmuting abandoned copper mines into silver or gemstone shafts; and painting fly-blown village whores with sores on their buttocks as virgin black princesses opening their thighs on beds of ostrich feathers to appetites as frustrated as their own.

Picot knew. He had been told of the Tel Aviv firm's involvement in the illegal diamond trade by a Greek trader who owned an appliance store in Djibouti. The afternoon the two men had talked of it, they were standing at the rear of the Greek's shop, leaning against a repair counter piled with broken compressors and electric motors. At the back of the bench were a few soft drink bottles; some were lying on their side, the drops of sugary syrup they'd spilled still fresh on the counter top. A trail of ants had discovered the syrup. The column of bright brown bodies led across the counter top, up the concrete wall, and out into the sunshine. Picot had expressed doubts about the

Greek's story. As restless as he was in his own boredom, he couldn't believe that diamonds from the Congo could find their way into the Sudan and Ethiopia across thousands of miles of jungle and savannah. The Greek shrugged his shoulders at Picot's indolent skepticism. It was a torrid day, too hot for argument or superfluous words. Then the Greek saw the column of ants. "*Comme ça*," he said, nodding toward the ants: "Just like that."

Picot followed his eyes, puzzled at first, but then reassured as he saw in that tireless, unending trail of insects the undeniable corroboration of all he'd been told. He saw above the spikes and spears of elephant grass an infinite column of African bushmen, pygmies, Bantus, Hottentots, Nilotes, and Nubians padding silently through the tropical forests of the Congo and out across the lush green valleys of Uganda and into the grasslands of the Sudan, carrying upon their ignorant, frazzled, kinky heads the plundered treasure of the Congo's gold and diamonds.

He believed that McDermott would be flying illicit diamonds and gold out of Sudan and Ethiopia, bankrolled by the Jewish diamond cutters of Tel Aviv.

It was after three o'clock when McDermott taxied the Beechcraft away from the hangar. The mechanic watched from the open door with Picot, following the shark-colored plane as it lumbered slowly down the tarmac and disappeared behind the shimmering tinted windows of the airport tower. They waited in silence. At last the plane went bulleting down the runway through the undulate heat waves and lifted into the air, silhouetted against the distant line of dusty palm trees, the buildings and clefts of blue sea between, and the pall of red dust hovering in the air from the new port where machines as grotesque as iron mantises were moving earth and rock in their hydraulic jaws. It lifted higher.

McDermott was over the ocean, Djibouti behind him, perched like a termite hill on the isthmus of rock and sand. The shore was outlined with surf, and where the breaking waves ended, the sea was dyed to turquoise as the tidal ichors dissolved. McDermott banked toward the north, sunlight filling the cabin again, and then climbed parallel to the coast, veering inland ten miles beyond to cross the beach along a long reef of corrugated sand. He lifted to ten thousand feet, and put the aircraft in a steep bank toward the west, increasing power as he maintained altitude. Dropping a few thousand feet, he nudged the plane toward a stall, using minimal power. As the nose began to buffet, he throttled forward and recovered, slipping away again in a long, looping glide. Two hundred feet above the desert he leveled off and throttled forward in level flight, horneting above the salt pans and the cracked volcanic earth until the hammering at the controls annoyed him, and then he climbed like a gull into the sun. He flew back over Djibouti but the city was lost against the sea—only a small fossilized polyp lying at the terminus of a few rhumb lines of road, desert track, and rail line as faint as hairlines in the crust of coastal plain. Far at sea he turned again and began the descent back toward the city.

After he had checked the plane out a second time on the ground, he walked over to the operations center and filed a flight plan for his return to Addis. As he walked back to the hangar to meet the taxi, he saw a small executive jet, as white as a gull, being pulled from an adjacent building. The jet made the other airplane look sluggish and dowdy, merely second-hand merchandise. He saw Bouchet leave the cabin and knew then that the white jet was the replacement aircraft for the Beechcraft, and that Bouchet would fly it for the oil company. Bouchet waved to him, beckoning him closer, but McDermott only shook his head, and walked away toward the taxi. He had flown F-80's, F-100's, and F-105's in his time, but that was finished now.

The taxi returned him to the hot, sultry square opposite the hotel. His skin was damp, and the sun stung his face, neck, and arms. He stopped under the canopy of the sidewalk cafe next to the hotel, and drank a cold beer. A few French civil servants were taking their late afternoon apéritifs at the nearby tables. Somali vendors sold skins, ivory, and animal teeth at the curb. He was still sitting there when he remembered that Penny was waiting for him and he hurried back to the hotel.

The room smelled of shampoo and fresh talcum powder. The bed had been slept in, the sheet cast aside, but the room was empty. Her nylon backpack was on the dresser near the bed, where neat piles of freshly laundered shirts, jeans, and cotton briefs were folded, but she was gone. Her sleeping bag hung outside over the iron balcony, turned inside out to dry in the sun. He pulled it in and folded it on the bed. The light was on in the bathroom; two soggy towels lay on the floor, soaking up the overflow from the shower stall. On the sink were a bottle of shampoo, a small box of detergent with Arabic characters on the front, a bar of pine soap, and a tube of toothpaste.

After darkness had fallen and she still hadn't returned, he went down to the lobby and spoke to the desk clerk and one of the Somali bellboys. The clerk was French and remembered seeing her leave about four o'clock. The Somali, whose skin was darker, wouldn't admit to seeing her at all. Neither would the taxi drivers outside. He sat outside at a table, waiting for her to appear. He waited until the dining room was about to close, and went inside and had dinner. A few middle-aged French couples sat at a nearby table, talking and laughing over coffee and cigarettes. Remembering that Djibouti was an army town, too, their laughter annoyed him. After dinner he walked the streets and ended up on the quay. He passed the governor's house, a massive, wedding cake confection whose white walls were illuminated by floodlights so bright that the house and parterre shone with a brilliance as bright as the Cap d'Antibes sunshine. Further along the quay a lone Arab fisherman in a flat-bottomed skiff was setting out fish traps by lantern light along the tidal flats. He walked past him and stood in the darkness at the end of the quay, looking out over the sea. A warm wind blew across his face, and he wondered if she'd gone swimming alone. A few ghostly whitecaps broke in the distance. He had only met her a little more than twenty-four hours ago. Now the lonely plain of black water reminded him only of her, her absence, and now his own solitude. He couldn't find the horizon to the east; there was no moon yet, only a faint scattering of stars overhead. He watched the heaving sea while the wind rattled a rusty Coca-Cola sign wired to the navigational lightpost at the end of the rocks. He turned away and walked back to the hotel.

She hadn't returned. He searched among her clothes for a bathing suit, and when he couldn't find one decided that she'd gone to the beach after all. He thought she might have met some kids there—Americans; maybe French, Swedes, or Brits. Probably she had moved on by now, maybe a bistro or a discotheque, time, place, and geography forgotten. But Djibouti was still a garrison town, and McDermott pulled on his jacket and went downstairs to the lobby. The night clerk gave him the names of a few local clubs where the French youths gathered, but said they closed at eleven on weeknights. McDermott went out into the street and looked for a taxi. He stood on the deserted street, aware for the first time that it was after eleven, when he saw a figure emerge into the lamplight across the square, half running, half walking. It was Penny.

"*Thank God*," she sighed, out of breath, when she saw McDermott. "I gotta get inside, quick."

On the second floor she staggered into the room, pulled her sweat shirt over her head, flung the sleeping bag on the floor, and collapsed down on it. "I've got to lie down," she moaned. "I've just got to. I'm dying." Her face was damp, her eyelids heavy.

"Where have you been?" She squirmed out of her blue jeans, flung them aside, and lay back again on the sleeping bag, her eyes focused on the ceiling fan. Her pupils were dilated. She moistened her lips with her tongue, tried to swallow, but couldn't, and flung her arm across her eyes. McDermott kneeled beside her and felt her racing pulse. He brought a cold washrag from the bathroom and put it across her forehead.

"I've had it," she said in a weak, dry voice. "I really have. I'm wiped out."

"What happened?"

"Something I drank. Smoked or drank. I dunno. *Oh, God*—" Her voice died away and she tried to lie quietly on the floor. But then her head began to thrash dizzily; she rattled her heels against the floor, and sat up: "Oh, Jesus. Not now! Not—" She bolted to her feet and into the bathroom, flinging herself across the bathtub just as the first convulsions racked her body.

After the retching stopped, he gave her a towel to wipe her mouth and face. She lay against the tub with her eyes closed. McDermott went to get his dop kit. He was still searching for something when she came out of the bathroom, crawling on her hands and knees. "Don't laugh," she pleaded. "Don't even look at me, please." She didn't have the strength to get into the sleeping bag, so she curled up on the quilted kapok, clad only in her cotton briefs and shivering from the loss of body heat. McDermott brought a pillow and spread and covered her, then slipped the pillow under her head. She was asleep by the time he finished cleaning up the bathroom. Her pulse was normal and her forehead cooler. He turned off the light and sat in the chair, thinking he'd move her to the bed when she stirred again. But she didn't, and he fell asleep in the chair. He awoke in the middle of the night and found her still sleeping. He took off his clothes and got into bed.

It was dawn when her voice woke him. She was kneeling at the side of the bed, holding the pillow. "I'm cold," she whispered, still half asleep. Her teeth were chattering. "It's like Siberia out here." McDermott lifted the cover and brought her into bed with him. Her skin was cool and she trembled as she huddled against him, arms drawn together, elbows against her ribs. When her body began to reclaim its warmth from his own, she relaxed. The smell of her hair and skin aroused him, and after a while her thighs yielded to the pressure of his knee. She opened her legs. But then, as if discovering what was happening, she muttered: "I don't think I can make it." Her breath was warm against his chest.

"You mean you're not going to try?"

She laughed and her head fell back against his shoulder. "Just trying's no good. My head's like a barf bag. Just wait a sec. I'll be okay in a minute."

But in a minute she'd fallen asleep again, not to stir until sunlight had flooded the room, and McDermott was already in the bathroom, shaving.

They had a late breakfast in the hotel dining room, where she described what had happened the previous afternoon. Tired of waiting for him, she'd left the hotel to find a beach where she could swim before the sun went down. She found one beyond the quay, but after she'd walked through the fringe of palm trees and out onto the sand, she found it littered with tar from the ships purging their tanks in the bay beyond.

The sand ended at the water's edge where the tidal muck began, too thick and smelly for swimming. She started back to the hotel; on the path under the palm trees she met three young Legionnaires leaving a taxi. They were carrying towels, saw her beach bag, and asked her about the beach just beyond. She told them about the tar and the mud bottom. They followed her back to the square, where a young corporal caught up with her and asked if she'd have a drink with them. So they had a few bottles of beer at a sidewalk cafe on the side street near the square, and afterward the three soldiers offered to show her a few souvenir shops in the Arab quarter. They took her to the shop of an old Somali trader who sold ivory and skins. He gave them glasses of warm tea. A Yemeni trader in the adjacent shop gave them tumblers of arak. One of the Legionnaires was a young Yugoslav who offered Penny a cigarette as they examined the Yemeni's collection of antique Arab jewelry.

"It was hashish, I'll bet," Penny told McDermott as she finished her second glass of orange juice, and then began her poached egg. "God, was it strong. Anyway, it made me dizzy."

"Why'd you smoke it?"

"Because he was a smart-ass. I wanted to show him I could."

By the time they left the shop darkness had come, but the Legionnaires persuaded her to join them for something to eat at an Arab restaurant nearby. She was hungry; she had gone without lunch; and meat was grilling on a charcoal brazier inside the front window. The smell of the roasting meat had won her.

"It was real smoky—like an opium den or something," Penny remembered, soaking up the egg yolk with a piece of buttered toast. "I'd never been in an Arab restaurant before, except for those fake tourist tea shops in Cairo. Anyway, I was famished—I really was." She lifted her eyes to see if she still had McDermott's attention. "The guy that served us was pretty far out. He had a little red beard, like a billy goat. It was stained with henna, so I guess he'd made the hajj. He had a turban on too. You can't fake stuff like that. They were playing tric-trac, too."

Penny and the Legionnaires ate grilled meat, an oily salad mixed with curds of goat cheese, and drank a decanter of wine. After they left the restaurant, the Legionnaires began to argue about their next stop. In a narrow side street they passed a bar where Western music was playing. Penny told them she wanted to go back to the hotel, but they insisted she have a cognac first. She was lost and didn't want to be left alone. Inside the bar French soldiers were sitting with Somali and Ethiopian prostitutes. The bar was dark and smelled of incense, heavy enough to make her ill. She took a few swallows of brandy, but knew she couldn't finish it. The Yugoslav ordered whiskey for her instead. The young corporal from Marseille was drunk by then, and vomited on the floor near the side door. She got up to leave, too, but the Yugoslav grabbed her by the arm and insisted that she first finish the whiskey. He was pretty drunk too. When he got to his feet a second time to block her departure, she pulled free and went back through the tables to the rest room. She was nauseous.

Ethiopian prostitutes were combing their hair and putting on their makeup in the washroom. They slammed the door in Penny's face when she tried to enter. She waited outside behind the cloth curtain, leaning dizzily against the wall. She waited for five minutes while more Ethiopian prostitutes entered the washroom. They held the door against her a second time. Through the curtain she saw the Yugoslav get to his feet drunkenly and stumble back through the tables toward the washroom. She fled back along the corridor, down through a low-ceilinged room piled with beer and whiskey crates, and slipped out the rear door. Rubbish was piled in the narrow alley behind the bar, and she could smell the sewage from the bay. At the end of the alley was a small blue light over a pair of iron doors. She thought it might be a clinic or a French hospital. She heard the Legionnaires' voices in the storage room behind her, searching among the stacked crates, and she ran down the alley. She thought at first she was in a cul-de-sac, and the Legionnaires were in the alley behind her by then. But suddenly she saw the second passageway, off to her right, and the lights of a small street beyond. She stumbled down the passageway and into the open street. A policeman in a blue pillbox hat was standing at the curb. She told him she was lost and asked the way back to the hotel. He walked with her for two blocks, and then pointed with his nightstick up a second street toward Menelik Square. She ran the rest of the way.

McDermott listened to her in the sunny silence of the dining room. The waiters were already changing the tablecloths for lunch. She had finished two glasses of orange juice, two poached eggs, a few strips of bacon, and three pieces of toast. The color had come back into her face and her hair was no longer damp from the shower.

"They were stoned," Penny said, "doped right out of their heads. I mean like Bastille Day, ready to gang-bang the town. It was okay when we were just talking at first, drinking beer and trading questions, like they'd never met an American before, but they were just setting me up. The Yugoslav was the worst—a real freak. His face was sorta greasy and damp, with big pores. He was a mouth-breather too. His jaw was always kinda hanging open, and he had a size fifteen shoe or something. He didn't say much. Just sorta laughed with his adenoids hanging out. You know the type—a sadomasochist with cosmic overtones, maybe. The kind that are just mama's boy around the farm, but then they get loose and wanna smash everything, murder everyone, zap God. You can never tell, can you?" She sipped her tea.

McDermott laughed.

"What's so funny?"

You, he wanted to say. "What can't you tell about?" he asked instead.

"What people are really like. I mean rock bottom, down there in the mud, where the warm-blooded mammals get stomped and the real reptile race begins. You never know when it's gonna happen. How come you're smiling? I'm serious." Her eyes had taken on the green of the porcelain teapot, the lime carpet, and the dark green shutters against the whitewashed walls.

"Why'd you go with them then?" McDermott asked, smoothing away the smile. "Why'd you string them along?"

"String who along?" she asked innocently. "I was waiting for you. I was killing time." She put the last edge of toast in her mouth and brushed the crumbs from her fingers. "You said you'd be back by three. You stood me up, you fink."

"Tagging along after anyone who comes along. Is that what you call killing time?"

"I wanted to see something of this town. Don't be so negative. Are you mad or something? Where'd you think I was, anyway?"

McDermott was already searching the dining room for the waiter. "I thought you'd gone swimming and were swept away by the tide."

"What!" She stopped chewing. "Swept away by the tide?"

"I was worried, for God's sake. Who wouldn't have been? I told you this was an army town," he said. "There's a difference between getting smashed with your college friends on a California beach, and drinking too much in a garrison town."

"I wasn't drinking. I swear I wasn't. I hate it. My parents used to drink. They practically swam in the stuff."

As they went into the lobby from the restaurant, a few waiters turned to watch her pass, looking at the faded blue T-shirt. She was bare-breasted under the shirt. McDermott called Picot from the lobby. He wasn't there. The office manager told him that the plane wouldn't be ready until five o'clock, too late for McDermott to leave until the following morning.

"Bad news?" Penny asked after he hung up. He shook his head. "Good." She smiled. "Maybe we can take a walk before we go swimming, okay? I wanna see the Arab market."

"Sure. But you'll have to change your shirt first. Maybe you could begin by putting something under it."

She looked at him, and then down at her breasts. "How come? There's not much showing."

"There doesn't have to be," McDermott said. "It's an Arab town. What they own, they keep locked up. If it's not locked up, they want to buy." He looked down at her shirt. "If you're not selling, lock it up."

"God! How crude can you get." She went upstairs and when she returned was wearing a brassiere. "I thought only the middle-aged guys got uptight about someone's knockers. You're supposed to be the macho type. What happened to your *Playboy* image, anyway?"

"Canceled."

"Yeah? Who canceled it?"

"Minnie Mouse," he said, stepping out into the bright street.

In the Arab quarter she stopped in a few Indian and Arab shops, looking for a gold ring to send to her grandmother in San Francisco. She finally found one in a small, dark shop smelling of camphor and beeswax. When they returned to the hotel, she was wearing it on her finger. McDermott wasn't sure about the grandmother in San Francisco. He thought it was only an excuse for her own self-indulgence.

In the early afternoon they hired a taxi to drive them to a secluded beach ten kilometers from the city. They packed a few sandwiches and a bottle of white wine. The coastal road was empty of cars and the beaches were deserted. After the red-and-yellow taxi drove away, they walked down through the palm trees and onto the white sand. "Do you think that creep's gonna come back and pick us up?" Penny asked dubiously. "Forget it."

"He'll be back." The beach was deserted. He found a strip of sand partially shaded by a few palm trees, put the basket down, and stripped to his bathing trunks and T-shirt.

Penny wiggled out of her jeans. "What makes you think so?"

"I didn't pay him."

"Didn't pay him!" She smiled in surprise. "You're kidding? "You mean he trusted you?"

"Some people do."

They waded together out into the sea. The water had the transparency of glass, but the bottom was a corrupt, powdery sand and stirred from the shallows like saline chalk as they walked. Deeper offshore the colors changed. The bottom grew firm as they waded waist-deep toward the breakers. Penny wore a fawn-colored bikini as brief as two elastic sashes, barely covering her breasts and hips; but a moment later she'd discarded both pieces, naked in deep water, waving the fawn sashes toward McDermott as she treaded water, her brown shoulders bobbing in the swell, her head thrown back. She was laughing, her hair darker from the sea, as glossy as a sealskin. McDermott's arms and face were tanned dark but his chest and shoulders were pale so he had kept his T-shirt on.

"God! Why don't you wear your pants too?" she jeered, floating away on her back, her long, slim body riding just below the bubbling surface. McDermott pulled off the gray cotton T-shirt and flung it toward her, then kicked over and dove underwater. Still kicking, he swam deeply toward the open sea. When he broke the surface, she was behind him and wearing his shirt. He drifted with the current, and she caught him, gliding with deep, clean strokes through the lifting sea.

"I've done it!" she cried exultantly, water cleansing her face as she lifted from the surface. "I've swum in the Indian Ocean!" She soared out of the water like an otter—head, neck, and shoulders stiff; and then dove for the bottom, her ankles disappearing last, halter tied to one, pants to the other. She surfaced again, crabbing and frog-legging intermittently toward him, nose barely above the surface, but still smiling, despite the slap of surf against her mouth.

McDermott said, "It's still the Bay of Tadjoura."

"Rats! That's just a technicality. You're so crappy about technicalities, McDermott." She splashed water toward him, her hands white under the lens of the sea. McDermott rolled over, kicking free, and began a slow crawl toward deeper water where the high draft of the sea rolled. In deeper water the sea was colder, the waves high and powerful. The rim of beach disappeared. The bottom was twenty feet below and he dove for it, seized a fistful of coarse sand, felt the ooze of ocean floor beneath as cold as winter earth, and kicked back into the hot sunlight, flinging the gout of bottom mud far out across the waves as he surfaced. She threw his wet shirt toward him. He caught it and stuffed it in his waistband, kicking over on his back. She swam under him, surfaced and then drifted, her long body suspended in the waves, crystal water breaking over her brown shoulders, white breasts, and the hard angle of her pelvis. She suddenly arched herself in a back somersault, head thrown back, and disappeared. He swam over her; she came up under him, sliding against him as she surfaced, her face only a few inches away. "Hi." She fluttered her wet lashes and cocked her head: "My name is Helen Browning and I'm drowning. Will you save me?"

"Sure."

"Good." She locked her knees to his hips, and let her shoulders drift away, floating easily, her long hair uncoiling like kelp. "There's just one thing." She smiled, batting her eyes again.

"What's that?"

"I came with my boyfriend. I'm standing on him. His name is Tim and he can't swim."

She released him and slid beneath the surface, reappearing an instant later and flinging her arms around his neck. Her weight pulled him down, but before they went under he kissed her and they sank beneath the waves—down, far down, farther still, where the light dimmed and the colder current touched their ankles first, then their loins, and trickled up their spines. She moved in his arms finally, and he released her. She arose, feet fluttering past his face, and he followed her bright, bubbling body to the surface.

"You all right?" he asked her as he caught his breath. She nodded, smiling as she closed her eyes, still nodding, and turned over on her back. They rested together in the trough of the sea, sculling lazily. The beach was still hidden behind the waves. After a while they rolled to their sides, and began the long, slow crawl back to the beach. They had drifted a long way.

In shallow water she put on her bikini and they walked back toward their food basket a half mile away, the sand hot under their feet.

"You swim okay," Penny smiled, still winded. "I mean for an old guy." She gave him a shove and scampered away, but he didn't break stride. She stood ankle-deep in the surf a few yards away: "What's wrong—you got the middle-aged jags or something?"

He feinted toward her, and she ran; but then he gave chase and caught her. They flogged together through the shallow water, falling finally, and rolling through the surf until McDermott could still her thrashing shoulders. She relaxed then, sitting on the bottom, her arms around his neck, her face close to his, smiling and looking up at him. He kissed her again, and lifted her out of the water, but almost immediately she was looking beyond his shoulder toward the beach.

"*Rats,*" she sighed softly. "Some guy's watching us."

An Arab stood watching from the fringe of palm trees, a charcoal scoop in his hands, bare-chested, wearing a pair of ragged shorts. He had pulled his donkey cart down through the trees, unloaded his tin drums, and was filling them with beach sand. He watched them silently. McDermott released Penny and she stood up. He waved to the

Arab, who waved back, stepped back into his trench, and began filling his drums again.

They spread the picnic lunch on a beach towel under the palm trees and ate the cheese, sausage, and bread. The wine was still chilled from the hotel refrigerator. After lunch McDermott stretched out in the sun.

Penny shielded her eyes. "We're going swimming again, aren't we?" she asked.

"Sure."

"I think I'll rinse off in the meantime. Don't go to sleep." She sat waist-deep in the surf twenty yards beyond, combing her hair and looking toward the sails of the dhows that marched along the horizon. A towel over his head and shoulders, McDermott studied her back, the way she moved her head as she swept the comb through her long blond hair, the curve of her spine, the graceful neck. The grace of her body pleased him, and he saw nothing to remind him of the frightened young girl who had sat next to him on the coach two days earlier. She'd turned and was watching him, the comb still in her hands. "What are you thinking about?" she called.

"Mermaids." She got up and started wading back toward the beach, and stopped suddenly in the shadow of a rock, bending over.

"Hey! There're fish in here!" McDermott didn't answer, and she bent forward a little longer before she came wading out of the sea, her wet legs dark in the sunlight, her bikini drooping on her hips. "Tropical fish," she said, sinking down on the sand next to him, pulling the towel from his head and drying her arms and legs. "Little bitty ones. Are you sleeping?"

"Sure." He lay back against the sand, studying the thin mackerel sky that had begun to appear from the east. The sun had sunk lower and pushed the shadows of the palm trees across the beach. Not a breath of wind stirred. A plane was coming in from the sea, just a silver mote against the sky, and he watched it, wondering if it was the oil company jet Bouchet flew.

Penny stretched out, rolling over on her stomach, her face at his shoulder. "Don't go to sleep," she said. "I want to talk for a minute. Really. No crap."

"Okay. What do you want to talk about?"

"Stuff. Me. Don't laugh, all right?" He couldn't see her face.

"All right."

"It's about me. What I'm gonna do?"

"What do you want to do?"

"That's just it. I dunno. That's my problem. If you were me, what would you do?"

"I don't know."

"Think about it."

"I don't know what your interests are."

"Doing my own thing," she said. "No rat race. None of that career girl, housewife jive. None of that crap. I just don't want to get shoe-horned into some nine-to-five box like everyone else I know."

"Neither does anyone else."

"C'mon. Be serious. The way we are now—that's what I want. Like, doing what we're doing today. How'd you manage it?"

"You're asking me what we should do. If you're doing it, you don't have to ask."

Her long fingers drew circles in the sand. "That's not what I meant. It's tomorrow I'm thinking about. You've gotta bring in the bread no matter what you do. I get sorta tired scratching around. Not today—that's great. It's getting here I'm talking about. Tomorrow it'll be gone. Sometimes it's pretty crummy," she continued. "I get claustrophobia, like maybe I'll self-destruct. Like last night—waiting around in that crummy hotel room. It's like I'm not living my life at all."

He thought for a moment, arms cradling his head, and then he said: "Why don't you settle someplace?"

"Sure. Where?"

"You like to swim. Someplace on the ocean."

"Sure, but what could I do?"

Another plane was coming in, farther to the south: "Be an airline hostess," McDermott suggested, watching it bank over the sea.

"Are you kidding!" she cried, seeing the plane too. "That's just hired meat. It's wrapped in cellophane, but it's just supermarket meat. Be serious for a change. C'mon. Stop looking at the sky. What would you do if you were me?"

"What I do," McDermott said. "Fly."

"Sure. Just fly. Spread my wings and fly. Be a hostess—spread your legs and fly." She watched his face, but McDermott didn't reply, and she sank back on the sand. "Okay," she conceded dejectedly, "say I can fly. If you could go anyplace in the world, where would you go?"

McDermott thought about it for a minute. "Back to Vietnam, maybe Laos. Maybe fly there."

She sat up. "You flew in *Vietnam!*"

"For a little while."

She crawled forward, gazing straight down into his face. "You flew in Vietnam and you wanna go *back?*"

"I liked the flying," McDermott said.

"Bombing people. Napalming villages. Kids and little old ladies and everyone else that got in the way. You liked that."

"Not bombs. Not against villages anyway."

"Yeah, I'll bet! But if they happen to be there . . ."

"It didn't have anything to do with villages and people. That wasn't my job," McDermott said. "Anyway, that was a long time ago—back in '66. How old are you?"

She hesitated, still on all fours, looking down into his face: "Twenty-three. Why?"

"Good," he said. "That was five years ago." He shut his eyes and folded his hands over his chest. "Maybe you're too young to understand."

"How old are you?"

"Thirty-seven," he said, smiling slightly, like a man long reconciled to the past.

"Maybe you're too old to understand. Did you ever think about that, Mr. Rip Van Winkle or John Foster Dulles or whoever you are?"

Her shadow lay over his face. He didn't want to talk about Vietnam. He'd flown over a hundred missions in an F-105 against military targets in North Vietnam from Thailand and knew the mountain ridges and the Red River area northwest of Hanoi as well as any landscape on earth—where the Soviet SAM-2's nested, where the MIG-17's and MIG-21's would come in from—but these weren't the things he remembered now. What he remembered still lay as lightly as her own shadow across his consciousness.

"Laos too?" she asked.

"That was later."

"How much later?"

"After I left the Air Force. I was on contract for a few months." He opened his eyes and sat up. "If it gets you upset, why don't we forget it?"

"How come you left?"

"I decided to do something else."

"Did the Air Force kick you out?"

"Would that make you feel better?"

"It might."

"I just left," McDermott dissembled, leaning back on his elbows.

"How'd we get on this anyway?" she sighed disconsolately.

"You asked me where I'd go to fly."

"Okay, let's forget about Vietnam. Where else would you go?"

McDermott's eyes swept the sea. "Over there," he said finally. He lifted his foot and pointed off toward the northeast. She turned and looked across the horizon.

"What's over there?"

"Arabia."

"What's so great about that?"

"The flying's cleaner. Not like the African bush. You can go anywhere, come down anywhere. The weather's cleaner, the sky bigger."

"You've been there too?"

"For a little while."

She sat looking over the sea, and finally slumped back against the sand. "You sure do get around, don't you?" He didn't answer. "With women, too, huh? Making out?"

"All over the place," he said grimly.

"I'll bet. A real sack artist. So how come you're not still in Arabia?"

"I had problems."

"What kind of problems? Did they find you in the harem one night like Ali Baba and the forty chicks or something?"

McDermott said, "It's not very interesting."

"Come on. What'd they bust you for? Tell me."

"I had a problem with the operations manager."

"Tell me. I wanna hear." But he didn't answer, and she said, "For God's sake. Don't you ever wanna talk about *anything*?"

"Anything always ends up being me."

"So what? What's wrong with that? Did you leave your life in the dead-letter office in some Turkeytown someplace, afraid to go back and pick it up? I hate guys who are always trying to be mysterious—trying to be cool—like their life had some metaphysical tragedy to it only Alfred North Whitehead could understand." She sat up. "C'mon! What happened?"

"It's not interesting."

"Tell me anyway."

McDermott told her. He and another pilot had been hunting grouse with the operations manager in southern Lebanon. The manager was the worst shot, but he'd claimed all of the birds. He'd been using a number five shot; McDermott and the other pilot, number six. At a cocktail party at the St. George Hotel in Beirut that night, the manager had been boasting to a few visiting oil executives about his luck that day. Someone had asked McDermott about his own luck, and he'd said that if the manager found any number five bird shot in the grouse he'd claimed that day, he'd have them gold-plated for his wife to wear around her ankle. The manager was middle-aged and ten years older than his footloose English wife. He demanded an apology. McDermott had knocked him into the pool.

McDermott was suddenly depressed. It was a stupid incident, like her comments about Vietnam, and he knew it.

She put her head against her knee and began shaping the sand with her hand. "That's what I want to get away from," she said. "Office politics. Public behavior. I want to be free of all that. I'd like to write, maybe. Just lyrics—music sometimes. I'd like to live a private life. You wouldn't think it, would you? Like I wanted to be a kind of spaced-out Emily Dickinson or something. I don't mean famous. Just private. But I'd want to know that it had some integrity too—that nothing outside myself could really destroy it." She lifted her eyes. "Do you know what I mean?"

"Who's Emily Dickinson?"

"A hundred-year-old virgin," Penny said. "Kind of, anyway." The sky was turning to brass overhead. She followed his eyes. "I'd like to live on the sea. I always have. What could I do to support myself? That's what I don't know." She sat up. "What about the tropical fish business?"

"What about it?"

"Maybe I could do that. This place is loaded with them, isn't it?"

McDermott shifted on the sand. "Sure." He watched the gulls and the sandpipers along the beach. "What would you do with them?"

"Sell them, I guess. There're jillions of them, aren't there?" When he didn't answer, she said, "I could sell them in Europe or the States."

"Sure you could," McDermott said, "in the PX's in Europe, or the supermarkets in the states. You could market them in little cellophane bags, like candy bars in the vending machines. That way the kids could buy them like anything else. Then after two or three days when they got tired of them, they could just flush them down the john without telling their parents. That way they wouldn't have to buy a fish tank. No capital investment. That's a pretty good idea." He sat up. She was studying him, horrified.

"That's gross!" she cried.

"Sure it's gross. So are a lot of ways to make a living."

"So you're really not into being in Africa?"

"I didn't say that," McDermott replied carefully.

"You've been talking about Vietnam, Laos—even Arabia. Everything but what you're doing. Anyway, even if you didn't say it, that's what you're telling me. I can feel the vibes."

"What vibes?"

"Your vibes. You're Aquarius, aren't you?" He didn't answer. "Aren't you Aquarius?"

He got to his feet. "How the hell do I know?"

She sat on the beach looking at him. "How come you're so negative all of a sudden? What are you walking away for?"

"I'm not walking away."

"You are." She got to her feet and pulled up her halter. "C'mon, let's take a swim." She walked away from him, and when he didn't follow, she stopped and looked back. "C'mon," she said reproachfully. "Don't be such a shit."

They swam far out, side by side, resting more often this time. The sea was cooler, and had lost its transparency. They floated upright, faces lifted into the peach-colored sky. Where the darker water began, she found a shelf and dove toward it, finally surfacing near him, smiling and tossing the water from her face.

"*Fish!*" she exhaled. "Jillions of 'em!"

He followed her beneath the surface. Above the coronet of coral shelf eight feet below were schools of iridescent fish suspended like multicolored gnats, drifting above the tentacles of sea grass and the beds of brain coral and orange fungus.

"We should have brought some masks," she said as they bobbed in the waves later, her hands on his shoulders. "Maybe tomorrow, okay? Couldn't we get some masks tomorrow, and bring some snorkel tubes?"

McDermott said, "Tomorrow I'll be in Addis. Wheels up at eight."

The light changed and she watched it, sitting on the beach with her knees drawn up under her chin. Arab and Pakistani families strolled down through the trees from their old automobiles, the wind lifting their cotton skirts and tissue-thin saris. A few dark-skinned boys and girls chased the gulls along the lip of wet sand. She got to her feet and slowly slipped on her jeans. McDermott was packing the beach bag. From the line of old laurel and palm trees that fringed the road, bats took the evening air, veering in eccentric flight out over the strand.

"Hey, McDermott," she called to him, standing in her jeans and halter and combing her hair. He came over to her. She didn't turn. She said, "Take me with you tomorrow."

McDermott studied her silhouette. "I can't take passengers."

Her face lifted toward him in surprise: "Why not?"

"It's not in my flight plan. The regs say no."

"No one would be wise to it. If anyone found out, I'd say I smuggled myself aboard."

"Sure, and I could tell them the sandman flew in the vent and threw sleep dust in my eyes. Only they wouldn't believe me. Catch a plane."

"It's not the same."

"It'll get you there."

"I wanna go the way you do—just pick up my feet and fly. Going by train's no fun. I wanna do it differently this time. It'd serve them right, the jerks."

"What jerks?"

"The guys I was with at Awash before you came along. It'd be beautiful, gliding into Addis like a big bird while they're still bouncing around in the dust someplace. God, would they be jealous."

McDermott laughed, watching her face. "What would make it so beautiful, revenge or the free ride?" He laughed again. "You're too much, kid. You really are."

"Don't call me kid," she said angrily. "That's moronic and patronizing."

"Okay," he said, still smiling. "Air France goes in a couple of days. Take Air France."

"Screw Air France!"

They walked up through the trees toward the beach road where the red-and-yellow taxi was waiting. "No one would know," Penny explained. "They wouldn't. I'd wrap myself up in my sleeping bag and you could say I was cargo or something."

"That's right," he said. "Then they'd wrap me up in the regulations and air-mail my ass off to Katmandu. You'll be okay here for a while. Someone'll come along."

She stopped in the road. "That's not what I want. 'Someone'll come along.' That's sick. It really is."

She didn't say a word during the drive back to Djibouti. When he unlocked the hotel room door, she shoved him aside, ran into the bathroom, and slammed the door. A few minutes later he heard the shower go on. Twenty minutes later it was still on; he knocked at the door, but she didn't answer. The salt from the sea prickled his face and tightened the flesh on his back and shoulders. When she finally opened the door, the boiling steam drifted into the room like the mist from a Turkish bath. She stood at the washbasin, her hair wrapped in a towel, a larger towel girdling her midriff. Gouts of talcum powder lay across her brown shoulders.

"You can come in now, Mr. Babbit Bureaucrat," she said.

"Don't you do anything but wash your hair?" The floor was wet.

"Is there a regulation against that too?" she said as she swept by him, slamming the door as she left.

McDermott showered and shaved. When he joined her in the bedroom, she was already dressed, sitting in the armchair near the open window, smoking a cigarette. He hardly knew her. She was wearing a sleeveless white cotton dress; her blond hair had been drawn back severely from her face and bound with a velvet band at the back of her neck. He'd never seen her in a dress before; the perfume and lipstick were different too. She looked ten years older—as far from sleeping bags and dusty backpacks as the golfing greens of Palm Springs were from the African bush. She didn't speak.

They went downstairs and sat silently at a table in front of the restaurant next door. The evening light was fading, but the street lamps hadn't yet come on. McDermott asked her what she wanted, and she took a gin and tonic. He ordered a Perrier water, remembering what she'd said about gin and her parents' cocktail habits. After the waiter brought the drinks, she looked at the bottle of mineral water and then at him.

"No hard stuff?" she said coolly. "You really have crawled back in your shell, haven't you? What are you afraid of—some Jesus freak's gonna crawl in there with you and start telling you Bible stories?"

"I'm flying tomorrow," McDermott said. She was a young girl again, living out of a backpack, and McDermott was just a bush pilot.

"That never bothered the pilots I knew." When he didn't turn, she said, "Aren't you gonna make some smart-ass crack?"

"I don't know the pilots you do."

"You're strange, McDermott," she said accusingly. "You really are. You can go a million miles to bomb Hanoi back to the Stone Age, but you can't even give someone a lift in your crummy airplane. It's not the regulations or whatever freaky book you preach by. That's just an excuse. You just don't want me with you, isn't that it? You just don't want to get involved with anyone. You wanna cut out like you're back in Vietnam or Cambodia again, and those little specks down there aren't people—they're just ants! Bugs! So you go on, light your burner and cut out. *So long, kid! Be seeing you, kid! Been nice to know you, kid,*' and all the rest of that big brother, 'Goodnight, Irene' shit that you think makes other people feel good! You won't lose your license. You just don't want me hanging around, bugging you, isn't that it? You've been living without a conscience so long you've gotten used to it. Why don't you be honest about it? I make you feel your age, don't I? Only you don't want to. So you wanna deny I exist. You wanna wipe me out of your mind like I'd never been there."

McDermott smiled. "Fat chance."

"Stop laughing! You're cruel with people. You're careless. You really are. Like that first day on the train, worrying that people might think I belonged to you or something, thinking I might embarrass you."

McDermott listened without answering, watching the people pass along the pavement and wondering what had happened to the young woman from Palm Beach.

"Why don't you say something?" she asked.

"It's funny about the people here. They'll all be here tomorrow. All of them. The same place, doing the same things."

"So what else is new? And you'll be someplace else, is that it? I want to go with you tomorrow."

"I'll lose my license," McDermott replied easily, although it wasn't completely true, and no longer seemed important to him. He smiled at her stubbornness, his eyes roaming the sidewalk. "You don't like Ethiopia anyway."

"My friends are there."

"Maybe they're gone."

"They're still hanging around. They're always making big deal plans to go somewhere else."

A gray Mercedes pulled up in front of the hotel, and McDermott recognized Bouchet, the French pilot, at the wheel. He disappeared into the lobby. Two French girls in Air France uniforms left the Mercedes to look at the ivory bracelets an old Somali was selling.

"People think it's so cool traveling around with guys that way," Penny continued, "only it's not. It's a bummer, almost as bad as being alone. Half the time you spend arguing about where you're gonna go next. You're in a train station in Rome or Cairo and the artsy-craftsy types wanna go to Florence, a couple of groupies wanna go to Cannes for the film festival to get laid, the acidheads wanna go to Turkey, and a couple of jocks wanna go climb the Khyber Pass or Kilimanjaro in their sneakers and college sweat shirts. And pretty soon it's nowhere, and you're sitting in some back-alley cafe getting ripped off, or in some crummy *pension* where someone has barfed all over your mattress the night before and a half dozen Danish or Swedish hippies are frisking you for bread, pot, or sex. Anyway, you do things. You get around. You, you don't sit on your ass getting high while you pick your toes and rap about what you're gonna do, like most guys I know."

"So why do you want to join up with your friends again?" McDermott asked.

"I didn't say I wanted to catch them. I want to show them. Hey, is that your girl friend or something?" McDermott was watching one of the French stewardesses. A bellboy came out of the hotel, Bouchet at his heels, and pointed to McDermott. Bouchet nodded, and joined McDermott, not realizing that Penny was with him until McDermott introduced them.

"You come too." Bouchet smiled, inviting Penny. He was on his way to the new beach hotel with the cabin crew from the Air France flight, and was rounding up as many congenial friends as possible to make the party interesting. After he'd dropped the stewardesses at the hotel, he was going back to the flying club to pick up the liquor, and offered to stop by and pick up McDermott and Penny too.

Penny didn't answer and looked at McDermott instead. "There's a pool there," he said. "Maybe you'll meet some people." She looked across the sidewalk at the French hostesses, and then at Bouchet He was wearing dark glasses; his tailored white shirt was open across his chest, where a silver medallion hung.

"*Allons*," Bouchet suggested, still smiling, but Penny shook her head. McDermott walked with Bouchet back to the Mercedes and stood for a few minutes, talking to the French girls. "*Ciaou!*" Bouchet called to Penny as he slipped behind the wheel. The two hostesses watched Penny through the back window as Bouchet drove away, both of them smiling.

McDermott told her Bouchet was a French pilot he knew. "I thought so," she said. "I'll bet he gets stoned every time he looks in the mirror. I know the type—an orgasm a minute. All his."

"I'm tired of that kind of talk. I'm tired of listening to it." He looked out over the square.

"I want to go with you," Penny said coolly.

"For God's sake." He looked around hopelessly, and the waiter came over. "Bring me a whiskey," he said.

"No whiskey," Penny said. "Make it two gin and tonics." After the waiter left, she said, "Why didn't you just go with them if you feel that way?"

"Why don't you just think about it and stop talking for a while."

She lifted her head sharply: "If you've got a late date with some French babe, don't let me stand in the way."

"Good God," McDermott complained.

"If you want to cut out for some French hostess, go ahead," she said huskily. "Just walk away—the way you did before. You don't have to wait until tomorrow."

"Stop feeling sorry for yourself."

"I'm not. I'm sorry for what's happened, that's all. Only I don't understand it. Why don't you just leave if that's how you feel?" Her voice had a catch to it. She fumbled with her purse and found a cigarette. The waiter brought the gin and tonics and she moved her hand to her forehead, hiding her eyes, as he stood there. After he left, she sat with her hand across her forehead, cradling her brow, leaning forward so that the couples at the nearby tables couldn't see her. Finally she wiped at her eyelids with her fingers.

McDermott said quietly, "Go ahead and finish your drink and let's get out of here." The stares from the nearby tables annoyed him, but he was even angrier with himself for being conscious of them.

She tried to sip from her glass, but her hand was shaking, and she put the glass back on the table. He heard her clear her throat, as he sat slumped in his chair, looking at her hand lying along the table next to the gin and tonic glass. The long, slender fingers were scrubbed white by the sea. He remembered how they had moved through the sea that afternoon, how fluid and free her body had been, so certain of its element. She was still wearing the ring, which had caught the sunlight as they swam, the sparkling water magnifying the slim fingers, as the sea itself had magnified her grace. He touched the gold ring on the tabletop, turning it between his thumb and forefinger. Finally he lifted her hand into his own. "That's not how I feel," he said. "I've been where you are. Don't worry. We'll work it out."

They had dinner at a small Greek restaurant behind the square and afterward walked out on the quay between the sea walls. She wanted to see the ocean one more time so they stood in the darkness, looking out over the sea. The stones radiated the heat of the afternoon sun. The Southern Cross was low on the southeastern horizon, and Mc-Dermott pointed it out for her. They walked back to the hotel through the quiet streets, Penny silent and thoughtful, carrying the half-empty wine bottle from the restaurant. She turned off the table lamp after they entered the room and he saw only her silhouette against the open window as she stood looking down into the square.

"Good-bye Djibouti-streets-after-dark," she said. "It's kinda sad in a way."

"They'll still be here."

"But we won't be." The light from the street lamps traced the outline of her face and her mouth. "Where are you?"

"Here."

Her face and the flesh of her back were still warm from the afternoon sun, but her breasts and hips were as cool and smooth as the glass of the sea. She clung to him as if being lifted by the wind, lost her breath, and suddenly soared, taken beyond, rising.

Only later did she finally stir—much later—moving against him as he slept, her body curved against his, pulling his arm around her waist to huddle even closer.

"People disappear, you know," she whispered.

TWO

1

She lived alone at the edge of the grasslands on the Baro River a few miles from the Sudanese border—a tall, solitary woman with the first traces of gray in her brown hair. During the hottest season of the year she would sit outside after a cold supper, watching the first stars come out as she waited for the moon to rise. If she came early and there was light enough to read by, she would bring a Nuer or Anuak phrase book to study. Sometimes she fell asleep in her chair. But when the full moon appeared, she was always there, watching the flushed, white body ascend over the grasslands to the west—not the anemic, one-dimensional wafer of other hemispheres, wasted by smoke, fog, carbon haze, or factory fires; not even the autumnal moon of her New England childhood; but the chaste, full-blooded creature of the African savannahs, rising like another earth into the night sky where nothing diminished its splendor or its majesty.

On the first night she'd seen the plane, she had come into the yard late after a solitary supper at the wooden table in the kitchen, her only companion the Grundig shortwave radio on the shelf above the sink. She'd listened to the eight o'clock BBC news from London, turned off the generator, and left the house in darkness, intending to sit in the yard for only a few minutes. The moon wasn't full, and she'd been up since dawn, fetched by one of the village women to the bedside of her dying grandmother. She'd remained with the old woman until late afternoon, when she'd died peacefully in her sleep. The remainder of the afternoon she'd worked in the village clinic, ministering to expectant mothers and teaching a class in nutrition. She was a registered nurse, not an evangelist. Her late husband had been both evangelist and physician at a missionary hospital in the Congo. Exhausted by the anarchy and rebellion, they'd planned to relocate among the forgotten Nilotic tribesmen of the Ethiopian frontier, but he'd died quite suddenly of malignant tertiary malaria. Her final vow to her dying husband was that she would carry on their work alone.

The Baro station where she had resettled after his death stood on an acre of lawn and wild garden, shaded by gum and ash at the edge of the Sudanese grasslands where elephant, buffalo, giraffe, and lion prowled. The whitewashed brick cottage was half hidden behind trellises of bougainvillea, wisteria, and honeysuckle planted by the house's previous inhabitants, an elderly missionary couple from Nebraska. Tulip and mango trees overhung the rear roof and grew along the wire fence that enclosed the mission station yard. Pale blue and white anemone grew in the flower beds along the old foundation and the fence line, while bean vines tumbled over the brick walls of the old washhouse behind the kitchen. Water for the house and garden was pumped from the Baro River, fifty yards behind the cottage. From November until May, the Baro slumped low within its banks, like a sleeping copper serpent, but in June and July was swollen to floodtide as the rains swept down the escarpment from the Ethiopian highlands. During those months the river was navigable from Gambela, Ethiopia, in the east, to its confluence with the Nile hundreds of miles to the west in Sudan. In front of the house was a narrow dirt track which meandered out over the grasslands into the Sudan. On the other side of the track was a grass landing strip used by the bush pilots who provisioned the Baro station; to the east was the small clinic she maintained in the village of grass huts a mile away along the river.

That evening, William, the Nuer night watchman, found her still sitting in the wooden lawn chair as he began his nightly rounds. He came around the cottage, carrying his spear, and saw her familiar silhouette under the trees. He moved forward quietly to the picket gate at the end of the brick walk, rattled the gate to make sure it was fastened, and turned to look back at her.

"I'm not sleeping," she called, her head back as she watched the clouds drifting across the moon. A fox barked somewhere in the distance, and William turned, following the sound. Two hyenas loped away from the copse of acacia trees across the landing strip. He watched them disappear, grunted to himself, shouldered his spear, and disappeared around the far corner of the cottage as he patrolled the fence line.

"She is still there," he said to Samuel Eko as he joined him in front of the wood fire outside the brick washhouse. Samuel Eko was the mission driver and mechanic. He sat on a wooden stool grinding coffee beans in a clay bowl as he listened to Radio Omdurman from Khartoum on his transistor radio. An Arab woman was singing a plaintive love song in a hushed, dusky voice. Like William, Samuel Eko was a Nuer from the southern Sudan; but he had grown up in Khartoum as a street orphan and spoke Arabic as well as English. He was over six feet tall and was as thin as a rake, with woolly black hair shortly cut, a wide, full mouth, and tribal scars across his forehead. Despite his fondness for tobacco, grain alcohol, and durra beer, neither his brown eyes nor white teeth had lost their youthful color. Among the alien Nuer of the nearby village where he lived, he was known for his independent ways and his Arabized manners.

After Samuel Eko had finished grinding the coffee beans in the clay bowl, he lifted the blackened tea kettle from the coals and poured three cups of Arab coffee. One he gave to William, and the other two he carried with his stool around to the front yard where Emily Farr was sitting.

"That's very thoughtful," she said, "but I wouldn't be able to sleep." He put his stool in the grass and sat down. "I didn't intend to stay very long, but it's so lovely tonight. So peaceful."

"No wind," he said.

"Did you hear the news from Khartoum?" she asked.

It was the same question she always asked. He told her what Radio Omdurman had said about the guerrilla war in the southern Sudan, claiming that sixty Anya-nya rebels had been killed by government troops near Juba. "Do you think it's true?" she asked.

"No." He didn't know whether the news report was true or not, but he knew Emily Farr would believe him more readily than she would

Radio Omdurman. But he didn't want to talk about the war in the Sudan, where his old Arab friends from Khartoum and his black tribal brothers in the south were killing each other. Across the border only twenty miles away Nuer villages like the one near the Baro station were being razed by marauding government troops as they searched for Anya-nya insurgents. Men were shot, crops burned, huts set afire, cattle confiscated. Rifles and ammunition for the southern black guerrillas found their way into the Sudan from Uganda and Ethiopia, supplied by Christian sympathizers and Western nations who opposed the Soviet-supported Arab government in Khartoum. That night on Radio Omdurman the government bulletin had accused Israel of giving guns to the Anya-nya.

"I heard on the BBC that Russian pilots were flying helicopters against the rebels," Emily said. "Have you heard anything?"

"Juba is very far away," Samuel Eko said. He knew that she was worried about the refugees. When the fighting in the southern Sudan increased, the survivors from the devastated villages fled across the border into Ethiopia, many of them passing by night along the track in front of the Baro station as they made their way toward the UN relief and resettlement camps a hundred miles inside Ethiopia. Emily Farr was permitted to provide rations and medical aid for the women and children, but none for the men, who might be Anya-nya insurgents seeking a temporary safe haven. The refugees were forced to move on.

"I suppose you know that we're low on rations," she said. The UN plane hadn't arrived as scheduled.

"The weather has been bad. The fighting has moved to the south again. The rations will come." He got to his feet. "It is late. You will fall asleep in your chair again."

"In a few minutes."

Samuel Eko went back to the washhouse and took off his *jalibiiya*, the long cotton shirt he had worn in Khartoum and later Juba, where he'd owned a taxi, and which he still wore in the evenings in the mission yard. But at night before he returned to his wife in the village, he hung the gown on the back of the washhouse door.

"Did she go inside?" old William asked, lifting his wrinkled black face from the coals, the spear across his knees. Samuel Eko said she hadn't, and William looked behind him toward the grasslands. "Will the rebels come?" he asked.

"They will come and take you away," Samuel Eko replied. "Then they will make you a soldier to fight the Arabs."

The old man laughed, and Samuel Eko went back around the house to the front gate. "It is still late," he told Emily Farr, "and if you fall asleep, William will be afraid to wake you."

"I won't fall asleep."

"That is what the old grandmothers say." He went out the gate.

"Good night, Samuel Eko."

"Good night."

But she did fall asleep, and William banged the gate several times, yelled at an imaginary hyena, even rattled the screen door, but she didn't stir. Finally he crept close to her, calling her name sheepishly, and finally, when there was nothing else he could do, he tapped her on the shoulder. She awoke at his touch, saw him shrinking away, and apologized, rising to her feet sleepily. He followed her to the front porch, and after he'd heard her latch the screen door, returned to the fire. She stood for a moment in the door, wondering whether she had taken anything with her into the yard that night—book, flashlight, perhaps her box of stationery—when she heard the sound of a plane. At first she thought the engines were deep in the night sky—a 707 or a DC-8 flying between continents along the Rome-Capetown-or-Nairobi axis, their passage overhead sometimes drawing a faint hairline of frost on the night sky, vanishing with a brief pulse of sound. But this plane was much closer. Dangerously close, she thought, going back out on the porch.

Looking east, she thought she saw a shadow pass over the trees north of the village and reemerge against the dome of silver sky. *But it can't be.* She gasped, her heart missing a beat. But it was. She ran down the steps and out to the gate, following it as it passed north of the landing strip, a small aircraft flying without lights, only the dark silhouette and the bluish-white flare of its engines visible. *He's lost,* she thought immediately. *He's searching for the field.*

At both ends of the strip and along its sides were clumps of dead thorn and scrub cut from the savannahs and gathered in piles for emergencies, when a single torch would set their tinder ablaze and illuminate the perimeter of the field. But she had no matches. She ran back into the cottage, stumbled across the living room and down the hall to the kitchen, knocking two saucepans from the old wood stove before she found the jar of safety matches on the shelf. She snatched up the flashlight from her bedroom table, and rushed back to the gate, searching the sky for the plane. She couldn't find it at first, but when she did, its shadow was still moving west, droning resolutely through the night, the sound of the engines fluttering with distance, changing their pitch; and she stood on the road, still clutching the jar of matches and the flashlight, the blood pounding in her temples as she watched the shadow dissolve like smoke into the mist of moonlight, knowing that it wasn't lost at all.

She felt betrayed at first, standing idiotically in the middle of the road, her missionary instincts gathered for mercy or catastrophe, but left there with nothing but the whisper of the savannah wind in her ears. These were the grasslands she knew better than anyone except the Nuer themselves, yet he seemed to know them as well. He was a trespasser—flying at night and without lights. It was lunacy.

The gate squeaked behind her and she turned to see old William cross the road with his spear. "It was a plane," she called out, angry and upset. "Did you see it?" Yes, he had seen it. She went back to the cottage, fully awake, prepared to turn on the generator behind the kitchen. But once inside she knew that if the cottage lights went on, the old watchman would think something amiss and send for Samuel Eko, who would probably conclude that the plane was lost and recommend lighting the brush piles. Then the entire village would be roused, and by the following day the Ethiopian authorities would hear and send someone to investigate. If the Ethiopians investigated, so would the Sudanese consul at Gambela, who would protest to the UN that an unmarked plane was violating the Sudanese border by night.

She left the generator off and sat instead by lantern light in the radio room behind her bedroom. She switched on the emergency batteries for the sideband radio and monitored the emergency frequency of the missionary headquarters at Moquo, a hundred and twenty miles to the northeast. The frequency was silent. She was tempted to call in and inquire about any overdue plane in the vicinity, but realized that she would have to give Reverend Osgood more facts. If she did, Osgood would rouse every mission operator within hearing, report what she had seen, and send his evangelists off into the bush to spread the word. The results would be as unfortunate as lighting the brushfires outside. The Ethiopian and Sudanese officials would come to investigate and, whatever the evidence, the Sudanese would contend that a plane was using the Baro station to violate the border in contravention of the agreement, and ask that it be closed and that the nearby village be evacuated. Khartoum had been seeking the closure of the Baro station for almost two years.

She turned off the emergency power, drank a cup of warm cocoa, and went to bed. Two hours later she awoke in the darkness. William's spear point was scratching at the window screen. She sat up in bed. She heard the sound of the plane again, drew her robe from the chair nearby, and hurried out to the front porch. It seemed to her the same plane she'd seen earlier, approaching from the same direction in which it had disappeared—a dark swift shadow flying without lights across the western sky. She moved out into the wet grass, head lifted, not frightened now, but simply puzzled. Standing at the gate, she watched it disappear over the trees beyond the Nuer village. How strange, she thought. How strange and remarkable. There were few mysteries left to her life on the grasslands. There were none that weren't shared by the Moquo station, by Osgood, or by the Nuer village, by Samuel Eko or even William. For reasons she didn't wholly understand, she welcomed this one, which seemed to belong to her alone.

"I don't think we should talk about the plane," she said to William as he followed her back the walk to the cottage. "It wouldn't do for the Ethiopians to come. Or the Sudanese either."

William agreed.

2

The plane came regularly after that. It passed near the station at least once every two weeks—always late at night or early in the predawn hours; always without lights. The pattern never deviated, even after the first month when she recognized that the sound of the engines was different and it seemed to be a larger plane. It would appear high in the night sky to the east and then drop lower over the savannahs, occasionally making a minor correction in its compass bearing before it disappeared into the moonlight to the west. After three hours or so it would return. Once during a rainstorm to the west she had seen flashes of lightning strike up the horizon and illuminate the canyons of black cloud as the plane crossed overhead, flying toward the storm; but less than thirty minutes later it returned, and she watched with relief as it returned to the Ethiopian highlands.

She never mentioned the plane to others. She knew that both William and Samuel Eko had seen it and sometimes talked about it as they sat in front of the woodfire near the washhouse. She wasn't so naive not to guess that the night flights weren't somehow related to the guerrilla war in the southern Sudan. The thought occasionally disturbed her, but only because she feared that the Ethiopians or the Sudanese might somehow identify the plane with the Baro station and seek its closure. In the past the UN administrator, Stone-Ashton, had recommended both the relocation of Emily's clinic to Moquo and the evacuation of the village to the east, well within the Ethiopian border. Whether the village was actually being used as a safe haven by Anya-nya guerrillas was beside the point, Stone-Ashton had explained. In diplomacy, as in war, the perception was what mattered. If the Sudanese regulars across the border suspected either the Baro station or the village of sheltering Anya-nya rebels, they would cross the frontier and raze the village huts and the station cottage too.

But each time the plane swam into view, Emily's doubts were forgotten as she watched it soar across the black sky, crossing a hostile frontier without lights, beacons, radio signals, or emergency landing strips, challenging a wilderness of grassland, savannah, and swamp as vast as the ocean itself. The sight of the lonely plane against the stars awoke in her emotions so strong that she was convinced the simplicity of its flight must surely reflect the ends it served. She thought they must be courageous ones. In that way she identified the plane with the station itself, with the lives of the Nuer villagers nearby, as well as her own ministry. She persuaded herself that the plane must be flying mercy missions to the suffering peoples beyond the frontier, ferrying in medical and food supplies, and returning with the critically ill and wounded. Only those needs seemed to her as heroic and compelling as the audacity of the flights themselves.

Late one afternoon only a month after the plane had first appeared, Samuel Eko mentioned the aircraft to her. They were together in the overgrown vegetable garden, pulling tomatoes and beans from the stalks. As they reached the end of the row, Samuel Eko mopped his face and looked at the sky. It was a bright, windless afternoon. He said that the plane would probably come that night or the next.

Emily looked up at him in surprise. "How do you know?" She was wearing a straw hat, a denim skirt, and rope-soled walking shoes.

"Because of the moon."

Samuel Eko saw her smile and knew she didn't believe him. They began picking beans again. She took off her hat so that she could better see his face through the bean stalks. There was little he didn't know. He talked to everyone who passed on the road or who arrived from else-where—the UN pilots, the Swedish doctors, the rebel wounded, old widows and children, fishermen and herdsmen, passing cattle boys. "Has anyone mentioned the plane to you?" she asked. He shook his head. "But the village knows?"

"They know," he said, "but they don't talk about it."

"I think that's wise. I think it's best not to talk about the plane. If people talk, then it will be misunderstood. Soon everyone will be talking about it, and we don't want that, do we?" She tried to see his face through the dusty vines. His head was turned away. After a min-ute she said, "Don't you think that's wise, Samuel Eko—not to talk about it?"

He spat out a bean string and picked a few more pods, nodding his head indifferently. He was often embarrassed for her because of her clumsiness. Because she had known him the longest and trusted him the most, she would often say to him what she hadn't the heart or the courage to say to others, knowing that he would carry her message to the village. But she sometimes spoke too much, telling him again what he already knew in his heart. He had already told the villagers that they shouldn't talk about the plane. He had told them because he knew that was what she wanted. How could he explain it to her? He knew her as a woman whose gifts lay not in her words or her commands, which were sometimes clumsy and unnecessary, but in her hands and her heart, which he knew as well as he knew his own. He was hurt because she didn't recognize what her silence had already told him.

He dropped the beans into the woven basket, picked another, and stuck it in his mouth. She picked a few more beans in silence, noting the look on his face. "I meant the others," she said after a minute. "I didn't mean you or I—William either. I simply meant that when others ask, we should be careful."

"I am going to pick some corn," he said. He lifted his basket and crossed to the edge of the garden near the fence where he pulled a few ears of corn from the young stalks, humming to himself, and then went back to the washhouse. He took his *jalibiiya* from the hook behind the door, folded the towel over his arm, and crossed through the grass on his way to the river. The old crocodile was sleeping on the clay shelf fifty yards downstream, his yellow eyes half-open, his huge dragon tail lying across the sorghum stalks the village children flung there from the high bank above to tease him from his noonday snooze. "Stay away from me, old grandfather," Samuel Eko warned, "or I'll bring you gunpowder fish and ten chains for your head." He shed his clothes across the old uprooted tree trunk, and sat waist-deep in the brown water, watching the crocodile and the high grasses far across the river as he soaped his body with a sliver of soap which he kept in the hollow of the fallen tree. He hummed as he bathed, singing first to the crocodile, and then to himself, but finally breaking into Arabic song. The sun had gone down; swallows had taken the air, sweeping for insects high above the channel of the Baro. He dried himself in the warm dusk, put on his gown, and climbed back up the bank.

An hour later he was sitting at his stool in front of the washhouse, lifting a few red coals with his tongs and dropping them carefully in the clay bowl with the coffee beans. Emily Farr joined them from the front yard, carrying her Nuer phrase book. William brought another stool from the washhouse, but she said she wouldn't stay. "I was thinking about something you said," she told Samuel Eko. He pinched a few more hot coals into the bowl.

"Will you drink coffee with us?"

She hesitated, and then sat down. "That would be very nice. I didn't mean that we shouldn't talk about the plane. That wasn't what I meant at all." Samuel Eko's head was cocked as he ground the coffee beans, his tongue between his teeth. Beads of perspiration shone among the tribal scars on his black forehead. "You said it might come tonight," she continued. "How do you know?" William lifted the battered tea kettle from the coals and Samuel Eko spooned the coffee dust into a small cup.

"I will show you tonight," Samuel Eko said, "when the moon is full."

It was after nine o'clock when he summoned her from the kitchen where she'd been writing letters. She took the flashlight from the table and followed him out along the walk to the hard clay of the road. "Where are you going?" William called from the gate. Samuel Eko told him a bustard with a broken wing was under the thorn tree.

"Is that what you want to show me?" she asked, following him across the loose rubble that littered the crown of the landing strip. The moon was high, bathing the savannahs. He didn't stop until he reached the first brush pile at the end of the field. There he turned and looked back toward the cottage.

"Look," he said.

She followed his lifted arm, gazing back toward the cottage. The moon lit the grasslands, but the trees and shrubs surrounding the Baro station were only obscure shadows. She didn't understand what he wanted her to see. But then she moved her head toward his, still looking back, and as she did the cottage roof shone like a heliostat between the sheltering trees, reflecting like a mirror the radiance of the African moon, the axis of its roofline pointing like a silver finger toward the Sudan border to the west.

"A *beacon*," she whispered. "Of course! He's using the mission house as a beacon!"

She felt betrayed. As poor a student of celestial or aerial navigation as Samuel Eko, she sensed that someone was taking advantage of her and her house. The plane's purpose no longer seemed so charitable to her. On the contrary, it seemed hypocritical and deceitful.

She spent a restless night and was already in the yard when the sun broke through the trees, lifting the mist from the night earth. She met Samuel Eko at the gate as he came up from the village. He knew she had something on her mind. She followed him across the wet grass toward the parked Land-Rover. "It's obvious that we'll have to do something," she said. "We can't let the Baro station be used in this way, can we?"

Samuel Eko looked down at her sleepily. She looked up through the blowing leaves at the cottage roof, already bright in the morning sun.

"We'll simply have to paint the roof," she continued, shading her eyes from its glare. "I'm sure we can find some roofing paint in Gambela, don't you think? If not, then we can certainly ask Reverend Osgood to send us some from Moquo. The more quickly it's done, the better for all of us."

Samuel Eko stood gazing up at the aluminum roofing panels he had installed three years earlier. He had chopped up the crude ladder he had built and used the timbers for firewood—chopped it up immediately to make certain he'd never be asked to use it again. He remembered the scorching heat of the metal panels, the cauldron of tar from which he'd drawn the buckets he carried aloft to daub the joints and nail holes and which, once spilled on the rickety ladder, had taken the hide from his arm and shoulder. Three months it had taken him.

He was still looking up at the roof when Emily Farr went down the path toward the clinic, carrying her medical kit and wearing her straw hat.

"Come eat my feet, old grandfather," he said as he sat on the mud shelf that evening, bathing in the river. "Come eat my feet so I won't climb that ladder and paint her roof."

THREE

1

He was flying on a southeasterly heading, drifting through the ragged rain clouds that blanketed the highlands along the edge of the escarpment. The clouds thinned after an hour and swept their shadows across the steep fields and peaks where teff and millet grew along the fertile slopes between the gorges. Swift water lay as quick as mercury in the plunging streams, brightening to dark blue as the plane dropped westward. The clusters of tin roofs of the monetized economy had long since passed away; below him the plane's shadow sped over ravines, gorges, and groves of eucalyptus—pleated, fragmented, and folded by the earth's facets far below as the sun moved to the west, like some indestructible engine of its will.

As the afternoon passed, the sun brightened the cabin where he sat alone. The escarpment behind him, he was lofted like a gull out over the mountainsides sloping toward the Sudan border, corrugated with coffee trees and towering strands of hardwood. He found the coil of river, cast like a rope across the landscape as it fell out of the mountains toward the savannahs to the west. He dropped lower and below him saw an antlike thread of movement along the road near the river. The sunlight, filtered through the gauze of yellow dust to the west, flattened the shadows against the track where they moved like insects, and for a moment he couldn't distinguish body from shadow. He brought the plane around and flew directly over them on his approach to the Sudi airstrip hidden beyond the trees two miles away. The shadows were army porters, moving supplies up from the foundered trucks to the airfield camp. He passed over them swiftly, the plane just a momentary shadow over their lifted faces before it dropped from sight below the trees, settling lazily to the strip, igniting behind it billows of dust, chaff, and penny-sized pebbles as it trundled toward the far end of the small, hidden airfield.

Along the southern edge of the airstrip lay a group of canvas tents, a dozen in all, lined in military defile along the mud path. Most of the tents had their flaps rolled up, their sides, too, airing their plank floors, cots, rolled bedding, and mess tables in the afternoon sun. A few Israeli military advisers sat in the shadows inside, watching the plane. The three tents at the end of the row were closed. Ethiopian paratroopers in khaki uniforms and olive green berets sat on wooden stools outside, their backs against the closed canvas, American M-14 rifles across their knees. Beyond the last tent was a high, corrugated metal roof supported by peeled eucalyptus poles. Fifty-gallon drums of aviation gas were stacked in the high grass beyond under a wet tarpaulin covered over with camouflage netting and green limbs.

McDermott taxied the plane back down the field and turned toward the shed, following the hand signals of the two Europeans in short-sleeved shirts and tan hiking shorts, as he eased the plane forward under the high roof. Both were Israelis. One was dark-haired, with olive skin; the other pale, with a flaming copper beard. Both wore high-topped leather boots with cleated rubber soles and heavy stockings rolled above their boot tops, like Alpine climbers. On their wrists were identical military watches with aluminum bands. McDermott climbed from the cabin, opened the double door on the port side of the fuselage, and lifted out the boxes of radio and truck parts. Then he brought out the aluminum cooler as the dark-haired Israeli adviser climbed into the cabin and began passing out the cartons of tinned milk, coffee, sugar, and flour to his red-bearded colleague. A third Israeli came around the corner of the radio tent. Younger than the other two, he wore a cotton cap pulled low over his eyes, steel-rimmed spectacles, and a wispy adolescent beard. "What about the letter mail?" he asked McDermott.

"On the front seat," McDermott said.

The copper-bearded Israeli pulled a bottle of beer from the

chipped ice of the cooler and held it aloft: "Amstel!" he shouted; and his dark-haired helper jumped to the ground. A short, heavyset Israeli with blond hair came into the shadows of the shed from the hot sunlight beyond. "Hey, Rozewicz!" the man at the cooler called. "Beer! Amstel! He brought it!" He held up the frosted bottle but Rozewicz only grunted and looked at McDermott.

"What about the weather?" Rozewicz asked.

"What about it? It'll be all right," McDermott said, uncapping a bottle of beer.

Rozewicz took a bottle from the redhead. "What time?"

"Eleven thirty."

"We need a Dornier, not a Beechcraft," Rozewicz said. "The DO-28. Very quick. Short fields don't matter." His eyes were a wintry gray, his hair a dirty blond beginning to gray. It stuck out over his ears like thatch. He was wearing shorts and cleated boots, like the others, but was stocky and more powerful, with heavy, muscular legs, like a rugby player. A major in the Israeli army, he had served as an aviation mechanic in the RAF during the war. Now he was the commander of the Israeli advisory team at the Sudi airstrip. Born in Poland, he'd married an English girl during the war, and still traveled on a Commonwealth passport. His wife lived in Tel Aviv with their two teen-aged children.

"There's no mail," the wisp-bearded Israeli said, leaving the cabin. "Just official mail." The others ignored him. He was a young, French-born linguist from Tel Aviv who specialized in Nilotic languages.

"Rozewicz is worried," the red-bearded Israeli said to McDermott as he put his beer bottle aside to help his companion to remove the seats from the rear cabin. With the seats removed, the plane could hold an additional three thousand pounds of cargo, three litter patients and four ambulatory wounded, or ten fully equipped combat troops.

"He's always worried," McDermott said. "Just don't let him worry me." Another Israeli adviser appeared with the Ethiopian porters from the gun tents, carrying cases of rifles, machine guns, grenades, and ammo, which they stacked near the plane. Included in the wooden crates were Belgian, German, and Soviet rifles, 9 mm Egyptian Suez machine guns, 7.62 semi-automatic NATO rifles, and a few Russian-made carbines. Some of the weapons were booty from the 1967

Israeli war; others had been purchased from munitions brokers on the Continent. McDermott studied the loading plan with Rozewicz and the Israeli with the red beard, the strip's cargo master. He checked the cargo weight and the distribution plan, gave back the clipboard, and told them to load. He left the shed and went back to the end of the air-strip and began to walk off the field. Rozewicz joined him, following McDermott's footprints in the ridges of fine sand and clay that washed down from the high bank below the coffee trees. Rozewicz despised the Sudi strip—despised it as much for its isolation, its monotony, and its unpredictable weather as he did the dangerous limitations of the strip itself. The field was too short, the clay base too fragile, the drainage too poor, the wash from the higher elevations unpredictable. There were too many trees. During the rains he was forced to bring up the guns by porter from the trucks that were mired to their axles in the deep mud of the road below. He had recommended that the Sudi operation be transferred elsewhere—to the airstrip at the Baro station, for example—but the Ethiopians had repeatedly denied the request. Either they flew from Sudi or they didn't fly.

"They're not serious," Rozewicz said, kneeling down to pick up a few green coffee beans washed down from the slopes by the previous night's rain. "The Ethiopians are not serious men. Why should we be serious then? They are playing games with us. It is suicide—this whole bloody landing strip. This whole bloody operation is suicide." McDer-mott didn't answer, pacing off the field until he reached the end of the strip and could smell the crocodile skins in the primitive wooden shed below the trees. "We could fly a DC-3 out of Baro," Rozewicz said as McDermott joined him again.

"Nothing's perfect," McDermott replied, looking out over the trees. A few ugly clouds drifted down from the slopes above, dissolving as they touched the sunlight further down. He looked west. "There'll be a moon tonight."

"A moon?" Rozewicz asked, awestruck. "Oh, God almighty, a moon tonight? Is that what makes it so bloody perfect?" His head rolled back and he laughed, his gray eyes shining under the massive brow bone. "Oh Lord, don't tell me."

"Everything helps," McDermott said, searching for the tractor driver. They walked back to the tents and McDermott told the Israeli tractor driver to take the Fiat tractor and scrape the northern edge of the field beyond the crown. On a wooden pallet, outside the tent the Israeli advisory team used as a ready room, were four cases of medicines and field rations. On the wooden map table inside were the cargo manifests and maps of Upper Nile Province in Sudan. Standing at the map table, McDermott once more calculated his fuel load and the cargo already aboard the Beechcraft, then told Rozewicz to load the medicines and rations. The young ethnologist came into the tent, complaining about the lack of personal mail from home. Two Israeli captains stood with McDermott at the map table, studying the navigational maps and the weather reports.

"They send us out here and abandon us," the ethnologist complained. "No one cares. The whole thing is absurd."

"Rubbish," Rozewicz said.

McDermott listened as an Israeli officer described the radio intercepts they'd picked up from the Sudanese army radio at Nasir. A Soviet-piloted helicopter had landed there two days earlier after a surveillance flight over the Pibor River and the adjacent grasslands. The young major thought the Sudanese army had put a launch with a sideband radio in the Pibor to monitor the Anya-nya's movements.

"I'm not assigned here like you others. I'm not a military man," the ethnologist complained. "My wife doesn't even know where I am. What can I tell her?"

"Ask our bachelor pilot," Rozewicz said. "Ask him what he tells his Ethiopian girl friends."

"What can I say?" the ethnologist asked him. McDermott put the maps in his briefcase. "What can I tell her?"

"Words of one syllable," McDermott said, closing the case and looking around. *They think they're going to get a little local color in the African bush*, he thought. Then the mail doesn't come and they think they're dead.

It was after five o'clock. He went into the adjacent tent, took off his boots and his tan poplin shirt, and stretched out on the cot near the door. Outside, the sun drew the shadows across the strip. A few Israeli advisers stirred from their tents after their afternoon naps and joined the Ethiopian paratroopers who were already on the field, kicking a soccer ball back and forth. Lying in the tent with his eyes closed, McDermott could hear the voices from the adjacent tents and the cries from the field, the soft thud of the soccer ball, the quick, jogging breaths that came to claim it and send it back to scrimmage, the soft whisper of the Ethiopian guards speaking in Amharic outside the gun tents, the wind stirring in the coffee trees high on the hillside.

Lying on the cot with his arm across his brow, McDermott heard these sounds and could see each segment of the field, the soccer players, the Sudi strip, the river far below, the hillside, the sky; and even with his eyes closed could bring sound and shape together, know from a heel's thud how near it was, whether the calf that flexed it was on the rise or fall, whether the blowing leaves rustling against the tent canvas were in sunlight or in shadow. Whether it was the acuity of vision, memory, muscular concentration, or the swiftness of his ability to knit brain, nerves, and muscles together—probably the only remarkable gift of an otherwise unremarkable man—McDermott saw it all, drifted through these forms and shadows beyond the tent canvas the way the plane had drifted through the mist of cumulus debris above the escarpment, trading its substance for another as it passed in and out of sound, transferring to the earth below a quick, small shadow fleeing across wheat and teff fields. His mind now was only this shadow, transferred under the imperial sun, floating across fields, forests, tukuls, rivers, and ravines, across dark throats and lifted faces, across fly-blown children and tubercular mothers, rotting sorghum, groves of eucalyptus silvered with sunlight, but crawling with disease and death—floating in that moment across everything he didn't understand, telling him in darkness not that he slept but in which form, in which shape had he passed so swiftly across the face of the earth he might never find again—a ubiquitous memory prowling among forms, possibilities, spectra of light and darkness, sleep and wakefulness, earth and sky, and finally the present was lost to him.

He awoke in darkness, the night absolute beyond the open tent flap. Slowly he sat up, his face and neck wet, and looked at his watch. He'd slept five hours.

He lit the kerosene lantern, bathed his face in the aluminum wash-basin, pulled on his boots, and went out onto the field. The disc of moon hung white and luminous over the trees. Inside the ready tent the two Israeli captains were bent over the map table. Locusts and tree frogs chirped from the shadows. From the ashes of the campfire a Galla orderly in a tattered uniform brought a blackened tea kettle into the ready tent and filled the porcelain teapot on the table. McDermott followed. His name was Tadessa; in 1940 he had fought his way back into Ethiopia from the. Sudan with the British army. He looked toward McDermott and dropped a bag of tea leaves into the bubbling water.

Across the field the tractor moved slowly down the strip, dragging the portable generator on its wooden sled. McDermott heard the tractor, made a few final notes, and pocketed the leather notebook. He left the ready tent and stood outside, the glare from the kerosene lantern falling across his dusty boots. Tadessa watched his boots from the mess table, and when McDermott turned back into the tent, he quickly lifted the pot and poured the tea into a glass, spooned in some sugar, and poured it into the earthenware mug to cool it further. He handed the mug to McDermott, who carried it back to his own tent, picked up the web belt and the Uzi submachine gun, and walked toward the plane, standing out on the field. Rozewicz sat in the copilot's seat, his face visible through the tinted glass as he throttled the engines. Ethiopian soldiers and Israeli advisers had gathered in the darkness to watch, and McDermott joined them, finishing the mug of tea. When he finally turned, the mug empty, Tadessa was there to take it from him. He entered the plane, climbed past the gun crates, and slipped into the pilot's seat. Outside, the sled of generator-driven landing lights had been pushed into place at midfield. He went over the aircraft checklist with Rozewicz, who climbed past him when they had finished, and dropped to the ground, locking the door behind him. McDermott buckled the web belt with its .45 pistol across the back of the empty copilot's seat, jammed the Uzi between the belt and the back of the seat, muzzle down, and taxied forward.

He waited at the end of the strip until he saw the flashlight signal from midfield, then began to throttle forward, the plane still locked in place. As the seconds passed, the engines' roar drove every other sound from the surrounding hillside, flattening the grasses and small shrubs behind the plane with its gale. The bank of lights at midfield suddenly swept on, illuminating the far end of the strip; and McDermott released the plane. It catapulted forward at full throttle, and as it moved out of the darkness and into the fog of light, it began to lift—unsteadily at first, clumsily—before it finally swept above the trees beyond the end of the runway. The instant its silhouette was free of the earth, the lights behind it faded and the field itself disappeared in the darkness below the coffee trees.

2

The Baro River was a bright beading of silver off his port engine. The moon bathed the grasslands, striking the glinting die-points of the plane's silhouette in the vacuum in which it seemed suspended, without visible thrust or motion. He was cruising at five thousand feet, his airspeed a little more than one hundred and eighty knots. The smoky moonlight filtered into the cabin as it had on hundreds of other nights, the vein of river below indistinguishable from others on other continents—the Ch'ongch'on, the Red River in North Vietnam, the Rhine, Canada's Labrador, the Moselle. From time to time he saw the frail ash of campfires below, weak braziers of acacia or dung chips, feeble cinders that were lost under his wings. He passed over the Baro station and reset his chronometer on the panel in front of him, changing course slightly as he moved closer to the river and brought his airspeed down. He was over the Sudan.

He moved the radio dial to the Sudanese military station at Nasir and slipped on the headphones; but he heard nothing, except the chittering static of the African night. Ten minutes passed and he banked toward the southeast, bringing the moon over his right shoulder. West of the confluence of the Baro and Pibor rivers, he veered to the south and began to lose altitude. He watched his airspeed, the wind-drift indicator, and his compass bearing constantly now, glancing only oc-

casionally at the shiny channel of the Pibor. When he found the familiar loop in the river, he dipped away toward the southwest on a new
bearing. As he banked, a flare burst ahead of him over the channel
of the river, and under the fading light of the two starbursts he saw a
small motor launch moored in midstream—

SAMs up at eight o'clock!

He kicked the rudder in reflex, his mind elsewhere, no longer in
Africa at all as he watched the orange balls still falling through the
night sky, a tide of bubbling voices rising suddenly in his earphones
after all those years—

*This is Neptune twenty eight! We've got a launch light! SAMs up at
eight o'clock. Do you read?*

*Rog, Neptune. Gopher lead. Read you five-by. Keep it moving, Go-
phers. Read out is three zero.*

*Gopher four! You've got two Migs at seven o'clock—maybe eight
thousand out!*

*Gopher lead, this is Otter one. Target's solid. Like concrete, all the
way down from six thousand. We can't get in. We're egressing.*

Go full burner, Gopher four! He's on your tail!

Light your burners, Otters! We're moving out!

Gopher four! You're out of control!

Gopher two, watch it! You've got flak off the ridge!

Oh, shit! Mayday, goddammit. Mayday.

Gopher three is down. Anyone have a tally-ho on a chute?

Dump your bombs, Gopher two.

Gopher two! Get the hell out!

Gophers, we got two more launch lights. SAMs up at five o'clock.

McDermott watched the last flare dissolve in the African moonlight, the voices again only a memory. He was alone: no SAM-2 mis-
siles, no flak, no MIGs, no F-105's around him from Otter Flight, no
F-4 SAM hunters above him. There was nothing now, and for a moment he felt the void in himself. He changed frequency and moved
away from the river on his new bearing.

Thirty minutes later he began his descent and leveled off less than
a thousand feet above the scrubland. He watched the cotton soil give
way to alkali pan, dropped lower and checked his chronometer, com-

pass bearing, and airspeed. Ahead of him a light pulsed below the horizon, glowed for two long intervals, and was extinguished. A second light flared closer, and he dropped the plane to two hundred feet. He switched on his landing lights, turned them off again, and ahead of him the two lights came on simultaneously from each end of the hidden airstrip. Accelerating his descent, he drifted against the two lights, trimming his glide as he brought them into line against the axis of his descent. He lowered the landing gear and the plane rumbled forward, yawing slightly as the flaps were fully extended. Switching on the remaining landing lights, the cracked alkali pan flared brightly beneath his wheels. He identified the parallel piles of gathered brush funneling his descent toward the strip and rode the corridor like a beacon. The soldier with the lantern was suddenly under his wheels, and he dropped the aircraft to the alkali floor thirty yards beyond.

The Anya-nya captain was waiting outside when he cut the engines and unlocked the cabin door. The officer was wearing a twill shirt and twill shorts, a lime-green beret with leather piping, and Israeli military boots. "Welcome," he said, shaking McDermott's hand. "Welcome."

"Are your men ready?"

"Ready."

McDermott dropped to the ground, unfastened the double doors, and pushed them back against the fuselage, bringing into the cool cabin the warm African night as the Anya-nya porters stood waiting for the guns at the door. They formed two lines, more than forty in all, Anya-nya guerrillas dressed in ragged shorts, twill shirts, but most of them barefooted; some carrying spears or bows and arrows, others armed with old Italian or British muskets. Tall, silent, as black as ebony, they were all Nilotics, Sudanese Negroes from the south, some Christian, some animists, but none of them Moslem. A few were old men; some were just kids, still wearing the dust-stained white robes of a village cattle boy. All of them smelled of rotting clothes, exhausted flesh, and empty stomachs. McDermott, the Anya-nya captain, and another officer moved the gun crates to the open door, and the guerrillas bore them away, four men to a crate. McDermott's back ached; his shirt was wet; his mouth and throat tasted of the dust that blew in through the open door.

They unloaded the plane in twenty minutes. Nearby, the gun and ammunition crates were opened by the Anya-nya captain's NCO's. Each guerrilla was armed and given an additional weapon and ammunition to be carried to other guerrillas waiting in the south. There were animals, too, and McDermott could smell them even before he heard the loose jounce of their traces and the creak of their baggage saddles. As he watched, three camels were brought out of the darkness to the circle of lantern light, where the guns were being distributed, and prodded to their knees by two Dinka camel men. The camels would carry the heavier ordnance. The arms and ammunitions that couldn't be taken away that night would be buried; in two or three days the Anya-nya bearers would return to dig them up and take them south.

The Anya-nya captain led McDermott away from the gun crates and back into the scrub to a clearing between two acacia trees. Kneeling down with his flashlight, he pointed out the tread of a truck tire against the cracked earth, then another, and finally a third and fourth, all turning in a wide radius some hundred meters short of the landing strip.

"There was an army truck here?" McDermott asked.

"Two days ago." The captain's eyes were bloodshot in the reflected glow of the flashlight.

"Did they find the field?"

The captain got to his feet with a shrug. "Only the Arabs know," he said. "We saw a helicopter two days ago. It flew along the banks of the Pibor. Did you know about it?"

McDermott said he did. The captain went back to the gun crates and McDermott walked alone out onto the field beyond the plane, looking at the sky. What could he do about a helicopter and a Sudanese army truck? Nothing. No more than the captain and his guerrillas could do about them.

The captain called to him. "The men said there are only two boxes of rations," the captain declared, puzzled, as if a mistake had been made.

"Just two, yes," McDermott admitted. "That was all the extra weight I could manage."

A few yards away the rations were being distributed, the crate lumber broken up to line the gun pits where the surplus weapons and ammo would be buried. The guerrilla captain studied McDermott silently, then turned and went back to his men. McDermott listened to their quiet voices and saw a few faces turn his way. There was nothing more he could say. He was a mercenary, like them, not their benefactor, although he knew they didn't understand that. He had landed among them a dozen times, each flight arming a new unit, freshly conscripted from the bush, but even so he didn't make the rules. He knew his descent from the night sky and the precision of the machine he commanded was evidence enough of the sovereignty of his power, which continued even where theirs ended here on this godforsaken patch of soil, abandoned by crops, by animals, and finally by men. Still, he could do no more about their hunger than he could about helicopters or army trucks.

He walked to the edge of the gun pit where the soldiers were carefully covering the weapons. A few looked up at him, smiling as they worked, while others gathered around, curious as to his interest in their work. In their labor he could smell the smoke of their rags, their huts, their campfires, their animals. In him they smelled beneath the bland, neutral sweat a scrubbed white skin and the ceremony of rooms, lamplight, odorless beds, and the machines that separated him from his own labor, as well as a thousand other magic surfaces that isolated his white flesh from the consequences of his existence. The sharp smell of the anodized cabin from which they brought the guns carried the mystery of men and machines whose identities they couldn't isolate or understand. Most of all it was the machine itself that overwhelmed them and he commanded it. It stood behind them in the darkness, poised and yet lifeless, empty but alive, its metal skin shedding like an animal the cold condensations of space, its glittering iron shell giving off the bitter metallic taste of its propulsion, of fires too hot to smell of fire at all, of cold too absolute to know itself; and so in its mystery and their exile, it smelled to them of death, the way the stars themselves might smell should they tire of their solitude and come down to claim their mortality here among their miserable rags, huts, and dungchip fires.

McDermott brought the engines to life and the guerrillas moved away—far away—from the stinging turbulence. Their hands clapped their ears as he advanced toward full throttle and sped forward. The plane bounced across the strip and soared into the night sky, trailing under its wings the dark racing figures who were already beginning to drag back over the hard earth the brush and branches that would obliterate his tire marks.

He climbed to four thousand feet and flew north-northeast, banking as he crossed the Sobat River, still in Sudan, and followed it east. The moon was high overhead; the earth bright beneath. The Baro station swam slowly into view, a small neat square on the ocean of savannah, as tidy as a New England meadow. He dropped away toward the north and came around again over the station.

They were sleeping below: the mission house, the Nuer village under the trees. He came in low over the meadow behind the airstrip and lifted over the trees and the cottage beneath, twisting its shape under his rotating wings. Looking down, he saw a figure standing at the gate, staring skyward. He saw it for only a moment—just a slim pencil of white, as solitary as a whaler's widow outside some New England saltbox with the sea of grassland sweeping away endlessly at her feet. It was almost as if she'd been expecting him, and he watched until he was far beyond her, until her own lonely figure and the riddle of her face were swept into abstraction again, like the savannahs around her.

He flew east toward the mountains. Leaning forward, he reset the chronometer, and turned toward the Sudi azimuth. It was three fifteen.

FOUR

1

O ccasionally during the rainy season the mist would rise from the gorge of the Baro during the early dawn, obscuring the tops of the trees and lying in thick drops on their trunks, on the heavy grasses, and the hard clay of the road. The thin blanket of air kept in the noises of the earth, like a glass bell, dimming the reverberations as they ascended through the fog—the cries of birds and animals, cattle, the Nuer herdsmen and their wives at the morning fires—so that the sounds came in a more intimate, personal way. In the mist the old baobab tree, midway to the village, looked like a pillar of the universe. On these mornings nothing seemed more real or eternal to Emily Farr than the life of the village itself. For more than ten years Africa had banished autumn and winter from her memory; but for those few hours on mornings such as these, the fog rising from the Baro was a recovery of lost seasons.

A light mist lay over the village under the trees as she came down the path from the cottage, carrying her medical kit. No new wounded rebels or refugees had arrived at the village for several weeks. Samuel Eko had been painting the cottage roof, but that morning had driven a Nuer child with an infected eye to the Swedish hospital sixty miles away. Emily had remained behind, expecting the UN aircraft from Addis bringing powdered milk and vaccine. Space permitting, the plane would also bring a consignment of hoes, spades, and mattocks from the mission headquarters at Moquo. But the plane would also bring a mail pouch from Moquo; she hadn't received mail from her parents and sisters in Vermont for over a month.

She worked in the mission clinic until noon, but by lunchtime the plane still hadn't arrived. At one o'clock she spoke to the mission radio operator at Moquo on the sideband and was told that the Swedish pilot was ill; the substitute pilot had been delayed because of engine trouble. When the plane hadn't arrived by midafternoon, she concluded that it wouldn't arrive at all. She sat in the kitchen and made a second cup of tea, hoping that she might be wrong, but the fifty-year-old Swedish pilot was undependable, even in the best of weather. His replacement, undoubtedly with less experience, would be even more cautious, quick to abandon the flight at the first sign of trouble.

She took her straw hat from behind the door and went out into the empty African afternoon. She heard distant thunder and looking to the east discovered an ugly anvil of gray thunderheads towering to twenty thousand feet along the mountains. She was sure it would be raining in the highlands, perhaps even at Moquo. Leaning against the front gate, she tried to think of something she might do to relieve her disappointment; but she could think of nothing—only her unexpected solitude and the emptiness of the grasslands stretching away in the distance. The sky was still clear overhead, a brittle blue, and the storm was drifting off to the southeast, away from the station; but the clouds had already drawn their veil across her mind. She thought of swimming in the river, but knew she hadn't the courage to swim alone. She could go to the village clinic and scrub out the cabinets and the small emergency room; but the smell of the clinic, its medicines and carbolic, still clung to her hair and skin from her work there that morning and the previous day. So she just stood in the road, looking toward the Sudan border. In planning her days at the mission, she'd conditioned herself to accept disappointment and conceive alternatives to rout the unexpected, but standing in the empty road that afternoon, she was impatient with the excuses which denied loneliness. She should have gone to the Swedish hospital with Samuel Eko.

Emily moved away from the gate, away from the village. She knew others thought her stoical in her acceptance of isolation. They wouldn't have understood her helplessness at the failure of the plane's arrival. Her solitude was hidden from them, her boredom concealed by habit and routine. The missionaries she knew were never bored. They met disappointment with prayer, solitude with Christian reflection, and emptiness or loss with more determined purpose. In recent years she'd found herself less able to recover these resources from her own existence. In the moral and physical depression that followed, she found only her own solitude, like a dry worm in an empty hull. "*Bored! Emily bored!*" Reverend Osgood once told a delegation of visiting Presbyterian clergy: "My goodness sakes alive. Never—not in a million years. She's got the good Lord out here with her."

She hadn't prayed in years. Most of the missionaries were simple people, and their simplicity, like their constant prayers, brought her pain. But Osgood's words had annoyed her. If she'd still prayed, she would have asked for forgiveness for disliking him so much. She continued down the track.

Standing beyond the far end of the airfield, looking west, she heard the plane—just a faint, momentary thread of sound waving in the wind at first, but then stronger. She turned. It veered low out of the sky to the north, far out over the grasslands, the sun striking across the wingfoil like a semaphore. She watched it come, astonished at the miracle of its appearance.

It flew almost directly over her, even the shriek of its engines a relief. Running back along the road, she watched as it waddled gooselike over the uneven strip and taxied back toward the cottage. She waved to the pilot and ran to meet it near the front gate. The windscreen was streaked with dust; raindrops hung suspended on the fuselage. As the engines were turned off, she slipped under the wing and stood at its trailing edge, hand over her eyes, hat off, smiling as she looked up.

"How glad I am to see you!" she called impulsively as the pilot stepped out on the wing. McDermott looked down at her and then at the empty track beyond. Except for her, the cottage, and the sunlight, there was nothing.

"I had a little trouble," he said. "You must be Mrs. Farr. My name's McDermott."

"You certainly are a sight for sore eyes, Mr. McDermott. Welcome to Baro station. I certainly didn't expect to see you." She took her hand away from her forehead, still smiling.

"I guess not," he said, not understanding why she was smiling. But that was the least of his surprises. When he'd first heard her name, he'd conjured up a woman of sixty or sixty-five, like a pioneer widow on the Nebraska prairie—with a calico bonnet, a strong pump arm, and a flinty eye out for cyclone weather, Comanches, or traveling whiskey salesmen. But this woman wasn't old; she wasn't even middle-aged. Her strong, lean face was burned by the sun, and her brown hair was tied in a fetching bun at the back of her neck.

"I'm certainly glad you're here," she said as he dropped to the ground.

"I've got some mail for you. Other stuff too. I don't have much time. I've got to get to Gambela before the field closes down. I've got a fuel problem."

"I'm sorry I don't have any aviation fuel, but it's forbidden here."

She smelled of the prairie—of open fields and windblown laundry. Why was she smiling? "Not the fuel," he said, realizing she was apologizing. "The fuel pump."

"Do you think there's enough daylight left?"

"In this place there's never enough daylight left." That was one of the hazards of flying the missionary frontier, and he supposed she realized that. The Swedish pilot did and it was his plane McDermott was flying. Twice that morning he'd called McDermott from his hospital bed to warn him that if he couldn't find the Baro station by two o'clock, he should abort the flight. He never flew after four o'clock in the African bush.

There was no truck, no Land-Rover, not even a road crowded with naked children and curious villagers. He unloaded the medical supplies and the agricultural implements with her help, gave her the mail pouch, and climbed up on the wing.

"I'm sorry you can't stay longer," she said. "I'd like to show you the station."

"So am I," said McDermott, who had wanted to walk off the field to see if it was as long and well impacted as Rozewicz claimed. "But maybe I'll get a chance later. I'll be substituting for Larsen for a couple of months. He's going back to Sweden on leave."

She waved him off, and he taxied to the end of the strip. She watched as the port propeller feathered and lost power. Three times the engine broke its rhythm as McDermott throttled in place; and the last time the port engine shut down completely. He taxied back to the gate and shut off the other engine.

"No luck," he said as he climbed down. "It's the godda—it's the fuel pump."

"Probably it's just as well," she said, encouragingly. "Better safe than sorry." They went into the cottage and she called the Moquo radio operator and asked that she relay a radio message to the UN at Gambela that the plane would be delayed at the Baro station. Two hours of daylight were left. She brought some men from the village to move the supplies to the clinic, and afterward sat on the front lawn under the trees and read her mail. McDermott worked on the plane. She sat in the blowing sunshine, raising her head from her letters from time to time to look out across the grasslands, thinking about the Vermont mountains. She had forgotten the storm in the mountains, her impatience in the road, even McDermott, who was working under the wing of the plane, hidden from her beyond the vine-covered fence. At last she went back into the cottage, put the letters away in her stationery box, made a pitcher of lemonade, and carried it out to the yard.

McDermott was kneeling under one engine, his shirt off, his hands dark with grease, his face dripping. Gnats and midges swarmed around him, sometimes getting in his eyes. On the canvas drop cloth at his knees were a few small fittings and a length of aluminum-fiber hose. He was swearing to himself as she came through the gate. She stopped and let the gate shut to tell him she was there.

"I thought you might be thirsty," she said, kneeling under the wing with the pitcher and two glasses.

"Thanks. You don't have anything for these gnats, do you?" She gave him a glass of lemonade.

"Just patience, I'm afraid. We don't use pesticides here." She sat down sideways on the grass under the wing as he drank the lemonade. Her eyes were dark brown, her face as cool as porcelain. "Is that the pump?" she asked.

He looked up at the exposed couplings in the recessed panel over his head. "It's the fuel line."

"Is the engine damaged?" She moved further under the wing, looking up too.

"It will be if they let the same mechanics keep working on it. The fuel line is fouled, perhaps the pump as well."

"How did it happen?"

"Poor maintenance and crummy supervision." The way he said it made her feel culpable as well. The mail pouch seemed insignificant and she was embarrassed that he might have sensed how much it meant to her, even at the risk of flying a poorly serviced aircraft.

"I take it then it's not your plane," she said, smiling as she said it, as if it were an important discovery. But he only glanced at her, as if she should have known that from the beginning.

"It's no one's plane," he said, reaching overhead to unfasten an aluminum fitting. "That's the trouble. It's public property." That was exactly what Samuel Eko might have said, she thought, watching McDermott pull down a length of hose and squint through it, holding it against the sky. "The line's garbaged up," he said.

"Then it's not the pump?"

"We'll see."

"What would happen if you had to fly the plane back tonight?" she asked, still thinking guiltily of the mail pouch. "The way the plane is and with the bad weather?"

"It would increase the sweat factor," McDermott said.

The gnats were still a nuisance, and she wished there was something she could do—not only with the insects, but the plane as well. "It's really a shame you can't enjoy what little time you have here," she said, wishing he'd not try to fly the plane back to Gambela that afternoon. "This is one of the loveliest times of day."

McDermott sank back against his heels, still looking up into the recessed panel. "Why don't we do it then," he said. "Gambela's probably closed down anyway." He looked at his watch, and began wrapping up the assembled parts in the drop cloth. "I can do it better and quicker in the morning."

She was relieved. "I'm sure you can. Even the most experienced pilots, like Mr. Larsen, never fly after four o'clock." He replaced the metal panel, returned the wrapped parts and tool kit to the cabin, and brought out a small canvas rucksack.

"Rations," he said as he joined her on the ground. "A survival kit."

"Self-reliance," she said, approvingly. "That's a very wise rule."

"Maybe you'd better tell the UN that," he said as he followed her across the road. He'd thought her voice mannered, a little prim, with a range that wouldn't carry any more emotion than a Methodist hymnal, but now he wasn't sure. He opened the gate for her. "I guess you know all about that."

"The UN?" She turned, lifting her face.

"Self-reliance."

He could see her face more clearly in the sunlight. She wore no makeup, but the sun and wind had brought the color to her lips and cheeks. A few gray hairs were visible along the part in her hair, but he thought them premature. Her face looked younger and he guessed she was in her middle thirties.

She led him into the house and said she'd planned on serving a cold supper. She hoped he wouldn't mind. McDermott told her not to trouble herself, that he had C rations in his bag. His shirt and trousers were damp, his hair wet, and he wanted to take a swim. She insisted.

The living room was meagerly furnished. Wooden armchairs were arranged along the walls and their stiff cushions showed little use: they could have been taken from a front porch in Elyria, Ohio, or Topeka, Kansas. A few locally woven rugs covered the wooden floor; a small upright piano whose varnish was cobwebbed with cracks sat in front of the window. Halfway down the center hall were two bedrooms whose closed doors faced each other across a strip of worn linoleum; farther down was the radio room; and beyond it a large kitchen with an iron handpump on the wooden counter next to the sink. The rear door led to the small generator room and through the screen door on the other side of the kitchen McDermott could see the river.

She showed him the guest room and the bath and shower opposite the radio room, brought him a towel and washrag, and went out, closing the door behind her. McDermott put the rucksack on the small, hard bed, stripped to his waist, and remembered suddenly that he had no pajamas. Next to the bed was a crude wooden table with a kerosene lamp. Behind the bed was a picture of Jesus and the Good Samaritan in a wooden oak-leaf frame. The dry curtains stood away from the small window like a hundred-year-old bridal veil; on the wall nearby was a framed sampler in bold needlework with the words *God Has Made Us Fellow Christians.*

To McDermott the house had a depressing uniformity, as lifeless as the simple utilitarian creed that had furnished it. It was as dusty as the choir loft in the chapel of the Methodist orphanage where he'd grown up, identical to every other rectorage he'd ever known, as if whoever had built it had walked away from a Methodist chapel or a clapboard parsonage near the railroad station some sixty years ago with the key in his pocket and the light in his head, and once resettled across the seas in the African bush had done nothing but replicate its moral sameness. Just work, devotion, and the Word, he remembered, sitting down on the bed. *For God's sake*, he thought, not sure what he'd gotten himself into. He started to light a cigarette, but found no ashtray and put it back in his pocket. He found his bathing trunks in the rucksack, put them on, and pulled on his damp trousers. Emily Farr was in the kitchen, standing on a kitchen chair, searching through the cans and Mason jars on the top shelf of the cabinet, looking for a tin of crabmeat she'd last seen two years ago. She was standing on tiptoe, and McDermott noticed her legs were as slim and lovely as her neck, despite the odd-looking clodhopper shoes. "I think I'll take that swim," he said, looking up. "Why don't you come, too?"

"I'd just hold you up."

"No, you won't. Come on. It's no good splashing around alone."

She hesitated, looking from him to the window and the late-afternoon sunlight. "It might be nice," she admitted. "The river's lovely this time of day."

"Come on then."

He waited for her outside, and when she joined him she was wearing a sleeveless sundress that buttoned down the front. She carried a towel and bathing cap.

Below the bank the river was wide and swift, well over sixty yards across where they descended the path—too swift for idle drifting. She led him along the bank to a fallen tree trunk, pointing out the clay shelf just below the surface where they could enter. McDermott pulled off his trousers and shoes, studying the high, swift current moving toward the Sudan and the Nile beyond. Then he saw the crocodile. He looked at her quickly, and back at the crocodile. He was the same color as the muddy yellow shale bank where he lay, eyes half open, his long ugly jaws and the serrations of yellow teeth as cruel as knife blades in the sunlight. He'd seen crocodiles on the Omo, but never one this size; and for a moment, looking at the incredible jaw, all he could think of was ten feet of chain saw driven by a twenty-foot hydraulic ram.

"Good God!" he said.

"I certainly forgot to tell you about him, didn't I?" She laughed, enjoying the look on McDermott's face.

"I guess you did."

"That's his pool upriver. He sleeps there most of the day."

"What's he do the rest of the day?" he said. "Push barges to Khartoum?"

"He's lived there for years now," she said and scampered down the bank to the tree. She slipped out of her sundress and put on her bathing cap. The black bathing suit with its short skirt reached a modest distance down her thighs and betrayed almost nothing of the body within—not a curve, dimple, or depression. But she was full-breasted, not even a twenty-year-old YWCA bathing suit could conceal the cleavage, and her legs were lean and supple, the muscles drawn out by walking. Her body intrigued McDermott, not because of its seductiveness, but because of her total lack of self-consciousness. She seemed totally unaware of it, and he was sure she had no inkling of its effect upon others. He thought for a moment that she didn't intend to swim at all, but would sit on the ledge, dangling her legs in the water as she watched the crocodile. But instead she waded out and turned, waiting for him to join her. She saw him looking at the crocodile and smiled.

"He frightened me at first," she said, "but he knows we swim here. He doesn't seem to mind."

She dove effortlessly out into the current and McDermott climbed the tree trunk, balanced himself, took a final look at the crocodile, and dove after her. As he fell forward, he remembered he should have been searching for flood debris too.

"*Oh, Christ!*" he yelled as he struck the water, his mouth torn sideways, river bilge and sediment in his teeth. He surfaced, blowing and spitting, but she didn't seem to have heard.

The water was refreshing, swift, and cold, and they swam together for some thirty minutes the way most strangers would—conceding space and distance to one another. She swam effortlessly, he noticed, but she seldom put her head underwater. Penny, on the other hand, swam like a seal, more often under the water than on it. Emily Farr swam with a certain buoyancy, like a pond duck who'd never been beyond the garden gate. Maybe it was the difference between the river and the ocean, McDermott thought. The bottom was too muddy for exploration anyway.

"I'm so glad I came," she said as they finally climbed the path back to the cottage, carrying their clothes. "It was lovely, wasn't it. Thank you for reminding me."

He took a warm shower in the small bathroom, dressed into clean khakis, and waited for her in the living room. The house was silent, the only sound that of the wind stirring through the leaves outside. He started to light a cigarette, but again couldn't find an ashtray. A small flower vase sat on a crocheted doily on top of the piano, but a few dried flowers were stuck in its throat. He returned to the hard chair, still waiting for her, and discovered a man's face within a gold frame on the bookcase at his elbow. He lifted it against his knees and studied the picture. The man was in his early or mid-thirties, with dark blond hair and a thin face, sitting on a summer lawn in front of an ivy-covered building. One knee was raised; the arm draped over it held a briar pipe. The other hand grasped a closed book against his seersucker thigh, as if he'd been reading it before the photographer had called to him to look up. McDermott supposed the book was a Bible, although it was too slim for both the Old and New Testaments. Maybe it was a book of poems. He looked at the picture again, discovering in it something vaguely familiar to him. Then he knew what it was. It was the sort of picture he'd seen many times before—the kind that Air Force dentists or parsons posed for on the flight line in front of F-105's they didn't fly; or junior-college history professors had taken while holding pipes they never smoked in front of bookcases they didn't own. He looked at the back of the picture, but found nothing. He supposed it was her dead husband.

The sunlight lay on the floor around him, lying in oblongs across the native rugs and the old pine boards. The house was silent. The wind stirred through the trees outside, and he looked through the window at the drifting leaves. He could never live in a place like this and he pitied those who thought they could. There was an emptiness in the house, in the wind, in the sunlight outside. It would eventually seep into their souls, the way the dust was embedded in the stiff curtains. Then the wind would blow them away and that would be all. It was as simple as that.

He went out into the yard, down the path, and out onto the airstrip, pacing it off, east to west. It was twenty-eight hundred feet, longer even than Rozewicz had claimed, well drained, with a clay base impacted to concrete hardness by the African sun. There probably wasn't a better strip within three hundred miles in any direction.

As he stood under the thorn trees on the far side of the field, she watched him through the kitchen window, still undecided as to whether she would fix a cold meal, as she had planned, or something more elaborate. A warm dinner would take longer, and he was probably hungry. Looking at the blue plates she'd taken from the back of the old cabinet, she saw how dusty they were; even chipped—quite odd-looking, in fact—and she hastily put them away. She would carry on as she usually did, as if she were alone—with neither the time nor the energy for pretense. She was already aware of how odd and empty he'd found her life there. How could she explain it? She'd seen it in his eyes as he'd come into the kitchen and discovered her searching for the can of crabmeat. When she'd showed him the shower and how to manage the balky faucets, she'd seen it again. Now he'd taken refuge out under the thorn trees, studying the sky.

She discouraged visitors because of it. Their presence always made the rooms seem smaller, the house emptier, the chairs more primitive. Her kitchen table, with its hodgepodge of crockery and broken-handled cutlery, was such a clutter of junk that she couldn't imagine why she'd been blind to it for so long. Some visitors had that effect upon her, particularly those visiting Presbyterian clergy from the US whom Reverend Osgood periodically herded to Baro station in his attempt to increase the church pledges. It wasn't their rudeness—they were never rude—but the tyranny of their presence. They left her with a world too demolished to rebuild, like drunken revelers departing a smashed shop. In the carelessness of their curiosity they corrupted what was most familiar to her, robbed her of what was most dependable. McDermott seemed to her less that way, but she recognized his restlessness and the fact that nothing he had seen at the mission held the slightest interest for him. He hadn't uttered a word about the house; and that was a sure sign of what he thought it to be—peculiar and uninhabitable.

He'd been annoyed about the plane; she'd recognized that immediately. Flying was probably the only thing that interested him; he was devoid of curiosity about the lives of the others—Samuel Eko's, William's, hers. Her existence had shrunk like a child's in his presence.

They ate a cold supper in the kitchen. When McDermott saw the cold fillet of perch, caught in the Baro by Samuel Eko and baked two days ago, he went out to the plane and returned with a bottle of white wine, borrowed from a case of Chablis he was delivering to a French mineral survey team camped on the escarpment. Accustomed to eating alone, with no spirits, she was uncomfortably aware of her own voice. She drank two glasses of wine with her meal and felt better for it. After dinner they washed the dishes, and she talked about Africa and her years in the Congo. Twice the lights dimmed as they stood at the sink, and as they were hanging up the towels, he asked about the generator brushes. She found the flashlight and showed him the generator room, where McDermott fiddled with a few wires, and then crawled under the generator itself. He told her that the generator brushes needed replacement and that until they were replaced, she wouldn't get full power. "Someone's been diddling with the alignment," he muttered cryptically, lying on the floor.

"I can't imagine who it might be," she muttered, unable to bring herself to mention Samuel Eko's periodic repairs.

"Maybe it's just old age," he said as he stood up. There was nothing accusatory in his glance.

A quarter moon lifted over the trees that night and they walked out beyond the gate. The dew was bright and cold on the skin of the plane. He walked around the wings, climbed up, locked the cabin door, and stood looking to the west, as if waiting for something. She touched the cold metal curiously, watching him from the ground.

"The war seems far away, doesn't it?" she said. She waited for his reply, but it didn't come: "I'm afraid it isn't," she added clumsily, her cheeks warm, embarrassed by her attempt at drawing him into conversation, of recovering her own existence and that of the mission station from the silence that had separated them since they'd left the cottage. To use the rebellion to provoke his interest was inexcusable, she thought. It must be the wine.

But McDermott hardly seemed to notice. As he climbed down beside her, he said, "Which side are you on?"

"Neither side."

He looked toward the cottage. "Why are you painting the roof?" He'd seen the drums of paint, the ladder, and the few half-coated roof panels as they'd come back from the river.

She was surprised he'd noticed. "For caution's sake, I suppose," she said as they went back through the gate. "We don't want anyone using the Baro station for his own purposes," she added innocently. She wanted to be honest with him. "For a landmark, I mean. Planes sometimes come at night."

"What kind of landmark?"

"Any kind. As a pilot, I'm sure you know far more about these things than I. The roof is quite bright, especially in the full moon. It could be used as a beacon. It could attract airplanes."

"You mean you're trying to make yourself invisible."

She turned, thinking he misunderstood. But then she knew he was right. "In a way, I suppose," she conceded, watching his face.

"You might as well change the channel of the river," he said. "Move the hills, bury the meadows, tear away the mountains."

She stopped on the path, her head still turned, afraid now that he was making fun of her. But his face gave her no clues. "I don't understand," she said, puzzled.

"Because it's not the cottage or the people. It's the land and the river. You can't change that."

The words emptied her mind like a rifle shot. She stood on the path in astonishment, amazed at the simplicity of the discovery, speechless at her own dullness in not recognizing it.

"Not with a paintbrush anyway," he continued, still looking at her face.

"Of course," she muttered in embarrassment. "*Of course*. It would be the river, wouldn't it. Of course it would. How absolutely stupid of me." She sank down on the porch step, looking up through the trees. "What could I have been thinking of?"

"A lot of people would have made the same mistake."

"I suppose it's a matter of perspective, isn't it?" She hardly had the courage to look at him, looking at the stars instead. She thought he must think her a fool. She would never share that kind of perspective, the simplification that compressed details into abstract contours: rivers, savannahs, mountains, and coastlines. But he had meant nothing else at all. "As a pilot, probably you're accustomed to seeing things that way."

"What things?" He sat down on the step.

"Navigation." She was still looking up at the stars. "Knowing the land below and what to look for. Knowing where you are at all times." The sky seemed vast tonight; the thought of drifting through empty space frightened her and yet drew her mind away. Even a photograph of the spiral galaxies, like the Crab Nebula or Andromeda, great wheels of drifting protoplasm millions of light-years away, so exhausted the simple muscle of her brain that to think seriously of them, measuring their meaning with her own, was to send chills down her spine. "I suppose you're quite comfortable up there," she suggested after a minute, her embarrassment forgotten.

"I'm comfortable down here," he replied.

She heard the sound of a motor and thought for a minute that it was the plane, moving without lights north of the village. She rose and went down the path, McDermott following, but it was the Land-Rover, its lights bouncing crazily along the deep ruts of the track as Samuel Eko brought the sleepy child back from the Swedish hospital.

She got her medical kit from the storeroom and went down the path to the clinic to meet them while McDermott went to bed.

2

The following morning when she awoke, McDermott had already dressed and left the cottage. The sun hadn't risen yet and the grasses were still wet; a chilly mist lay over the field. She dressed and went out to the gate, prepared to bring him a cup of coffee or tea while he worked before breakfast, but then she heard Samuel Eko's laughter. He was sitting under the wing, too, his own tool kit opened, laughing as he compared his own eclectic, improvised, and sometimes hand-forged tools with McDermott's own.

"That's the wildest-looking wrench I've ever seen," she heard Mc-Dermott say. "Wait a minute. Let me try it—"

She listened to Samuel Eko's laughter a little longer, staying out of sight, and then went back to the kitchen and began breakfast. After their meal, she saw him off.

"I'm sorry you didn't get to see more of the Baro station and the village," she said as she stood with Samuel Eko below the wing, saying good-bye. But McDermott was ready to go; she could see the impatience in his face.

"Maybe next time," he said, already looking east toward the dark weather gathering along the mountains. "Thanks for everything. If you need anything, tell the UN radio at Gambela to give me a call."

And then he was gone.

The storm clouds remained for the rest of the week. She told Samuel Eko that he needn't finish painting the roof. Lying alone in her bed five days later, she awakened to the sound of thunder far in the distance, rolling across hills and meadows, through lonely woods and across empty mountains. The sound made her tremble for an instant, remembering how she would awaken as a child to the distant peal of thunder booming down from the Vermont mountains during a summer night, reverberating through the open window and the blowing curtain, to where she sat bolt upright in bed. The same emptiness that had frightened her then still frightened her now: all that lonely distance, all those dark miles devoid of people. She stirred. The clock on the bedside table showed twelve o'clock. Then she heard the sound: the plane, flying out from the Sudan. She hadn't heard it pass over during its flight toward the west, and she wondered if it was now following a different flight path as she pulled on her robe and went out onto the porch.

The plane was lower in the western sky, barely three hundred feet above the savannah; and she stood in the wet grass of the yard, watching in astonishment as it flew directly toward the cottage, passing only a few hundred feet above the roof itself, the roar of its engines shaking doors and windows, its turbulence lifting violently through the treetops. Then it was gone, as quickly as it had come. She stood at the gate, searching for its shadow against the sky, but could find nothing as she listened to the sound fade away.

She knew that the flight over the house had been deliberate. But there was no menace in it. It was a gesture, she thought—an impulse, like the wave of a hand in passing.

FIVE

1

"What happened to the plane?" Penny asked McDermott as Rozewicz helped him unload the freight from the cabin doors. It was late afternoon and the two men had just returned from the Sudi camp. Penny had been waiting in the Land-Rover near the hangar since three o'clock, when she'd called the tower and learned McDermott's arrival time. "It's got mud all over the tires, like some kind of farm tractor. What kind of crummy place were you, anyway?"

"Just that," McDermott said.

"Just what?"

"Crummy." His shirt was damp, his khaki trousers stained with red clay, and his boots caked with mud the same color. Rain had fallen at Sudi as McDermott returned from his night flight into the Sudan, and he had had difficulty landing.

Rozewicz laughed and Penny looked at him irritably. She'd never seen him before that afternoon.

"A crazy place," he grunted. "Bloody crazy and stupid." He brought his suitcase from the cabin. "I am going to get very drunk. Then I'm going to sleep for two days. Then I'm going to get very drunk once again." He waved and went out the hangar doors to where Cohen's car was waiting.

"What'd he mean by that? How come he's gonna get snockered?"

"He's been out in the bush a long time."

"Who is he, anyway? Is he British or what?"

"He works with one of the French mineral survey teams," McDermott lied.

"You mean he just hitched a ride? What about the regs?"

"He's a pilot too."

"How come you're so late?" she asked as he drove the Land-Rover out across the apron and through the side gate. Penny had thought McDermott was delivering supplies and seismic equipment for the French geologists surveying in the interior.

"Bad weather," he said finally.

"You might as well be a truck driver, flying all that machinery and nitro and junk around the boonies. Sometimes I don't think flying is what it's cracked up to be." She was annoyed and hurt. For three days she'd looked forward to his return, thinking he might have missed her, too, but Rozewicz's unexpected presence had ruined it. McDermott wasn't demonstrative, and even less so in the presence of others. His face had told her nothing; now Rozewicz was gone and she still felt left out, not a part of his life at all.

He turned off the main road two miles from the airport and drove down a narrow gravel lane between green fields and a few isolated stone houses mostly hidden by stone walls overgrown with vines and creepers.

"What'd you do this time?" she asked. "Anything interesting?"

"Pretty much the same." He never talked about his trips.

"Always is, isn't it. When are you gonna take me with you?"

"When I've got room. Maybe in a couple of weeks. What have you been doing?"

"I bought some furniture. A few chairs and a rug. A couple of pots. We've gotta have some place to sit down, don't we?"

She got out and pushed open the gate and he drove forward into the small compound. Blue-green eucalyptus trees grew within the stone wall enclosing the one-story stucco villa. A small square of green grass lay in front of the house and a flagstone patio behind. The high walls and eucalyptus trees concealed it from the other houses in the neighborhood.

When Penny had first seen the place a few months earlier, the emptiness of the villa had surprised her. There were no photographs, no pictures, no souvenirs, and little furniture. Two chairs occupied the living room, and a single bed comprised his bedroom. The other rooms were empty, as were the closets, except for the one in his bedroom, where a few shirts, some khaki pants, and a single cotton cord suit hung on the iron pipe behind the louvered doors. At the back of the closet she found two expensive leather suitcases, which she'd examined during his first absence. In one was an old shoebox containing a pair of military dog tags, a pair of major's oak leaves, two sets of pilot's wings, three bars of brightly colored campaign ribbons, a few tape cassettes, some odd book matches from hotels in Bangkok and Saigon, and a pair of tarnished silver cuff links with his initials in scrolled English letters. In the second suitcase wrapped in a Bangkok newspaper was an odd-looking piece of statuary made from a twenty millimeter cannon shell mounted on a wooden base. Screwed to the pedestal was a silver plate, inscribed:

To
Major Scott McDermott
F-105D
355th Tactical Fighter Wing
Ta Khli AB Thailand
"Who Gave Us Back Our Honor"
April 19

There was nothing else. A few paperback books lay on the nightstand near the bed and on the shelf below was a Zenith shortwave radio. The bookcase in the living room was empty except for a pair of stereo speakers and a phonograph on the lower shelf. She found no records. McDermott explained that he'd bought the stereo from the former occupants of the house, a UN couple retiring to New Zealand. They'd offered it to McDermott at half price.

"How do you stand it?" she had asked him after exploring the empty rooms. Her voice reverberated from the polished floor and blank walls.

"Stand what?"

"This house. There's nothing here except echoes."

"You don't notice it much when you're alone," he'd explained.

The second day she had bought the chairs and a rug. The night he returned she was grilling hamburgers on the patio and burned her finger. She stuck it in her mouth instantly, frowned, and said: "Thinking about fingers, you know what Kierkegaard said, don't you?"

"No."

"I stick my finger into existence and I can't smell anything. Nothing—nothing at all. Who am I? Who are you?" She started grilling the hamburgers again. "That's the way I feel around here sometimes."

"Who's Kierkegaard?"

"A philosopher."

"No wonder."

"There's nothing," Penny had complained, standing at the grill, an apron wrapped around her shorts, barefooted. "Nothing at all. A few chairs, a bed, a couple of dishes. Like, you're permanently camping out. Existence is temporary, sure—all flesh is grass, okay—but *this temporary*? You gotta be kidding. Where are you, anyway? I've been looking around this place for two days, trying to find you, but you're no place. Where do you keep your life, at the dead-letter office?"

Penny opened the front door and waited for McDermott to bring in his bag from the Land-Rover, making him take off his muddy boots at the door.

McDermott showered, changed his clothes, and went out on the patio, still buttoning his shirt. The sun was setting and to the east the first shimmer of evening stirred through the trees behind the wall. Penny was on the flat roof above, sitting on the stone coping, watching the sunset. "I'm up here," she called. "You wanna come up?"

A crude ladder, made by the gardener from eucalyptus poles, led from the patio to the roof where Penny sunbathed during the day. He climbed the ladder with the gin bottle, two glasses, and a bucket of ice cubes.

"It's a good thing you don't get vertigo," she said as she met him at the top of the ladder and took the glasses and bottles.

"It's happened."

"Not flying, I'll bet."

"Sometimes."

"Where?" He'd never again talked about Vietnam since that day on the beach at Djibouti, but the shell casing and the inscription had made her curious. She'd probed occasionally, but without success. "Where'd *you* ever get vertigo?"

He opened the gin bottle. "When I used to refuel from tankers out of Thailand. If the weather was bad, it was pretty hairy. You'd lose the horizon, couldn't trust your instruments, and pretty soon you'd think you were flying upside down, hanging there on the end of a boom at thirty-five thousand. Hey, when did you get those tables?"

On the roof were two small reed tables near the straw mat where she sunned in the afternoon.

"Pretty cool, don't you think? I got them at the market yesterday." On one table were a few college catalogues a Peace Corps volunteer named Lizzy had borrowed for her from the United States Information Service library in town. "What do you mean, refueled from tankers? You got your gas from another plane?"

"On the way to Vietnam. We didn't have the range otherwise."

"What if it was bad weather?"

"It increased the sweat factor." He remembered the question Emily Farr had asked as he sat under the plane at Baro, when he'd given the same answer, and smiled.

"What's so funny?" Penny asked immediately, afraid he'd discovered she'd been snooping through his luggage. "How come you're smiling like that?"

"I just thought of something."

"What kind of plane did you fly?" she asked, hoping the question would convince him she hadn't. It was there on the pedestal: an F-105.

"An F-105."

"I'll bet it didn't have mud all over the tires," she sighed with relief, eager to change the subject. They drank gimlets and watched the sunset.

"Which school have you picked out?" he asked her finally, lifting one of the college catalogues from the table. They were all graduate-school catalogues: one from California, Harvard, Michigan.

"I dunno. It's all just crap. The same old dishonesty, the same old shell game. Hiding the pea under the same old Socratic walnut. School's always the same. Who cares?"

"You do, or you wouldn't be looking through those catalogues."

"It's just something to do. I get so damned bored around here."

"What about your Peace Corps friends?"

"They're all screwed up. Half of them hate it here—the regime's so rotten. The embassy's so fucked up. I don't know whether I want to go to grad school or not. What would you rather be—a philistine who lives without thinking, or an intellectual who thinks without living? That's a stupid choice, isn't it? Why do I have to keep categorizing like that? It's suicidal—black and white alternatives. Life and death options. That's what thinking does, and I'm sick of it. I really am."

"What got you interested in anthropology?"

"I dunno. Maybe it was just a fad. Thinking about people, I suppose. Other life-styles. Maybe that's the problem—trying to hide out from your own, try another shell on, like the hermit crab." She sank back, her head against the lounge pillow, looking at the sunset. "I think I'd like to find that point in a culture where language is first cosmicized—language with a glow on, when it first discovers itself, and all words are fresh, new. A sort of verbal LSD, if you know what I mean. I think that would make me happy. There was a guy I used to know at Berkeley. He did a thesis on erotic herbs in Vedic ceremonials—can you dig that? He got me interested. He had a head shop on the side and I guess I was pretty tight with him for a while, but it didn't last. He was such a creep, and so was I for not seeing it. All the time he was so heavy into anthropology, he was just trying to snitch ideas about what would be big commercially. He wasn't anything but a counterculture capitalist looking for 'in' stuff he could merchandize in his store. He was pretty bright, I guess, but what'd he do with it? He used to program computer runouts up at Cal Tech with a math-freak friend of his, breaking down population curves so he'd known how many teenyboppers would be entering the economy every year. He was kinda weird, come to think about it. A real jerk. Now he's into something else. The record business out on the Coast. Guys like that are always into something else." She sighed. "What a waste. What about you? When did you decide what you wanted to do? When you were in college?"

"Before that."

"How old were you when you took your first flight?"

"Twelve or thirteen. I went up with a crop duster down in Texas."

"Texas. I thought you were from Pennsylvania."

"I hitchhiked to Texas one summer, looking for a job."

"When you were thirteen! Jesus, you didn't waste any time, did you? God, when I was thirteen, I didn't know squat. Hitchhiking? Forget it! I used to go to a summer camp in Wyoming." She put her head back. "That was the only time I was happy, really happy. I was taller than anyone in my dancing class. Did you think much about it when you were growing up?"

"No."

"You're lucky then. One of my biggest problems was possessive parents. They wanna own everything, even me. I don't wanna own anything or anybody. And I don't want anyone to own me, whether it's money, kids, a job, or anything. Money's owned my pop since the day he was born."

She'd given him her money belt and asked him to put it away for safekeeping. She carried five hundred dollars in traveler's checks but inside the belt were five thousand dollars more, together with a San Francisco savings-account book with an equal amount on deposit. She said that some of the money she'd earned, working in vacation lodges in Idaho, California, and the Canadian Rockies; but most of it had been given to her by her grandmother over the years. Her grandmother, a banker's widow, had carried on a kind of guerrilla war against the estate lawyers. Her father was one of them, a specialist in estates and trusts, but actually in cahoots with the West Coast utility, banking, and timber interests. The fascist money machines, Penny called them. Her grandmother was the only person she spoke of with any affection.

"It's okay if he lives on Nob Hill and earns his eighty or ninety grand a year or whatever his rip-off law firm pays him, but he's still a cheapskate," she continued, "especially when it comes to other people's money. I even had to sell my stereo at Christmas one year when I wanted to go skiing with the guys in Idaho and he wouldn't fork over."

"Who paid your way through college?"

"He did, sure. But it didn't mean anything to him. Social gestation. Rites of passage, or whatever you wanna call it. Like the dancing school or the country club and yacht club dues. He wanted me to study art history or something safe. You know, nonutilitarian. Herding philosophical unicorns or centaurs, maybe. No *real* goats in his plastic backyard. My mother was a French major, can you believe that? A French major and she doesn't even know the difference between Malraux and Mauriac. She doesn't even know who Camus is. The only thing she says in French is 'Penny, dear, when are we going to have our little *tête-á-tête*?' Anyway, that's what my pop wanted. He didn't want to feel threatened by anything I'd learn in college, which was why he didn't want me to go to Cal in the first place. He wanted me to go East, to one of those junior-league finishing schools where you learn how to put the right books on the library shelves and the right pictures on the walls. When I told him I was going to major either in anthropology or sociology, he practically had a seizure. He thinks all the sociologists do these days is teach the black kids in Watts to make Molotov cocktails and pipe bombs. So he called up this golfing friend of his whose wife is a shrink. Not a real shrink either, but one of those chic shrinkers who go around decorating people's skulls with the latest pop psychology, like an interior decorator. Anyway, he wanted to make an appointment for me. He didn't call up this female Sigmund Fraud himself. Oh, no. That would have been too embarrassing. He mentioned it to this golfing friend of his, and had his wife call *me*." Her voice trailed off, and she sat looking at the sky, the gimlet balanced on her knee. "How'd we get on this, anyway?" she asked disconsolately.

"You were talking about money."

"Yeah," she remembered, sitting up. "Money doesn't own you, for instance. Whatever you're doing, it's not for the money." McDermott laughed and she looked at him. "It doesn't," she insisted. "I know it doesn't. Maybe I can be fooled about a lot of things, but I can't be fooled about that." She sat up again. "Only sometimes I think this is a pretty down place for you to be."

"You mean you're getting restless?"

"I don't know. Right now, I feel okay. I dig being here, but it's different when I'm alone. This house gets pretty empty. How much longer are we going to be here? I know it's nothing permanent. Nothing is, so I'm not worried about that. I've been tight with guys before. But I was wondering."

McDermott was surprised she'd stayed as long as she had. He liked having her there, but his reasons were selfish ones. He had no claims on her. He knew that once she decided to leave, nothing he could say or do would change her mind. He would miss her for a while, and probably she would miss him too; but both accepted the fact that transience had brought them together and would inevitably separate them. In the yard below, the watchman lit the lights along the perimeter wall, and she stood up, pulling the shawl over her shoulders. The watchman called to McDermott and said the fire was built, so they climbed down the ladder and went into the house, where eucalyptus and acacia logs were roaring in the fireplace. Penny disappeared into the bedroom, and when she returned she was wearing a white madras dress and brown sandals. Her hair had been brushed as smooth as flax. He turned on the table lamp to see her better, but she didn't look at him.

"It's no big deal," she said, recovering her half-finished gimlet from the mantel. "I just felt like it, that's all."

She moved to the stereo and slipped a long-playing record from its jacket. In the weeks she had been there, she'd bought more records than McDermott had owned in a lifetime.

"I thought maybe you'd like to go out for dinner for a change," she suggested, putting the record on the turntable.

"You mean a party?" He'd met none of her Peace Corps friends. She kept them away from the house when he was home.

"No, just the two of us. I ironed a shirt for you. It's on the bed."

He heard the record as he went into the bedroom to change, first the drum and guitar, and then the lonely harmonica.

> Think I'll pack it in
> > an' buy a pick-up,
> Take it down to L.A.
> Find a place to call my own an'
> > try to fix up:
> Start a brand new day—

2

They packed the Land-Rover the following day, took a tent, sleeping bags, food, and beer, and drove down to one of the Rift Valley lakes to the south. They stayed for two days on the shores of the lake, sleeping out under the stars. They swam in the lake, fished, read, and walked the rock-strewn hills and canyons. In the early morning the flamingos would gather nearby from the far shores of the lake, and in the evenings the baboons would come down from the cliffs and sit silently in the distance, staring at their campfire.

"Chaperones," Penny said the last night.

"Don't be so sure," McDermott said. "The big guy's got his eye on you. He wants to take you home to meet his mother."

She didn't laugh, but only moved her head against her lifted knee, watching them through the darkness. "Maybe he's bashful," she said quietly. "Like you."

Later that evening as they were spreading out the sleeping bags near the dying embers, she said, "I'll bet we could find a place like this in Idaho or Wyoming. Don't you think we could?"

"Maybe." He didn't want to think about it.

"Why don't we talk about it then," she suggested, stretching out with her head toward the embers. "Why don't we? I get tired of moving around like this. Always having to pack up and go just when I'm getting used to it."

SIX

Emily Farr was awakened before dawn by William, scraping at the bedroom screen. She heard the clanking of pots and kettles, the jounce of cartridge belts, knives, and canteens, and the occasional moans and low cries of wounded. From the front porch she watched the shadowy column of refugees moving along the track beyond the gate, like beads on a string, scattered by the distance they had traveled since leaving their burned-out villages in the Sudan. The old women were first, followed by the children, the mothers, and the old men, protected in the rear by the retreating Anya-nya guerrillas. She dressed quickly and brewed a cup of tea on the kerosene burner as she packed her medical kit in the dispensary. She ate a piece of bread spread with honey as she went down the track toward the village. Overhead, the sky was beginning to pale to a dull oyster gray. A few elephants had crossed from the river during the night and she smelled their passage on the morning wind.

The village was a clutter of mud and grass huts and a few cattle kraals that lay under the thorn and hardwood trees a hundred yards from the river. On the western edge, facing toward the mission, was a small clinic built of mud block and enclosed by a pole fence. More than forty refugees were squatting in the dark enclosure when Emily arrived. Her two Nuer nurses aides were already passing out rations of com, sorghum, and powdered milk to the mothers while a village elder stood outside the clinic itself explaining to the refugees that they could remain twenty-four hours, no longer. They must continue their trek eastward to the UN resettlement camps, or the Ethiopian soldiers would come.

She paused in the clinic only long enough to make sure that none of the mothers and children was wounded, and then hurried back through the village to the large hut on the eastern slope surrounded by a pallisaded fence. The morning cooking fires were already burning in the yards of the huts nearby; a few dusty chickens stirred along the paths flanked by the thorn scrub rolled in coils around the yards to keep out the goats and animals. Inside the pole fence were tethered a few undernourished cattle. An iron kettle was boiling over a woodfire near the door to the hut. A dozen guerrillas stood in the enclosure, their weapons over their shoulders. Four kerosene lanterns burned inside the hut and two more from the ceiling beams. The hut and kraal belonged to William Latu, the Anya-nya leader in the village, who'd fought in the Sudan but had returned to recuperate from a bullet wound. He was waiting for her inside the door, a tall, gentle Nuer with long gangling arms and neck, and smallpox scars on his cheeks.

A young Sudanese Nuer was lying on a pallet under one lantern, his trousers slit to the knee, his ankle and calf dark with crusted blood. Two other wounded guerrillas squatted on the floor next to him; and the fourth lay stiff and cold under a cotton sheet on the litter that had borne him from the Sudan. The wounded were all younger men, like William Latu; the older men died on the road or in the bush, like the dead man on the litter.

She examined the youth's shattered ankle, and found no infection, then gave him something to ease the pain and tried to clean the wound, but the blood encrusted his foot like a boot and he cried out in pain, trying to force her hands away. Each time he did, his breath gave back, like fecal decay, the exhaustion, dehydration, and parasital infection of his body. "He'll have to go with the refugees," she told William Latu helplessly. "There's nothing I can do for him. He must go. The foot will become infected." She brought the second youth under the lantern, and as she lifted his hands from his bandaged head, feared the worst—a head wound no surgeon could heal in time. But as she removed the bandage, she found only a scalp laceration, the skin of his head torn away, and some forty stitches required to restore it in place. She could only clean the wound and rebandage it. "He must go too. He must be hospitalized. The Swedish hospital will take him. Dr. Ahlmark will take care of him."

The final casualty was also the most difficult, shrinking away in the shadows as she approached. "I must look at you—don't be frightened." She drew him forward into the lantern light and found the left side of his face swollen and discolored, as if he'd been stung by bees. He wore a dirty bandage over one eye, but resisted as she attempted to loosen it, his hand clapping it firmly in place. "William Latu. Would you help—" But he'd left the hut. "Please take your hand away. I must see your eye. If your eye is injured, then I can help." Again she tried to remove the bandage, but again he resisted.

At that moment William Latu reentered the hut, followed by three Anya-nya officers.

"Excuse me, missy," said the shortest of the three, moving into the lantern light. It wasn't Sudanese English—at least not the English she was accustomed to. He wore a uniform of green twill with the red, white, and black of the Anya-nya flag sewn in crude masculine stitches over the breast pocket. She'd never seen the emblem so conspicuously displayed. A clean new rifle was slung over his shoulder, the leather of the sling as bright as the bluish muzzle and dark stock. His face wasn't black, like William Latu's or the other Nilotics, but coffee colored. She guessed that he was perhaps from far to the south, from a tribe she wasn't familiar with. "My men have no rations," he said.

"William Latu has told you why."

"My men need rations."

"Our rations are for the refugees—for the women and children."

"I am a Christian," he said.

"We are all Christians here."

"The brotherhood is in Christ," he said. But the words had no effect on her. "I was told that this was a Christian village," he began again. "I was told that you were a Christian healer."

"My mission is with the village and the women and children."

He studied her silently, his eyes a pale brown, like the coffee beans in Samuel Eko's bowl before he roasted them. Then he took off his cap respectfully. "We want only to rest and eat, missy."

"I can give you no rations."

He put his hat back on, turned, and told the other Anya-nya officers to leave the hut. The guerrilla with the bandaged eye attempted to leave, too, but Emily restrained him. "Please stay where you are. I haven't looked at your eye."

After the others had left, the short Anya-nya said, "You give my men medical treatment, but not rations. You save them from dying but not from starving." His voice grew shriller when she didn't respond: "How is it that the one they call William Latu has rations?"

"William Latu has his own crops and animals."

"You are *not* a Christian!" the captain shouted angrily.

"I must account for my rations. They are entrusted to me. If I were to give you rations, then there would be none for anyone. They would close the mission, evacuate this village."

"You give medicines!" He pointed accusingly at her medical kit.

"These are my own."

"You are not a Christian!"

"You judge in me what isn't yours to judge," she said calmly. "If I give you rations, then I'll be accused of supporting the Anya-nya. If the Sudanese soldiers didn't come, then the Ethiopian soldiers would, taking all these village people to the refugee camps. I have no choice."

"I was told that there were rations here, food and medical care, huts in which we could sleep and rest!"

"Then you were misinformed."

"We will talk about this later," he said coldly.

"There is nothing more to talk about. I will give you no rations. Now would you please ask your soldier to remove his hand so I can look at his eye."

The captain turned savagely and kicked the wounded soldier in the side. "Take off your bandage! Take it off! Are you afraid of a woman!" He stormed out of the hut. She would have gone after him angrily, but at that moment the young Anya-nya rebel tried to flee. She seized his shoulders and held him in place, lifting the bandage from his forehead.

"I *must* look at your eye. Now sit still."

But there was nothing wrong with his eye, which flickered and darted in the beam of her probing pencil-flashlight, like some frightened atom of protoplasm alone in a terrifying universe, searching for darkness as deep as its own in which it could hide. He was not hurt. He simply wanted to join the refugees in their flight to the east, away from the battle.

The yard outside was spangled with drifting sunlight filtered through the blowing foliage overhead as she left the hut, carrying her bag. The Anya-nya captain stood talking with his staff quietly in the far corner of the enclosure. All were dressed in green twill except for a small black man wearing ragged serge trousers, rubber sandals, and an incredibly dirty white shirt without a collar—like a clergyman's shirt. A few wiry white hairs mixed with the wool of his head; flat-nosed, with thick lips and a small jaw, he looked to Emily like a Bantu from the savannahs of the central Congo. Pinned ostentatiously to the front of his dirty collarless shirt was a cheap aluminum cross outlined with plastic pearls. He carried no rifle or revolver, like the others, but stuck through his leather belt was an ugly black panga, a machete.

He turned to watch her as she crossed the compound to speak to William Latu. The other Anya-nya officers stopped their conversation and watched her too. She ignored them, pausing only long enough to tell William Latu that the three wounded men should accompany the refugees to the east. She walked back to the clinic, where she spent the remainder of the afternoon examining the women and children among the refugees, who would take up their journey again before the sun went down.

It was after four o'clock when she climbed the track to the mission house to find Samuel Eko working on the Land-Rover under the trees. Only his black feet were visible, flung out across the grass under the front bumper. Nearby were two rubber buckets he'd made from old truck tires and sealed with pitch, both full of muddy water drawn from the pumphouse. She asked him what he was doing as she sank down on the grass nearby, the earth cool against her legs. He said he was fixing the radiator. "What's wrong with it?"

"There is an animal inside," he said.

"Really? What kind of animal?"

"The kind that drinks all my water and spits it out again at me." He slid from beneath the vehicle. His black face and hair were splashed with reddish-yellow water, so that he looked like one of the Nuer herdsmen from deep in the bush who dyed their hair foxy-red with cow urine.

"I wish I had a mirror," she said. "You wouldn't recognize yourself."

"I recognize myself."

"Do you?"

"I see my feet," he sighed, hands on his knees, studying his scaling black feet. "They are my feet. I know them too well. If I could trade them, I would." He took a package of cigarettes from his pocket, still looking abjectly at his thin ankles and long toes, and put a cigarette in his mouth.

"But you're smoking again," she said in surprise.

"Yes," he admitted, searching for a match. "I decided I would do something else."

His decision to stop smoking had been made impulsively, more for Emily Farr's benefit than his own—a vow given after Emily had told him that his wife was pregnant. His wife was no longer a young girl. She had a withered foot, and the disability had affected her spine as well; but Samuel Eko had taken her as his wife more for convenience than from love or affection. Her father had been anxious to marry her off, and Samuel Eko, living alone in the village, had needed a house-keeper. It had never occurred to him that she might bear his children. The old village woman had declared her barren, a condition which had reinforced the practicality of the marriage, since it could provide him with an excuse for abandoning her after the Sudanese wars were ended and he could take up his old life in Juba or Khartoum. His wife's motives in marriage were as practical as his own: she wanted a hut and a fire, to gather faggots and dung chips as her married sisters did, to have reasons to plant corn and sorghum, or draw water from the river. Her marriage also relieved her solitude and the shame of her disfigure-ment, which had made her painfully shy. As a wife she was welcome again at her father's fireside, where she could sit as an equal with her sisters, listening to their gossip as she wove her own baskets and raffia cloth, and not merely help them with theirs. Although Samuel Eko had seen his wife change in the two years since they had married, it had never occurred to him that this change had anything to do with him. If her carriage now seemed more erect, her foot less a hindrance, even her dark eyes more youthful, he attributed her flowering more to her recovery of her parents' and sisters' respect, the only bounty she'd ever expected from their marriage.

When Emily Farr had told him one day that his wife was pregnant, he was dumbfounded, his wife suddenly a stranger to him. He had no words to express the shame or the isolation he felt, his own finite existence suddenly lost in the mystery of his wife's, which held the miracle of life his own would have denied her. "I will do something," he'd announced in confusion after Emily had told him. He hardly knew what he meant at the time, but when he saw his wife again for the first time after hearing the news, he suddenly understood that the miracle of his wife's being lay so far beyond the grasp of his own mortality that he knew he would never find the means to express it.

A week later Emily Farr had remembered the vow. They were returning from Gambela in the Land-Rover. He knew she had misunderstood, believing that he'd intended to build a new hut or at least repair the old one, perhaps buy a new Arab bed, a few cotton waxes, or a transistor radio from the Greek emporium in Gambela. Her literal-mindedness sometimes disturbed him—her determination to lay bare the world around her in words or phrases; to coax the waters of the Baro into the decrepit garden pump; to tempt the wind of the savannahs through her open kitchen window, the lore of the old grandmothers into her twopenny copybooks, and the furnace of the African sun into the windows of the glass cucumber frames where she cultivated the wild herbs of the grasslands. That shopping day she'd noticed that he'd bought nothing for his wife at Gambela, and reminded him of his vow.

"I've decided to stop smoking," Samuel Eko had replied recklessly, throwing his cigarette out the window, a gesture intended more for her than for his wife or the vow he hadn't the wit to explain to either because he didn't completely understand it himself. But a month later he'd started smoking again—beginning again because he was weak, because he found it almost impossible to deny that old pleasure, and finally because the renunciation inhibited that quiet reflection that was necessary—helped too by grain alcohol or durra beer—to find the meaning of his vow.

So now he was smoking once more.

"I have decided to do something else," Samuel Eko told Emily Farias he looked over the Land-Rover, averting her eyes.

"When?"

"When the child comes," he promised, getting to his feet.

She brought glasses of tea from the kitchen and afterward they took the vegetable baskets from the generator room and went into the garden. As they moved between the rows, she asked him if he knew the Anya-nya captain who had arrived during the night. He knew many things, but was indifferent to politics. He rarely talked with her about the politics of the Sudan, but she knew that he was contemptuous of politicians and the rebels' claims to the loyalty of southerners like himself.

Samuel Eko nodded. "He once lived in Juba."

"What did he do there?"

"He was a politician from the border. A coffeehouse politician. Now he has a gun. Does that make him a soldier?"

"I'm afraid I don't care for him."

Samuel Eko laughed, stripping a bean pod with his fingers and chewing the beans. "He is just an ant. They are all ants. They don't know what they are doing. Black or brown, Arab or Christian, Pagan or Catholic. To the eyes of God, if God had eyes, they are just all ants—small, busy, crawling ants. Pieces of dust." He glanced at her through the dusty bean stalks, smiling as he waited to hear her answer. "So small that the differences between them don't matter," he continued.

"I'm sure we are much more than that," she chided. Sometimes she heard in his words echoes of the Nuer cosmology, a view so remorseless and frightening that she could only understand it not as an act of reason or faith, but as an act of revenge, of malice against whatever cosmic purpose had brought life to this brutal wilderness. But sometimes he teased her with the same words, which she recognized were only intended to provoke her response. "I'm sure you don't believe that," she added.

He laughed good-naturedly, and she knew he was teasing her. "How do you know what I believe?"

"I don't. But someday perhaps you will tell me."

"How can I?" He laughed again. "They are not in the words. And if they are not in the words, how can they be in my head?"

"You're teasing me," she said.

After he left the garden, Samuel Eko sat on the riverbank, his back against a fallen tree, playing an Arab melody on a small harmonica. The air was alive with dust drummed from the scrub beyond the bank by the cattle driven to the byre at the edge of the village. Beyond, a few clouds floated. The river's plunging copper surface was broken by eddies, riffles, and whirlpools marking hidden tree limbs or sandbanks. He was gazing along the far shore, the harmonica silent in his mouth, when he heard rapid footsteps behind him. He thought at first that village children were playing in the grass, but suddenly two khaki-clad figures leaped from the bank and crouched along its flank, hugging their muskets. Two more followed, carrying bows and arrows; and within a few minutes eight Anya-nya were strung out along the riverbank, like soldiers in a mud trench. Their dark faces were shining with sweat, their wiry black arms streaked with dried mud and chaff. After one of the soldiers lifted his head and whistled, like a jackdaw, the plump Anya-nya captain appeared, clad only in drooping undershorts with clothes folded over his arm, on his way to bathe in the river. Only after he descended the bank did he see Samuel Eko and stop suddenly, looking suspiciously at the *jalibiiya*.

"Who are you?" he demanded.

"Samuel Eko."

He knew the name. "Yes," he nodded, but at that moment two of the Anya-nya spotted the crocodile surfacing near midstream, and called out to the captain, gesturing wildly. The captain saw him too. Samuel Eko got to his feet, moved to the river's edge, and sang out to the crocodile. As they watched, the reptile thrashed his huge tail and disappeared.

"He will go up the river now," Samuel Eko said, "and everyone can swim."

But the Anya-nya captain didn't swim, squatting instead on the bank at the water's edge, dousing his head, arms, and legs with his cupped hands, taking the sliver of soap Samuel Eko offered him, but only after he'd sniffed that suspiciously too.

"Why aren't you in the army?" he asked Samuel Eko as he dried his face and arms.

"Whose army?" Samuel Eko asked, seated again on the bank, his back against the tree trunk. There were a dozen Anya-nya armies. Some fought because the foreigners gave them guns, some to liberate their villages from the tyranny of the Arabs in Khartoum, some because they were Christians who feared the Moslems, some because they were ambitious, some because they felt more powerful with guns than with plows, some because they were thieves—brigands. Samuel Eko thought the Anya-nya captain on the riverbank was a brigand. His village was deep in the south, near the Ugandan border. The soldiers with him were semiliterate rabble from the southern scrubland, most of them Acholi, like the captain himself, who claimed to be a Christian, but had claimed Islam when Samuel Eko had been in Juba.

"The Anya-nya," the captain said, pulling on his twill shirt. The right sleeve was stained with blood, and Samuel Eko wondered if it was the captain's blood or that of the dead man he'd taken it from. These were not the Anya-nya Samuel Eko knew. They foraged alone. A buffalo or elephant who forages alone is driven by fever, grief, starvation, sometimes madness, and so Samuel Eko mistrusted the Anya-nya captain for that reason. They would burn a Sudanese or a Christian village as easily as an Arab village if it didn't give them succor.

"There are many Anya-nya. There is a brigade across the border, just a few kilometers away. I talked to the commander this morning," he lied.

"Does the white woman give them rations?"

"No."

The captain looked downstream toward the border. "Do they protect her?"

"She treats their wounded," he replied, picking up his towel. The captain's soldiers still crouched along the bank. "Old grandfather is up the river now. Your men can swim here. He won't eat them."

"Do you know him?" the captain called out to Samuel Eko, who was already climbing the bank.

"I have talked to him," he answered over his shoulder.

Emily was in the kitchen when she heard the living room screen door ease closed. The afternoon light was fading, but the western windows were still glazed with the setting sun. She thought Samuel Eko or William had entered the house and called out: "I'm in here—in the kitchen." But she heard no footsteps down the hall and thought it might be the wind. But the trees beyond the kitchen window were motionless, and she turned, listening. *Strange*, she thought, her head cocked, standing near the door, still puzzled. She'd started to take off her apron when she heard the sound of the piano from the living room—a single chord, no more. She stopped again, her hands at her back, a chill moving up her spine. Another chord followed, then a second and third, all of them like the first—mechanical and primitive; meaningless— struck by a hand that knew nothing about the instrument.

She went silently down the hall and discovered him there, standing at the keyboard, the fading sunlight falling across his dirty shirt, his black hand poised over the keys. His bare feet were cracked, the black panga sagged in his belt. As he turned, she saw the small metal cross, with its beading of seed pearls, pinned to his shirt.

"I was in the kitchen," she said, her heart pounding. "Didn't you hear me call?"

His face was small, eyes protuberant. "No." He looked at her feet.

He was a head shorter, she realized. "I'm afraid the piano's out of tune." He was still staring curiously at her feet. "It belonged to the missionary couple who once lived here. Do you play the piano? I've never learned—"

She sometimes said silly things when she was frightened, and she was frightened now. Her words made no impression on him, but she knew that she must keep talking, that it was the voice that mattered even if the words did not.

Old William's shadow loomed suddenly across the screen and she called out to him. He came into the living room. "It's all right," she said as he moved across the room, not seeing the small figure at the piano, who'd slipped behind him and through the door, as silently as a shadow, before he could even turn. He'd come to tell her that the Anya-nya captain was in the road outside and wanted a word with her.

"Samuel Eko is an Arab," the captain began, removing his hat as he spoke. His two lieutenants did the same. The small black man with the cross on his shirt had joined them and stood watching her silently as she left the gate. "He is more Arab than Nuer," the captain continued. "He is not of the Brotherhood of Christ. He is not a Christian."

William asked Emily quietly if he should fetch Samuel Eko, who'd gone down to the village, but she shook her head, listening to the captain.

"He speaks to the crocodiles," the captain said and waited for her reaction, but her face was expressionless. "I have asked Dr. Botewi to speak to you, missy. He is my counselor and has worked for Christ with the white missionaries for many years."

"Dr. Botewi?" She looked at the Bantu with the panga through his belt and the seed-pearl cross on his shirt.

"Dr. Botewi is a member of my military council, a soldier for Christ. He is a Christian, like all of us."

Dr. Botewi began to speak, his voice strange, his English stilted. In his cadences she recognized the songs and hymns of some primitive Christian mission station, far from the national or even provincial capitals of central Africa. He told her he'd gone to a Methodist mission school deep in the bush near the great river. He asked her if she knew Mr. and Mrs. Reuben Golden from Hastings, Nebraska, who were butchered by the Simbas during the Congo rebellions of 1964. They had taught him his first hymn and saved his sister's soul when the long penis of the gods was making demon children in her head. Now they were gathered by another river and the soldiers of Christianity needed her charity. There was a piano in her house, but that would be only the beginning. Hers was the only piano between Khartoum and the Great River. From Khartoum to Juba and the Ugandan border below, he babbled, they were watching the rape and pillage of a black civilization. The smell of burning flesh awoke with them each morning and crept into their nostrils each night. They were responsible for the orphans and widows of God and she had to open her heart with song, and open up their lives with prayer. The black population of the Sudan would be scourged from the face of the earth by the infidel Arabs from the north, who wanted their daughters for the brothels of Cairo and Babylon. There was a piano in her house. The new day would dawn from the windows beyond when the first chords were sounded. They would sing together, work together, grow crops together. Ambassadors, bishops, and generals would be sent out to every corner of the world. Troops would arrive—

Emily listened silently, watching the dark, wet face, the rapidly blinking eyes as Dr. Botewi babbled on in his stilted, singsong, mission-school English, which lay as weakly over his mind as the dust of the road over his face. Finally he took a dirty slip of paper from the small New Testament he carried in his pocket, and asked for sugar, tea, coffee, sorghum, durra, millet, flour, and kerosene. He asked her to render them up from the Christian larder in her mission house.

"He is a Christian like you," the captain said when Dr. Botewi had finished.

"Are you not a Christian?" she asked.

"I am a Catholic."

"I have none of these things in my house," she said. "What I have is for the village. There are vegetables in the garden. You're welcome to them, but that is all I can offer you."

"You have UN rations!" the captain replied.

"For the refugees."

They stood facing one another in the growing shadows of the road. Old William stood near the gate, and Samuel Eko had appeared, accompanied by William Latu and a few of the young men from the village, some of whom had served with the Anya-nya. William Latu carried a carbine.

"My men could take the rations!"

"So they could," she answered. "And then the Ethiopian troops would come to evacuate the village. The mission would also be closed. Is that what you want?"

The captain put his hat on his head, looked at Samuel Eko, William Latu, and the youths squatting in the twilight near the gate. He shouldered his musket and turned away down the road toward the Sudan border. Dr. Botewi didn't move. He stood watching Emily silently, and when the captain called to him, he also turned to go, took a few steps, stopped, and looked back.

"One day I will sit in your parlor, sister," he said. "I will sit in your parlor and play your piano."

She stood in the road watching the guerrillas until they were out of sight. Then she turned, went through the gate, and into the house.

Samuel Eko, William Latu, and the old watchman sat in front of the small fire near the brick washhouse, troubled and silent. Emily Farr hadn't left the house, the generator lights had gone out, and the three villagers William Latu had sent to follow the small group of Anya-nya hadn't returned.

After a while the watchman sighed, looking into the embers, and lifted his head. "They eat rats," he said to Samuel Eko.

William Latu looked up at him, the carbine across his knees: "Who eats rats?"

"The little one with the panga," Samuel Eko replied.

"Do you know who he is?" the watchman asked.

Samuel Eko nodded. He was the captain's witch doctor.

"Rodh," the old man whispered, speaking the name of the ghoul who disinterred the Nuer dead.

"Shhh," William Latu muttered. The moon lifted above the roof of the washhouse, a slender crust of silver visible through the broken clouds. They were sitting there as silently as before when the whistle came from the front gate. The three villagers were back. The captain and his group had crossed into the Sudan. Their vigil was over.

As William Latu and his party headed back to the village, Samuel Eko changed his clothes in the washhouse, took a sorghum knife from the workbench, and let himself out the front gate. He turned down the track toward the huts, but pulled off his white shirt as he walked, stuffed it in his pocket, and when he was sure the watchman could no longer see him, turned out onto the landing strip. He crossed to the far side of the strip, stopped for a minute under the thorn trees, listening, then moved out into the moonlight again toward a clump of acacia shrubs. He stretched out near the shrubs, stuck the sorghum knife in the ground nearby, and pulled away the divots from an abandoned burrow. Reaching into the burrow, he removed a damp wad of musty flour sacking, unwrapped the old bottle of grain alcohol, and removed the wooden plug. Stretched out behind the shrubs, he watched the moonlit track leading to the Sudan border. Nothing moved there, no one came, but he continued to watch for over an hour, drinking occasionally from the old bottle. But it wasn't merely the foraging Anyanya captain he was worried about, or his deranged little witch doctor. He couldn't understand why Emily Farr hadn't sent for him when she'd discovered Dr. Botewi in the parlor, or had been summoned by the captain to the front road. Why? Was it because he hadn't stopped smoking, as he'd promised, or because he had teased her that afternoon in the garden? Why hadn't she asked for him? Had he spoken too carelessly, come too late in the morning, taken too much sugar with his afternoon tea, or laughed too loudly in the clinic? Why?

The grain alcohol was musty on his lips, but as quick as silver in his mind. The Arab song came as easily as the wind:

I have followed the wadis, followed the stars;
I have seen the white moon and the white stones.

What had he done? Was it because Amina was now to become a mother, he to be a father? He drank again, the track ahead of him forgotten, the words growing stronger in his mind, his heart broken as he lay on the grass, remembering her standing in the garden that afternoon, remembering Khartoum on a warm African night, as soft as this one, the evening before him and ready to be spent, like a pocketful of pound notes:

I have seen the wadis and the stars;
The moonlight dying upon the sand;
The desert wind drying my life like bleached bones.
Why have you done this, my Heart?
Why have you left me alone?

SEVEN

1

"They wanted to see the plane," Emily said to McDermott. "They were curious, and Samuel Eko has told them about you."

Her hand was on the shoulder of the youngest village boy, who was no older than seven or eight. Three other village children stood in their rags on the track near the gate, looking up solemnly at McDermott, whose shirt and face were still wet from unloading the UN rations. Samuel Eko had just driven back to the village clinic. She'd heard the plane on its approach and had walked up from the clinic to meet him, accompanied by the four children who'd been helping her sweep out the clinic yard. On his three previous trips to the Baro station she'd missed him, climbing the hill too late, the plane already preparing for takeoff at the end of the strip. "You're a regular visitor now, but we seldom see you."

"There's never much time, is there?"

"Too little, I'm afraid."

He showed the children the plane, but only the youngest had the courage to climb into the cockpit; but as always happens, too, his legs were the shortest, and when the other three ran off down the track to carry the news of their adventure, he was far in the rear, denied the greater victory of telling the other children.

"I missed you the last couple of times," McDermott said as he watched the children run off. "I suppose you've been pretty busy?"

"I was in the clinic. I tend to lose track of time there." She didn't know whether he was apologizing or not, and for a moment she was as unsure of him as she'd been that first afternoon. "We're busiest in the morning." She shaded her eyes against the sun. "I watched you take off."

"I see you stopped painting the roof."

She turned to look back over her shoulder. "Yes, we have. I think Samuel Eko is pleased. It seemed rather silly, didn't it. I suppose it was the uncertainty more than anything else." She turned back.

"What uncertainty?"

She hadn't intended to draw him into her own world. Now she regretted it. "What's going to happen to us, I suppose. Would you like something cool to drink?" He walked with her back to the kitchen. "Whether we'll continue as we have or whether the station will be closed. The politics is certainly confusing, isn't it? We hardly seem to know from one day to the next who our friends are and who our friends aren't." She was thinking of the Anya-nya captain and his group, as well as the group of Ethiopians who'd visited two days earlier. "Do you follow it—the politics, I mean?" She studied his face as she held open the screen door.

"Not much. Thanks."

His indifference suddenly reassured her. "Sometimes I can't make heads or tails of it. I'm not sure that's really important." *It's the land and the river*, he had said. *You can't change that.* But she had never wanted to, and his remark had struck home for exactly that reason. "I suppose the roof was simply a symptom of our uncertainties here."

They drank iced tea at the table in the kitchen, and afterward walked together down to the river, which was hot and uninviting in the midday sun. Insects swarmed over the surface, turgid and muddy in the gassy heat. They walked along the bank in the shade of the trees and climbed to the wild grass of the garden.

"Maybe you have some work you'd rather be doing," McDermott said as they stopped in the shade of an old mango tree.

"Oh, no. Not until four." She looked up at him, her face in the shadows of the blowing leaves, her forehead and nose damp from the heat as she pulled a few wet strands from her forehead. In her lifted face and the immediacy of her gaze it seemed to McDermott that there was nothing he didn't know about this woman, and its recognition came to him so sharply and so painfully that he knew it must be true. She was lonely. For a moment he thought she'd known what he'd discovered, too, but then the moment passed.

"I usually spend some time in the garden after lunch," she said, stooping to gather a few green and yellow mangoes. "On Thursdays, especially." She turned. "Is it Thursday?"

"I'm not sure."

"We'll pretend that it is." She smiled. She showed him the garden with its bean, melon, squash, and tomato plants, brought a basket from the house, and began filling it with ripe tomatoes.

"Are you going back to Addis today?" she asked.

"No. I've got another stop."

"That's rather a luxury, isn't it?" she asked. "Dropping in all around the countryside like that?"

"Like a traveling circus," McDermott said.

"A circus?"

"Fun for the small-town crowds and every day the same day for the peanut vendors and the acrobats."

"But you're more than that, I'm sure."

"No, I'm not. I'm a horse-and-buggy bush pilot, like the Swede, Larsen. That's all."

"I'll keep your secret," she said. "But I won't believe you." It wasn't until they returned to the plane that he realized that the tomatoes were for him.

The shadows were long across the Sudi strip when he came in below the coffee trees. "You're late," Rozewicz said, looking at his watch as McDermott dropped to the ground.

"Late for what?" It was almost five o'clock.

"They've moved the strip. We got the radio message this morning. They've moved it eighty kilometers to the south. The Arab troops are bivouacked at the old field—two companies brought in by helicopter."

He followed Rozewicz back to the ready tent and stood at the map board, looking at the charts two Israeli advisers were studying. The new field was marked in red pencil.

"It shouldn't be too difficult to find," the Israeli captain said cautiously, moving aside as McDermott leafed through the other maps.

"For God's sake!" Rozewicz shouted. "It's a bog! The whole bloody sector's a bog!" He turned and slammed out of the tent. The red-bearded cargo master was back from the plane and intercepted Rozewicz on the path outside. He asked for his loading instructions. "What am I, a magician?" Rozewicz cried. "Ask him. Does he land on bog water too? Ask Cohen in Addis, the big-shot field marshal!"

"Probably our maps are wrong," the other Israeli captain said uneasily, wiping his face with a handkerchief, as Rozewicz's voice died away. He was embarrassed too. They were all embarrassed. The three different sets of maps on the map table all showed the new landing strip lying in marshland. McDermott asked the obvious questions: how carefully the coordinates had been given by the Anya-nya radio operator, whether they had been given in the clear, or encrypted, and whether they might not be reading from different sheets of music.

They'd checked with the radio operator three times, using three different codes, but each time the answer was the same. Rozewicz had requested a fourth transmission, in the clear, but the radio operator had already shut his transmitter down and was on the move.

"When did they finish this new field?" McDermott asked.

"Last week," the captain said. McDermott compared the three maps with his own air navigation charts, looked at his notebook and his flight log, and went back to the three maps. Two were from British intelligence sources, dating from the colonial era, and the third a more recent Israeli map marked *Top Secret*. He folded the three maps along the bog and marshland areas, and compared the contour lines and the terrain notations. In some areas the detail differed, but in the vicinity of the new landing field the detail was identical, taken from a common source.

"What do you think?" the Israeli captain asked finally.

"Cartographers are like everyone else. They repeat each other's mistakes," McDermott said, comparing the contour lines again. "That's the trouble with the bureaucracy too. They'll give you an answer that looks plausible because someone else said it was, but they'll never discover what they don't know. That's the trouble with these maps. No one's ever been there."

The two Israeli advisers leaned over the map table, comparing the tracing McDermott had just made of one set of contour lines with those on the second and third maps. They were identical. McDermott sat down and took his slide rule, compass, and notebook from his briefcase. Rozewicz slipped quietly into the tent and stood looking over the shoulders of the two Israelis.

"What is it?"

"*Terra incognito*," one Israeli said. "He said no one's been there—that it's never been mapped. See, there are few details."

"Except the rebels," McDermott added. "Go ahead and load," he told Rozewicz. "But give me less weight to play with. I don't want to get hung up with a maximum load. With the additional space you can give me some light stuff. Medical supplies. More rations."

"What—bully beef? Beans and marmalade?" Rozewicz said in despair.

"Something lighter," McDermott said without changing expression, writing in his notebook. "Bagels maybe. Dried chicken soup."

"*Bagels?*" Rozewicz turned and went out. "Good God!"

McDermott worked out his flight plan, left a copy on the map table, and walked down the path to watch the plane being loaded. He remembered the tomatoes Emily Farr had given, brought them from the cabin, and passed them around. Rozewicz only pocketed his absentmindedly, his mind on the loading of the plane. McDermott walked off the field and returned to his sleeping tent. Tadessa came up the hill from the village below, carrying his staff and tea kettle, his chamma over his shoulders. He stopped on the path as he saw McDermott, took off his cap, and nodded, his heels together, the way the British had taught him when he had carried their rifles and their tea trays. McDermott waved. Farther down the path two Ethiopian paratroopers sat outside the straw watch tukul, keeping the rabble of small children from climbing the hill to look at the plane.

A circus, he had said. It was a circus all right. He slept for three hours. When he awoke, he heard thunder to the east and knew it was raining on the escarpment, but the sky to the west was clear and luminous under a quarter moon.

He found the newly built strip lying along the coordinates the Anya-nya radio operator had given Sudi. Marshes and swamps lay to the north and west of the field, but the strip itself lay along a spine of cotton soil that the rebels had dragged clear and then impacted with oxen-dragged logs brought up from the river bottom a few miles away. The strip was fringed with fire, like the fields farther to the south where the African farmers burned the wild grasses and undergrowth before planting. The drifting smoke obscured his visibility, and he overflew the field twice before he came around over the swamps on his final descent, the strip firm beneath his wheels.

A few dozen Anya-nya were gathered at the end of the field, waiting. Beyond he saw a group of beehive huts on the slopes toward the swamp. After they had unloaded the plane, the Anya-nya captain drew him aside and told him there was a white man in the village and that he was ill. He touched his head as he said it. McDermott took his gun belt from the cabin, and followed the captain back through the village to a small beehive hut above the swamp where the hill fell away sharply. A few dugouts lay at the foot of the bank.

The captain nodded toward the raffia curtain hung over the low door. McDermott ducked his head and went inside. A white man with long gray hair and a thin yellow face sat inside, his eyes bright in the light of the oil bowl that flamed at the foot of the bed. "Welcome," he called immediately. He was Belgian. In the hut with him were two black women, shorter and plumper than the tall Nilotic women of the village. The Belgian wanted to talk, but not about McDermott's plane—no. He had heard the plane, but it meant nothing to him. He had owned a tea plantation in the Congo that had been burned out in the rebellions and was now foraging for illegal ivory in the southern Sudan and smuggling it by truck into Kenya. The southern Sudanese wars had moved into his poaching area, and government troops had burned his storage sheds only a few hours after he'd fled. Forced to abandon his Mercedes truck a hundred kilometers to the south, he'd buried two tons of ivory in the field nearby. After the rebellions moved to the west, he'd go back and dig them up. His English was erratic and rusty, and he occasionally lapsed into French; but the compulsion to talk was stronger than both his fever and his memory. In the smoky stupor of the hut his voice seemed to be the sole justification for his existence.

"You're American, eh?" he said. The older and heavier of the two Negro women was cutting his gray hair with a pair of rusty scissors. He was shirtless, wearing a pair of filthy trousers that hung in tatters about his ankles. His bony chest and hollow rib cage were the color of wood ash. "I don't care what you're doing, no! Christ, no! What's the gun for? To shoot elephants? It won't do, lad!"

McDermott asked him if he needed medicine.

"Medicine? What for? Christ, talk about diseases! I've had my share! What was Schopenhauer's, incidentally?"

McDermott said he didn't know.

"Don't you know?" He laughed. "Migraine, maybe. Worms? I lost my books, by the way—all my medical books! I was self-taught! A whole bloody library. No, wait a minute! I have two left. But the *Larousse Médical* is gone. The two? Diseases of the liver, maybe. What a sickness that is, incidentally. No alcohol! What a worse one is emptiness. I mean it. Have you ever been sick for two years? Three? I mean it—blank! Not atheism—shit no! Emptiness. Take your color from the jungle back there, just beyond the water's edge. Green and black! That's good, honest decay for you, not what they teach in Bruxelles these days. The scum on the swamps around here, the wall of rotting banana trees. That's life! Not scholars' snot. Take a look when you go out, but watch your step. Raise your children to that, and see what a coward it makes of you. Do you have any children, by the way?"

"I'm not married."

"Not married! A bachelor! Lucky man. *Ce sont les garçons très dangereux.*" McDermott stood in the shadows inside the low door, wiping his face on his arm. It was terribly hot.

"Hey! Watch my scalp!" The Belgian jerked his head under the plump woman's scissors, and laughed. "She wants me to look handsome again, the way she remembers me from the old days in the Kivu. She was fourteen when I found her. Look at her now." He pinched her loose belly under the cotton shift, and she moved back with solemn dignity. "If you have any books with you, newspapers, too, leave them for me. Throw them out the door when you leave. I'll find them. Anything you have. Did you ever live in a world without print—no memory at all. The day dies with you, lad. The roaches feed on the glue

135

here—like molasses. Take the pages apart. I think I've got two left."
He called in Swahili to the younger of the two black women and she
arose obediently and began searching through a tin footlocker. "She's
hardworking, that one, never sleeps. Look at those tight little buttocks.
I love that one—the little one. She sucks me out of my loins like a
leech. My life goes with it—existence, life, biology too. All the philosophical puzzles. There it is—in that tight little ass. Soul of my soul!"
He laughed and looked at McDermott. "Why shouldn't I love her, eh?
Where else could I find it at my age—a reason to get out of bed in the
morning? Bruxelles again? Fuck Bruxelles! Two, maybe three years.
That's all the young ones last here. The fat one is good for a few years
more. Then someone younger. Look for a good screw first, and who
cares what the face looks like. When I'm eighty, I'll still have someone
younger, two or three to straddle. They'll ride my pole like I'm Don
Quixote. Do you know what the old man said, by the way?"

"What old man?"

"Don Quixote! Don't you know Spanish? 'Don't look for this year's
birds in last year's nests.' There's no medicine that can cure that, is
there? Anyway, I'm not afraid of dying. God, no!" He laughed. "Not
like you. What's the gun for, by the way? Do you think I'm boasting?
Not at all. It boils it out of you—the fever and everything else. When
I'm too old, the women won't care anymore. That will make death
easy, won't it?" He laughed again. "Acceptable, I should say. That's the
perfection we reach. No place to go except over the edge. Everything
sucked out. Death knew what it was doing when it made our bodies
smell, our flesh rot. But it begins long before." He moved aside and let
the smaller Negro woman sit alongside him on the bed. "What's ivory
bring in Nairobi these days?"

"I don't know," McDermott said. "I'm not in the trade."

"If I don't make it next month, maybe the month after. There's no
hurry. It ages better underground. It can stay in place for a while. Not
like the women, though." He laughed, showing his crooked yellow incisors. "You've got to be careful, especially with the black ones. Come
home two hours late and you'll find her in bed with someone else—
with the houseboy or cook, maybe. When you do, you'll know there's

nothing new under the sun. Take my word for it, lad. You look young enough to learn still. 'Africa makes swine of men, and you're the worse of the swinish lot, Henri!' my wife in Bruxelles told me. It's true!" He laughed quietly. "Look at the Portuguese, the French, the Belgians— even the British! They've paid the price for their African empires! Why is it they're not on the moon these days, like the Americans, eh? Why is it? I'll tell you why. They're swine like me. Afraid their wives and whores will climb into their servants' beds while they're gone!" He laughed for a long time. "Do you remember that song the woman sang in the Luxembourg Gardens the night Paris was liberated? Do you? You could hear her voice on Boulevard St. Michel, where the crowds joined in. By God, that was a night for you! When was that? Forty-three?"

"Could have been," said McDermott, looking at his watch. "I've got to go. Do you want me to do anything for you?"

"Nothing—unless it's the books. *Rien! C'est tout!*" He waved his hand. "Go ahead then. Go on. My truck is just to the south. You'll see it on its side in a ditch. Two of the tires are gone. I pulled off the carburetor, too, just to be on the safe side. But don't waste your time looking for the ivory! You'll never find it."

McDermott left him there, still talking, the plump Negro woman still cutting his hair.

2

Penny sat on the airport terrace, drinking a cup of cappuccino and reading the *International Herald Tribune* from Paris which she'd bought at the news counter below. It was after four o'clock. She'd driven to the terminal from the hangar after a mechanic had told her that McDermott would be two hours late. She'd been excited as she'd left the house for the airport that afternoon. But now, on the terrace, she found herself slipping back into the same terrible depression that had haunted her for three days in the empty house. She could summon no interest at all in the newspaper and finally put it aside, suspended in time. The vacuum in which she waited was an agony for her.

A Peace Corps group climbed to the airport terrace for espresso after putting a colleague on a flight to Nairobi, saw her sitting there alone, and joined her.

"Who are you waiting for this time, your old rat pack or your new pilot friend?" Eastwick asked, lifting the *International Herald Tribune* from her knee to study the headline. "What's the latest on our blue-collar war?" He frowned, looking at the front-page photograph from Saigon.

"If you're talking about Vietnam again, fuck off," Penny said. Eastwick was Penny's age, dark-haired, wearing a button-downed shirt open at the collar, Levi's jeans, and polished loafers. He worked as a Peace Corps Volunteer in the prime minister's office. He was a legal adviser, one of the few PCV's without a beard or long hair.

"What's happening to you? You becoming a hardhat these days?"

"The rat pack bugged out for good," said Lizzy. "When are we going to meet your pilot friend, Pen? How come you're so mysterious about this guy? Gimme a cigarette, Murph."

"You've already smoked my last cigarette," Murphy complained.

"He keeps busy," Penny said.

"You're not busy," Eastwick said, still scanning the headlines. "How come you never answer your phone these days?"

"I've got things to do."

"You know what we should do about Vietnam, don't you?" Eastwick said, looking at Murphy across the table. "Let the AFL-CIO finance it. Maybe the United Mine Workers. The Four-H Clubs. The Future Farmers of America. Why not? It's their war."

"The small towns are already financing it," Murphy said irritably. "So are the ghettos."

Lizzy lifted her small head: "You're fulla shit, Eastwick!"

"It's their war. They want it." Eastwick laughed, folding the paper to the editorial page. "That's all I'm saying."

"It's nobody's war," another volunteer said. "So why do we have to keep talking about it."

"That's what I say," Lizzy said. "Who's gotta cigarette?" Eastwick brought a pack from his shirt pocket together with matches and lifted them toward Lizzy, still reading the paper. "Wow!" she exclaimed, holding up the book of matches. They were official matches, with the State Department seal in gold on the white cover. "From the embassy yet. Are the fags duty-free, too?"

"Why didn't you get the ambassador to autograph it?" Penny asked. "Like he did the letter to your draft board."

Eastwick ignored them, reading the *International Herald Tribune.*

"Hey, is that this McDermott guy's plane?" Lizzy asked, looking toward a DC-3 circling in from the north. Eastwick lifted his eyes too. Murphy and the other volunteer turned in their chairs.

"No, that's not him."

"Is he still flying for Cohen, like you said?" Eastwick asked, still watching the plane.

"Maybe. He doesn't talk much about it. Neither do I."

"If I worked for Cohen, I wouldn't talk much about it either," Eastwick snickered, picking up the paper again.

"I think that's him," Penny said, rising from her chair, her eyes turned to the west. "Yep, that's him. See you guys."

"Bring him around," Lizzy called after her.

"Yeah," Eastwick agreed, handing her the *Herald Tribune.* "Don't be such a hermit."

Sitting on the rear patio that evening, her depression forgotten, she thought she was happy again, even if he'd told her nothing about his four days in the bush. But she thought of what Eastwick had said about the blue-collar war in Vietnam, what Murphy had observed about the small towns, what she remembered of her parents' friends in San Francisco who were McDermott's age, and wondered. She knew no more of his present life than she did of his past.

"How'd you escape it?" she asked him impulsively as they sat together in the twilight, waiting for the charcoal to burn down in the grill.

"Escape what?"

"Everything. Peer-group pressures. Expense-account waistlines.

The nine-to-five rat race. That little town in Pennsylvania. The whole scene."

"As the crow flies," he said quietly. She wondered whether his reply was as thoughtful as her question. Some of his responses were merely mechanical. She wanted to think that this one wasn't. It seemed so appropriate to the answers she was searching for.

EIGHT

On a bitterly cold day in December 1940 a seven-year-old Plymouth sedan, with one fender missing and a set of mud-splattered Kentucky license plates, circled the main square of a little hillside town in western Pennsylvania near the West Virginia and Ohio borders, and drove east out of town. It drove past the funeral home, the tall gingerbread houses behind the oak trees, and the iron gates belonging to the community's doctors, lawyers, and mine owners, and proceeded out the ribbon of asphalt into the open countryside. At the edge of town the old Plymouth slowed as it passed a tall red-brick building standing on a bank of dead grass sifted with old snow above a wet stone wall. To the east was an expanse of open field. On the highest shoulder of the bank, in front of the old Victorian mansion, was a black metal sign with the gold letters: *Chesley Children's Home 1886.*

"Hit's got a far a-burnin!" Pursley Amis shrieked, his small chapped face pressed to the back window of the old Plymouth as he saw the gray scarves of smoke lifting from the orphanage chimneys. Four other small, dirty faces were pressed with his against the car window.

"Hit's a horsepittle!" Buford Amis yelled, remembering where they'd taken his mama recently, his blue eyes shocked, too, with the recollection of that painful absence. He began to whimper. He was six years old.

"Hit ain't no hospital neither," their father said from the driver's seat. "You 'uns doan go tellin' Scotty no fibs now. He's got enough to think on without all that talkin."

Next to him on the front seat sat an eight-year-old boy who was not his son. The driver was Will Amis. His oldest daughter, Wanda, sat on the other side of the eight-year-old boy, who was wearing a leather

141

aviator's helmet with isinglass goggles, and a cracked, hand-me-down sheepskin coat with a fleece collar. At his feet was a cardboard box which contained everything on earth he possessed. His eyes seldom left Will Amis's movements at the wheel, the gearshift, and the floor pedals. Wanda was attempting to hold his hand, but it eluded her. She tried to cradle his shoulders with her arm, but he leaned away.

"Yore gonna make a whole buncha new frens where yore a-goin'," she whispered encouragingly, her breath sweet with thick chocolate which Will Amis had bought to keep their minds elsewhere. "Maybe they'll even give you yore own bed." Wanda was wearing a cloth coat with a fur collar that had once belonged to her mother, who was awaiting her family's return in a Wheeling boardinghouse, nursing her two-week-old baby. A two-year-old was also in bed with her, suffering from a fever. On Wanda's feet was a pair of her mother's old bedroom slippers. "We'd be a-packing you along with us to Daddy-Jesse's house iffen you wuz kin," she whispered, her hand over her mouth so her father couldn't hear. "Only you ain't kin. I wisht you wuz."

"Daddy-Jesse ain't got no room!" Pursley cried, leaning over the front seat excitedly. "Me an' Buford gonna sleep in the chicken house!"

"You 'uns hush now," Will Amis said as he turned the old Plymouth into a service station, drove around the closed pumps, and back out onto the highway. He drove back past the Chesley Home while the small dirty faces studied the old Victorian building through the side windows.

"That's where yore gonna live," Buford said to the boy on the front seat. "Did you see it!" He tapped Scotty on the head. "Hey, Scotty. Wuz you a-seein' it?"

"Sure, he seed it," Wanda said with the superiority of a ten-year-old. "Turn loose of his hat 'fore I bust you one."

"Hit looks like a nice place all right," Will Amis said aloud, trying to spark himself up. He still didn't know whether he could do it or not. The boy had lived with the Amis family since his father had died in a Wheeling Veteran's Hospital six months earlier, the mother already dead back in the Kentucky hollows two years before Nate McDermott brought his son with him to find work in the steel mills. Will Amis and Nate McDermott had grown up together in the mountain hollows twenty miles from Hazard, Kentucky, and it was Nate McDermott who had found work for Will in the same Wheeling mill after the coal tipple had closed down. The McDermott boy called him Uncle Will, but they weren't kin.

Now Will Amis had lost his Wheeling job with the closure of the extrusion plant and was taking his family back to the Hazard hollows, where he'd help his father-in-law mine a little dogleg, crawl-in coal mine nearby. There wasn't hardly enough room in the cabin for his own family, to say nothing of those who weren't even blood relations. His wife had told him there wasn't enough room in the old Plymouth machine to get them all to Hazard anyway, but what she meant was that her Jesse wouldn't be any too happy with all those children. What then would Daddy-Jesse say if they brought a stranger too? Will Amis had thought about it for weeks. A Methodist woman in the Wheeling boardinghouse had told him about the Chesley Home. But she'd also told him about the Chesley school, which was as fine a school as there was in Pennsylvania. School had been Will Amis's problem all his life. He'd only had six years, like Nate McDermott. He thought that if he ever died like Nate had, he'd want his youngsters put in a good home with a good school. But he didn't know whether he had the heart to do it.

He drove back into town and around the square again, but as he saw the open road in front of the Plymouth, he knew he couldn't take the boy back—not after the talks they'd had about it all those evenings, not with Daddy-Jesse's problems—not with the money problem either, which was even worse after spending the gas and candy money he had to spend to bring them up to Pennsylvania from Wheeling. Tomorrow night they would be on the road, clean down the Ohio River and on into Kentucky if the tires and the water pump held out.

He drove back toward the Chesley Home, turned the car into a driveway, backed out again, and parked next to the broken sidewalk. The children tried to climb out, too, but he told them to stay in the car. Buford started to cry; then Pursley, Andrew, Donna, Ashford. Finally even Wanda, who put her head in her hands and sobbed as Scott climbed out alone, carrying his box of possessions. "You say good-bye to them, son," Will Amis told him. "They'll understand better iffen you say it." He walked up the street and away from the children as Scott said good-bye, looking out over the winter countryside.

"It'll be all right," Will Amis said as the boy joined him finally, struggling to control himself. "It'll work out all right, the way your mama and daddy would have wanted it to. They'd know it wuz the right thing, being good Christian folks like they wuz. Them folks up in the house there can make you into something better than ever I could. Give you a trade, make you a doctor or a lawyer, maybe a preacher even. All you'd ever learn from me would be coal an' factory work, being up an' down the road all the daggone time." His voice broke and he looked away, tears in his eyes, his rough fingers brushing them away, but the grief was as much for his own youth and its smashed hopes and innocence as the trusting face he saw looking up at him.

During the past half year Scott McDermott had come to love this man as he'd loved his own father. He was the only surviving link with the past—the smell of his oil-stained clothes, the creases in his shoes and neck, the graphite-stained fingers that would pinch a nickle or dime for him from his tobacco-littered pockets. Will Amis knelt down on the pavement.

"You'll be all right now, won't you? The way your daddy learned you. You know what to tell them—that your daddy died in that Wheeling vet'rans hospital, an' you got no folks no more. You ken tell 'em you run away from the boardin' house because I whupped you, but tell 'em you're Methodist, too, and that your Granddaddy Parkins tithed ten percent, which is the Bible truth. All right. You got your mama's Bible there too. All right then, I'll be a-coming back when the mill opens again. I'll be a-talking to you then." Will Amis and the boy embraced on the sidewalk.

McDermott knew that the mill would never again open in the same way. He watched the car drive away. Even after it had disappeared, he stood motionless on the sidewalk, looking down through the empty streets, unable to bring himself to move his eyes in any other direction. For a few minutes he thought that the car would come back, but as more time passed, he knew that it would be crossing the river at the toll bridge, and that it would not come back. He turned finally and looked at the old Victorian house.

The two tall chimneys were smoking and he watched them as he had watched the car and the empty streets. Watching the smoke eddy in the wind and drift out across the wintry sky, he discovered something else too. His eyes traveled out across the raw countryside to make sure he hadn't been mistaken. On the winter panorama of grays, black, and dirty umber, nothing moved. The landscape was empty. He stood there for a long time before he finally stirred himself. Carrying the box, he turned up the steps, paused a final time at the end of the long walk by the foot of the wooden steps and searched the fields a final time.

"*Christian* gentlemen remove their hats in a lady's presence," the gray-haired woman said from the doorway, looking down at him. She wore a wine-colored dress, a black velvet throat band, black hose, and black shoes. And she held a small black book to her chest.

McDermott gazed up at her solemnly, searching the thin, harsh face for clues as to kin, children, family, or understanding. There were none. Behind her trailed a long bright corridor carpeted with a flowered runner. He continued to study her face as she waited; and finally after he had found nothing there he could recognize or identify with his own past, not even his dim recollection of Granddaddy Parkins, who tithed ten percent, he yielded to hers. He shifted the box in his arms and obediently pulled the aviator's cap from his head, his damp-combed hair springing up like spring onions from his scalp. Her expression didn't change. Neither did his—not that day or the next, nor the long months that followed. But as the year passed, and then the next, when her lips finally softened, and her face, too, as she sat with him for hours, helping him recover those lost years when his education had suffered and left him behind the other children his age, he knew he would never forget her as she'd greeted him that first day when he'd stood on the porch with nothing alive about him but the beat of his own heart.

"She must have been a marvelous teacher," Emily Farr said as they walked on the grasslands beyond the strip.

"She was," McDermott said. "That's all she had—just her teaching. Just her school."

"I don't know western Pennsylvania. But your family wasn't from there?"

"From Kentucky," McDermott said, lifting his binoculars. He'd seen a few buffalo on his approach to the strip but now they were gone.

"Do you have a home there—in Kentucky?"

"No, not anymore."

"I suppose it's a mistake to ask that question these days. When I was growing up, it was the question one usually asked. Now it has less relevance—with younger children especially. Were you in the military?"

He nodded, bringing the binoculars down. "I was in the Air Force for a time." They walked back toward the cottage.

"In Vermont a stranger is someone whose family has been there for less than two generations." She smiled.

"It's probably the same way in the Kentucky hollows."

"Kentucky is a lovely state. At least I've always thought so. The bluegrass country in particular."

"Hazard, Kentucky, isn't bluegrass. Only the music. Was your husband from Vermont?"

"New Jersey. His father taught at the seminary." She stooped in the grass near the gate to lift a few, pale anemone blossoms into the sunlight. "It's the dust that does this to them—the dust and the wind. Why do they insist on growing here?"

He didn't answer, looking instead at her face. *Why do you?* he considered asking, but thought he knew the answer she would give him, and he didn't want to hear it on a day when everything he had detected in her voice and seen in her actions denied the claims of her ministry. She paused at the fence to gaze back out over the grasslands. Her head didn't move for a minute, her eyes fixed upon the distant horizon. A moment passed before she spoke. "How time passes," she murmured, rousing herself. "How quickly it goes."

"Too fast," McDermott said, opening the gate.

"Next time you must bring a picnic lunch. And your fishing rod. We could picnic along the river."

"I will," he promised.

NINE

1

Penny sometimes drove with McDermott to Cohen's villa on a steep hillside up the mountain behind the city. Usually she waited in the car or walked in the garden with Mrs. Cohen. The villa made her suspicious. It stood in a large compound shaded by silver trees and surrounded by a high stone wall with shards of broken glass razoring the concrete beadwork atop the wall. The iron gate was covered with sheet metal to conceal the courtyard from the foot and animal traffic along the rocky road outside. Inside its portals was a small gate-house; a pair of brindled Alsatian dogs were staked to a post nearby, snarling and growling whenever the gates were opened for a vehicle, the hairs bristling along their spines like porcupine quills. Some-times they roamed free when the gate was closed, as lean and feral as timber wolves. The two watchmen at the gate weren't Ethiopians, like most of the local watchmen, even at the diplomatic compounds, but Europeans. Their presence made her suspicious too. "A guy with all this protection must have something to hide," Penny insisted after her first visit. "Are you sure he's on the up-and-up?"

McDermott had told her that Cohen was simply a temporarily transplanted Frenchman who was uncomfortable in Africa, a descrip-tion that was half true. He'd described him as the operations manager for the French survey team exploring the interior, but this was false. Although Cohen traveled on a French passport and had been born in France, he was an Israeli intelligence officer with Mossad, controlling the gun-running operation into the Sudan. Rozewicz worked for him as commander of the Sudi strip; so did the other advisers, as well as a few Israeli military officers attached to the Israeli military assistance group that was training the Ethiopian army. The Ethiopian government cooperated with him, too, but only up to a point. Although Mossad also paid McDermott's salary, Cohen had no direct authority over McDermott, who'd drawn up his own contract with Mossad in Tel Aviv. McDermott was carried as a consultant, free to fly under circumstances or conditions of his own choosing.

Cohen had once been a pilot but his experience was limited. He'd flown a small transport for the RAF during the war and hadn't touched the controls since. McDermott and Rozewicz both thought Cohen knew far less about combat or all-weather flying and the systems they required than Cohen gave himself credit for. He was a small, bony man with sparse gray hair, closely trimmed, high cheekbones, and lips so thin and bloodless they looked like the mandibles of a tortoise. As a result of a racing-car accident in France years earlier he had only partial vision in his right eye. In recent years the optic nerve had begun to atrophy and he wore dark glasses to conceal the impairment. Strong-willed, often ruthless, he had little sense of humor, no talent for small talk, and little interest in ideas that weren't of his own divination. He considered himself a strategist and tactician, but in fact was a theoretician who could better manipulate the abstractions of *Realpolitik* than he could motivate the men who served him. His parents were born in Germany and he looked more German than French, or Israeli. In a high gray collar he would have resembled a *Junker* on the German general staff circa 1939. The name Cohen was a *nom de guerre*. In Tel Aviv he was Efim Yacob, and some claimed that he'd been a member of the Stern Gang. Rozewicz referred to him in the privacy of the bush as "The Field Marshal." After her first meeting Penny had been as graphic: "*That* guy's an operations manager?" she'd said skeptically as they drove out the gate. "*That* guy? He looks like a lab rat to me. I'll bet he's got pink eyes under those shades."

So once again Penny had driven McDermott and Rozewicz directly to the villa from the airport and had disappeared with Mrs. Cohen among the roses of the rear garden while the men talked. Cohen wore a white shirt, open at the collar, gray trousers, and gray leather sandals on his sockless feet. His arms were thin and hairless, with a tallowy tint to the muscleless, almost translucent flesh. McDermott and Rozewicz were still dressed in their bush khakis, their shirts and boots covered with the red dust of the road below the Sudi strip. They had spent two days bringing the guns up from the road where the trucks were mired. The new strip within the marshes had been discovered by Sudanese military helicopters. The village had been razed. A new field was now being built farther to the south, but even when completed, it would lie just within the limits of McDermott's flying range.

Cohen sat in his lounge chair, head reclining, as Rozewicz explained the operational problems from the leather ottoman nearby, his maps unrolled on the floor between his feet. Cohen's logistics adviser, an Israeli colonel, and his secretary looked on. McDermott sat slumped on a bamboo footstool, listening to Rozewicz argue for a larger plane or the relocation of the Sudi operation to an airstrip closer to the Sudanese frontier. His briefing was slow and repetitious, as were his arguments, and Cohen lost interest.

After he'd finally finished, Cohen suggested that an auxiliary fuel tank be installed in the Beechcraft. Rozewicz said that an auxiliary tank would decrease the payload too much.

"Then make more flights," Cohen replied, his eyes closed under the dark glasses. He'd neither lifted his head nor turned to look at the maps.

"More flights! It's impossible! Once every two weeks conditions are right—weather, visibility, wind, Anya-nya in place. Not perfect, no. Minimal conditions. How can we increase that? Can mothers make more children? Five a year? It's bloody dangerous now. To increase the flights would make each ten times more dangerous." Rozewicz turned to McDermott. "Tell him."

"We take what the weather gives now. We can't do any more," McDermott said. "Not from Sudi."

"Then put in an auxiliary tank," Cohen replied.

"A DC-3 from a field nearer the border is all we're asking," Rozewicz said.

"If we ask the Ethiopians for a DC-3, then we must give something in return," Cohen said distastefully, lifting his head. "If we ask for another field, closer to the border, then we must pay for that too. What are we going to give? Nothing. We have nothing more to give. Tel Aviv has nothing at this time. Why are we forced to use Sudi? It's perfectly obvious. As far as the Ethiopians are concerned, it's our war. Never mind the Arabs in Khartoum, Aden, San'a, or Jidda. Never mind Ethiopian talk of Arab encirclement; the war in the Sudan against the Arabs is still Tel Aviv's war and the southern black man's. If we were willing to give the Emperor more money, more guns, boats, or something else, then he might be willing to share something else with us. But Tel Aviv has given enough already. What has it gained us? The strip at Sudi, which you say is too dangerous. That's all. Nothing. But even so the Emperor complains every month that Israel is overexposed in Ethiopia, and that he pays a political price for it—the enmity of the Arabs, Arab support for the Eritrean guerrillas in the north, the hostility of other African nations. The political price isn't so great that he wouldn't accept a financial or military gift to offset his political losses, however. So he'll take more. To help Israel? No, to strengthen himself. But this is how Ethiopia has survived all these years, and survival has made them duplicitous. We asked for a DC-3 last year, you remember—and a better airfield. The Ethiopians said they would consider it. They are still considering it. That is to say, they are waiting to learn what we will give up in return. But Tel Aviv will give nothing. So you see what Sudi symbolizes, don't you? Our condition. Our task is to make it work." Cohen put his head back, his voice tired.

"We've helped those buggers!" Rozewicz protested.

"We're here to help ourselves," Cohen reminded him.

"They're not serious men."

"But we are serious men. Whatever we do, we must do for ourselves. There is no one else. That is our lot. That is Israel's lot as well."

The dust of Sudi dissolved with the afternoon heat on Rozewicz's thick face. He knew nothing about political or diplomatic maneuvering, unlike Cohen. All he knew was that the Sudi operation, dangerous from the beginning, was now even more dangerous. He was a mechanic and his suggestions had been offered with the same logic that told him to replace one missing bolt with a new one, to pull a piston head when compression failed, or repack a bearing when it overheated. Any of these failures could ultimately spell disaster, and Rozewicz, like McDermott, dealt in survival. Nations could survive, so could diplomatists, bureaucrats, and the ministries that paid their salaries, but not always the men that executed their orders.

"Our most dangerous habits are mental ones," Cohen resumed after a moment. "Believing that others will either solve or survive the problems we cannot resolve. They won't, not any more than Israel will. We aren't Frenchmen, or Ethiopians. Not the United States either. Many forget this. America will survive without men like Mr. McDermott, just as France will survive whether or not the French ambassador carries out his instructions in Moscow or Bonn. But Israel will not survive without us."

McDermott watched him silently, knowing how much Cohen despised Israel's dependence upon other nations. This was the one quality he most admired in Cohen, whatever his flaws; it was also the quality which made him dangerous, and Sudi was its proof.

"Then give us another plane," Rozewicz cajoled, mopping his face.

Cohen laughed. "They gave you the Beechcraft. If no one else will fly it, perhaps I will."

Rozewicz had no more to say. Cohen had denied him the only logic he understood—common sense—and now he felt clumsy and betrayed, listening to Cohen's voice:

"Our problem also is that we're merely soldiers, and that our enemies are not merely the Arabs, but our own politicians who think they're generals and the diplomats who think they're both. They're the ones who seem to be making many of the decisions in Tel Aviv. Ask McDermott. He can tell you. He flew in Vietnam, and so he understands that. What other lesson is there from that war except that it wasn't left to the soldiers to fight it."

McDermott listened to Cohen's disquisition, but his mind gradually withdrew, past Cohen's logistics adviser, past Rozewicz's silent brooding, and the tired face of Cohen's middle-aged secretary who was taking notes as her master spoke. A spinster with a smudge of ink on her white chin, she wore neither lipstick nor rouge, and smelled to McDermott like the winter cloakroom in the old grammar school in Pennsylvania.

He thought he knew what Cohen's problem was. Tel Aviv was reexamining its enthusiasm for supporting the southern Sudan insurgency, and now Cohen was awaiting instructions, committed to the status quo, to holding on—nothing more. In conception Tel Aviv's Sudan strategy had been simple: support the black Anya-nya in the Sudan with guns against the Soviet-supported Arab government in Khartoum, and the political environment of the entire region, if not the continent, could be altered to Israel's advantage. Militarily, a full-scale war in the southern Sudan—perhaps drawing in Egyptian troops—would reduce the pressures on Israel's own frontiers. Politically, a war in the southern Sudan, pitting black Africans against Soviet-supported Arabs, would polarize black Africa against both Islamic and Soviet imperialism. The territorial gains Israel had won in the 1967 war could be again justified in Africa, the West, and the Third World, not in terms of Israel's own security, but as essential to the defense of Western and African interests against the dangers of Soviet and Arab hegemonic ambitions. If this was the theory and Cohen one of its architects, it hadn't worked out that way. The southern Sudanese war was fragmenting; attempts at a settlement were under way; and African nations themselves were too deeply divided and too threatened by secession at home to mobilize themselves in defense of the rights of the Sudanese Negro.

But McDermott had been skeptical from the beginning, since those first months when he and Cohen had spent hours together on this same verandah talking about the Sudan and Africa. Before McDermott had been assigned to Thailand to fly an F-105 against North Vietnam, he had been briefed by Air Force and DIA intelligence officers who spoke as plausibly of historical inevitability in Southeast Asia as Cohen had spoken to him about Arab and Soviet designs in Africa. History seemed to McDermott little more than selective recollection, whose most dangerous or untold element was plausibility. Belief or conviction was the sum of its story, but as a pilot McDermott had also learned that truth was most often the least plausible of the certainties he searched for, as well as the most elusive. The truths of the DIA analysts were never elusive: they were as self-evident as fiction could make them. So McDermott had been privy to far too many strategic intelligence briefings not to keep these ambiguities clearly in mind as he listened to a theorist as seductive as Cohen talk about historical inevitability. This was his advantage over Rozewicz. He had heard it all before—on another continent and in another war. He believed none of it.

He slumped on the bamboo stool, listening to Cohen's tireless voice reexploring the old Soviet/Arab chessboard: "Arab and Soviet intentions are clear, from the beginning. First the Sudan, then Chad, soon the Congo. The White redoubt in the south would be threatened: cobalt, gold, diamonds . . . shipping lanes. Who would awaken the West to the menace? Africans themselves? Never. Someone must show the way, help fix the azimuth, begin the creation of a *cordon sanitaire* across Africa from Djibouti to Port Harcourt in Nigeria . . ."

The sun had begun to set. The porch was still windless, and Rozewicz's wet jaws leaked drops of sweat as large as claret-colored raindrops to the map of Upper Nile at his feet. The laterite dust had also soaked to a rubious paste on the back of McDermott's hands, and he moved from the stool to the railing, hearing Penny's voice in the courtyard below:

"You sure are frisky, aren't you, boy? Frisky and shedding too. Doesn't anyone ever brush your coat? What do they feed you, anyway? That's right—sniff. What good's a wet nose if you can't sniff. What do you feed them?"

In the courtyard below, Penny was petting one of the unleashed Alsatian dogs, her blond hair tumbling over her face.

"The guards feed them," Mrs. Cohen said from nearby.

McDermott watched her from the railing. It was funny, he thought. Wars were all alike, but you could never tell about animals. Penny looked up and saw him. "Hey, are you guys about finished?"

"In a minute."

"What about the auxiliary tank?" Cohen asked as McDermott went back to the stool.

"It might work, but let's wait awhile. The new field will be within reach. We can still make it."

"I have another idea," Cohen said, "in addition to the auxiliary fuel tank. This would complement it." He told them that he'd been considering establishing small, mobile ammunition factories in the southern Sudan. The equipment would be flown in, and the Anya-nya cadres could manufacture their own ammo. A few ammo lines in the bush would greatly reduce the Beechcraft's weight problem. "Do you think the Anya-nya capable of manufacturing their own cartridges?" Cohen asked McDermott.

Rozewicz lifted his head in a raucous laugh, half amused, half disbelieving. "You send them guns and you ask *that*—if they can make their own cartridges?"

"I think so," McDermott replied. In Rozewicz's half-astonished look McDermott found again what had been bothering him all afternoon. Rozewicz understood the war and the others on the porch didn't. He was linked in a direct, personal way with the strip at Sudi and the Anya-nya of the Upper Nile. The others weren't. Cohen could invent strategies for pursuing the war, but he couldn't create emotions for understanding their meaning. But if he hadn't shared the war, he couldn't understand it. McDermott had been drummed out of the air corps in Vietnam for trying to teach the same lesson.

"What were you guys talking about?" Penny said as they drove back to the boulevard.

"Problems with scheduling."

"Was that what Rozewicz was so teed off about?"

"Not teed off," McDermott said. "Just disappointed. He thinks the operation could be better organized."

"You can say that again. God. I never see you anymore. You're always on the road these days. Between Cohen and the UN flights, I hardly ever see you. When are you going to take me with you, like you promised?"

"One of these days," McDermott replied.

2

The Peace Corps deputy director was giving a buffet dinner that evening for a few visitors from Washington and Penny was invited. She'd declined the dinner invitation, but had said she and McDermott might stop by later. She'd been working in recent weeks with a few Peace Corps volunteers on a crafts project helping local carvers, weavers, and potters set up a cooperative in an old Italian brickworks. Although some volunteers had begun visiting Penny at the house during McDermott's absences, he'd met none of them.

"C'mon," she pleaded after dinner as they were sitting in the living room. "Just this once. You've never met any of them. You don't even know their names and they're my friends. If you don't want to stay, we can just have a drink and cut out. Okay?"

When Penny and McDermott arrived, the gates of the compound were open, and a dozen cars, Land-Rovers, and motorbikes were parked inside the gate and along the road. On the open porch overlooking the courtyard a dozen Peace Corps volunteers stood in the shadows or leaned against the iron railing. A bar was set up at the end of the porch. The buffet tables had been cleared from the dining room inside, where a few white-coated waiters were circulating with trays of coffee. Some of the American volunteers were in coats and ties; others wore sweaters or denim jackets.

"This is Ed Murphy," Penny said, introducing McDermott to the barrel-chested young man who greeted them at the top of the steps.

"How are you doing," Murphy said. He wore a bushy blond beard, had a friendly Irish face, and the arms and hands of a stonemason. He brought them drinks from the bar. "Sorry you missed the speeches."

"What speeches?" McDermott asked.

"The two congressmen inside. Didn't Penny tell you?"

"You guys missed the chow line," another volunteer informed Penny as he joined them.

"This is McDermott," Penny said. "We've eaten anyway."

"Hi. I'm Ted Eastwick." He stuck out his hand. "I borrowed your timing light once when you were out in the bush. Hope you didn't mind." He was in his twenties and wore a tweed coat and faded jeans. "Penny tells me you're with Cohen's outfit."

"Where are your congressmen friends?" Penny interjected.

"Still interrogating," Eastwick said.

"Looking for anarchists and acidheads," Murphy explained to Mc-Dermott as a few more volunteers joined them.

"I wish they'd leave so we could get a party going," a young girl declared.

"I think the little guy's stoned," Murphy guessed, looking through the door and into the foyer, where the two men were shaking hands as they moved toward the porch. "He still thinks he's in Nairobi."

"Which one is he?" Penny asked.

"The one from the Appropriations Committee," Eastwick said, "a real troglodyte. From Texas, where they founded the breed."

"That means cave dweller," Penny quipped sarcastically. "Is that one of your fifty-dollar Republican law school words?"

"Are you two arguing again?" another girl sighed dramatically as she joined them, her face small and pale as an orchid. She wore a red flower in her thin, brown hair. Her long white dress of undyed cloth looked as if it had been made on a small village loom in Asia or India. "You must be McDermott," she said.

"This is Lizzy," said Penny.

"Hi," Lizzy said. "I thought you were middle-aged."

"I am," McDermott said.

"Lizzy makes everyone feel middle-aged," Murphy drawled.

"Why don't you be a little more discreet," Penny complained.

"What's indiscreet about that?" Lizzy said. "Do you think I was indiscreet?" she asked McDermott innocently.

"God!" Penny rolled her eyes.

"If anyone cares, the troglodytes are coming," Eastwick pointed out. The two congressmen had moved to the porch.

"Hey, Murph!" a volunteer called from the railing behind them. "You'd better close down the hard liquor bar or we'll never get those guys out of here. They're drinking our Scotch dry."

"Us beer drinkers don't worry," Murphy said, opening another can and offering it to McDermott. "You know what'll happen, don't you? The embassy crew will pour those two guys into bed tonight at the Hilton. Then tomorrow they'll go back to Washington and tell everyone on the Hill that the Peace Corps punks aren't potheads at all. Shit, no. They're lushes."

McDermott laughed. "What's so funny?" Penny asked immediately from across the dark porch. She'd been talking to Eastwick and hadn't heard Murphy's remark.

"Nothing," McDermott said as the two congressmen moved closer, shaking hands near the bar.

"You two guys were laughing about something."

"Lord, do you have to know everything?" Lizzy sighed.

"They were laughing about something—"

"It's been real nice," the smaller congressman drawled. "It's been real nice. Talking to you folks makes these trips worthwhile. Good to see you, son. Ya'll come see me when you come to Wash'nton, hear? Good to visit with you. You're from Arizona, right. I reckon that's close enough to Texas." The two men moved across the porch. "Enjoyed talking to you, I sure did. Hello there, young lady. I don't believe I had the pleasure of talking to you. I'm Tom Grayson from Texas." He stood holding Penny's hand, a small, silver thatched man, each white hair immaculately in place, his blue eyes slightly glazed from too much whiskey or too much travel, the smile of the political hustings stamped as clearly on his lips as the American flag in his buttonhole. He wore a dark blue suit, white shirt, and—despite the bourbon—smelled of hair oil and after-shave lotion.

"I'm Earl Dawson from South Carolina," his colleague said. He was taller, stoop-shouldered, wearing a gray knit suit. "You musta slipped in a little late, I'll bet."

In the lantern-lit shadows of the porch Penny's face seemed to Mc-Dermott more genuinely American than the faces of the other girls, and he supposed that the two congressmen had recognized that too.

"What do you do here, little lady?" Grayson asked, still holding Penny's hand. "Looks like you got you a whole caboose full of young admirers here too. I bet your daddy had to run 'em off the front porch with a stick, didn't he." He winked at Eastwick. "How do you like the Peace Corps?"

"I'm not a PCV," Penny said, her cheeks flushed.

"Well, I declare."

"What brings you out this way? Your daddy with the embassy or the MAAG people?"

"No. I just sort of decided to come out and help," Penny said awkwardly. A few of the volunteers laughed.

"Tell us a Mau-Mau story," someone hooted from the bar.

McDermott suddenly felt sorry for her, standing alone with the two congressmen, her face flushed, helpless in Grayson's grip. He put his beer can on the railing, and moved toward her.

"Well, I'll be," Grayson intoned. "Come to hep out. Real neighborly of you. You must be from Texas." He laughed and squeezed her hand. "Where's your home, sugar?"

"Penny," McDermott said, moving between the two congressmen. "Let's go." Neither congressman turned. Penny ignored him.

"Oakland, California," Penny said.

"Is that right? Oakland. Must have cost you a pretty penny, getting on that aeroplane and coming out here to hep these good folks. Show 'em what a little grit can do."

"Free enterprise." Penny shrugged, her face bolder. "Grit and corn bread. Down home stuff."

"Free enterprise, that's the ticket." Grayson nodded. "Making your own way. Not letting Uncle Sugar do everything. That's the spirit. What's your daddy do, honey?"

"He's a plumber."

"Well, I declare. What are you gonna do when you go back?"

"I dunno. I thought maybe I'd get on the gravy train—go into PR work or politics, maybe run for Congress. You know—feet in the trough. Shit like that."

"Well, I declare," Grayson sighed, his eyes a little dimmer, but the smile still on his lips. He patted her on the shoulder gallantly as he let her hand go. "Nice to talk to you, little lady. Howdy, son." He shook McDermott's hand, his face lifted, but there was no enthusiasm in his grip, and a moment later both congressmen were stooping at the foot of the steps to get into their black limousine.

"*Congress sucks!*" Penny yelled as the car went through the front gate.

"Those sexist jerks," Lizzy muttered bitterly.

"How come you got so mad?" a volunteer asked, still amused.

Penny saw his smile and grew even angrier. "Because he was put-ting me on, you jerk! He was putting all of you guys on."

"Don't you ever relax?" Eastwick asked.

"About what? For God's sake, didn't you hear him? Don't those guys ever communicate? Don't they ever listen? How long do they think they can get away with it?"

"So everybody knows it's a put-on. So what's the problem?" East-wick said blandly. "So they embarrassed you, so what? Come on. Let's change the music." The lights in the living room had gone down.

"Change the music! When are you people going to change the mu-sic! What music—'The Stars and Stripes Forever' all day long? Their music!"

"Come on. I brought some records," Eastwick said.

"What were you going to say to those airheads?" Penny asked Mc-Dermott. "When you called to me, what were you going to do?"

"Tell them we had to go, I suppose. Something—"

"If you're going to play some music, you'd better get started," Mur-phy said. "Lizzy brought her Bombay zither with her. You'd better change the music before she does."

McDermott had forgotten how much beer American kids in their twenties could drink, how loud their music, and how casual their inti-macies. Most of the couples were dancing inside, and he watched from the shadows of the porch, leaning against the railing, sipping the beer that had long grown tasteless to him.

"You okay?" Penny asked, standing suddenly in front of him, car-rying her sandals, her face damp from her exertions on the dance floor. "Everything all right?"

"Sure. Why not?"

She took the beer can from his hand and drank from it. "God, this beer's warm." He didn't answer, and she studied his face, her fingers wiping the moisture from her forehead.

"Yeah, I kinda get the message," she sighed and she put her hand on his shoulder to steady herself as she got her sandals back on. "It's late anyway. What have you been thinking about?"

"Not much. It's a nice night."

"Yeah, for being someplace else. C'mon. It's time to go."

3

McDermott and Penny drove south from Addis in the Land-Rover on their way to a campsite on the shores of one of the Rift Valley lakes two hundred kilometers away. They stopped for lunch at an old Italian restaurant overlooking a small crater lake. As they got back into the Land-Rover, she told him that a few Peace Corps Volunteers might be there too. "Liz, Murph—maybe a few others. That won't bother you, will it?" He said no, and she sat back, reassured. "You'll tell me if you ever think they're crowding you, won't you?"

She slept for an hour in the front seat and awoke finally, and watched the villages pass, dusty and somnolent in the midafternoon heat. "Do you still wish you were back flying someplace else," she asked him after a while, "in Vietnam or Cambodia?"

"I haven't thought much about it."

"What were you doing when you left?" She sat up and pulled a cigarette from her purse. "When you left Vietnam?"

"Flying frags against North Vietnam."

She turned. "Flying what? *Frags?* What's a frag?"

"An operations order. A piece of the whole that'll never add up to the sum of its parts. Your part of the puzzle."

"I don't get it."

"It's not complicated. Call it a unit of work. Say the operations order is the big picture. Say headquarters, maybe the Joint Chiefs, wants to take out all of the road and rail facilities in North Vietnam. Some of the job is given to one fighter wing, some to another. Maybe your wing gets the fragment giving you the Dong Dau railroad bridge and everything else in the area. So that's the wing's frag. Maybe one squadron in the wing gets the Yen Vien yards, another the Duc Nol yards. Maybe your flight gets a few buildings. Maybe your plane gets

THE ANTS OF GOD

the roundhouse. So the roundhouse is your part of the frag." Her eyes showed her puzzlement, a quick green in the glare of the sun through the windshield. "It's like an assembly line," he began again, "building a machine, an engine. Someone's drilling a hole. Someone else is threading a bolt. You may not know what it means, your bolt or the steel you're milling, but that's your part of the frag. Someplace else—maybe in Saigon, the Pentagon, or the White House—someone else is totaling up the sum of its parts. You never see it."

"You can say that again," she sighed. "Like you could be building a Frankenstein and not realize it until the lab rats in the Pentagon turn him loose. That's awful." She stared out the window at the sunny hills beyond, and moved closer to him on the front seat. "So that's what you were doing—dropping bombs on roundhouses and locomotive yards, doing whatever they told you to do?" She leaned her head against his shoulder. "So what happened then? Did you leave when you saw what the big picture looked like? When Frankenstein got up off the table?"

"It's a long story."

"You can tell me."

"It gets complicated."

"Make it simple then," she murmured. "Go ahead. Like you always say—words of one syllable."

"I was court-martialed."

She sat up. "Court-martialed!"

"That's right."

She didn't know what to say as she studied his face. Was that good or bad? It had to be good, didn't it? she thought. Someone who went against the regs? She remembered the words on the funny-looking trophy in the suitcase: *Who Gave Us Back Our Honor*. How? By being right, of course. If the regs were wrong—the Pentagon, the White House, the State Department hawks—then he must have been right. He'd disobeyed orders and been court-martialed for doing what was right. Everyone in his squadron had known he was right, the regs wrong.

"Thank God," she breathed, her head dropping back against his shoulder.

"It's not that simple," McDermott cautioned.

"I don't want to hear any more," she said, terrified for a moment that he would deny her what she had learned, that he would set her adrift again, unable to understand. "I don't. Please. Let's think about camping out instead. Forget the crummy war."

A shooting star streaked across the black bowl of sky, like a silver raindrop—its arc clearly discernible against the heavens so alive with stars, so dense and so vast, that everything else was forgotten as they sprawled around the dying campfire near McDermott's tent. The lake waters lapped quietly against the shores in the darkness. Murphy saw a satellite. He sat near the fire like a bearded Buddha, head back, beer can on his knee as he studied the stars. Lizzy couldn't find it. Penny found it immediately. "My God," she sighed, head against her sleeping bag. "How far do you have to go to get away from tin cans and junk. Can't they even leave the stars alone, for God's sake." McDermott sat against a piece of driftwood, eyes lifted, watching the small satellite moving steadily across the heavens. He pointed it out to Lizzy, who finally identified it too. Another group of Peace Corps Volunteers camping down the lake had joined them after darkness had fallen. Penny had been annoyed.

"How'd you explain that to your Ethiopian goatherd friends?" Murphy asked, still watching the satellite. A few Ethiopian village youths had been there that afternoon, foraging for tin cans.

"The two cultures," suggested a girl from the other group.

"What two cultures?" Lizzy wanted to know.

"The sacred and the profane," Eastwick ad-libbed from across the fire, where he'd arrived with the other group.

"Who said that?" Penny complained, lifting her head. "Would you visitors kinda hang it up and stop garbaging up our sky with your preppie philosophy."

Fingers strummed a guitar from the darkness. "Why don't you sing 'Danny Boy' for us, Lizzy?" said the guitar player.

"I'm still trying to figure out which two cultures," Lizzy said.

"Abercrombie and Fitch," Penny suggested, looking at the stars again. "Ask Eastwick."

"Haves and have-nots," said someone else.

"How do you know it's not a plane?" a girl asked Murphy.

"Because I know it's a satellite," Murphy said.

"Are you sure?"

"Sure I'm sure."

"What's it doing?"

"I don't know. Ask McDermott."

"For God's sake, is this a ten-party line or something?" Penny yelled.

"What about the two cultures?" Lizzy wondered. "Where's the counterculture fit in?"

"It doesn't," Murphy answered, opening another beer. "Artsycraftsy isn't culture. If you don't know the difference between a satellite, a 707, and Ursa Minor, you're artsy-craftsy. With a couple of exceptions, all you fire-squatters are artsy-craftsy."

"Yeah," Penny agreed. "So if you don't mind, would you artsy-craftsy crowd take your zithers and nose flutes down the beach and play a few lute songs for the baboons while we quasar types think about the Second Law of Thermodynamics."

"Tell us all about the Principle of Uncertainty," Eastwick proposed, "the physicists and your own."

"Drop dead."

"I still don't know what Murph is talking about," Lizzy confessed. "Is he talking about the counterculture or isn't he?"

"What's your definition of artsy-craftsy?" a voice asked.

"Someone who thinks he invented the wheel and the Navajo rug," Penny announced.

"I was asking Murph."

"An amateur," Murphy said. "If you can work in a welding shop or a plasma physics laboratory and not feel put down, you're not artsy-craftsy. If you can't, you're a literate amateur. The Peace Corps is fulla literate amateurs."

"That's an oversimplification," Eastwick disagreed.

"Yeah, what's your technological ticket?" asked Murphy, who was a physics major.

"He's got a water bed," Penny answered.

"I don't think I need one," Eastwick said, "any more than I think a law degree bars me from the other culture."

"You gotta be kidding," Lizzy joined in. "How would you ever make out without your water bed?"

"That's the problem," Murphy summed up. "You lawyers never think you need one—that a good brief will tie all the loose ends together. That's the way the bureaucrats think, too, and that's the gap I'm talking about. They don't live in the real world at all. Ask McDermott. He knows what I'm talking about."

"Yeah, which culture do you belong to?" Lizzy asked. "You're a dropout, aren't you? Didn't you leave the Air Force and all that stuff?"

The satellite was gone. McDermott looked back toward the campfire. "I suppose so," he said.

"I thought we were talking about the two cultures!" Penny reminded them.

"What'd you do in the Air Force?" asked a girl from the shadows.

"He *flew* a plane!" Penny shouted defensively. "For Christ's sake, what do you think he did." She sat up angrily. "Why don't you guys take your twenty-question hootenanny down the beach. We came here to get a little peace and quiet—not to hear all this garbage."

"So what's wrong with flying a plane?" the girl asked coolly from the other side of the fire.

"Why don't we just knock it off," Murphy proposed. Penny got up and went to the cooler, rattled around noisily in the ice, searching for a cold can so she wouldn't hear what they were saying, and then opened the can as she walked down to the edge of the lake, head back, looking at the stars. She stood in the darkness, beyond the reach of their voices. *Call it a unit of work,* he had said. *A unit of work?* She still didn't understand. She doubted that she ever would, now or ever. Did he still think she was a child or something? She walked up the beach, moving farther into the darkness before she stopped again, looking up at the stars. She heard footsteps behind her and thought they might be McDermott's, but they weren't. It was Eastwick.

"We didn't mean to drive you away," he said. "If you want us to go, we will. No harm done." He was alone.

"That's not it." She was too depressed to argue.

He stood looking up at the stars. "It's incredible, isn't it. Jesus—"

"Yeah." She supposed he was talking about how close they seemed in the African sky.

"How come you're always pissed off?" he asked. "If I've done anything to piss you off, I'm sorry. But it wasn't deliberate. Maybe we ought to talk about it."

"You can stop calling me up."

He smiled in surprise. "What's wrong with that? Don't shut yourself away. You're not married to him, so what's the big deal? He's gone most of the time anyway."

"It's no big deal. I just don't want any problems."

"Relax then. I'm not trying to beat him out. So why don't you relax and enjoy it. He isn't defensive about what he is. Why should you be?"

"How do you know what he is?" Penny asked coolly.

"He's just a pilot—a jock. So he flew in Vietnam. So what? A blue-collar pilot in a blue-collar war, flying his tin lunch pail to work every day. So what? So now he's flying for Cohen, running guns. It's the same thing. No one cares. Don't be so defensive about it." He laughed and turned and walked back up the beach toward the campfire.

TEN

1

"Y"ou know about the plane?" Colonel Mohamed El-Hassan Hamid inquired that sunny morning at the Sudanese consulate in Gambela, brows knitted, his dark eyes resting on Emily Farr's cool, slim face. "You've heard it?" The colonel was tall and dark-skinned, with jet-black hair as fine as silk, a dark moustache, and the erect carriage of a cavalry officer.

"What plane?" They sat together in Colonel Hamid's office, a wooden table between them, drinking tea. A few flies stirred listlessly in the cage of light over the table, searching for the sugar bowl, and the colonel chased them away with his hand.

"The plane that comes at night along the Baro."

"I hear so much gossip that it's sometimes hard to remember." She was dressed for town, wearing a white cotton blouse, a plain tan skirt, and her hiking shoes.

"Not just gossip, for sure," Colonel Hamid protested, his voice lifting toward its parade ground register, of which he was especially proud, as he was proud of everything else about himself—his voice, figure, his face. Colonel Hamid sat a chair as he did a horse, his shoulders always lifted to full height, as if to give him full command of the tactical terrain. "A plane is flying rifles and mortars into Upper Nile Province, for sure." He stood and offered her a cigarette from the carved wooden box on the table and she declined, as he knew she would. But the gesture gave him the opportunity to study her eyes. He believed that she had never lied to him, but she was a white woman and a Christian, while he was a Moslem and a Sudanese, as well as a man powerful in his own personality, and he believed that while women's words might attempt to deny the magnetism of his presence, their eyes were as helpless before it as the flutterings of a compass needle. Colonel Hamid disliked most of the American and British missionaries in the vicinity, not because they were Christian or white-skinned, but because most had served previously in the Sudan, had been expelled by the Khartoum government, and had resettled along the Ethiopian frontier, bitterly anti-Sudanese and anti-Moslem, as bigoted in their own rustic, provincial way as the Egyptian *fellaheen* whose insults he had suffered as a young Sudanese military officer studying in Egypt. But he trusted Emily Farr, who had never lived in the Sudan, was independent, fair-minded, and, he often thought, not unflattered by the attention of a personality as seductive as his own. He was also an intelligence officer, seconded from Sudanese military intelligence to the diplomatic and consular corps, and knew that she had repeatedly denied rations to the Anya-nya rebels seeking safe haven in Ethiopia.

But the light was in Emily's eyes, and as she lifted her hand against it, Colonel Hamid quickly lowered the Venetian blind at the window opposite—returning too late, her face again in shadow, telling him nothing. "Where do the guns come from?" she asked.

"They are Zionist guns," he sighed. He offered a chocolate from a box of English nougats, but she declined. He took one himself, chewed it reflectively, discovered a disagreeable flavor, and extracted it quickly from his molars. "Zionist guns, yes," he complained, studying the chewed nougat distastefully as he deposited it in the ashtray.

"You're certain of that?"

Colonel Hamid was certain of nothing. "It is true," he said sadly.

"When do the guns come?"

"At night. Very late at night, along the Baro."

"And so if you know that, you must also know where they come from, don't you?"

"From Ethiopia."

"Then there's nothing more to know, is there? When is your wife returning to Gambela?"

The colonel's frown died away, his confidence unseated, his

mount gone, afoot now, ambushed by these tea-time pleasantries. He shrugged, hoping to win her sympathy instead. "Politics," he muttered enigmatically, the way an army officer would. "Diplomacy." He sighed and offered her another chocolate. "For sure, some of your villagers have heard the plane at night—very late at night."

"Then I shall certainly ask them."

But Colonel Hamid wasn't interested in what the Nuer villagers said or reported. All that mattered to him was what she had heard or seen. The villagers were simple, illiterate, rumor-plagued blacks, no more dependable than the other spies and informers scattered throughout the surrounding countryside who took the colonel's money and then told him what he wanted to hear. They were undependable; she wasn't. Moreover, he'd never paid her a shilling. Khartoum would credit a rumor which she might corroborate when it would believe no other.

The difficulties which Colonel Hamid faced were not so much with the Anya-nya, with Zionist guns, or his own network of informers, as with his own ambassador in Addis Ababa. Colonel Hamid had reported that an unmarked plane was flying by night along the Baro and into Sudan. Some of his informers had reported seeing such a plane. But the Sudanese ambassador in Addis Ababa had dispatched his own telegrams to Khartoum, most especially a recent one that forwarded the solemn pledge of the Ethiopian prime minister that no flights were taking place. In giving these assurances, the prime minister had admitted that a few flights had occurred in the past, but had sworn that such activities had now been suspended on the orders of the Emperor himself. The Sudanese ambassador in Addis refused to believe Colonel Hamid's reports from Gambela. As an ambassador and diplomat the Sudanese envoy to Ethiopia was an experienced and worldly man. He knew that the world was full of deceit and hypocrisy, that his own staff would sometimes lie to him, as he would sometimes lie to his capital, the press, or the public, as diplomats frequently lie to one another; but as an ambassador he would never admit that the government to which he was accredited, with all of the pomp and dignity therein bestowed, would ever lie to him.

So in this atmosphere of sanctimony and priestly trust, Colonel Hamid had been unable to persuade Khartoum that a plane was flying guns into Sudan from Ethiopia. Khartoum acknowledged that a plane was regularly entering Sudanese airspace by night and unloading guns and ammunition at unmarked airfields, but was convinced that such flights originated in Uganda to the south.

"If you have a minute, I would like to show you some pictures," Colonel Hamid said desperately as Emily rose to leave. "Pictures from Upper Nile. They would interest you, for sure." He removed a large manila envelope from his desk drawer, withdrew a dozen glossy photographs, and took them to her. "These are the guns the plane carries into Upper Nile," he explained as she leafed through the photographs, which showed captured stacks of rifles, muskets, small mortars, and pistols lying along a dusty Sudanese road.

"From the plane you mentioned?"

"For sure," the colonel assured her. "One hundred percent." The last two photographs showed no guns, but a dozen corpses instead, face up in the African sun, their limbs flung out akimbo, their flyblown faces frozen in death. All were barefooted. Some were mere boys who carried no guns, only spears and bows and arrows.

"I'm sorry. I didn't want that you should see such pictures," the colonel said sorrowfully, but without making an effort to take them back. "It is a pity. Without weapons there would be no war." He studied her face secretly. She was looking curiously at the trees along the road and skyline. They were not the trees of Upper Nile or the Baro River regions, but were those instead from a landscape much farther to the south.

"They must have been taken near the Uganda border," she said quietly. "The trees are quite different. Did you notice? I'm sure it's not Upper Nile."

"Excuse me." He peered over her shoulder. "I did not notice the trees," he muttered disingenuously. "I was thinking only of those dead cattle boys lying in the road." The photographs were over a year old and had been taken by a Sudanese Ministry of Information photographer below Juba. They had been circulated in Khartoum as well as in Arab newspapers in the Middle East since that time.

"Yes, I'm sure it's far to the south," she said, returning the photographs. "But you're quite right. It's the principle that matters."

The audience was ended.

Twice ambushed, twice thrown, Colonel Hamid stood at his office window, watching Emily Farr leave the front gate and turn toward the village.

Gambela was a sleepy town lying along the river, with unpaved streets, no electricity, and few guest accommodations. To Emily it was similar in many ways to those small river towns along the Ohio or Mississippi rivers in the early nineteenth century. The road was white with dust in the late-morning sunshine; a few Anuak women passed her, carrying faggots and water jars on their heads. A few goats with salt sacks over their udders cropped at the wild grasses growing along the verges of the road. She entered the broken picket fence in front of the Ethiopian provincial government offices and went back the dirt path to the porch, where a few Ethiopian policemen in gray uniforms lounged dissolutely under the trees, listening to a young Amhara girl gossiping in a low, liquid voice. Flies stirred through the open door and into the shadows where an Ethiopian clerk sat at a bare wooden table amid the decrepitude of civil administration—broken chairs, rugless floors, shadeless windows, and files gathering dust in cardboard boxes. The office had been without electricity for a week because of a broken generator.

The clerk told Emily that Ato Tefari, the provincial administrator, was too busy to see her, and resumed his conversation with the two young Ethiopian teachers who sat on the nearby bench, rolling a soccer ball between them. Emily had stopped by the office earlier, but Ato Tefari hadn't arrived and she'd continued on to Colonel Hamid's office. Ato Tefari had passed along the road in his Fiat as she'd turned into the Sudanese consulate, and had recognized her. He was new to his position and still sensitive about matters of protocol. Arriving at his own office, he had told the clerk that he wouldn't see her that day.

"Perhaps I can call later," Emily proposed, dabbing at her cheeks with her handkerchief.

"Not today," the clerk muttered. The two young Ethiopian teachers were newly arrived from Addis, like Ato Tefari. They had heard of

American missionaries who lived and worked with the blacks of this godforsaken corner of the empire, but had never seen one in the flesh. The clerk saw their smiles, and smiled himself.

"Perhaps tomorrow," Emily said. The clerk tore a corner from the Addis newspaper he'd been reading. "Ten o'clock, if it would be agreeable."

The clerk wrote *ten o'clock* in block letters on the paper. Behind him the door to Ato Tefari's office squeaked closed. Ato Tefari had closed it himself. He wanted to hear no more. Like most of the other government officials, he was an Amhara, but his face was a muddy brown color, his eyes flecked with yellow, and his expression held the coarse, sleepy insolence of a half-caste, awaiting some racial slur. In Addis the Amhara bar girls and secretaries believed he was half Negro, like the Shankalla or blacks he now administered. But he was suspicious of Emily Farr because he didn't know her, because her call on Colonel Hamid prior to calling on him offended his vanity, and because she was a white woman. In addition she worked closely with the Nilotics, whom he despised, not because he knew anything about them, but because his father had been an Ethiopian civil servant, serving for many years in the more remote reaches of the empire, whose third son, Ato Tefari, was said to have sprung from the same pagan womb as the half-clothed black women of Gambela.

"I asked the mission driver to pick me up here," Emily said, looking from the doorway back to the clerk. "If he comes, would you tell him I've gone on to the UN offices?"

He looked at her without answering. The Ethiopian policemen moved aside indolently to let her pass down the steps. A blind old Nuer woman led by a small child had entered the picket gate and came back along the path, begging for coins. The policemen on the porch and the Ethiopian youths inside watched as Emily stopped, opened her purse, and gave the woman and child a few coins, speaking to both in Nuer. The officers smiled to themselves and spoke to each other in Amharic, laughing, and watched together in amusement as Emily turned down the road toward the UN offices, her umbrella raised against the sweltering noonday sun.

2

Emily remained overnight in Gambela as a guest of the Shepherds, a UN couple who lived in an old cottage on the road along the Baro River with geckos on the walls, mango trees shading the roof, and the bright sheen of the river reflected from the old ceiling. Thomas Shepherd was an Englishman, responsible for the Gambela refugee programs funded by the UN—a solitary little man who looked less like a UN technician than a carpenter or cobbler; his hands were rough and gnarled, his arms too short for his body, his head too large as well. His wife was a clergyman's daughter from the north of England, a plump woman with nervous brown eyes, coal-black hair which she tinted artificially, and a moist chin and upper lip which she dabbed at perpetually with the small scented handkerchief she kept in her hand. She also had a fondness for painting—for tepid watercolors and washed-out pastels, the impoverished, anemic renderings of an impoverished, anemic disposition.

The Shepherds had persuaded Emily to stay because they were giving a small buffet for Stone-Ashton, the deputy UN commissioner from Addis who was visiting Gambela that day. Guests were in short supply. Colonel Hamid and Ato Tefari had both sent their regrets, and several of the UN technicians from the Gambela office were on annual leave. Accompanying Stone-Ashton on his trip was an elderly English-woman from the UN offices in Geneva.

The evening began a little before sundown with drinks on the front verandah facing the river. "I'm sorry Colonel Hamid won't be coming," Stone-Ashton said. "Rather a Commonwealth group, now, isn't it?" he quipped. "But a bit incestuous, too, don't you think," he muttered to Emily with a disappointed smile. He was a plump, raffish Englishman in his mid-fifties with damp chestnut hair, which he kept slightly oiled. With his pink cheeks, he always looked as if he'd just emerged from the shower. He was dressed for the bush on this occasion, an informality that suggested something midway between a Northumberland snipe shoot and a North Atlantic crossing on the *Queen Elizabeth*. He wore a tan shirt and ascot, brown whipcord trousers with slash pockets, and brown suede shoes. He had come in the door carrying a bush jacket over his arm. Stone-Ashton had the diplomatic look about him—a quality he'd carefully cultivated—but he'd failed for the British diplomatic service after the war and had transferred his ambitions to the UN instead. With an Oxford degree and no technical abilities to speak of, save his French, which he'd mastered with the same mechanical application as others master calculus or physics, his strongest professional suit was tact and good manners.

The UN technicians thought him effete, more a ceremonial than a substantive officer; he treated them with the same mixture of bonhomie and condescension with which a squire might treat the keeper of the hounds. Because he took so little notice of the skills that shaped their character, he had to be constantly reminded of the details of their individual lives—the fact that the Shepherds had no children and that Simon was therefore their Yorkshire terrier, that the Canadian agronome was a soybean expert, not a cowboy, and the New Zealander an accountant, not a sheep farmer.

Emily studied the bottles on the bamboo bar at the end of the room, trying to decide what she might drink, already regretting her decision to remain overnight. Shepherd, after offering her a choice, had gone off to show Miss Gresham, the visitor from Geneva, the majesty of the river at sundown. Remembering that Emily was a missionary, not that familiar with spirits, the wife of the New Zealander came to help out, identifying aloud the whiskies, ryes, brandies, and cordials.

"Oh, this is very nice," Mrs. Frazier murmured, fondling a dusty bottle of apricot brandy. "But I believe I know this," she discovered suddenly, returning it for another. "This one too." She brought her spectacles from her handbag and was soon able to describe the pedigree of four more. The apricot brandy, crème de menthe, and port had belonged to an Indian doctor with the UN; the Dubonnet and vermouth were once in the cabinet of Dr. Fouquet, the French entomologist. The throats of the bottles were dusty, their labels watermarked, sun-faded, or illegible, like the bottled sauces in a Torquay boardinghouse. They were the vintage of an earlier UN generation, passed on with transfer, medical evacuation, or retirement, sold to the newly arrived like the handmade furniture, the cracked dishes, and tin cutlery on this remote edge of the wilderness. Eccentricity, emptiness, or inebriation characterized the idle hours of the UN clerisy that waited here in transit along the Baro, most of them living like impoverished clergy on their local currency earnings while they repatriated their dollar earnings to London banks, or Spanish and Portuguese real estate.

Miss Gresham sat in a cane-bottomed chair, dabbing at her sunburned face as she sipped her second gin and tonic, the river a broad shimmering plain in the twilight. Nuer and Anuak women passed along the road, carrying baskets of mangoes and smoked fish on their heads. "How stately they are," Miss Gresham exclaimed admiringly. Shepherd agreed with a silent nod, cracking an almond between his teeth. Following Miss Gresham's gaze, her handkerchief at her forehead, too, Mrs. Shepherd told her guest that the river was indeed lovely, but one had to beware. She told the story of the German groundwater specialist who'd attempted to swim the Baro just fifty yards downstream from where they sat and had been eaten by a crocodile. "Mercy!" Miss Gresham exclaimed.

The buffet table was lit by candles, despite the warmness of the night; the gin and tonics and whiskies supplemented by wine.

"Difficult days ahead," Stone-Ashton sighed as he sank down on the sofa next to Emily, balancing his plate on his knee.

"Difficult days?"

"The southern Sudan," Stone-Ashton admitted. He traded in political gossip as other men traded in foreign exchange, commodities, or postage stamps. "Have you heard about the latest Russian enterprise?" He lowered his voice so that he wouldn't be overheard.

"I heard a few radio reports."

"Flying helicopters against the Anya-nya rebels. Dreadful business."

"Did you hear it on the BBC?"

"Can't reveal my sources." He dropped his voice even further. "It just wouldn't do, you understand." Stone-Ashton had heard the report that afternoon from an Egyptian parasitologist at the UN clinic. Shepherd had been present as well, but it would no more do for an international diplomat of Stone-Ashton's pretensions to let it be known that his sources were idle clinicians and bored bureaucrats than it would for a Wall Street banker to have it found out that he regularly visited a Gypsy palmist.

Across the room Mrs. Frazier was describing the disappearance of a young Belgian bush pilot some six years earlier. When finally found only a few weeks after his crash, the pilot was still inside the plane—heels up, still in harness, but only a medical-school skeleton after the ants and termites had finished their work.

"Mercy!" Miss Gresham declared.

After dinner Mrs. Shepherd was persuaded to bring out her pastels and charcoal portraits. Most were pictures of the local Nuer and An-uak women, painted not from life, but from the postcards she bought at the Greek emporium. Included also were pictures of donkeys, a ver-vet monkey, and a zebra with a rhinoceros horn on its snout. Mrs. Shepherd explained that she had begun sketching a rhinoceros, but it acquired a shape of its own and emerged as a zebra. She'd left the horn in place, deciding that it would be a unicorn.

"How clever of you," Miss Gresham exclaimed.

"Doesn't the unicorn's horn grow from its forehead?" Stone-Ash-ton muttered sleepily to Emily.

"You're quite right, I believe," Mrs. Shepherd agreed, overhearing the remark.

"Oh, yes, but a magical unicorn," Stone-Ashton corrected grace-fully, sitting up and looking at his watch. "'Fed not on grain alone, but the possibility of being,'" he remembered, quoting Rilke.

"Quite possibly," Emily agreed, but no one else had turned; no one else was listening; they were all awaiting the next portrait in Mrs. Shepherd's portfolio.

On the path back to the guest cottage an hour later, Emily stopped under the trees to look up at the stars. She didn't move for a moment, her head lifted. In the silence she found herself listening for the plane along the Baro.

ELEVEN

"Hajii Mazoot?" McDermott asked, turning from the small black child to look at Emily, who was standing behind him as he dug for worms at the back of the garden.

"Samuel Eko," Emily said. "They also call him Hajii Mazoot. He's brought the dugout up the river." The child ran off down the path toward the Baro, and McDermott stood up.

"Why do they call him that?"

"Ask him."

"He hasn't taken the hajj, has he—to Mecca?" She laughed and shook her head. It was two o'clock in the afternoon. Too hot to fish, McDermott had said, but she said Samuel Eko knew where to go. He picked up the baitbox, the two rods, and the landing net. "You're sure you're not coming?"

"Next time," she said. "I have some work to do in the garden."

The dugout didn't drift far downstream and she heard their voices as they fished—Samuel Eko's and McDermott's. Then she heard only Samuel Eko's voice, speaking slowly, interrupted sometimes by laughter; and as she heard McDermott's laugh, too, she knew that Samuel Eko had told him about Hajii Mazoot.

The name had been given him by a Greek mechanic in Khartoum. He was a young boy at the time, a homeless street orphan who owned a donkey cart, hauled charcoal, water, and stores for the Arab shops, and slept in a packing case near the Greek mechanic's shop at the edge of Buuri Abu Hashiish. During the mornings and afternoons he would bring tea or coffee to the Greek mechanic and his Sudanese helpers from the surrounding coffee shops for a few shillings. If he wasn't busy, he would stand in the shop and watch the men work. His ambition was to own a taxi one day; and the Greek mechanic repaired many taxis.

Late one afternoon near the end of Ramadan, the Moslem fasting season, he entered the old garage to find the mechanic lying under a battered truck, only his feet visible from beneath the rear axle. The two Sudanese helpers had left for the day and Samuel Eko squatted down to see what the old man was doing. The mechanic called out to him in Arabic and Samuel Eko thought he was asking him to fetch him a pail of crankcase oil. *Mazoot?* he wondered to himself. *Oil or gasoline? But it must be oil.* It was growing dark and, as he entered the small shed behind the garage, he could barely distinguish one tin from another. He looked into two small drums, but the smell of gasoline was overpowering, even after he had replaced the lids. With the reeking gasoline still in his nostrils, he had difficulty identifying the contents of a third can. He knew that oil had the viscosity of molasses, so he lifted one tin after another, trying to determine which was the heavier. The mechanic called to him again, and in his impatience he struck a match and peered into the heavier can. The flame leaped first across his eyes, and as he recoiled, the explosion blew him backward through the open door and ten feet across the courtyard among the rotting banana trees.

When he opened his eyes again, he saw hovering over him the pale faces of two Egyptian nurses from the Red Crescent clinic, their hair hidden in white caps and snoods, their crisp, starched uniforms framed against the snow-white walls. Lying in the white hospital room under the white sheets, Samuel Eko saw his own thin black arms resting against the sheets, and thought he was dead. He thought he was in paradise.

When he left the hospital and told the old Greek mechanic and his two helpers his first thoughts as he'd awakened in the bed, they laughed. They laughed most of all at the presumption of the young black pagan from Upper Nile who believed that his soul had finally escaped the world of his ancestors in a celestial hajj. His hajj, they told him, had been as brief as his flight out of the gasoline shed and back through the banana trees, as brief as his few days in the Red Crescent clinic before his return to the muddy alleyways and the squalor of Buuri Abu Hashiish. Did he believe he could so easily escape his fate as that? In the hovels of Buuri Abu Hashiish they called him Hajii Mazoot.

Samuel Eko and McDermott caught two Nile perch, the largest one weighing thirty-five pounds. After they'd eviscerated the fish, Samuel Eko insisted that McDermott take both with him, but McDermott was reluctant. Finally he packed a few fillets in his ice chest. Samuel Eko drove off with the remainder in the Land-Rover.

"You'll have to fish in the late afternoon," Emily said after McDermott packed the chest in the plane.

"Yeah, but there's always someplace I have to go," McDermott said. "That's the hell of it."

"I suppose so." They stood in silence for a minute.

"Maybe next week then," he said finally.

"Next week." She nodded, as if it were a promise.

A minute later they heard the sound of the Land-Rover coming back up the track from the village. Samuel Eko had brought his wife with him to see the plane, and McDermott shook her hand through the open window. She was in her eighth month of pregnancy and didn't leave the vehicle.

That night, after his wife had fallen asleep, Samuel Eko crossed the moonlit airfield and slumped down in the grass beyond the thorn trees near the burrow. The lights had gone out in the cottage. He pulled the moldy flour sacking from the crypt, uncorked the wooden plug, and sat drinking.

After a while he said, "He will take her away, old grandmother. He will take her away and it will be all right. He won't leave her here for the dust of the savannah."

TWELVE

1

When McDermott flew in from Sudi Penny wasn't waiting for him at the hangar. He had with him in the ice chest the Nile perch he'd caught at the Baro station, fishing with Samuel Eko. He caught a ride in Cohen's carryall and the driver dropped him outside the front gate of his villa. His Land-Rover was parked in the drive and he could hear the stereo speakers in the living room. He carried his bag and ice chest around to the back of the house and in through the kitchen. In the kitchen he left the ice chest and carried his bag into the bedroom. When he opened the door to the bathroom, a young girl was standing there in her brassiere and blue jeans, leaning over the wash bowl as she washed her hair.

"Do you *mind?*" she asked. "Close the door, for Christ's sake."

"Who are you?"

"A friend. Who are you, anyway?"

"It's my house," he said. "That makes it my bathroom. Now beat it."

She straightened, pulled a towel over her shoulder, wrapped another around her head, and picked up her shampoo and comb. "Sor-ry," she said acidly. "Pardon me for living."

McDermott was standing at the wash bowl when Penny came in. "You look like you got some sun," she said. "How come you got here so fast?"

"Who was that girl in here?"

"I didn't know she was here until a minute ago. I told her to use the back bathroom. How come you didn't call me from the airport? I've been waiting."

"You wouldn't have heard me if I had. Not with all that racket going."

"Sure I would. I've been waiting."

"Who was that girl?"

"Some Peace Corps kid. She's with a group that just came in from the boonies. They didn't have anyplace to stay, so I said they could stay here—just for a couple of days. C'mon, don't be so crabby, okay. Jesus, what's that smell? My God, you've got it all over your shirt."

"Nile perch. I put it in the refrigerator."

"Not again," she groaned. "Do you know what it's like to cook all that fish? I mean it's okay to be the Great White Hunter and all that, but who does the scullery work? I do. Did you ever think about that? Who brought you home anyway?" she asked.

"Cohen's carryall."

"That schlemiel! God, that fish stinks as much as he does. You should have called me." McDermott had enjoyed the fishing on the Baro the previous evening, but its memory wasn't enough to ease the dislocations of Penny's world. He wished he was back on the grasslands again. She stood watching his face in the mirror. "Don't get mad at me. It's not my fault if those fish are so gross."

"I want to take a shower." He took off his shirt.

"So do I." She smiled and pulled off her T-shirt, slipped her arms around his waist, and stood against him, bare-breasted, her head against his shoulder. "It's okay if they stay a few days, isn't it?" she asked after a minute. "They can use the other two bedrooms, can't they?" She didn't lift her head. "I mean you don't know how crummy it gets around here sometimes, being all alone in this house."

"Sure."

She rested against him. "It'll only be for a little while. They're going to Greece next week." She slipped away from him and pulled her shirt back on. "Don't take all the hot water," she said as she went out.

There was no hot water. He showered and shaved anyway, changed his clothes, and went out through the living room to the patio. The stereo was still playing but the volume had been turned down. Penny sat on the rear terrace with the four Peace Corps volunteers, two young men and two girls, all Penny's age. All were sunburned, freshly scrubbed, hair damp, still barefooted as they drank beer and smoked, sprawling in the camp chairs and on the cushions Penny had brought out. The four had been working for six months with a smallpox vaccination team among the Galla and Somali nomads of the Ogaden region, sleeping in tents or out under the stars, often sharing the camel's milk and the goat meat of the nomadic herdsmen in their camps. Now they were on their way to Greece before they returned to the US, their Peace Corps service completed. All planned to go on to graduate school. In their weariness McDermott thought he saw satisfaction; in their lack of affectation, grace. He watched Penny's face while they answered her questions about nomadic life, and found the vacuum that told him how insulated had been her life in the capital these past several months. Darkness had come when a Land-Rover came through the gates and they were joined by Murphy, Lizzy, Eastwick, and a girl McDermott didn't know. From the way they were dressed, he knew that they were going to a party. "Some kind of weenie roast someone's giving for the smallpox guys," Penny explained after she'd changed clothes. "Don't you want to come too?"

McDermott said, "You go ahead. I'm a little tired."

"Did you just get back?" Eastwick asked.

"This afternoon."

"Don't you get sick of flying all the time?" Lizzy wondered. The volunteers from the smallpox team straggled back out onto the patio one by one as they changed their clothes too.

"It beats this turkey town," Penny sighed.

"Where'd you come in from today?" Eastwick asked.

"Gambela."

"That's where the action is, isn't it?" Eastwick continued. "The Sudan and Eritrea?"

"Don't be so nosy," Penny interjected.

"What action?" Lizzy wanted to know.

"The insurgencies," Eastwick said.

"Oh." She looked at McDermott. "I think it'd get awful monotonous," she sighed, her voice wearied by the very thought of it. "Just flying all day and nothing else."

Penny took McDermott's Land-Rover, her four guests with her, and followed Murphy's vehicle out of the drive. "If you change your mind, I'll be back in about half an hour. I'll run the guys over first," she told him as she drove away.

He thought she'd probably stay. He mixed a drink in the kitchen and went back out on the patio. In the darkness, without Penny, and with the camp chairs and cushions where they'd been abandoned, it didn't seem like his house at all.

He was still sitting there when the lights from the Land-Rover flashed against the rear wall and the tires crunched across the drive. A few moments later he saw Penny's silhouette on the porch above him. She was alone.

"Are you still sitting out here?" she asked as she came down the steps. "Nothing's wrong, is it? You're not sick or anything, are you?"

"Just sitting here. I thought you went to the party."

"It was full of noise. Everyone's trading stories about nomads, the boonies, camping out, and how crappy this city is. I couldn't stand it. Anyway, they can get a ride back with Murph, so I just cut out. Where's Venus?" She stood in the darkness, looking into the night sky.

She was deep into astronomy, Vedic ceremonials, black holes, quasars, and relativity, but she couldn't find Venus or Mars except when someone pointed them out to her. McDermott did, guiding her eyes over the tops of the eucalyptus trees.

"Oh, yeah, I see it. Aren't you cold? It's freezing out here." She turned and picked up his drink, holding out her hand: "Let's go inside. There's a fire going to waste."

She stood in front of the hearth, her hands behind her as she warmed herself in front of the burning eucalyptus. "Everyone's always going someplace. When are we going to leave this town?"

"I don't know."

"You promised." He lifted his eyes, and she hesitated: "You did . . . in a way."

"My contract's not up."

"How soon then?"

"I don't know."

She went to the stereo and put a record on—Mendelssohn's *Italian*

Symphony. "Doesn't that make you want to get up and go?" she asked as she came back to the fire.

"It might if I played a five-string banjo."

"Play it with your feet then. We've got to get out of this place. We really do. What's the trouble, anyway?"

"The trouble with what?"

"With you. Me, too, maybe, but you mostly. I've noticed it recently. What is it—have you got another girl friend back in the boonies? How come you're such a grouch?"

"I'm tired, that's all." He sat on the couch, looking at the fire.

"You've been gone four days, and you haven't even said anything to me. Then that jerk Cohen picks you up and I don't even get to talk to you." She came across the room and sank down on the couch beside him. "Other people are doing things and here we are, just sitting around. You couldn't be having any fun, so there's got to be more to your life or what you're doing than I know about. I know it's not just the flying that keeps you here. Not the money, not the flying. What then? Maybe another girl friend?"

"Maybe it's you," McDermott said.

"Yeah. Sure. You didn't even say anything to me when you came in this afternoon, just stomped through."

"I wanted to get the fish in the refrigerator."

She laughed. "Oh, sure. Sure." She put her head back against the couch. "That's so stupid it's got to be true. What is it you don't want to tell me? Afraid I'll be mad or something?"

"There's nothing to tell."

"Don't say that. There is. I can feel it. Going to bed isn't the answer anymore—not the whole answer, anyway. I mean, just climbing into the sack isn't all of it. It can't be."

"What do you want to do?"

"Go somewhere. Do something. Get us out of this blasted country."

"You ought to go back to school," he suggested. "That's one thing."

"Okay, let's do it, then. We can go to Hawaii and I'll study oceanography or Zen Buddhism. You could open a flying school or charter service."

"Why don't we just open the window there," McDermott said. "We could find a moonbeam and climb up to Mother Goose land. That way we wouldn't have to work, just sing nursery rhymes all day."

"Stop joking around. Be serious for a change."

"I am serious."

"You're not." She shifted on the couch and put her head in his lap, looking up at him. "C'mon, let's be serious for a while. You can't tell me you make more money here than you could make in the States."

"It's not just the money."

"What then?"

"The job. The flying. I've got a contract."

She lay looking up at him silently. "You know who this guy Cohen is, don't you?" she asked. "You know what he does?"

"What does he do?"

She watched his eyes. "He runs guns." McDermott looked down at her without answering. "Someone told me you were helping him run guns." She didn't move again, studying his face.

"Who told you that?"

"Some Peace Corps guy. Eastwick, as a matter of fact. He said you probably didn't even know what was behind it. Do you know Rimbaud? Did you ever hear of him?"

"No."

"He's French. Or was. A poet, a kind of fag, but that doesn't matter."

"Maybe that's why I don't know him."

She sighed. "Be serious. He's dead. He came to Africa about eighty years ago to run guns into Ethiopia from Djibouti. That was when the British didn't want Ethiopia to have guns. Anyway, he was working for the French, like Cohen. Expanding or maintaining their sphere of influence. The French have a kind of neo-colonial tradition of supporting the status quo in Africa."

"Who told you all of that?"

"Eastwick."

"He's full of information, isn't he? Have you been seeing a lot of him?"

"He sort of hangs around sometimes when you're not here. He's not a bad guy when he keeps his hands to himself. He's got some cushy job as legal adviser in the prime minister's office. Basically he's a Harvard Law type camping out in the Peace Corps so he won't get his little ass drafted. But he knows a lot about what's happening in this rotten country. He gets around too." She continued to study his eyes. "Cohen is running guns like Rimbaud used to do, in case you didn't know. Is that what you're doing—helping Cohen?"

"Where does Cohen take the guns?"

"That's the worst part. He takes them into the countryside. They've got hidden arsenals in the boonies, so that if a coup ever comes and the army turns against the Emperor, they'll have a peasant army already equipped to help him. The peasants here are the most conservative. The Emperor doesn't trust the army or the university students. Divide and conquer, that's the Emperor's motto."

"Is that what Eastwick told you?"

"He said you were running guns. What's so funny?"

"You are."

She was annoyed. "Just because you don't like Eastwick doesn't mean he might not be right. I think he's a jerk, too, sometimes, but he's got a feel for internal politics in this country, and they're pretty Byzantine, like Carolingian Europe. Serfs and lords." McDermott smiled again, and Penny sat up awkwardly. "Stop laughing."

"I don't even really know Eastwick. When did he tell you all this?"

"Not any one time. Over the past couple of weeks he's been filling me in. He sees all sorts of reports in the prime minister's office. Some of them he's not supposed to see." She sat on the edge of the couch, watching McDermott cross the room to turn off the phonograph. "You think he's wrong? Maybe there are two sides to every story, but that's how he sees it."

"There are always two sides," McDermott said, "but you don't have to stand on your head to find the other."

"You think Eastwick is standing on his head?" she asked irritably. "He was worried about you—thinking you might not know what was going on, and that Cohen might be taking advantage of you."

"Why would he think that?"

"I don't know," she said uneasily, "maybe because of Vietnam. How everybody got conned there. You think Eastwick is wrong?"

"Sure he's wrong."

"You mean it's not true?"

"No. But what difference would it make if it were?"

"Cohen's a fink for the local establishment! A shill for the status quo, making money hand-over-fist doing it, keeping this rotten regime in power."

"Is that what bothers you?"

"Sure it bothers me. Doesn't it you? People want change! It's crummy—the whole system!"

"Like Vietnam?" McDermott asked. "Does my working with Cohen bother you as much as Vietnam, as my flying there?"

"It might." Her eyes hadn't left his face. "Anyway, you told me you got court-martialed, so it was okay."

"Okay with who?" McDermott asked. "The Peace Corps crowd? What's okay with them is okay with you, is that it? Whatever they approve of—whatever you don't have to be too embarrassed about or too apologetic for? When are you going to learn to stand on your own two feet. What did you tell them, that I was court-martialed?"

"Sure. It's the truth, isn't it?" she said uneasily, her face flushed.

"Why is it any of their business? What the hell is it to them?"

"I wanted to tell them so they'd understand. I got tired of making excuses."

"Excuses for what? Why did you have to make excuses?"

"God, because they're my friends!" she cried. "The only people I see!"

"What kind of friends are they if you have to keep apologizing to them?"

"Is this an interrogation or something?" she shouted. "Did I do something wrong! Tell me if I did!" In that moment she saw the ugly, vicious triviality of the whole affair and was sickened by it. "You got court-martialed, didn't you! Didn't you? Didn't you refuse to fly and they kicked you out?"

"No."

She looked at him in disbelief. "You were court-martialed!"

"I did things I wasn't supposed to do."

"Like what?"

"Bombing targets that were off limits, that were sanctuaries, not to be bombed. They court-martialed me for that."

She suddenly felt sick. "I don't believe you," she muttered, far too committed to turn back. "I don't believe you. You just don't want to admit I'm right." She picked up her sweater woodenly. "What about Cohen? Is that a lie too?" She couldn't look at him.

"Your friends can believe what they want to believe. I don't think it makes much difference."

"You mean you just don't give a damn."

"Not about what they think. I never did."

"Thanks a lot. Neither do I."

McDermott carried his glass into the kitchen, and when he returned, Penny was gone. A moment later he heard the Land-Rover start up, and the sound of the gate being opened. She hadn't returned when McDermott awoke the following morning, the bed empty beside him. His Land-Rover was parked in the drive outside and one of the Peace Corps volunteers from the smallpox team told him that he'd driven it back himself, that Penny had had too much to drink and had gone to Lizzy's flat to sleep it off. At eleven McDermott carried his bag out to the Land-Rover and was just leaving as he met Murphy and Lizzy in Murphy's Jeepster. They'd come to see if Penny had gotten home all right. They'd left the party at three and she was still there, still dancing.

"I guess she was a little smashed," Murphy said apologetically. His eyes were red and he smelled of stale beer.

McDermott told them that Penny wasn't there and drove off to the airport.

2

"There is a pristine beauty to this land," Reverend Osgood told the group of UN officials as they stood at the edge of the grasslands beyond the airstrip, his hand sweeping the landscape north to south. He cited Isaiah 18:1–2: "'Woe to the land shadowed with wings, which is beyond the rivers of Ethiopia,'" referring to the Sudan, yet immediately returned to his own unmistakable cadences: "But we know, too, that there is a virgin goodness to its people here along the frontier, and they are in our care. Mine, yours, Emily's there—even our good pilot, Mr. McDermott, who has flown through foul weather and fair to provision these poor souls with the victuals from the United Nations larder. But most of all, in *His* care. So there is a pristine purity to this terrain you see stretching away in grassy verdure as far as the feet can trod, or the inquiring eye can reach. Pray God that it is so."

Osgood's voice rose and fell. As the senior Presbyterian official at the Moquo mission headquarters, he had accompanied a UN refugee team to Baro station to survey the results of the UN refugee effort. Osgood was a spider-legged man of medium size, with a thatch of white hair, bushy black eyebrows, and restless gray eyes that had a perpetual shine to them. The impression they conveyed was not one of spiritual calm, but of a rapacious curiosity. He was ordinary and even rustic in appearance, as plain as an Ohio feed merchant, but the small-town theater and the Chautauqua circuit were in his voice. He was full of sumptuous phrases and archaic expressions. His testimonials were often punctuated by dramatic pauses and reflective silences.

Osgood's words made Emily Farr restive and uncomfortable as she watched the faces of the UN team to see their effect; but they were foreigners and strangers as well. She could read nothing in their polite attention. She glanced at McDermott, who had known within two minutes that Osgood was a fool, and she knew from his expression that he wasn't listening to him at all.

At one o'clock McDermott flew the UN group back to Gambela and immediately took off again with Reverend Osgood for the Moquo station. On the way he overflew a herd of fifty or so buffalo. Osgood unfastened the lens flap on his .35 mm camera and asked McDermott to overfly the herd again. McDermott flipped the plane into a steep bank and Osgood found himself looking straight down through the side vent at the puny shadow of the aircraft bouncing along through black thorn and galloping buffalo. *"Great God Almighty!"* Osgood cried out, clawing in panic at the ceiling panel for something to hold to, his feet braced against the instrument deck, his loose neck and gray lips set in rigor mortis. The camera bounced off the window and rattled to the rear, but Osgood couldn't unlock either hand from the death grip along the rail overhead to retrieve it. By the time he did, the buffalo had scattered.

From Moquo McDermott flew on to the Sudi strip, settling down through the trees a little after four o'clock in the afternoon. "It may rain," Rozewicz said as they walked back to the ready tent.

"I hope to Christ it comes soon then," McDermott replied, stopping to look to the west and then back up the mountain, realizing that he hadn't been thinking of the weather at all.

"We should stop hoping about the weather," Rozewiz declared. "We should stop being victims of the weather and take the bloody thing in our own hands. Have you talked to Cohen again about the plane?"

"The answer's the same."

He flew down the Pibor River that night, monitoring the Sudanese military radio from Nasir that was transmitting to a portable receiver somewhere in the bush below. A small group of Anya-nya guerrillas had attacked a riverboat near Nasir and Sudanese military units were searching for them. As he turned toward the marshes from the Pibor, a few scrub fires were burning along the horizon, but as he droned deeper into the Sudan, he found the plain below ablaze with ribbon after ribbon of fire, sending curtains of smoke and ash into the night sky. The wind had carried the flames over miles of prairie and scrub; as the wind had died, the pall of smoke had settled over miles of savannah not yet touched by the flames.

The Anya-nya airfield was somewhere below him. He circled the area three times but couldn't find it. On his final pass he identified a light and dropped lower but found only a few acacia trees blazing in the darkness. He was still carrying a full load. Sudi had reported heavy rains and violent winds lashing the airstrip. At the foot of the escarpment he called in a second time:

"Gopher check. Baseline is three five. How do you read with a full payload? I read negative. I read negative. Can you check it out? Over."

Rain suddenly splattered against the windshield and he lost visual contact with the hills ahead of him.

Rozewicz's voice came back on the air, broken with static: "Gopher, this is Baseline. Bloody awful here. Gale winds and no visibility. We read negative, too. Sorry. Over."

"Rog," McDermott called back. "I'll go second alternate, dump a few, and wait it out."

McDermott's alternate field was located at an abandoned inland mission station to the north which he'd used on two occasions to wait out bad weather. Gambela was a last-ditch option, but would mean compromising the operation, perhaps fatally: the plane would be confiscated, if only for the sake of appearance; the pilot would be arrested, ultimately declared persona non grata. But McDermott had always told himself that he had another option, if it came to that, and this night it seemed the simpler choice. He turned back, out of the storm clouds, moving again to the west under a pale moon barely touched by a few wisps of gray cloud. He found the Baro below him and flew out over the grasslands, turned, and came back in toward the Baro station.

She was frightened at first, believing the plane might be a Sudanese military aircraft, swooping in over the fields totally without warning. She knew it intended to land.

"Fetch Samuel Eko!" she told old William, "quickly now," sending his awkward, resisting body out through the gate. She was convinced she would be dealing with Sudanese soldiers who spoke only Arabic, come to search for the foraging Anya-nya marauders that had ambushed the river steamer near the border, killing six civilians. What if they have guns? she asked herself suddenly after William had run off, following the plane's shadow as it descended toward the strip. Then she saw the plane's silhouette more clearly and realized it wasn't a transport at all. She pulled the sweater over her shoulders, still clutching the flashlight, and went out onto the road. Should she stay inside the fence or run to the village? If they were soldiers, as William had thought, wouldn't they spill out immediately in all directions, like beads out of a bottle, shooting their guns wildly in the darkness? She remained in the road, her heart pounding, following the plane's descent, and then recognizing it suddenly, totally bewildered by then. But it wasn't until the aircraft taxied to a stop and McDermott stepped out on the wing that she was certain.

"Is that you?" he called. "How come you're not in bed?"

Her knees went weak. "You've no idea," she muttered, leaning with relief against the wing. "I was terrified."

"Sorry."

"Are you alone? Is there anyone with you?"

"No—just me."

"What on earth happened?"

"It's raining in the hills," he said. "I've got a full load and couldn't get in. I've got to wait until the weather breaks. Maybe drop off a few boxes." Her face was calm in the moonlight, lifted toward him silently. "Otherwise I can't climb the hill."

"What kind of boxes?" she asked, her voice suddenly very tired.

"Rations, for one thing."

She stood leaning weakly against the wing, her eyes still lifted, her expression unchanged even after he had climbed down and was standing next to her. "Just rations?" she asked in sorrow, the knowledge painfully complete in her mind after all of this time, the mystery solved. She should have known and now was astonished that she hadn't, more disappointed with herself than with him. "It was you," she said sadly. "It was you all this time."

McDermott studied her face without replying. He didn't need to answer. It was already in her eyes. He thought she had known and now was as surprised as she that she hadn't. What the hell did she want him to say? You fly a plane and they think you're Charles Lindbergh. Then you put guns in the wings and dynamite in the cabin, and they think you're the Boston strangler.

"It was your plane that came at night," she deplored.

"It's still my plane."

She put her head against the wing and shut her eyes: "I can't imagine what I was thinking."

"Neither can I." Why hadn't she known?

"I suppose it was your intention to use this field all along?" Her head was still down.

McDermott laughed and she looked up in surprise. "If I had any intentions when I began this half-assed operation, I've forgotten what they were," he said.

"You're sorry then?"

"I'm always sorry about something. Tonight it may as well be this."

"That's not very encouraging." He climbed back into the cabin and she hesitated, then followed him. "I said that's not very encouraging," she repeated as she stood behind the pilot's seat. McDermott lifted the headset, turned on the radio, and called the Sudi strip. The rain had slackened and the tractor was working on the field. If McDermott could wait for a few hours, Rozewicz thought he might be able to bring the plane in. Emily stood watching him. The cabin behind her was stacked with wooden crates, and she could smell the oil and cold metal beneath the balsam of pine. In the seat next to him was a small, ugly machine gun. "It's a wonder you ever managed to get off the ground," she murmured, afraid to touch anything. "Who was that you were speaking to?"

"A gremlin that helps me with the weather reports."

"It's all very discouraging," she said as he helped her to the ground. Samuel Eko and old William were standing on the track nearby, waiting for them.

"Is he an Arab?" Samuel Eko asked with a smile. He had known all along. "William said the Arabs were coming."

"William and I made a mistake," she answered. "Mr. McDermott was driven off course by a storm and was forced to land here. He was carrying medical supplies to Gambela when the storm came up." It was such a transparent lie and she was so humiliated that she said no more.

"I'll be taking off in an hour or so. It'll be all right. I won't be needing anything."

"I feel like a hypocrite," Emily said after they'd left.

"I think they understood."

"That's certainly no comfort. They know I've misled them."

"Why didn't you let me do it?"

She faced him in the moonlight. "Why? Do you do it more easily? Are you accustomed to it?"

McDermott could see her dark eyes and hear the anger in her voice. He didn't want to argue with her.

"No, but maybe I've got less to lose."

"In what? In telling the truth?" When he didn't answer, she said, "I assume you would have told me in time."

He turned back toward the plane. "About what?"

"The plane. That it was your plane we'd been seeing all this time."

"I thought you might have known." She was still standing in the road. He stopped and looked back.

"You certainly know very little about people, don't you?"

"What's that got to do with it?"

"You would have known how I felt about giving guns to the Anya-nya. How it jeopardizes everything we're doing here at the Baro station." He turned back to the plane and she followed him. "What are you going to do now?"

"See if I can't get rid of a few crates." He pulled open the cabin door.

"You certainly can't leave those guns here."

"I've got some crates of medical supplies—rations too. If you can't use them, I can pick them up next time."

"I certainly have no intention of using them."

"Why not?" He looked back at her.

"It's a matter of principle."

"You mean you don't want to get involved. Don't tell me you're not involved. You're involved every time an Anya-nya soldier comes by with a gunshot wound."

"That's completely different."

"Sure it's different. Different for you and different for me, but it's the same war." Kneeling in the hold, he unstrapped the first tier of boxes and pushed open both cargo doors. She stood nearby, holding the flashlight.

"That has nothing to do with guns."

"Guns don't make war. People do." He lifted a crate to the door and eased it to the ground. Two more crates followed as she watched him silently. A minute later McDermott heard her laugh and stood up, looking over the stacked crates. "What's the trouble?"

"This is absolutely ridiculous. Do you know what time it is?"

"No. Maybe two o'clock. Why?"

"Two o'clock and there you are, trying to find rations, guns all around, and a field too wet to land on. It's ridiculous, all of it. Don't your friends realize that?"

"What friends?" He dragged another crate to the cargo door and dropped to the ground to lift it out. She moved aside and sat down on one of the wooden crates.

"The man on the radio. The people helping you do all this."

"There's no one helping me. That's the problem." He pulled the crate toward him from the hold, standing on the ground, but it was heavier than the others, and its weight carried him backward, reeling clumsily and barely able to control it as it smashed heavily to the ground. She recognized the sound of metal inside and immediately flashed her light against the lettering on the side. "Don't get excited, he said, breathing heavily. "I'll put it back. The rations are in the back." He unloaded two more crates that were equally heavy and rested afterward, mopping his face. She sat on the box nearby, legs crossed, still holding the flashlight.

"I still haven't seen any rations or medical supplies."

"Give me time. They're in there someplace. What time is it, anyway?" His poplin shirt was dark with perspiration.

"Ten minutes past two."

"Good God." He got to his feet and climbed back into the hold. After he'd manhandled two more crates toward the door and lifted them slowly to the ground, he heard her say:

"Obviously you didn't load the plane, did you?"

"What gave you that idea?" He was resting, hands on his knees, still breathing heavily.

"Watching you. If you imagine you're going to leave those crates of weapons lying about on the ground, you're quite mistaken."

"Maybe I won't have to. Maybe a few Anya-nya will come by and we can just pass them out, like Popsicles." He climbed back into the hold.

"It's much easier when you just have to do the flying, isn't it?" she called out a few minutes later. "When other people have to do the loading and unloading. Or the fighting."

McDermott's head reappeared in the door. "Yeah," he said. "You must have some military experience yourself, figuring that out. What branch of service were you in, the Dental Corps?" He nearly fell trying to control a box of ammo.

"I was just thinking. Of how easy it is to set plans in motion and then leave it to others to carry them out. With absolutely no comprehension of the pain or suffering those plans create."

"You can say that again." He crawled back into the plane on his hands and knees. A few minutes later he said, "Goddammit!" and when he reappeared, he was pushing another ammo crate.

"Are you sure that rations and medical supplies were loaded?" she asked skeptically, standing at the door and probing the hold with her flashlight. McDermott's back was braced against a crate and he was pushing it backward toward the door, feet against the deck.

"They're behind me," he said through his teeth. "Just a couple of more to go."

He found two boxes of rations and three crates of medical supplies, loaded them in the Land-Rover, and stored them in the cottage supply room behind the kitchen. He reloaded the weapons and ammo alone, thinking she'd gone to bed, and was stretched out on the grass, the cabin doors secured again, when she reappeared, carrying a Thermos of coffee and a package of sandwiches wrapped in wax paper. The birds were moving in the trees and the sky had begun to lighten faintly to the east.

"I thought this might help," she said. "It's been a long night. Would you like some now?"

He lay stretched out in the grass, his eyes closed, his arms motionless at his sides. She poured a cup of coffee and sat holding it until he moved finally and sat up. "Thanks," he said, taking the plastic cup.

"I wasn't deliberately trying to make it difficult for you," she said.

"I know you weren't," he answered after a minute. The light was stronger and he could see the bones of her face, the dark eyebrows, the details of the cottage behind her, through the trees. "Few things are deliberate in this business." He sat looking at the cottage, his shirt cold and clammy against his back. "Funny," he remembered finally. "I saw you one night, standing over there, near the gate. Right at the edge of the road."

She remembered too. "It seems like ages ago," she said, looking back herself.

"I guess it was."

"Someday you'll have to explain to me what this is all about," she observed as he pulled on his Windbreaker next to the plane. "What it's about and how you got involved."

"Someday I will." He nodded, taking back the Thermos and the package of sandwiches.

It was six o'clock in the morning when McDermott dropped unexpectedly out of the overcast skies and came thundering into the Sudi strip. The mist hovered over the trees and the rain had been gone for four hours, but the field was still glazed. He used every inch of runway coming in.

THIRTEEN

1

Penny had packed her backpack three times and three times she'd unpacked it again, sitting on the sunny floor of the bedroom with the door closed so that her four Peace Corps houseguests couldn't see her. She didn't know what she wanted to do. She was depressed, her body ached, and a cold wind blew through her, a nullity where no light showed, as gray as a San Francisco fog, a sea bottom from which there was no recovery at all and where her body drifted, hair, face, and limbs as colorless as sea kelp. She could hardly stir from bed in the morning. Everything she saw or thought nauseated her; both fear and loathing paralyzed her, and for the first time in eight months she'd thought again of suicide. *Maybe I am psycho*, she thought helplessly, looking again at the pair of faded denims she was putting back in her rucksack again, forgetting that she was unpacking. Her head still ached, her tongue was thick in her mouth, her body still poisoned by alcohol.

She remembered Eastwick's apartment—the water bed, the local rugs, the baroque records on the stereo, and the abstract expressionist prints on the wall—with the same nausea a mental patient might remember a padded cell. When she'd left the house the day after she'd returned, Eastwick had been waiting for her on the patio outside, his Toyota in the drive, ready to move her things to his apartment. He was tossing a Frisbee back and forth with Lizzy, wearing a crew shirt with a college letter over the pocket.

"For God's sake!" she'd shouted from the top of the steps. "How trite can you get, anyway. Do you still watch the boob tube in your

Mickey Mouse ears." Eastwick had looked up in surprise and she'd fled back into the house and locked the door. The next day he'd sent Lizzy to talk to her. Penny had seen her drive through the front gate in Murphy's Jeepster, and had jumped up from the mat, slid down the roof ladder, and vanished into her room, locking the door.

"C'mon, Pen. Open up. Please. I've got to talk to you."

"No!"

"C'mon, be nice. We're worried. All of us are—"

"*Get the fuck out of here, you goddamned little witch!*" she'd shrieked from the middle of the bed. "*Get out! Get out! Get out!*"

That had been two days ago. Now she sat on the warm floor, unpacking her backpack again. After she had finished, she pushed it forward into the closet, too tired to stand, lying stretched out on the floor, her blond head in the closet, her legs and hips outside. She lay there for a long time, staring at the wall, at the cobwebs in the corner, the grains of plaster, the small brown spider that was busy along the molding, the same seams of McDermott's leather suitcases. She pulled beneath her cheek the pile of folded blankets they'd taken with them to the Rift Valley lakes, shutting her eyes. For a moment the smell of the blankets and the cedar chips in which they'd been packed reminded her of the lodge at Lake Tahoe, but then she smelled the smoke from the campfire at the lake, still embedded in the fabric, and opened her eyes again. The sun was shining outside and she moved her head, looking out through the top of the window toward the patch of blue sky.

The kitchen door slammed suddenly, and she heard her Peace Corps guests assembling on the patio. Someone called to her through the bedroom door, but she shut her eyes and didn't answer. After a few minutes the voice went away, and she heard their feet on the gravel outside as they walked toward the front gate. The iron gate slammed, and she heard nothing:

"Please," she whispered, closing her eyes. "Please—"

For a moment she was back at the Awash station, standing in the hot sunlight, but her mind someplace else—at the bottom of the sea, darkness all around her.

She may have slept. When she opened her eyes again, her mouth was wet, and the blanket wet against her cheek. She lay with her head in the closet, listening. She heard nothing; the house was empty. Slowly she lifted herself to her feet and crept to the bedroom door, her ear against the crack. Still nothing. She washed her face and hands, changed her blouse, and sat on the bed, combing her hair. Barefooted, she crossed the living room, as light as a shadow, and stood in the kitchen, looking at the coffee cups and beer bottles left on the counter. The afternoon sun fell through the blowing leaves along the rear wall beyond the patio. She stood on the warm flagstones, head lifted, listening to the leaves rustling in the wind, the only sound there was.

That night as she lay in bed alone, her eyes open, she tried to see herself, lying in this bed on this dark night, tried to see the house within the compound, the road between the eucalyptus trees, the mountains in the distance, the hairline of railroad down through the wasteland and across the volcanic rock, the deep Prussian blue of the Indian Ocean, the strip of beach and the blue lagoon where they swam that day, and she had been happy.

2

The airfield was drowsy in the afternoon sun. McDermott left the plane in the shadows of the hangar, walked across the oiled concrete, and looked out into the sunlight, shading his eyes, looking for Cohen's carryall. He couldn't find it, but a moment later he saw his own Land-Rover at the corner of the building, Penny sitting behind the wheel.

"How long have you been here?" he asked through the window, throwing his bag in the backseat. "I came around the other way."

"Not long," she said, biting her lip and pulling down her sunglasses. She'd been there for two hours. "Maybe you'd better drive." She scooted across the seat, giving up the wheel because she didn't want him watching her. "You sure took your time coming back." It wasn't what she wanted to say, and as she said it, she knew it would never again be the same, not with the constriction in her throat, or the tightness at her eyelids, and quite suddenly she felt like weeping. It would have been simpler that way. "What happened?" she asked, fighting to control her voice.

"Bad weather," he said. "Rain and more rain."

She looked desperately at the sky, searching for thunderheads, but the sky was blue, with only a trace of cumulus to the west. At least the beginning was over, and she'd dreaded that. She had seen him again; they had spoken; and their eyes had met. If it wasn't as natural as she'd prayed it might be, it was over. She continued to study the sky through the windshield. "It doesn't look too bad now."

"It wasn't bad coming back."

"What was it—sleet, or hail too?"

"Just rain."

"Didn't you say you once got vertigo?" She turned to him, the reflex simple and spontaneous, the question brought from memory at a time when spontaneity seemed lost to her forever.

"Not on days like this."

The Peace Corps smallpox team had departed the same morning for a final excursion to the Rift Valley lakes. They'd left behind their suitcases and had borrowed McDermott's tent. Penny told him that they would be leaving for Greece in a few days—that the offer of the tent was a small enough price for McDermott's having a few days of privacy.

"I guess that means there's plenty of hot water," he concluded, sitting on the bed and pulling off his boots.

She studied the crust of clay on the sole and the flakes of dried mud on the floor beneath, still not knowing where they'd come from or what they meant. She went into the hall to get clean towels from the cupboard.

"I guess you're pretty tired too," she said as she returned, but the bathroom door was already shut and she heard the sound of the shower. She sat on the bed a long time, holding the towels and looking at the dried mud on the floor. When she became aware of the empty room around her, she stirred herself and got up. McDermott came out of the bathroom, toweling his hair.

Dusk had fallen and the light from the glass doors of the living room fell across the flagstones. "It's no big deal anymore," she said, her face in the shadows, "what you did or didn't do. It was stupid of me, running out the way I did. I hate myself for it. I always will. I get so mixed up sometimes. I do. A lot of people don't, but I do. Anyway, I found a trophy in the closet—in your suitcase—and the whole thing sort of added up. I didn't mean to snoop—"

"What trophy?"

"The one in the suitcase. Made from a shell, or something . . . with your name on it."

"I'd forgotten about that. It was a joke, I suppose."

"For being court-martialed?" He didn't answer, and she sat back again. "Anyway, it's pretty obvious I'll never understand, but that's okay. It's no big deal anymore either."

McDermott said, "Understand what? Why I was court-martialed? It's a long story. It doesn't interest anyone anymore."

"It does me. It always will."

He thought about that first day on the beach at Djibouti, when everything had seemed simpler. Questions could be postponed until they didn't matter or had been forgotten. "It was a stupid, filthy war," he said without anger. "Anyone who doesn't know that doesn't understand the problem. I broke the rules."

"So what rules did you break?" She waited patiently, looking at his silhouette in the shadows.

After a few minutes McDermott said, "I bombed a North Vietnamese airfield near the Red River. It was off limits. I bombed it anyway—Phuc Yen."

"But they do it all the time, don't they?" she asked. "I mean bomb airfields, towns—even Hanoi?"

"Not in '66 and '67. Everything was off limits: Hanoi, the SAM sites the Russians were manning, the airfields the MIGs were flying from, the fuel dumps, the ships at Haiphong."

"Why'd you do it, then?"

"MIG-21's were flying out of it, hitting us as we came in for our bombing runs. There were MIGs on the runway the day I hit it."

"And that's all—that's all you did?"

"That's all."

"Tell me. Tell me what happened."

He told her. He'd led an initial flight of four F-105's against rail facilities northwest of Hanoi, part of a larger strike of F-105's flying from Ta Khli Air Force Base in Thailand. His flight had been the first into the target area. Before they began the bombing run one of his wingmen had been hit by ground fire and had turned back; he'd lost a second wingman over the rail yards. McDermott's bomb load had hung without releasing, and he'd left the target area low over the trees with the 750-pound bombs still in the rack. He was preparing to jettison his bombs and bomb rack when a MIG-21 screamed over him. A Soviet air-to-air missile came fishtailing past him at ten o'clock, so close he could read the Cyrillic letters on the shank. Behind him, his only remaining wingman was hit by a second MIG-21 and went out of control. McDermott limped after him through the overcast, watching for his parachute. The plane exploded in the trees before the pilot could eject. Below the overcast McDermott saw the Phuc Yen airfield ahead of him. Behind him Gopher and Hacksaw flights were approaching the target area, with two more flights coming in behind them. Three MIG-21's were trundling down the Phuc Yen strip, and McDermott had two 750-pound bombs in his rack. Even if the MIGs on the runway wouldn't be airborne in time to hit Gophers and Hacksaws, they'd be ready for the others. He did what his training had taught him to do. He swept up the Phuc Yen strip, toggled his bombs ahead of the MIGs, and screamed off into the overcast. The second time around he came in lower, hanging over the treetops in a strafing run that smashed the control tower and detonated a MIG-19 on the runway. Then he lit his afterburner and blew out, his tanks almost dry as he refueled from a KC-135 over Thailand.

He'd done minimal damage to Phuc Yen, had disabled a few planes, scored one hit, and knocked out some radar equipment. MIGs were using Phuc Yen later the same day. By the time he landed at Ta Khli Airfield, his chief and crew already knew what he'd done. So did the base commander. Within a few days so did the Pentagon and the White House. Both Gopher and Hacksaw flights had reported that someone had hit Phuc Yen. It could only have been McDermott, the only Otter pilot to return from the bombing run that day. The press corps picked it up; so did Saigon. He was grounded pending an inquiry but the base commander couldn't keep the lid on. Three days later the instructions came from the Pentagon. He was to be court-martialed. After the court-martial he resigned. Ta Khli gave him a trophy.

Penny didn't say anything for a long time. "Who made the decision then," she asked finally, "the politicians?"

"I don't know. I resigned."

"But it had to be the politicians, didn't it? Army or Air Force brass don't put airfields off limits, do they?"

"No. They just follow orders too."

"That's what I mean. Those bastards in the White House! All those crummy little TV dots that spell out Johnson or Nixon or whatever shill is peddling his public image. All those weirdo gimmicks that are going to win a war without killing people!" She put her head in her hands. "Oh, God, no wonder I couldn't understand it. It doesn't make any sense at all."

"Don't try, then."

"Yeah, but there's got to be an answer. There's got to be. I mean, things seem pretty crazy sometimes, sure, but that doesn't mean they have to be that way. Sometimes things work out."

"Like when?" McDermott asked.

"I don't know. Like other wars, other problems—the way they work out. This one will too." It wasn't the answer she was searching for and she sat back in her chair in defeat. "History, I guess. Maybe that's it." She still wasn't convinced. "I don't know. I mean it's not like history were irrational or anything, is it?"

"It doesn't have to be irrational," McDermott said. "Not irrational, not homicidal. Not even a paranoid. Just a simple, well-intending moron."

"A *what*?"

"A moron."

"Is *that* what you think? That history's a *moron*?" Her spirits lifted suddenly, despite herself: "A *moron*?"

"I think if any psychiatrist ever wrestled what everyone else calls history into a straitjacket, he'd find he had an IQ of about thirty. Maybe less."

"You're not serious."

"Sure, I'm serious. That's the history everyone talks about. The only thing dangerous about him is his own stupidity. What's the matter?"

He saw Penny smiling from the shadows. "That's the most cynical thing I ever heard anyone say. History a *moron*. My God, they'll have to rewrite the history books."

McDermott left at the end of the week and Penny drove with him to the airfield a little after seven in the morning. The air was fresh and brisk, the sun pale on the wet green fields. The concrete aprons near the hangar were still wet from the previous night's rains. As she saw the silhouette of his plane in the hangar, her heart began to beat a little faster.

"I think I've had it," she said in a quiet voice. "I think I really have."

"Had what?"

She took a deep breath, looking out through the windshield. "I think I'm going to Greece with the guys. They've got a pretty cool trip lined up, and I might as well go. I feel sort of useless around here."

"Who's going?"

"The smallpox gang. Murphy, Lizzy, Eastwick, and a couple of others."

McDermott drove around the hangar. "Greece will be nice this time of year. Not too many tourists."

"You know how I feel then." She knew he hadn't the slightest idea of how she felt.

"Sure."

"How do I feel?"

His eyes didn't leave the tarmac. They drove past two parked planes. "It's like all the kids are in school and you're upstairs in bed with the mumps or whooping cough."

"That's the craziest thing anyone has ever said to me," she said. "It is. We just don't communicate anymore. We just eat, drink, talk; and sleep together. Then you pack your ditty bag and I don't know where you're going, or what you're doing, or even how long you'll be here. I'm just in limbo, that's all. So they asked me to go to Greece with them. So I am."

McDermott climbed from the Land-Rover and unloaded his bag and the cooler. Rozewicz had already arrived and gone to the operation center to file a flight plan. She sat in the front seat, watching McDermott talk to the two men who'd been unloading boxes from a panel truck. He came back to the Land-Rover and asked if she wanted to go with him while he gassed the plane. They taxied out into the sunshine to the fuel depot. She waited alone in the cabin while McDermott walked with the two attendants around the plane, looking through the tinted glass and remembering the day they'd flown up from Djibouti. Clipped to the board on the flight deck was a map. The airstrip at Sudi was marked with grease pencil in bold black letters, and she studied the map emptily. The name meant nothing to her. "Sudi," she whispered in agony, remembering Djibouti. "Oh, God, McDermott. Why can't we go someplace real?"

McDermott returned.

"Is that where you're going?" she asked him as he climbed back into the pilot seat, wiping her eyes on her sleeve. "Sudi?"

"Tomorrow. You all right?"

"I'll be okay."

They taxied back to the hangar where a UN Land-Rover was waiting with medical supplies. McDermott and Penny stood outside near the wing as the plane was loaded. She finally turned and walked away. McDermott followed her. "You're sure you've made up your mind."

"I think so." She looked across the field.

"I wish you'd told me earlier."

"I didn't decide for sure until this morning."

"When are you leaving?"

"Tomorrow morning. Eight o'clock to Cairo and Athens."

She knew he'd be surprised. He stood with his hands on his hips, studying her face, and then the field beyond. "I always knew you would," he said. "I didn't think I'd be surprised either but I am. Tomorrow morning." He shook his head. "That's pretty soon."

"I think sometimes you could have made it easier. More part of what you were doing. More of your life."

"Yeah. Maybe so."

"You never took me on those flights you promised."

"I should have, I guess. I always thought there would be time for it."

"I sort of got the message after a while. You didn't want me along. I don't know why. I still don't. Anyway, when I talked about going some-place else—Hawaii, or Wyoming maybe—you just kind of laughed it off and I felt like an idiot. It was like I was okay in the sack, but didn't know beans about anything else. Just someone you had to put up with."

"That's not true. It was more than just that."

"Maybe so, but that's how I felt." Her head was turned away from him. "I tried to find excuses, until I sort of ran out. We just weren't talking about the same things. You thought I was being defensive about what you did—that I cared more about what other people thought than you. I don't care what they think. It just hurt me, not knowing as much as they did, or claimed they did. Then that night you gave me the third degree, and I ran off—" She stopped and took a deep, slow breath. "Anyway, it's over. It doesn't make any difference anymore."

McDermott studied the sky, eyes narrowed against the piercing sunlight, grimacing as he searched the open fields nearby. "I'll be back in a few days," he said finally. "Maybe we could talk then."

"The guys are leaving tomorrow. I don't want to be alone, even for three days. Sleeping alone, sitting alone, thinking alone—"

"Maybe I could come back tomorrow."

"It'd be the same thing all over again. That's just the way you are. I thought I knew guys that were pretty far out—pretty spaced out—but they're nothing compared to you. Then everything got screwed up all at once—" Her voice broke, and her eyes filled with tears, but she caught herself. "It was fun, and you just about saved my life once. I'll never forget that, the day on the beach, and then up here—" Those days came flooding back and she covered her eyes with her hand. "Oh, God," she wept miserably, "why is it always me?"

"I didn't do anything," McDermott said painfully.

"You *did*," she whispered fiercely, "you did. I was almost suicidal that time in Djibouti, rock bottom, just like the other night."

Rozewicz came around the corner of the hangar and Penny turned and walked farther away from the plane, McDermott following her.

"You can do anything you want," he said. "You know you can."

"I used to think so," she said, drying her face. "But you didn't do much for my confidence. Would you get the Land-Rover for me. I don't want those jerks seeing me crying like this."

He brought the Land-Rover out and stood at the window as she got in behind the wheel, leaning forward, her head against her arms.

"I'm okay now," she sighed, sitting up. Her face was still wet, and her eyes red under her damp lashes. "You'll let me know how you are, won't you?"

"How long will you be in Greece?"

"A few weeks. We're going to the islands. Lizzy has a friend with a house on Paros. I'll be okay. It's not like it's the end of the world or anything."

"If you have any problems, I'll still be here."

"Thanks. I'll send you a card. Take care of yourself."

"You too."

He watched the Land-Rover drive away, and then went back to the plane. "Anything the matter?" Rozewicz asked. He shook his head. "You're a bloody liar," Rozewicz laughed.

FOURTEEN

1

A group of refugees had arrived during the night, accompanied by thirty Anya-nya guerrillas. Two Anya-nya had suffered gunshot wounds and Emily doubted they would survive. As she left the hut where she'd treated the two casualties, the Anya-nya captain was arguing with Samuel Eko. The group he led was well armed: all carried automatic weapons. There were no young boys or old men among them; they were better disciplined and more professional than any of the groups she'd seen. The young captain was brisk and uncompromising, a product of the wars in the south, like his men. It occurred to her that they might have been responsible for the raid on the Sudanese riverboat that had left so many Arab passengers dead or wounded a few weeks earlier.

As she heard the captain talking to Samuel Eko, she realized that he was attempting to shame him into joining the Anya-nya. A new training camp had been established in Upper Nile, and the captain was searching for recruits.

"His wife is expecting a child," Emily interrupted quietly. "He is far more useful here than in Upper Nile."

The captain turned and looked at her coolly with his dark, weary eyes: "It is not for you to say."

"He has a wife."

"I have a wife too."

"She is his other wife," an Anya-nya lieutenant said to the captain in Nuer.

"Why did you come here?" Emily asked. "This village is peaceful. These people know nothing of your war."

"Villages across the border were peaceful too," the captain replied. "Now they are being burned."

"The captain and I were friends in Juba," Samuel Eko explained.

"This isn't the Sudan," Emily said. "Juba either."

"It isn't for you to say," the captain repeated. "These people are Nuer. The blood is the same. Blood knows nothing of borders."

"You can't recruit soldiers here."

"Your house is up there," the young captain replied, pointing off through the trees. "This is a Nuer village."

"Your two wounded men can't travel," she said, turning away. "I came to tell you that. Nothing more."

She left the enclosure but as she came out into the morning sunlight saw that the refugees who'd arrived at dawn had spread their possessions on the meadow behind the village. Some of the more energetic old men had begun to stake out hut sites. A few women were beginning to dig up garden plots with their mattocks. She sent a village child to fetch Samuel Eko to explain to them that they must move on, and as she waited she moved among them herself, trying to discourage their wasted labor. They paid no attention to her. *How long will this madness continue*, she thought as she sank down on the grass in the shade. Nearby a young woman with a child on her back was hacking at the turf with a mattock. Samuel Eko didn't appear. She started back into the village, and met William Latu on the path, sent by Samuel Eko in his place.

"But why? Where is he?" she asked, bewildered. Samuel Eko had never failed to heed her summons. William Latu shook his head awkwardly. Emily Farr had embarrassed Samuel Eko in front of the Anya-nya officers, but it was impossible for William Latu to tell her that. "I'll talk to him later," she said. "We must hurry. They have a long walk ahead of them and they don't seem to understand they can't settle here."

It took William Latu and Emily almost an hour to assemble the refugees under the trees at the edge of the meadow, where William Latu explained to them in his gentle voice why they couldn't settle at the Baro station village. His oratory was much less spectacular than Samuel Eko's. A dozen village children were sitting in the front row, listening to William Latu with growing disappointment, his words wholly lacking the color of Hajii Mazoot's, who would have conjured up visions of Galla soldiers arriving to sell them into slavery, smoking huts, devils, demons, and Galla slave raiders with sticks fanged with fire.

William Latu had almost finished his explanation when the children heard the sound of a plane overhead, flying low over the trees. Full-blooded drama was better to them than dry oratory, and instantly they were on their feet. "*Galla! Galla!*" they shrieked as they flew down through the trees to the safety of their huts. The refugees began to flee too: some toward the river, others into the village, a few back along the track to the east.

The plane was a small two-engined Ethiopian military aircraft painted olive drab. Upon landing Ato Tefari deplaned, followed by an Ethiopian colonel from the Ministry of Interior, then Colonel Hamid, and an Ethiopian major. Unlike the usual inspections, which were to ensure that no Anya-nya were in the village, no new acreage under cultivation, and no additional huts under construction, no advance word had preceded their arrival. Emily Farr was waiting on the track with Samuel Eko—who'd miraculously reappeared as she was climbing the road. The visitors filed solemnly past. Colonel Hamid's presence told her that this was no ordinary inspection.

In his thin, petulant voice Ato Tefari informed her that a group of Anya-nya had attacked a Sudanese river steamer for the second time on the Baro River just inside the Sudan border. Four Sudanese soldiers and three civilians had been killed. The crew reported that the terrorists had fled east, toward the Baro station.

"We saw some figures running across the meadow," Colonel Mulegeta from the Ministry of Interior added. "We saw them as we approached." He was moon-faced, wearing gold-rimmed spectacles. Each of the visitors carried either a walking stick or a riding crop; Colonel Hamid's was folded under his right arm; a pair of binoculars hung from his neck.

"They were refugees, frightened by the plane," she replied impatiently, still annoyed at the plane's unexpected appearance and the turmoil and panic it had created. "I should have been frightened, too, if I'd never seen a plane before."

"Planes land here quite often, I am told," said Ato Tefari dryly, his muddy eyes fixed on Emily's face.

"These were refugees, not village people."

"Who is this man?" Ato Tefari inquired, his walking stick lifted to Samuel Eko's shoulder and resting there lightly.

"This is *not* a Galla cattle market!" she cried angrily, thrusting the cane away. It fell to the ground and the four men stood looking at it, transfixed. "Samuel Eko is my driver and mechanic," she continued, controlling her temper, her impulse regretted. The villagers, not she, would pay the price. "He has been here for years. I'm sure Colonel Mulegeta remembers him." Samuel Eko moved to retrieve the thin walking stick, but she stooped to recover it first, handing it back to Ato Tefari.

"Yes, I know this chap," Colonel Mulegeta recalled in his soft, London-acquired English. "There is nothing personal in this visit. We came at the direction of the minister. The deaths on the riverboat have shocked all of us. Serious accusations have been made."

"What kind of accusations?"

Ato Tefari drew Colonel Mulegeta aside and they spoke softly together in Amharic. "That the Anya-nya find refuge here," the colonel replied, lifting his head again.

"The charge is untrue." She looked toward Colonel Hamid, whose eyes were concealed suddenly behind his binoculars.

"We will investigate," Colonel Mulegeta murmured. "Perhaps we might begin with the house."

"My doors are open." She knew she didn't have the courage to accompany the group through her cottage.

"You won't show us?" Colonel Mulegeta asked.

"I asked the refugees to wait in the meadow. They're frightened and they must leave quickly. I must go reassure them."

After consulting together in Amharic, Colonel Mulegeta and Ato Tefari decided that it would be more prudent for the group to accompany her. Samuel Eko drove them down to the village in the

Land-Rover. They walked down through the huts, inspecting the few that lay along the main path. Colonel Mulegeta quickly lost his appetite for his duties. After leaving a second hut, he stood mopping his neck. Gnats swarmed near his face; a smell hung in the air he couldn't identify. "Smoke, musk? Campfires?" he mused as he caught his breath. "The cholera has been here?" He didn't enter another hut.

William Latu and the Anya-nya guerrillas had vanished, melting like the midday sunlight through the trees downriver. The refugees were waiting alone at the edge of the meadow. Emily and Samuel Eko followed as the visitors moved among the refugees. The old men and women sat on the ground, their exhausted faces still dusty from their long march, their eyes bloodshot, the flesh of their arms and necks gray with mud and ash, the skin hanging from their bones like rags from a scarecrow. Ato Tefari prodded a woman with his thin cane, but the bulge in her dress held only a sack of sorghum. "They are very old," Colonel Mulegeta concluded, dabbing at his wet face. Ato Tefari circled through the old people like a camel trader, prodding legs and shoulders, his café-au-lait face inscrutable, his sleepy eyes half-closed.

"There are no Anya-nya here," she said angrily as she watched him, turning to Colonel Mulegeta.

"They would be dead if they were," Samuel Eko said to Emily in Nuer.

"What did he say?" Colonel Hamid asked.

"He said the refugees must be leaving. It is a hot day and they have a long walk," Emily answered.

They climbed up through the village again and Ato Tefari stopped at the entrance to a cattle byre, looking through the rising dust stirred by the animals inside toward the hut beyond. A small cattle boy squatted on his heels inside the gate, staring up at him. "What is this?" Ato Tefari asked.

"For the cattle," Colonel Hamid said with distaste, grimacing through the drifting dust. Cakes of steaming dung littered the byre, which also smelled of fresh urine. Flies blew in and out of the shafts of sunlight falling down through the trees. They resumed their climb toward the Land-Rover. As they turned along a mud fence, two small village boys were lying in wait for them:

"*Galla! Galla!*" they shrieked, flying away through the trees. "*Galla! Galla!*"

Colonel Mulegeta was upset. "Galla? Where do they learn this—here? In this village? We give them land. We protect them." He looked at Emily in disappointment.

"They are just small boys," she said.

"Small boys hear what their parents say. They repeat what the parents say. If there is fear in a village, they know it."

"It must be reported to the minister," Ato Tefari said. "There is something in this village. What it is, I cannot say. But there is something here."

"For sure," Colonel Hamid agreed. "There is much more here than what we are seeing. More than meets the eye."

After the military plane departed with its passengers, Samuel Eko drove Emily back to the clinic, where one of her nurse's aides was waiting with her medical kit. "He is in the byre," she told Emily, who ran quickly down the path to the cattle byre where the fleeing Anya-nya had left one of the two wounded men. A few thin spokes of sunlight radiated from the smoke-hole overhead and down across the earth floor. The dust of the byre blew across her damp face as she crouched next to the wounded man, his chest dark with blood. The flies were everywhere; a few crawled across his hollow cheeks and open lips. He had been dead for an hour or more; the dressing with which she had covered the wound now lay in the dust beside him. She sat for a few minutes next to him, the brine of cattle urine and dung stinging her eyes. She was still there when Samuel Eko entered with the Anya-nya captain.

"The other man is dead too," the captain told her, slinging his automatic rifle over his shoulder as he lifted the dead man by the heels. Samuel Eko took his arms, and she turned away suddenly, her head averted, unable to watch them remove the body.

The same week the Sudanese embassy in Addis Ababa issued a demarche protesting the Baro station's support of the Anya-nya insurgents and appealed to both the Addis government and the US ambassador to close the station. Stone-Ashton, accompanied by Osgood and

Colonel Mulegeta, flew to Baro to present Emily with a full text of the Sudanese allegations. She prepared a statement defending the mission station's activities. Osgood said he would take the subject up with the mission board and then meet with both the UN and Ethiopian officials to discuss a course of action. Two days later a motor launch appeared on the Baro near the cottage. It came up from Nasir in the Sudan in the afternoon, its boiler sending billows of black smoke into the sky, its pistons racketing noisily out across the grasslands. During the day it would pound upriver toward Gambela, but at night would drift with the current back past the Baro station, its boilers silent, its lights extinguished. There were armed men aboard. Samuel Eko believed it was a Sudanese military launch sent from Nasir to watch the village, the mission house, and the airfield. He believed the armed guards were Sudanese soldiers.

2

McDermott and Emily swam in the Baro at the end of a scorching African afternoon. McDermott was scheduled to pick up a UN survey team in Gambela the following morning but hadn't decided whether he would fly into Gambela that afternoon or remain overnight at the Baro station. He was curious about the launch Samuel Eko had described for him, but he was also troubled by the recent official visits to Baro.

"They're all lying," he said as he climbed out of the water after her. "All of them."

"Sorry?" Her thumbs tugged at the bands of her suit hidden beneath the skirt, then lifted the fallen shoulder straps. She pulled off her rubber bathing cap, her body shining with water, and let her brown hair fall across her shoulders. "That feels so much better," she said, arms raised to bind her hair with a rubber band at the back of her neck. The rubber membrane covering her ears always made her voice strange to her, and that afternoon in the river she was uncomfortably conscious of it and how tiresome it had grown. "What did you say? They're what?"

"I said maybe you need a vacation."

"Maybe I do, but I couldn't possibly leave. Amina's child is coming soon—any day now, I suppose—and I promised her I'd be here. In the meantime there's this other business. I'm absolutely caught in the middle. I couldn't leave now." She sat down on the tree trunk, drying her arms with the towel. "I don't have very much confidence in Osgood either. He's anxious to please the government for the sake of the other mission stations here, and I'm sure he'd recommend closing Baro. I don't quite know what to make of Colonel Hamid. Or Ato Tefari either, for that matter."

"They're all lying," McDermott said. "All of them. That's what keeps the bureaucrats and diplomats busy, inventing excuses for lying to each other." She looked up at him in surprise. "So they're all lying—to each other and to you. The Ethiopians are running guns to the Anya-nya and the Sudanese know they are. So does the UN. But refugees keep the UN salaries going, the same way poverty and misery do. Anyway, they're playing games. If that's their game, deal yourself a hand too."

"Myself a hand? I don't understand?"

"Play your own hand. Let a plane fly a few guns and rations out of here into Upper Nile, resupplying the Anya-nya. Then they'd really wonder what the hell was going on. They'd be so screwed up they'd never get it all sorted out—trying to figure who was doing what to whom. That's how you short-circuit the bureaucrats."

"Are you serious?"

"Why not?" It was just an idea to McDermott, more the product of his irritation with everyone or everything that was victimizing Emily Farr than anything else. "What's the best that could happen now? Probably they'll close you down. Those are the same odds you'll get if you deal a hand for yourself."

"I can't believe you're serious."

"Why not? Okay. I could fly rations, not guns. Just rations and medical re-supplies."

"You're the last person in the world I would ever expect to make a suggestion like that."

"Me?" He frowned. "How come?"

"You certainly know how I feel about the war."

He shrugged. "Okay, the—"

"It's certainly not okay."

"Maybe we'd better forget it."

"What on earth made you think I could ever approve a plan like that? If you're embarrassed, I'm sorry, but I'm embarrassed too. Flying weapons from the Baro station. It's senseless!"

"Yeah, maybe it is." He pulled the towel around his neck and picked up his shirt.

"I'm surprised. I'm really surprised."

Good God, he thought, looking at her lifted face. "Yeah, I guess maybe you are."

They climbed the bank to the cottage in silence and he changed clothes in the guest bedroom, looking out the window at the waiting plane. He'd brought a bottle of Chablis from the house in Addis, and he pulled it from the flight bag and left it on the dresser where she'd find it. Then he slung the bag over his shoulder and went down the hall to the living room, where he waited for her to finish dressing. She took a long time. She came down the hall, still combing her hair, and saw the flight bag over his shoulder.

"But I thought you were staying."

"It's not too late yet," he said, squinting out through the screen door at the late-afternoon sky. "Maybe I can still make it to Gambela."

She didn't move for a minute, studying his face, her arm still lifted with the comb. Then she completed the stroke. "But you can't," she said simply. "The airport will be closed." She took the strap from his shoulder. "Please."

"Look—"

"Please. It's over and forgotten now. I didn't mean to criticize you, and I'm sorry I did. I don't like being lectured to either and I'm sorry I lectured you. I'd feel dreadful if you left now."

"That wasn't it," McDermott said. "You've got things on your mind. I know that. You don't have to put me up too."

"It's no trouble. Have I made you feel it was?"

"No. Never." He dropped the flight bag to the empty chair behind him.

"Did I ever tell you about the Land-Rover tires?" she asked, the comb put aside as she tied a ribbon at the back of her neck. "Samuel Eko once bought two tires in Gambela. They were the wrong size and I told him so at the time. He didn't believe me. Later he found out for himself. I lectured him too, I suppose; the wrong way. We never spoke of it again." They moved across the porch and out into the yard. "I suppose I was more embarrassed than he was." Her voice trailed off as she grew conscious of it again, as she had earlier in the river with the bathing cap fluttering the sounds of her larynx through the rubber membrane. Spontaneity had never been a gift with her, her husband had often reminded her. Emotions discovered within herself had lost all of their naturalness or simplicity by the time they broke the surface of her mind. The fear of self-betrayal ruled her life more than the need for self-discovery. A church psychologist had told her that at a missionary seminar her husband had insisted they attend before going to the Congo for the first time. She thought it was true. She remembered his spatulate fingers and his Masonic ring.

They stood at the gate, McDermott's face opaque to her in the late-afternoon sunlight as he looked out across the field. "I thought I saw a few antelope there this afternoon," she told him quietly, remembering the buffalo they had searched for a month earlier when they'd talked about Kentucky and Vermont. They circled the plane and he brushed a few crumbs of dried mud from the rivets of the recessed light panels, looking at his dusty fingers afterward. "Where is it from?" she asked.

He didn't know. Sudi perhaps, maybe the Upper Nile. Someplace different—far from where they stood. The wind moved across the meadow and stirred the trees along the fence. The late-afternoon light was as thick as honey, golden yet translucent still, dense with the accumulations of its passage—light filtered across thousands of miles of savannah and prairie; the dust from yoked animals, woodfires, the heat of the alkali pan, and the blowing grasses—all distilled to an amber clarity that lay as soft as silk on her face and skin.

"Sometimes I don't quite understand why you're here," Emily said. "Somehow, I'd never quite have expected it of you."

"Me either," McDermott laughed. "I don't worry about it."

"I can well imagine you someplace else. But not here."

"Sometimes I have the same problem. What about you?"

They walked out on the grasslands beyond the field. "I used to think about it quite often," she admitted. "But I don't suppose I do anymore."

"Did you ever think you'd like to just keep walking?" he asked as they stopped, watching the sun drop toward the horizon.

"Sometimes."

They had a cold dinner in the kitchen, which was warm and sultry. She dropped a dish. "I suppose you wish you'd gone to Gambela after all," she apologized as she cleaned it up, her cheeks flushed, perspiration across her forehead and temples. "Nothing seems to be going right."

"That's okay. We can do without potato salad." He pushed open the window over the sink and lifted the sash in the window opposite so that the breeze moved across the table where they sat. He remembered the bottle of Chablis and brought it from the guest room. "What's wrong with this?" he asked as he uncorked the wine.

"I'm afraid it's not much—fish and deviled eggs."

"It's fine. With a headwaiter and a fifty-dollar corkage bill, we could be in Paris."

"Do you like Paris?"

"In the winter," he said. "When the snow is on the ground."

"That's not very often, is it?"

"No, not too often."

"I know Brussels better. I studied French there for nine months before we went to the Congo. The recipe for the fish is Belgian, by the way. I'm not sure what it's called. I found it in an old cookbook last week. I wasn't certain I should try it. Do you know Brussels?"

"Not very well."

"I remember the rain," she said. "Days and weeks of it. That's about all." She lifted her head from her plate. "How do you remember Brussels?"

"The rain and the fog. I was grounded there for three days once."

"You remember cities because of the weather?"

"Usually. What about you?"

"The people, I suppose. The weather as well. Sometimes the architecture."

"You miss it then."

"I miss quite a lot of things sometimes."

After dinner they cleaned up the kitchen as they listened to the BBC and the Voice of America. The moon was out and they sat under the trees on the lawn, she in the lawn chair, McDermott stretched out in the grass nearby. The stars hung low on the southern horizon beyond the river. She told him that she'd once been invited by a Belgian priest at Luluabourg in the Congo to learn something of astronomy. He'd built a telescope in his parish workshop. But she hadn't had time, unfortunately. Now she regretted it. McDermott fell asleep in the grass but some time passed before she discovered this. She was uncomfortable at first, not sure how she should awaken him. Her husband had been unpredictable in sleep, flinging out an arm or a leg, stirring to her slightest touch. McDermott's breathing grew even deeper, and she sat forward, the grass damp. She touched his shoulder lightly. He didn't respond, and she kneeled in the grass next to him.

"Mr. McDermott," she called, shaking his shoulder. "*Mr. McDermott.*" Calling his name in the darkness of the lawn, she was suddenly struck by the absurdity of their relationship. *Good heavens*, she thought, *this is ridiculous*. She took his shoulder more firmly, and McDermott stirred and sat up. "You've been sleeping," she whispered.

"What time is it?"

"Almost eleven."

McDermott sat stupidly in the grass, not sure for a moment where he was or what he'd been doing. "Sorry."

"I'll see if I can find the flashlight," she said. "I think the lantern's here too. It's time to go in."

They groped together in the darkness under the trees, searching for them. Still only half awake, he said, "I can't see a damned thing."

"Maybe I left them inside." He followed her groggily back the path to the porch and stood at the foot of the steps until his head had cleared. "Watch the first step," she called.

The house was pitch dark. He tried to find her silhouette but saw only dim shadows and the gray rectangle of window. He struck a flame from his lighter, and her pale face hovered just ahead of him.

"I must have left the lantern in the kitchen," she conjectured as the flame flickered out. Moving after her, he walked into the wall, banging his head against old plaster as hard as concrete:

"*Goddammit!*"

"Shhh." Her voice was closer, and as he turned he collided with a small table, steadying it in reflex but not seeing the lamp, which toppled to the floor with a crash.

"Jesus Christ! Is this place booby-trapped?"

"To your right, I think—through the hallway."

He found the doorway and struck his lighter again. She joined him before it flickered out, and they groped their way down the hallway and into the kitchen. "Is the flashlight here?" he asked.

"I must have left it on the table."

There was nothing on the table except an empty saucepan which McDermott's hands knocked immediately to the floor. "Why don't we just forget it," he capitulated, colliding with her as he retreated, his hands steadying her. "Sorry."

"It's my fault. I can't imagine where I left either the flashlight or the lantern." Her face was close to him, her voice even closer. It may have been the softness of the voice or the warmth of her arms under his fingers, but McDermott suddenly saw her standing on the banks of the Baro, the water shining on her arms and shoulders, saw the brown hair, the full breasts, and the sunlight across her forehead and cheeks. He felt her arms move and her body stiffen.

"*Don't,*" she whispered, but he kissed her anyway. Her head twisted against him; her lips were clamped shut. "*No—*" she breathed as he released her shoulders, but even before the words were gone, he kissed her again. She suddenly twisted away and slipped sideways against the table, out of breath.

"I'm sorry," she insisted, "but you mustn't—"

He took her by the waist and moved her toward him. Her head was back, as if she were about to yield to him.

"Please listen," she asked, but he only kissed her harder.

He thought he felt her mouth soften, her lips open, but just as suddenly she broke away. He found her waist again, and was moving against her when fire flashed across his eyes, his cheek stung painfully, and he realized she'd struck him. She slid away along the table, shoved it backward across his path, and fled into the hall.

"Wait—" He went after her, but was only a few steps into the hall when the bedroom door slammed closed ahead of him and he heard the key turn in the lock.

He waited in the dark hall, calling out to her from time to time, but the room within was silent. His foot fell asleep, and he finally limped back across the hall, closed the door, and went to bed. The room was gray when he awoke, but beyond the window the birds were moving in the trees, and the morning sun lay on the open fields beyond the fence line. Down the hall water was being emptied into the iron bathtub. She was fully dressed when she knocked lightly at the door casing, wearing a sleeveless seersucker sundress.

"I filled the tub for you," she said quietly.

"Thanks. I'll hop right in," McDermott said. *What did you put in it?* he wondered. *A bucket of lye? That'd take the hide off bad habits, wouldn't it?*

"I'm sorry for last night," she said. "I'm very sorry. How is your cheek?"

"It's all right. I'm sorry too." But he was sorry most of all for what she might have thought. What did she think—a quick score on the widow's bed before he hit the road again? Chasing your pecker all the way out here to the edge of the prairie where there was nothing but prune juice in the pantry and Jesus on the walls? But he didn't know what she thought.

He took a quick bath, shaved, and got dressed. Still buttoning his shirt, he wandered down the hall and into the living room, standing at the screen door, looking at the morning sky. The day would be clear, without clouds until late afternoon. The sun had emerged from the trees behind the Nuer village. He watched Emily Farr come back from the vegetable garden, a basket over her arm, the straw hat on her head. He watched her stop near the brick washhouse to give instructions to old William, the night guard, who went off toward the gate at a lope. She was a determined woman, he'd always known that; but he'd never fully appreciated the strength of her determination. He'd been right about the pump arm too: his face still stung slightly. He watched her move the lawn chair in the yard, pick up the cigarette package and glass he'd left there, then saw her find the electric lantern and flashlight in the wet grass where they'd been under the chair.

Hadn't she said she'd left them in the house? Or did she conveniently forget them there in the grass and then get cold feet inside at the last minute? He went back to the bedroom and had just pulled on his shoes when she came down the hall and knocked at the half-closed door, carrying a cup of coffee. The flashlight was under her arm.

"I thought I might bring you this," she said, putting the coffee on the bedside table. "I don't know whether you prefer coffee in the morning or not. But you've got a long day ahead of you."

"That's real fine," McDermott said in his most authentic Air Force voice, still not sure he hadn't been hoodwinked.

"I found the flashlight on the lawn. The lantern too. I should have known that's where they were. I really wasn't thinking very clearly about anything."

McDermott had decided that if he'd been deceived, his best defense was to behave as if he were unaware of it. "That's okay. It happens sometimes. Happens to all of us." Nothing was more wooden in intent or more false in execution than McDermott's idea of himself acting naturally. Emily discovered the falseness of tone almost immediately, but listened to his nonsense a little longer. "I think it's going to be a real fine day. A-OK," he was saying. "Good flying weather. It's the kind of day that makes you good to be alive—"

"You mean glad to be alive, don't you?" she wondered, looking at him curiously. "Is everything all right?" Her sympathetic brown eyes traveled to the flushed skin of his cheekbone. "Is it painful?"

Discovering her face raised to his in the morning light, McDermott was stirred in the same way he'd been the previous night. His resolution collapsed. "Forget it," he breathed in his usual monosyllabic way. "Forget all of it." He took her bare arms in his hands and moved her back into the room, closing the door with his shoulders.

"I hope we're not going to begin where we left off last night," she said.

"Why not?"

"Because I'm afraid the conclusion would be the same."

He took her shoulders more firmly, and they struggled—Emily trying to reach the doorknob, McDermott trying to control her thrashing shoulders. He moved her steadily across the room, and when she made one last effort to free herself, slipping momentarily from his grasp, he caught her and they fell together across the bed. She was angry, breathing heavily, but McDermott wasn't angry at all. He held her wrists locked across her chest as she stared up at him coldly.

"I just want to tell you something," he said. "Stop squirming. I'm not going to let you go until you listen."

She turned her head away. "I won't listen."

"You will listen. You've got it all wrong." She thrashed again wildly but he only held her more tightly. "Stop it. Just stop it for a minute."

Her head was still turned away; the cords of her neck stood out. "I'm ready to listen to anyone, but not like this."

"I don't give a damn about what you think I'm up to, last night or any other time. But just take the blinders off for a minute and listen, okay?"

She turned her face toward him. "What are you talking about?"

"You," he said. "Just you. Nobody else. Just you. You're better than any of them. The whole idiot crowd. The UN. The creeping Jesuses at Moquo. Osgood. The Ethiopians. The Sudanese crowd. Stop thinking you're not. You've done more than any of them could do. Don't you know that? Goddammit, stop fighting and listen to me! No one could have done more—"

She watched him stubbornly, her eyes dark. "Are you finished? You're hurting my wrists."

"No, I'm not finished." He relaxed his grip, but when she tried to sit up, he held her again. "Did you hear what I said?"

She turned her head away and didn't answer. Still they lay on the bed, McDermott holding her arms. Finally she turned her head and looked up at him. "Yes," she said. He lifted himself, still over her.

"Okay. Remember that then. You're better than any of them." She stared up at him as he studied her face. "Okay, I'm through then. That's all I wanted to say." He released her wrists and kissed her suddenly on the mouth and stood up.

She sat up very slowly, rubbing her wrists, and then rearranging her hair, watching him silently. Still sitting on the edge of the bed, she buttoned the front of her dress, her face finally rediscovering the room again. "Your coffee will get cold."

"So will a lot of things." He opened the door and then picked up the cup from the bedside table.

"I sometimes think you're bound and determined to have your own way," she said as she stood up.

"What about you? That makes two of us, doesn't it?"

"I suppose so." Through the window she saw Samuel Eko go around the side of the house. "If you're to get to Gambela on time, I suppose I'd better fix breakfast."

Samuel Eko and William were already waiting at the plane as Emily and McDermott left the front gate. She moved into the road, looking away toward the east, shielding her eyes from the glare of the sun as McDermott unlocked the cabin. While McDermott readied the plane for takeoff, she turned and walked back along the wing toward the open grasslands, her hand at her eyes. She was still standing there when she heard his footsteps and for a moment hadn't the strength or the courage to say good-bye.

"I think I'm about ready," he said. She took a last desperate look at the empty fields beyond before she turned.

"I think you'll have good weather," she said, finding the will to lift her voice to her throat. "I'm sure you will." She didn't look at him.

"Maybe so." When she finally lifted her eyes, she didn't know what to say. Neither did he.

FIFTEEN

During the first week of Dr. Botewi's imprisonment in Gambela, the Ethiopian soldiers would often watch him through the barred window in the wooden door, squinting through the rusty steel grating so thick with dust and cobwebs that it was difficult to see in, watching the little Negro as if he were an animal in a cage. Dr. Botewi sat on his wooden bench during the day, scratching his woolly black head and rubbing the sweat from his face and neck as he jabbered to himself in a language none of the local soldiers could understand. They had taken away his sandals and belt, so he sat barefoot in his shapeless serge trousers and his collarless white shirt, with the small, cheap cross outlined in plastic pearls over his heart. He'd tried once to sell the cross to an Ethiopian prostitute locked in the cell across the passageway. She sold herself to the Ethiopian guards, hoping to accumulate enough money to buy her way out of jail, but the guard who'd transmitted Botewi's offer was an Amhara, like the girl, and believed Botewi was asking for an exchange of favors, not money. He cuffed Botewi across the ear and kicked over the small metal bowl he'd just filled with millet gruel. After the guard left, Botewi scraped what he could from the bottom of the bowl, kneeled down on the stone floor, and lapped up the remainder.

There were rats in the old stone prison, living within the thick walls and in the deep burrows beneath the foundation. Shortly after Botewi's arrival a guard surprised a large gray rat limping along the passageway near the grain bin, too old or too sated to scurry away, and stunned him over the head with his club. The rat's muzzle was brindled with white whiskers and old scars, one of its yellow incisors was broken, and its tail was as long as a garden snake.

"Like the little black man," said the guard who flung the stunned rat into Botewi's cell. Botewi was sitting on the bench talking to himself in his singsong voice as the rat arrived in the middle of the floor. Abruptly he grew silent, studying the stunned rat. Finally the rat opened one eye and looked at Botewi, who said something to the rat. For ten minutes the two contemplated each other while the guards waited. After ten more minutes the guards grew restless and drifted away. Late in the morning one of the guards looked into the cell, but the rat had vanished. Botewi was lying asleep on his bench pallet, his small face lifted somnolently to the ceiling, oblivious to the flies that crawled across his face and the small metal bowl that still lay on his chest. Because the guards were convinced that Botewi had eaten the rat that morning, they flung any rat found in the prison or the nearby garden into Botewi's cell in the expectation that he would eventually betray himself. The rats disappeared one by one, but no one had ever witnessed Botewi's killing or eating them.

The guard most suspicious of Botewi was the jailer who twice a day brought him millet gruel and the water bucket. Although prisoners with families or friends nearby were permitted to receive food from outside to supplement the prison diet, strangers like Botewi were out of luck. Botewi survived on water and millet gruel. The guard was skeptical. When he questioned Botewi about it, his little prisoner told him in his stilted English that more ample fare was on its way—that his friends would soon bring him plump chickens to eat, cassava, squash, roasted goat, corn, and beans. He claimed that the doors of the prison would soon swing open and he would return downriver to establish his mission station in the virgin countryside where all of his countrymen would soon gather. He had found such a kingdom, a nation with ten thousand hectares of virgin soil and a piano in the parlor.

The guard knew the story by then. Botewi's attempts at recruiting townspeople and villagers from the surrounding countryside to settle his up-country plantation had landed him in prison in the first place. He had appeared on the dusty streets of Gambela from the African bush, chattering to himself and harassing everyone who passed, black and white alike, soliciting money, asking questions, cadging food, and issuing threats, none of which was entirely comprehensible. Stuck in his belt was a black panga with a rust-pitted blade. At the Greek emporium he had attempted to buy a refrigerator, an electric fan, some chairs, and an iron bedstead, asking the Greek owner to send them downriver by steamer to the Baro station. The Greek merchant totaled up the bill, looked at the small dirty card Botewi had given him—

Dr. Cleophas Botewi
Doktor of
Pharmakology
& Religion

examined a little more closely the tattered Belgian franc notes Botewi had given him and which he knew to be worthless, and threw him out into the street. The Ethiopians who saw Botewi in town those first days thought him the demented product of the same evangelism still practiced by the Protestant missionaries among the Nilotic pagans of the Ethiopian frontier. To the Nilotic peoples themselves, however, Botewi was a man to be watched—a sorcerer or fetisheur from a region they didn't know, and whose magic was all the more troubling because it was unknown.

After the local policemen drove Botewi from the streets of Gambela as a nuisance and troublemaker, he roamed the surrounding countryside attempting to solicit money and win converts among the Anuak and Nuer villagers, hectoring children, women, and young girls whom he invited to join his downriver kingdom, promising them garden plots and new houses at his new settlement where game abounded, the soil was more fertile, water as plentiful as the Baro at floodtide, and squash, beans, corn, and cassava grew as thick as the hairs on a man's head. Botewi quickly became a pest in the countryside as well.

He tried to enter the hut of a pregnant Anuak woman; but her husband and sons drove him off with sticks into the hills, where he hid for three days. On the fourth day the pregnant woman's daughter fell ill with fever. On the night she was taken to the Swedish hospital, a villager saw Botewi hiding in the woods behind the family's hut. The girl died and after the burial her father and brothers searched the woods with lanterns. They found nothing. The next day a herdsman driving a few goats through the same woods came upon a small wooden box made of dried twigs and crudely bound with vines and wild grass. In the box was a candle stub, dried viscera, a broken mirror, a few animal teeth taken from the bleached jaw of a calf or a goat, a few tiny bat bones, and the still-bloody heart of a small lizard.

In banishing the dead child's soul to the underground and her mother's unborn child to the body of a bat, Botewi had also delivered himself to prison, not for being a sorcerer but because the aroused countryside drove him to seek refuge in Gambela, where the police discovered that he had no identity papers. He told the police that he'd accompanied a group of Sudanese refugees across the border, but the UN officials who were summoned to document his case were unable to attest to either his refugee status or his ethnic origins. Until then they had assumed he was an Ethiopian Bantu from deep in the south-western wilderness. The Ethiopians threw him in jail.

There he would have remained had it not been for the increasing hostility of the prison guards—the same guards who'd thrown the stunned rats into Botewi's cell. One day Botewi dropped his dirty metal bowl into the bucket from which the guard had been ladling his water ration. The guard thought it deliberate and threw the entire contents in Botewi's face, leaving him gasping and drenched to the skin from the deluge. Botewi's movements in the presence of the water or gruel bucket thereafter became more circumspect. The week following, the guard had finished his rounds with the water bucket and was returning down the corridor when he heard something rattling in the bottom of the bucket. He went out into the sunny courtyard and looked into it. The magnification of the water sluicing in the bucket, brilliantly clarified by the noonday sun, brought the evil eyes even closer. Glaring up at him malevolently from the bottom of the bucket were the eyes of a rat in a dead white skull.

The prison captain was brought out into the courtyard amid a babble of voices—not at all sure what he would find in the bottom of the bucket—an asp, a live rat, a rat with a serpent's head, or a diminutive, wizened Botewi, hiding like a shrunken toad in the pail. Taking a broom from the guard, he carefully tipped over the bucket, and what slid to the stones was neither a rodent nor a reptile but the wet white

skull of a very large rat. Its yellow teeth gleamed like fangs, one inci-
sor broken. Pressed into the eye sockets were two small cowrie shells
whose serrated inner folds might have resembled a serpent's pupil.

Not long afterward another prison guard experienced a similar hallucination. He'd been feeding the prisoners corn gruel from a
bucket, had almost finished his rounds, and had paused in the shadowy corridor to ease his own hunger from the ladle before the final
feedings denied him the opportunity. Lifting the dipper to his mouth,
he confronted in the half-light a disembodied, reptilian head ascend-
ing by levitation toward his throat as his arm raised—the jaws leaking
gruel, pulverized flesh, and God-knows-what-else, the glittering serpent eyes fixed hypnotically upon his own.

His cry brought the prison captain, who conducted an investiga-
tion. Had Botewi done it? There was no proof. The guards thought
so but, at the captain's orders, were forced to continue providing him
with the water and rations they would have denied. But they did so
reluctantly, perhaps even conspiratorially, and two weeks later Botewi
fell ill. The Swedish doctor summoned from the rural hospital thought
Botewi showed symptoms of food poisoning. The captain thought his
guards responsible and asked Mr. Shepherd of the UN if Botewi's con-
valescence might be arranged for at some UN-supported clinic far
removed from Gambela. Shepherd thought of the missionary station
at Moquo and suggested that Botewi might be released to Reverend
Osgood's custody while he recovered. Osgood was also agreeable, not
simply for humanitarian reasons. Taking custody of Botewi, whom he
knew nothing about, gave him the opportunity to ingratiate himself
with both the UN and provincial authorities and perhaps put both in
his debt. He didn't realize that except for Shepherd and the prison captain, no one of any real authority was even aware of Botewi's existence.

So Botewi, still giddy from food poisoning and dehydration, was
taken from Gambela to Moquo in the rear seat of one of the mission
Land-Rovers. He was put to bed in the mission clinic and at the end
of the first week had recovered sufficiently to be examined for parasites and other diseases. One of the nurses thought him tubercular,
a second found evidence of bilharzia, while a third thought him in-
sane. He was a cheerful but high-strung patient, chattering incessantly

to himself, whistling occasionally through his occluded teeth as he plucked strange tunes on the small thumb harp he'd made from reeds and sticks. He was finally released from the clinic, dazed and disoriented from his treatment for parasites, given the freedom of the mission grounds, and enrolled in the Moquo vocational program for local youths. By this time he had stopped speaking English and spoke only in his native tongue. Among the gadgetry Osgood had accumulated at Moquo—cameras, a photo lab, a sound system, and amplifiers for the Moquo social hall—was a tape recorder which he used to tape Botewi's speech and which he forwarded to the Bible Society in London, the repository of African tribal dialect, both living and dead.

"Why, for heaven's sakes," Osgood explained to Bertha Ivy, the Moquo librarian as he composed the explanatory letter to accompany the tape, "this little fellow might be God's last man speaking this particular language nowadays—the last man on the face of the earth."

Botewi correctly interpreted Osgood's interest in his native tongue as interest in himself and his tribal past and future as well. He attempted to teach the language to other missionaries, to his vocational counselor, as well as the Nilotic youths with whom he was learning carpentry.

Enrolled as a student in the vocational program, he was given a cot in a small cottage with four other students boarding at Moquo—all Anuak youths, younger than Botewi, none of whom had ever been away from his native village before. After less than ten days in Botewi's company, they asked to have him removed. They complained of his language lessons, his disquieting habit of making strange noises in his sleep, as well as other obscure practices, which they refused to describe. One of the mission nurses was more specific: she told Osgood that one evening at dusk she had seen Botewi on the roof of the schoolhouse, trying to snare the departing bats with a fish seine as they flew from the air vents.

By a combination of circumstances there was no piano at the Moquo station. The old upright piano in the chapel had been trucked overland to Addis for repairs and hadn't been returned. In the corner of the social hall was a small, dusty pump organ, but Botewi couldn't discover how to operate it and lost interest. He was reasonably certain that the mission contained a piano, as all mission stations did, and that he would discover it in time. But after a month had passed and no piano turned up, his suspicions increased. A variety of other instruments held his interest in the meantime—a few clarinets, a saxophone, a guitar, a few harmonicas, even a snare drum. At the Moquo station's Wednesday social hour some of the instruments were heard one week, some another, but rarely did they all appear together. Botewi waited.

The Wednesday night Botewi realized that he had heard all of the musical instruments Moquo had to offer, and that among those assembled for this evening's entertainment no piano was included, he understood his fate. He slipped silently from the back of the hall before the first chorus commenced and went back to his hut. He lifted his mattress and took out the stolen panga, pocketed the leather pouch of bat bones and dried viscera, hoisted a milk jug over his shoulder, and went out the door. He walked back through the trees in the direction the sun had fallen, climbed the fence, and disappeared across the grasslands in the direction of the Baro station. The panga was thrust through his belt, a clay-and-fiber jug slung over his shoulder, and the light was in his head, as surely as it was in the heads of those he left behind in the social hall where hands were clapping and voices raised to join Bertha Ivy from Muscatine, Iowa, who was playing "When the Red, Red Robin Goes Bob, Bob, Bobbing Along" on the clarinet, accompanied by her sister, Bernadette, on the snare drum.

SIXTEEN

1

The disabled launch was a shallow-draft vessel forty feet long with peeling gray paint and Arabic letters on the bow. One rusty boiler was exposed amidships, no longer in use, its pipes sealed with flanges, but a new boiler was behind it, still serviceable. Aft was a diesel engine so covered with grease that McDermott couldn't guess its manufacture. A dirty canvas tarpaulin patched in places with cotton cloth or burlap was lashed to an iron frame that overhung the boilers, engine, and deck. Two planks had been lowered from the deck to the bank as a gangway. Three Sudanese in khaki shirts and shorts sat on the gangway in the sun, their rifles across their knees. A fourth leaned against the deckhouse and crew quarters behind the boiler, rifle over his shoulder.

The launch had been idled for three days at the bend of the Baro below the mission station, its engine useless, waiting for a steamer from Nasir in the Sudan to come take it in tow. It was the same launch that had surveilled the Baro station for the past several weeks, pounding upstream by day and drifting back silently with the current at night.

McDermott squatted on his heels under the canvas awning, tinkering with the diesel engine, a crew member crouched alongside him silently, watching McDermott's hands, as if waiting for them to show him something he hadn't discovered already for himself. He was the engineer, an African, like Samuel Eko, as black as ebony and wearing filthy blue coveralls cut off at the knees. Unlike the Sudanese with rifles, who wore high-topped army boots, he was barefooted.

"He is Dinka," Samuel Eko said to McDermott, hands on his knees as he leaned over, watching. The black man smiled at McDermott, as if realizing that he had found the same problem.

"They've sheared the drive shaft," McDermott said, standing up and wiping his face. The metal of the drive shaft had crystalized long before and had snapped like a candy cane.

The launch captain stood behind McDermott, a fat Sudanese half-caste wearing a dirty gray *jalibiiya*, his river-wise blue eyes fixed on the sheared shaft. His cinnamon face was stubbled with white whiskers, and his lips were wet as he chewed one of the tomatoes Samuel Eko had brought from the station garden.

"Ask him how they did it," McDermott said, and Samuel Eko spoke to the launch chief in Arabic.

"Logs in the river," Samuel Eko explained.

"That's what they get for running at night."

Samuel Eko laughed and the launch captain smiled too. His name was Mustapha. "Can you fix it?" Samuel Eko asked.

"No, not unless he has another shaft."

The captain didn't have another shaft. He brought a few bottles of warm beer from the wheelhouse, and they moved across the gangway to the riverbank. A few pieces of driftwood had been pulled about a small circle of ash-strewn rocks where the remainder of a campfire was still visible. On the largest rock was a battered tea kettle; a few tin cans and clay pots, recently rinsed in the river, were drying in the sun nearby. A few fish had been cleaned on a flat boulder. The dried scales glistened like mica in the sun; flies swarmed over the entrails nearby. McDermott studied the wheelhouse and the small antenna, wondering about the radio. Mustapha had shown them everything but the wheelhouse, and he wondered which of the crewmen operated the radio. The Sudanese soldiers stayed in the shadows of the deck under the awning.

"Do they know the risks they take," McDermott asked Samuel Eko, still studying the wheelhouse, "tied up here on this side of the river? The other bank would be better."

Samuel Eko translated and Mustapha nodded in agreement. "He knows the other side is better," Samuel Eko said.

McDermott nodded and watched Mustapha take a deck of dirty cards from the pocket of his *jalibiiya*, tap them with his discolored thumbnail, and say something in Arabic to Samuel Eko, who nodded as he listened, first puzzled, and finally laughing.

"He wants to know if you play gin rummy. He learned gin rummy from the British in Khartoum during the war. His engineer plays but he always loses." McDermott looked at the Dinka mechanic, who had seen the cards, too, and was smiling expectantly, the way he had smiled as McDermott had tinkered with the shaft, hoping that he might teach him something he didn't already know.

"He always loses?" McDermott asked, watching the Dinka engineer nod his head emphatically, smiling broadly. "What about the soldiers?"

Samuel Eko asked Mustapha, who grinned as he replied. "He says the soldiers are too stupid to play. You fly a plane and he pilots a launch. He can't fly a plane but he can play gin rummy."

McDermott laughed. "Tell him thanks, but I haven't played gin rummy in years. Maybe next time." The Dinka watched Mustapha pocket the dirty playing cards, and looked back at McDermott, still smiling, as if Mustapha had won the hand, as if McDermott's unwillingness to play had only confirmed what he already knew—that they were both prisoners of predestined events, ruled over by the river and a half-breed Sudanese with his sly, English blue eyes.

"He says next time is all right," Samuel Eko said.

Samuel Eko and McDermott drove back to the mission house, where Emily was in the garden. McDermott joined her and Samuel Eko went back to the village. "Did you speak to the captain?" she asked.

"They sheared the drive shaft." He sank down in the grass.

"Then it *is* disabled."

"I think so." He watched her fingers gathering the beans, saw her shoulders moving under the white blouse, her lean calves flex as she stood and kneeled alternately.

"You're awfully quiet today," she said as she picked up the basket and moved past him to the next row. He could smell the scent of her hair, the fragrance of her blouse, and the softness of her throat. He saw her picking beans, packing her medical kit, filling the bathtub, and the kerosene lanterns on the kitchen table, sitting in the lawn chair, or on the edge of her bed, rubbing cold cream or lotion on her hands. He saw these separate acts in the silence of the African afternoon, concealed in a solitude as remote as the Baro station's—weeks, months, and years of them—saw this solitary, independent, and yet insecure woman accepting each day as calmly as she had accepted the one before. For what? What logic did she find in it? Not God's will; she never talked about God or doing God's work, like every other missionary he'd ever known. Why was she here then? McDermott believed less in the missionary vocation than he did Penny's or the Peace Corps crowd's, who probably thought Jesus a kind of psychedelic turn-on—a sort of twelve-string acoustic guitar in the universal road show.

Emily had moved out of sight behind the tomato plants. He rolled over on his back, closing his eyes. *The mind is a black mirror*, an Air Force psychiatrist had once said in McDermott's presence, the image recalled by McDermott's return to the flight line after six hours of night interceptor exercises along the NATO perimeter in Europe. A team of aerospace doctors had tested him following his return, interested in night fatigue; optical, muscular, and mental aberrations; motor control; endocrine behavior; sugar and carbon dioxide in the bloodstream. The doctors had climbed over McDermott's aircraft like locusts, carrying their testing equipment, but as the cockpit canopy was lifted, the medical team saw not a man at all but only a smoky visor of helmet on which the lights from the incoming jets splintered, gases flared and dissolved, the lights from the tubes along the blast wall bent and warped by fields of gravitation their biological devices knew nothing about. Fifty pounds of physiological monitoring equipment had accompanied him aloft that night, but the medical team saw only the black mirror of helmet returned to them, as if there were nothing within at all. "*The mind is a black mirror*," the young psychiatrist had recalled over coffee in the mess: "That's what I saw—"

"What are you thinking about?" Emily asked, standing over him.

McDermott opened his eyes and looked up, his peripheral vision showing the curve of her leg above the knee where the skirt was flared. He wanted to touch her leg and the warmth of her inner thigh, but sat up instead. She didn't move and for a moment he wondered whether she would have resisted. How many years had it been since he'd made love in the grass with an open sky overhead?

"You finished?" he said, getting to his feet.

After dinner that night he sat in the small radio room, monitoring the radio frequency out of the Sudanese military post at Nasir. The signal was strong as it directed a mobile unit somewhere in the field; but the return signal too weak to be coming from Mustapha's disabled launch. He was certain that the Sudanese were using the launch to monitor the rebels' movements along the Baro, but he doubted that the radio was in use that night. But his mind wasn't completely on his work. He was listening with more attention to the sound of crockery rattling in the kitchen sink.

She stood at the sink in front of the window, washing the dishes and trying not to think of what she would do after they were rinsed and dried, the towels folded, and the pots and pans returned to the shelves. She'd prepared a hot meal that night because it would give her something to do after dinner. Her mind was a blank. A few night moths rattled against the screen. She lifted the skillet, scoured it with the soap pad, listening to the noises from the sideband radio down the hall. She brought the tea kettle from the stove and rinsed it with boiling water, which sent steam against her damp face. Grease clung to her knuckles; the smell of burned gravy and fried potatoes was in her hair, which clung in damp curls to her temples and forehead.

The memory of their last night and morning together had grown stronger as time passed and had become the strongest emotion to her existence, awakening her a dozen times a day to its miracle as she climbed the footpath to the cottage, worked in the clinic or the vegetable garden, leaving her flushed and astonished and shaking her head in dismay.

He had kissed her and tried to make love to her. In the recollection her feelings had assumed a sovereignty of their own. Now they frightened her. They had the power to transform her life, but they were still feelings so profoundly personal that she doubted she would have the courage to share them with any living person, so deeply did they seem to her to deny the past as well as the present. Her hands had stopped in the dishpan, and she stood motionless at the sink, her heart beating faster, not knowing what she would do.

Down the hall McDermott sat listening to the voices on the sideband. One of the voices was quite strong, speaking excitedly from a radio deep in the bush. The second voice was much weaker, and McDermott wondered whether he should go get Samuel Eko to help him interpret the Arabic. But then he heard Emily run back the corridor from the kitchen. She was filling her medical kit in the storeroom when he found her. A small group of refugees had just arrived from the Sudan, some seriously hurt. He watched from the front door as she ran down the path, went back to the radio, and sat listening for a few minutes. "Who gives a damn," he muttered finally, turned off the radio, and followed her.

Twenty Anuak tribesmen fleeing their burning village had been attacked by Sudanese soldiers at their encampment a few kilometers beyond the border. The Anuak had fled in disorder from their evening fire out across the grasslands, leaving their animals and their possessions. Led by a Nuer cattle boy, they had crossed the border north of the Baro station. A few had gunshot wounds; some had knife or bayonet wounds; others had been burned.

Emily and her village nurses worked steadily in the hot, smoky clinic, and McDermott kept out of the way, watching from the side as the wounded were brought to the old surgery table. But when one of the nurses holding the gasoline pressure lantern began to tire, McDermott took her place, holding the light high over Emily's shoulder, moving as she moved, adjusting the light with the arrival of each new patient. She didn't speak; he wasn't even sure she knew he was there. The heat brought water to his face, arms, and shoulders. They worked in the clinic for almost three hours, and when Emily went out into the enclosure to look at her initial patients, he followed her.

"It's all right now," she said. "The flashlight will do."

He left the enclosure and sank down on the cool earth under the trees, his eyes closed. At last he heard her voice as she left the enclosure, too, and roused himself.

"I thought you'd left," she said. "Were you sleeping?"

"Maybe a little."

They walked up the path and out onto the open meadow under the stars. In the kitchen she lit the butane stove and put the kettle on, then filled the tub. She brought him clean towels, but he said he'd use the shower in the brick washhouse. There he took a cold shower under the old galvanized tank while William sat nearby, holding his spear in front of the night fire.

He was waiting in the kitchen as she came out of the bathroom. The kettle was boiling again, and he didn't know what to do with it. Her hair was damp, falling across the collar of her cotton robe; traces of bath powder clung to her throat.

"Maybe I'd better pack it in," he said ruefully, remembering the other night.

"No tea?"

He waited in uncomfortable silence for the pot to be poured.

"Thank you for what you've done," she said afterward in the twilight of the hall. The generator had been turned off; both held flashlights, the beams lowered to the lino of the floor, protection against uncertainty or misunderstanding. Neither had much to say. Both seemed to understand, moved in a direction in which words had lost their potency; speech, its need. Both were tired, both awakened at the same moment to the same postponed possibility—something to be explored at whatever cost. Both were awkward in its discovery.

She resisted his touch for an instant, head back, his face against hers, and then the cry died in her throat as the response arose within her, not impulse at all, but something deeper, flooding her body and lifting her with it. Her mouth suddenly lost its stubbornness and was as soft as a young girl's, opening in the darkness as he lifted the robe from her shoulders. The nightgown slid to the floor and he discovered her body naked against his, his hands along the cool of her back, and the curve of her hips. Her awkwardness was forgotten, like his. They found the moonlight bright on the windowsill, the curtains ghostly white beyond the bed. They were together on the bed, nothing separating them, moving together at last, and when he finally found her and took her and she him, her cry shook him at first. When it came a second time, he started to lift himself, but her arms brought him back against her, and they flowed boundlessly into each other, her cry forgotten, moving beyond the bright bed, the bright window, and the small moonlit rectangle of the Baro station—all just an infinitesimal mote in the vastness of the African night around them.

He awoke in the gray hour before dawn to find her asleep beside him, the chill of the room lying coldly on her arms and shoulders, her hair twisted on the pillow. He brought her against him and she responded sleepily at first; but then her eyes opened, her face, shoulders, and breasts were flushed with warmth as she received him again, without a cry this time, her face and mouth locked softly to his.

When he awoke again, the sun was in the white curtains and the bed next to him was empty. She wasn't in the kitchen. He thought she'd gone to the clinic. He shaved and dressed, waiting for her at the gate as she climbed the path with her bag.

"What are we going to do?" he asked as she fixed breakfast. She glanced at him with a smile, as if to confirm the question, and moved to the stove.

"I'm not sure."

"We've got to do something." Her back was toward him. He unbuttoned the first two buttons of her blouse and kissed her back. She turned and he took her by the waist, his face against her forehead.

"What do you suggest." She knew she could no longer conceal her feelings toward him. Samuel Eko would know; so would William, and then the entire village, Osgood, Hamid—everyone. She couldn't ask anyone to conceal what she could no longer conceal herself.

"I want to get you away from here," McDermott said. "We'll go someplace, wherever you want. The sooner the better."

"Yes, I've been thinking about that too."

That morning McDermott said good-bye to Samuel Eko and William in the road, but took Emily's arm and walked with her toward the plane. "I'll work on something," he said.

"Soon?" she asked. She looked back toward Samuel Eko and old William, who were still watching from the road.

"Soon. As soon as possible."

She nodded. He knew why she had looked back, just as he knew that they were still watching, but he kissed her anyway, and it was a long time before he let her go.

2

Penny had been bored for over two weeks, despite the sunny skies and the turquoise bay at Paros where she swam twice a day and sometimes alone in the evening. The stone villa was on a small promontory overlooking the Aegean six miles from the main fishing village where they sometimes went by foot, by donkey cart, or by taxi. The villa belonged to an American university professor who was a friend of Lizzy's father. There was nothing to do on the island but sunbathe, swim, read, eat seafood, drink the Fix beer they brought by the taxiload from the village, screw, or play cards. Murphy was sleeping with Lizzy again; Eastwick had finally given up on Penny and was chasing one of the smallpox girls, a heavy, almost bovine girl from Oregon. In a bikini and with her white thighs and arms burned to bronze by the Greek sun, she'd acquired a mannered insolence which Eastwick found irresistible.

Penny didn't know whether Eastwick was making out or not and didn't care. She slept alone on the villa roof, out under the stars. Lizzy thought she was playing a role from *Love's Labour's Lost*. Penny couldn't remember whether *Love's Labour's Lost* ended happily or sadly, and Lizzy refused to tell her. "You really ought to go on the stage, Pen," Lizzy advised her on the beach that afternoon. "That way you'd get to *know* the parts you're playing or just discovering."

"*Fuck you*," Penny said, pulling her sunglasses on and sinking back against the beach towel with her three-week-old copy of *Newsweek*.

"It's no use trying to remember what you probably never read in the first place," Lizzy baited. "I'll bet you've never even seen *Love's Labour's Lost*." She sat on a towel near Penny, wearing a one-piece bathing suit, the only one on the beach. Her bony, birdlike body was ultimately defeated by anything other than the shapeless, sacklike garments of the Near East or East Asia. "I'll bet she hasn't," she repeated to Murphy, who slumped down on the sand next to her, winded from his swim.

"Then why don't you whistle it up the old kazoo and play it for me," Penny cried in exasperation, flinging the magazine aside. She'd found an article on the southern Sudan war and had been trying to finish it. "You know what you look like in that sack—some kid from a fresh-air camp!" *Words of one syllable*, she remembered, and just as suddenly heard McDermott's voice. "Oh, God," she moaned.

"What the hell are you two squabbling about?" asked Murphy. Lizzy looked solemnly at Penny, sitting yogalike on the beach towel, her hands on her bony knees. A mist descended over her eyes and she raised her head, trancelike:

"*Cuckoo.* Cuckoo, cuckoo."

"What's that?" Murphy asked.

"*Love's Labour's Lost*," Lizzy muttered, still gazing off into the middle distance. "'When daisies pied and violets blue / And ladysmocks all silver-white / And cuckoo-buds of yellow hue—'"

"Hey, kinda pipe down, will you," Penny called, flat on her back again, the magazine lifted.

"*Shhhh*," Lizzy continued: "'Do paint the meadows with delight, / The cuckoo then, on every tree, / Mocks married men; for thus sings he, *Cuckoo. . .*'"

"You're stoned," Murphy chided.

"Cuckoo. Cuckoo," Lizzy continued, even after Murphy had picked her up, slung her over his shoulder, and carried her off into the sea: "*Cuckoo! Cuckoo!*" Both toppled headlong into the surf.

Eastwick and a few other PC Volunteers came climbing down the rock path from the stone villa, Eastwick carrying a cooler of beer, the girl from Oregon following with a beach umbrella. Penny watched them cross the sand and drop their towels nearby. "I thought you were gonna walk into town," Penny said.

"It's too hot," the girl complained.

"Oh, Christ," Eastwick muttered, looking toward the scrub behind the rim of beach. "We got some more goddamned spectators again." Penny rolled over and looked behind her. A young Greek was driving a donkey cart along the road, but three of the donkeys following him had started to graze in the undergrowth nearby.

"Just the guy I've been looking for," Penny declared, lifting herself to her knees. "Hey, mister!" she yelled. "Would you kinda tell your donkeys to stop shitting all over our beach! It kinda queers up the surf, okay!" The Greek youth didn't hear her, or, if he did, didn't turn. "It's sorta hard on the tourist trade too!"

"I don't see any crud," said one of the volunteers.

"That's because Murph and I cleaned it up. If you climbed out of the sack before noon, maybe you'd see it too."

"Who cares about tourists anyway," Eastwick said.

"Jesus, I forgot," Penny recalled sarcastically. "We're not tourists, are we? We're PCV's, roughing it. Hey, mister! Bring back the shit brigades, get some elephants, too, plenty of them! Constipated cows, camels, anything! Only we're not tourists, okay?"

"*Cuckoo!*" Lizzy sang, sitting on Murphy's shoulders as he stood deep in the water.

"This whole place is freaked out," Penny sighed, sinking back against her towel.

"Why don't you go over to Mykonos then?" said the Oregon girl coolly. She was trying to open the beach umbrella, but each time it collapsed. "I mean if you're so *enthusiastically* unhappy here, maybe you can find some fun over there."

"Because it's fulla tourists," Penny said, shading her eyes with the *Newsweek* to look at the girl. "I mean why do you think we've got these boatloads of donkey manure coming over here after dark, just to dump on our beach. It's because we're not tourists." The girl didn't answer. "The flies are okay. They just live here, like the sand fleas and the sea urchins and the empty beer cans." She swatted a fly with the rolled-up magazine and lifted it from her thigh. "Did you ever see a real Greek fly?" she asked, holding it up toward the girl, still shading her eyes. "This is a real Greek fly. No kidding. He's got a moustache, bedroom eyes, hair on his shoulders, and everything. He'll even be yours if you want him. Like Eastwick." Still the girl didn't look at her. "*Gross!*" Penny threw the fly away and stood up. "God, is this place ever dead."

"Will someone please help me with this *blasted* umbrella," the girl from Oregon complained. Eastwick came loping across the beach. Penny pulled up her bikini and walked down the beach until she reached the rocks on the far side of the cove. She loafed out through waves, her back against the wind, cycling with her legs. She turned and swam out between the rocks at the neck of the lagoon and into the deep sea beyond, where she'd not dared to go alone before. The current was colder and the seas high, just as she'd feared. The wind carried her farther than she'd intended to go but she floated on her back, resting, looking up at the sky. She took off her bikini and tied her pants around one ankle, her bra about the other, just as she had that day at Djibouti. She drifted and swam in the open sea, as solitary as a porpoise, the waves of the Aegean breaking over her slender figure. But the more she swam, the more she remembered the Bay of Tadjoura, and she knew she wanted to weep.

She kept her arms and legs busy, trying to free her mind, but at last her body began to tire and her arms lost their thrust. She turned back toward the lagoon, exhausted, reducing the frequency of her strokes, and rolling her body more emphatically as she swam. Her arms and legs ached as she entered the lagoon, and she barely had the buoyancy or the strength left to keep from being driven against the rocks. Murphy and Liz were standing atop the rocks, watching her, as they'd been watching since they'd seen her enter the open sea; and she gave them a weary wave and swam on. She reached the warmer waters of the beach, sank beneath the water, and put her bikini on. Crawling out of the sea on her hands and knees, she lay full length on the hot sand, her heart pounding, her breath gone, her body drained of its strength. *I did it*, she thought. *I did it*, but even as she remembered, the tears gathered in her eyes, and she lay alone on the beach, heartbroken, her body shaken by sobs, her head turned away from the umbrella far down the beach.

"She was skinny-dipping," Lizzy announced as Penny joined them twenty minutes later.

"Thanks for watching out," Penny said, her voice heavy, her eyes rimmed with red.

"Especially Murph with his binoculars," said the girl from Oregon. They were playing bridge under the umbrella.

"Ophelia, this time," Lizzy sighed. "Definitely suicidal."

Penny lay down on her towel, head down. Murphy splashed cold beer on her back. She sat up and he handed her the bottle. "Here, even if you're too proud to ask." His wild hair sprang out in goatish tufts, wild from the sea; his sunburned Irish face was beet red.

"Are you going to play cards with us or are you going to play busboy?" Eastwick complained.

"Gimme a chance," said Murphy, who didn't like bridge on the beach any more than he did at the frat house. He sat down and rearranged his hand. "What's trumps?" he asked. Eastwick groaned.

Forgotten by the others, Penny drank the cold beer and read *Newsweek* as the sun began to slide against the sea. The foursome argued as they played: Lizzy and Murph wanted to walk into the fishing village for some fried squid for dinner; Eastwick and the girl from Oregon wanted to have a cookout on the villa roof.

"You gotta be kidding!" Penny cried out, on her feet suddenly, holding the *Newsweek* with both hands. "*Sudi!* Are they sure! *Sudi!* Oh, God! I can't believe it!" The others looked at her in surprise. "Of course! How stupid could I be! No wonder he didn't say—*Jesus!* I wouldn't have either!" She was smiling, then laughing as she read. "Oh, my God, I can't believe it!"

> Arms are being flown into the Sudan in unmarked planes and unloaded at remote, hidden airstrips. Sudanese officials have long claimed that the night flights originate in Uganda, but this week's accusations from Khartoum are the first involving Ethiopia. The Sudanese Foreign Ministry claims the Ethiopian night flights originate at Torit or Sudi and are directed by Israeli military advisers. The identity of the pilots is perhaps the best-kept secret of the forgotten war.

"Believe what?" Lizzy asked, slipping from beneath the beach umbrella. "Don't be so cryptic. What is it?" She reached for the magazine but Penny had torn the page out and stuffed it in her halter.

Penny snatched up her beach towel and bag. "I'm on my way," she laughed, running away up the beach. "What time's the boat for Piraeus?"

"You've got three hours," Murphy called after her. "What the hell was it?" he asked Lizzy, who stood leafing through the *Newsweek* blankly.

"I dunno. Something she tore out."

"Look in the table of contents."

Eastwick recognized the cover. "Christ, that's three weeks old. What's so goddamned newsy about that. It didn't even carry the Kissinger speech. Are we playing bridge or aren't we?"

They looked toward Penny, who was still running up the rocks toward the villa.

SEVENTEEN

1

A light rain had fallen that morning and the strip at Sudi was still wet in places from the downpour the day before, when McDermott's mission had been aborted. Gray clouds still drifted over the coffee trees and dragged their shifting tails over the heights above the field. The roads below were muddy and impassable. It had taken two days to bring the weapons up by donkey.

McDermott walked off the field three times that afternoon, but in the ready tent afterward Rozewicz wasn't certain that he wouldn't cancel the flight again, as he had the day before. But McDermott told them to load the plane and went into the tent next in line and lay down. He slept for a little while, but was awakened by the sounds of rain beating suddenly against the canvas. But the sounds died away. A second deluge came a few minutes later, and McDermott knew it was the wind, ripping at the trees below the tents and driving the water from leaves heavy with two days of rain. It was after ten when he awoke—his fingers cold—dressed, and went out on the field with a flashlight, walking it off for a final time. Tadessa was waiting with the mug of hot tea, too hot to drink. He retrieved the Uzi, the web belt, and the .45, left the tent, and walked back to the plane, still carrying the tea mug. An anemic moon shone above the trees to the west where patches of mist still drifted. He stopped, looking back at the moon, the ground soft under his feet, and Tadessa stopped and looked back at the moon, too, smiling.

The moon told him McDermott would fly and that there was nothing to fear. Rozewicz was already in the cabin, readying the plane for takeoff. McDermott looked again at the ground nearby, lifted his shoe, and looked at the sole, as muddy as it had been the previous night.

"Stupid," he said quietly, studying the muddy sole. "It'll be better tomorrow."

An Israeli standing near the wing heard his voice, turned, recognized him, and moved aside. "Sorry," he said,

But McDermott didn't move forward. He watched Rozewicz through the cockpit window, finishing the mug of tea. Tadessa waited nearby for the cup. Always the same ritual, wasn't it? McDermott remembered, his mind not yet made up. A cup given and returned. Someone called to him, but he didn't move. What else was there for Tadessa in all of this—here on this brutal mountainside with its rotting village below, holding his six tubercular children and the wife with the malarial eyes? What conferred status or distinction except this—the cup given and returned—his participation in these night flights which maybe once every week enabled him to hold his head up among his children, his villagers, and his countrymen? Holding the cup and studying the waiting faces nearby, McDermott felt himself linked in some senseless, irrational, and yet absolute way by bonds as slight as these—expectation, habit, pride, trust. Dignity— the only organizing principle he knew, a cycle he had not set in motion yet which he couldn't break. Engines that are fueled must fly; bombs that are armed must drop; lives that are shared together must be protected; duty that is given must be returned. McDermott stood in the darkness of the half-dry field, looking at the silver surfaces of the plane and then to the west, down the misty hills toward the Sudan where the Anya-nya guerrillas were waiting, knowing that it was the wrong night, the wrong field, the wrong plane, and the wrong continent; but knowing, too, that he was now linked too closely with those lives to deny it, linked by a common purpose and a common dignity, too subtly dissolved in their individual lives to be called madness, however irrational their collective goals or ambitions might be.

Didn't he know that the bombing of Phuc Yen or any other airfield in North Vietnam was prohibited, the prosecution had asked.

"I knew."

"But you chose to ignore those orders."

Gophers entering target area. Look alive! he remembered. His friends. *"Yes, I ignored them."*

He stood in the darkness at Sudi, where the mist came like smoke down through the trees. He gave up the cup to Tadessa and crossed to the plane, the Uzi and gun belt over his shoulder.

They waited in darkness from the verges, only the bright coals from a few cigarettes showing. The wind flung itself in wild gusts down the slope, bringing raindrops from the distant trees against the shed roof. The moon cleared the thin haze, but it was the wind that caught Rozewicz's attention until the roar of the engines drove everything else from his mind, the wash of the propellers taming the grasses flat, rattling pebbles and grit like bullets through the undergrowth. The whine of the engines seemed to diminish.

"He's not going," Rozewicz cried in relief, starting forward, but the roar came back and the plane released in a furious thrust and hurtled down the strip. As it swept into the foggy bank of lights, McDermott still hadn't rotated, but twenty yards beyond it did, lifting clumsily into the night sky, Rozewicz moving after it. He heard the wind flattening the treetops higher on the slope, and watched the plane slip sideways, the port wing dipping dangerously. His heart came into his throat. At the same moment he saw the furious thrashing of the wind in the trees along the hillside, cold against his own face, and turning the dark leaves to ghostly white. Then the fierce turbulence overtook the plane and hammered it sideways, its shadow plunging in a half-glide toward the earth, shattering through the treetops in disintegrating fragments and coming to rest with an ugly thrashing of metal against the far slope. Rozewicz sprinted after it.

At the end of the strip he plunged down toward the far slope where the plane rested, tilted precariously, its port wing folded back, the smell of aviation gas already in his nostrils.

"McDermott! McDermott!" The wind had passed and the meadow was deathly quiet. *"Get out!"* he cried. *"Out!"*

He saw the bright worm of flame dance across the folded wing and disappear beneath the fuselage, flinging himself sideways into the wet, shoulder-high grass only an instant before the meadow erupted in a gassy glare, white hot at first as the fuel tanks ignited, sucking the wind from the trees. A tongue of black smoke billowed skyward, obscuring the moon. Only the flames remained, cracking the charred bones of the aircraft and curling away the leaf of aluminum plate in a light furious enough to fully reveal the faces of the advisers who stood behind Rozewicz at the top of the far slope. They approached as close to the plane as the heat permitted, shirts and jackets held in front of their faces.

"*The cabin door's here!*" an Israeli captain called. A few officers joined him quickly, looking down in disbelief at the door lying in the high grass fifty yards from the plane.

"Look for him!" Rozewicz cried. "Below the plane!"

"No! Toward the trees!"

Rozewicz flogged through the high, wet grass, circling beyond the plane toward the trees in the intense light, but he could find nothing— no evidence of any debris or equipment blown in that direction.

"*He's here!*" the captain called from behind him. "*Over here!*"

McDermott was in the grass down the hillside, half-kneeling, half-crouching, almost hidden by the wet undergrowth. His right arm dangled uselessly at his side. His shirt was scorched black and still steaming from the heat of the explosion. Blood covered the right side of his face and he was muttering to himself, dazed and semiconscious: "*Let go. Goddammit, leggo—*" He was still dragging the Uzi, but the holster had snarled itself in the undergrowth and he was pulling at the web belt awkwardly. He didn't see them at first, but even as he finally lifted his head and saw them gathering about him, either he didn't recognize them or his own semiconscious desperation transferred itself to them as well. Every vein in his forehead and every muscle in his neck stood out.

"*Get out of here, you bastards! Get out! All of you! Get out of here!*"

But Rozewicz, too relieved to understand anything except what his heart told him, led the way, believing that he at last understood the truth about this proud, complicated, and tormented man confronting them on the fire-lit hillside.

They carried him to safety, four men lifting the stretcher, and once beyond the danger of the exploding ammo boxes, Rozewicz embraced him like a brother, too moved to say a word, too gratified to remember anything but his own awakening from a similar nightmare in London so many years ago, tormented and death-seeking because life had survived in him, but not mother or father, sisters or brothers—all dead in the concentration camps of Poland. How could he explain to McDermott what he could hardly understand himself? He knew that McDermott had flown in Vietnam and that the experience had been a bitter one. But until that night on the flaming hillside at Sudi, Rozewicz had never understood that McDermott, like himself at an earlier age, might have wanted to die.

The plane burned for six hours, the explosions from the ammo boxes periodically lighting up the night sky like Roman candles. The wind sprang up again, whipping down from the hills above in the same bizarre way that it had as the aircraft took off. Rozewicz thought McDermott had lost power or that the port propeller bearing had failed; McDermott said the vortices of the wind had caught him and hammered him to earth. He'd managed to get out of the plane and had just jumped to the high grass when the explosion came. The Israeli medic thought that the high, wet grass had probably saved McDermott's life. Twenty stitches closed the laceration on his scalp and two bearded advisers helped the medic thrust the dislocated arm back into joint.

The mood in the briefing tent was one of jubilant catastrophe. Beer, whiskey, and vodka were broken out. Everyone was awake; everyone joined in—even the radio operator, whom Rozewicz told to close down for the night. The operator had been trying to raise Addis, but without success. He'd sent an encrypted message, but the acknowledgment was garbled. He had no better luck with the service repeat, and Rozewicz told him to wait until the following day. Everyone was jubilant, festive, even a little self-congratulatory. Those who had been at Sudi the longest, like Rozewicz, got a little drunk. McDermott sat on the cot, drinking with them, still dazed, an olive-drab blanket across his shoulders, his head bandaged, his arm in a sling. He accepted the good wishes, listened to the toasts, and heard the drunken songs, identifying in the noisy, relieved faces the same emotions he had seen among military men elsewhere. He knew that what they were celebrating was not only his own survival, but Sudi's closure, and he celebrated with them.

He awoke at dawn, his arm and shoulder stiff. The Israeli officers lay sleeping on the cots around him in the thin, gray light. A light mist fell over the field as he went outside, wrapped in a poncho. The coals from the campfire behind the tent were still smoldering, despite the rain; but there was another smell—bitter, ammoniac, lying over the field like a pall. He walked back through the rain toward the wreckage, heard Rozewicz's hoarse voice calling to him, and waited, watching Rozewicz come floundering through the mud, boots untied, a blanket over his shoulders, eager to share his contemplation of the previous night's disaster. But McDermott had nothing to say. They stood in the shelter of the trees and looked across the meadow toward the embers of the plane. Nothing was left but the twisted skeleton, outlined in white char. A few wisps of smoke curled up from the ashes here and there. The devastation was complete. A handful of villagers stood on the hillside opposite, gazing down silently at the wreckage. Some had been there since the first light; others had already slipped away, carrying the news of the disaster back to their people. More would come before the day was over.

It was the first time McDermott had ever lost a plane.

2

She sat in the yard that evening at the Baro station, despite the thick cloud cover that hid the moon. To the north and east veins of lightning raced along the horizon like filaments of fire. Earlier that evening a violent wind had thrashed through the trees suddenly, blowing a limb from the old mango tree above the roof. Samuel Eko had come around the house from the fire and said that he'd been unable to get either Radio Omdurman or Cairo on his transistor radio; she'd been unable to find either VOA or the BBC. Atmospheric conditions were responsible, she'd said. Both she and Samuel Eko had been waiting impatiently for the radio reports. The evening before, the Anya-nya marauders who'd been foraging along the border for the past several weeks had fired on Mustapha's disabled launch, the rifle fire audible from the mission cottage. That morning she and Samuel Eko had driven the Land-Rover downriver, but the launch was gone. All they found were the circle of stones, the mounds of ashes, the stakes still driven into the clay bank, and the severed hawsers drifting with the current. Samuel Eko thought the hawsers had been cut by the crewmen during the attack and that Mustapha hoped the current would carry him safely downriver and across the border. When they returned to the village, William Latu was waiting for them. He told them that two of the attacking Anya-nya had been there and gone. They'd claimed they'd killed the launch captain and one of the guards.

She watched the horizon, waiting for the lightning to come again and tell her the direction of the storm. A series of flashes illuminated the savannah to the north, and in their light she saw the vaults of towering gray cloud rising ugly and ominous toward the Ethiopian highlands. A bolt of lightning suddenly lit up the cottage and yard, and she flinched from the shock of the thunder which followed. Samuel Eko had moved to the gate just before the lightning struck, and she saw his figure as clearly as if in broad daylight. A moment later he ran by her and around the house; she got to her feet, thinking the washhouse or one of the trees behind the garden had been hit; but a moment later he returned, carrying his flashlight and machete, followed by William, clutching his spear and sorghum knife. She followed them through the gate, watching Samuel Eko's flashlight beam dart through the high grass at the edge of the airstrip. The thunder rolled to the south, beyond the river.

"Where did you see him?" she asked when Samuel Eko gave up the chase and came back to the road, angry and still winded. He pointed down the track, where old William was moving cautiously through the roadside grass, searching for something. They joined him, searching themselves, and a few minutes later Samuel Eko found it, lying on its side in the wet grass where Dr. Botewi had dropped it the instant the lightning had struck, bounding across the field like a frightened rabbit in the same reflex as Samuel Eko watched. It was as primitive as the other boxes they had found, made entirely of dried twigs and reeds, tied together with vines. This one had broken as it struck the ground, but its contents still carried the message of Dr. Botewi's impotent rage. There was a small, dead frog with a thorn stuck carefully between its eyes, a black beetle, cattle dung, a helix of broken shell from some bird nest, a tuft of animal hair, and the rusty tin from an old tomato-paste can. The frog perhaps best expressed Dr. Botewi's desperation. The eyes were gone and the frog had been dead a long time before Botewi stuck him in the box. He was also desiccated and flat, probably run over by a truck tire.

Emily stood looking down at the broken box. Botewi's antics on the grasslands annoyed her, but she didn't fear him. She had seen him once from the Land-Rover as Samuel Eko's churning wheels flushed him from a roadside ditch—a small, deranged figure scampering through the grass, his rags flapping, weed dust and milkweed in his hair. She pitied his threats, but she feared for his safety. She knew that if the nearby villagers ever caught him, they would kill him with a single blow of their sorghum knives, not because of his foolish boxes, which no one feared, but because they believed him to be the ghoul who fed on the bodies of their dead and whom Nuer tradition permitted them to kill without fear of retribution.

Samuel Eko kicked apart the twig box at his feet, scattering its obscene relics. "Tomorrow we will catch him," he said.

Emily spent the following morning in the clinic and afterward examined Samuel Eko's wife in the confinement hut. The baby was overdue and she was concerned. At noon she spoke to the Moquo station on the radio and was told that a light plane had crashed somewhere in Ilubabor Province and that the pilot had been killed. The Moquo station had been trying to verify the report, learn the identity of the pilot, and confirm an additional rumor that three passengers had died as well. The Moquo operator asked if Emily had seen or heard a plane in distress the previous night; she said she'd seen and heard nothing. But after she closed down the radio, she remembered the storm of the previous night and thought suddenly of McDermott. Her heart skipped a beat, and she stood up, listening. She went out into the hall and stopped again. The house was still.

Turning, she ran down the hall to the porch and it was only there as she saw the grasslands and airfield in sunlight that she was suddenly reassured, Moquo's and Ilubabor's disasters as remote to her as they'd seemed when the radio operator had mentioned the plane crash in her Kansas twang. The sky was blue overhead and she walked out on the track beyond the gate. She knew how carefully McDermott read the sky, just as she knew that he would never have flown in weather as threatening or ominous as that of the previous night.

But that evening Osgood himself was at the microphone of the mission radio at Moquo, the moderator of a round-robin inquest seeking additional information from all of the scattered mission radios in the area regarding the as yet unverified report of a fiery plane crash somewhere in the mountains the previous night. Villagers throughout the area had heard about it and reported the accident to government officials as well as their pastors, but Osgood wasn't privy to the government's information and he'd been unable to identify for himself the location, the aircraft involved, or the pilot. That night on the mission radio network, Osgood was both moderator and pastor, both prattler and physician, but to deliver the eulogy he had first to find the body.

Emily sat in front of the sideband radio, hemming a cotton skirt. The moon was pale through the trees and a fresh breeze lifted at the window curtains. Having convinced herself earlier that McDermott was safe, she was now troubled by Osgood's voice. She listened in the hope that one of the more remote mission stations further inland might have information that would relieve her growing uneasiness. But Osgood gave them little opportunity. She knew that men like Osgood, who carried the Bible so handily in their memories and God so familiarly in their consciences, carried also a complementary obsession with catastrophe. Her years in Africa had taught her that no one lifted his voice so quickly or so loudly to the rumor of disaster as those whose lives had been spent in portentous dedication to words and words alone, Old Testament or New, just as she knew that for men like Osgood only the cruelty of catastrophe enabled them to pluck from their hearts and minds the full-blooded root of their belief in all of its barbarous simplicity. Osgood was admonishing God to deliver up the missing plane when Emily turned off the radio in aggravation. She'd learned nothing that might reassure her.

Late the following morning a plane appeared unexpectedly at the Baro airstrip. She was with Samuel Eko's wife when she heard its engines, and she ran out of the confinement hut and up the path toward the field, thinking it might be McDermott. *It is!* she thought as she ran: *it must be!* her joy and relief told her; but as she reached the strip, out of breath, she didn't recognize the plane that was taxiing toward her. But even as the cabin door opened and she looked past the emerging Ato Tefari, Stone-Ashton, and Shepherd, she didn't give up hope, her hand shading her eyes from the sun. Only as she moved to examine the face of the pilot through the tinted glass did she realize that McDermott wasn't aboard.

"Sorry to come unannounced this way," Stone-Ashton apologized, "but it's rather serious." Ato Tefari stood looking at her expressionlessly, his heavy lips prominent, his thick lids half-concealing his cinnamon eyes.

"Won't you come into the yard out of the sun," Emily said, bitterly disappointed, her face still flushed from her dash up the hill. She avoided Ato Tefari's gaze.

The three men had flown into Baro to inform her of the joint Ethiopian-UN decision to close the Baro station and evacuate the village to the UN resettlement area to the east. As a result of the most recent Anya-nya attack on the disabled launch—an attack which had taken place within rifle range of the mission house—the Sudanese government had vowed to seal off the border with troops and end its cooperation with the UN refugee effort unless the Baro station was closed and the village evacuated. Thousands of Sudanese refugees seeking escape from the war would suffer if the nearby border was closed, denied the food and medical aid available in the UN resettlement zone. The UN and the Ethiopian government had agreed that closure of the Baro mission and the removal of the village would serve everyone's interests. "We certainly recognize that you don't cooperate with the insurgents and that you don't condone what they do," Stone-Ashton said sympathetically, "but nevertheless, more effective measures must be taken if we are to secure the tranquility of our relief effort."

"I understand," she said quietly, without surprise. She'd expected it. Avoiding Ato Tefari's repellent face, she looked at Shepherd. A simpler, less heroic man, he was silent and embarrassed. "What about the village?" She was troubled by the sheer physical problems of resettlement. "I assume they will be given land of their own."

"The village will be evacuated by government truck," Ato Tefari said dryly. "That is my responsibility."

"I would hope that the UN will help out."

"It is not the UN's responsibility, not in any way," Ato Tefari declared.

"We'll do what we can," Stone-Ashton murmured, "but I must say, we have full confidence in Ato Tefari's judgment in this regard, as does Dr. Mulegeta. I'm convinced that it will be managed splendidly."

"It must be done quietly, without disruption," Emily said, looking calmly at Ato Tefari.

"Our soldiers are disciplined," Ato Tefari said coolly.

"Soldiers?"

"Soldiers," he repeated, his face as expressionless as before as he returned her gaze. He folded his cane under his arm, turned, and went back under the trees toward the gate and the waiting aircraft. She stood watching him, but not thinking of him at all. It was as if her mind had simply failed to respond to what they had told her.

"I'm sorry, terribly sorry," Stone-Ashton said.

She nodded. "It would be helpful if you might send some observers from your office to oversee the relocation. UN observers."

"We'll do everything we can. But I am sorry. I want you to know that."

"I'm sorry too," she admitted. "Terribly sorry. But I can't think about it now." She looked out through the trees toward the open savannah. "It's been a busy week."

"Indeed it has. Frightfully. Guerrilla attacks, drought, plane crashes—"

"Plane crashes?" She turned toward him.

"Yes. Didn't you hear? Dreadful thing. Bloody awful—"

"I heard a rumor, nothing more. Whose plane was it?"

"Then you didn't hear. McDermott's. The chap that flew for us. Didn't get out, poor fellow. Bloody awful the way it went. Crashed in a storm. Lit up the entire mountain, they say."

She didn't move, rooted to the spot, her eyes never leaving Stone-Ashton's face, her cheeks as white as chalk. He realized his blunder at once. "Look here. I'm dreadfully sorry. But I thought you knew. How clumsy of me. Please—"

"I must go into the house," she muttered through her frozen lips, turning away. She went across the porch and down the hall, moving like a somnambulist into the bedroom, where she shut the door and sat down on the bed. But as the moments passed, she knew that she would get sick if she sat still, so she crossed to the guest bedroom across the hall. But the sight of the empty bed made her physically ill. She turned blindly away and went into the bedroom and locked the door. She washed her face and dried it, trying to keep her hands busy, but the paralysis of her mind at last released her as she held the towel to her face.

She heard a sob from within the towel, an ugly, lacerating sound that stabbed at her throat like a knife blade. She sobbed unnaturally once, twice, then a third time. Lifting her head in fright, she saw her face in the mirror, as if discovering another face hiding there, and recoiled in shame, falling heavily against the iron tub. She lifted the jar of cold cream from the table and with all her strength smashed the jar against the mirror, splintering the surface in a thousand facets. The old mirror collapsed forward, leaving the frame blank as it splintered in the washbasin, showering fragments over her head and shoulders as she sat on the floor, finally alone, and sobbed like a schoolgirl.

Stone-Ashton and Shepherd waited outside on the front steps. "I had no idea," Stone-Ashton muttered for the tenth time, "no idea at all she'd be so upset. I feel a bloody fool. Did you have any idea she'd take it this way? Did you? Did you have any idea?" he continued, wanting to blame Shepherd as much as himself.

"She always kept her feelings bottled up inside," Shepherd drawled. "She always has. As long as I've been here."

"Of course she keeps things bottled up," Stone-Ashton cried. "It's discovering what's kept bottled up that I'm asking about! Should we go in or shouldn't we? Think, man. You've dealt with her. What do we do?"

Shepherd chewed reflectively on a few blades of grass, his head turned toward the grasslands, like a farmer studying his fields. Stone-Ashton waited for an answer as the sun beat down furiously on his head. But seeing Shepherd sitting there stupidly, a few weeds sticking out of his mouth, he knew that Shepherd had no answer either, and quite suddenly the vanity that had kept Stone-Ashton's courage intact all of these many years snapped like a broken brace.

He knew what he should have known from the beginning—that the UN was no substitute for the Foreign Office; that men of substance, promise, or accomplishment didn't waste their careers in godforsaken backwaters like these, consoling neurotic women shut up hysterically in abandoned cottages; that governments worth dignifying with the name didn't lie to each other so consistently or so outrageously, exchanging fraudulent diplomatic notes in resolving the crimes committed by murderous brigands who killed and looted in the name of the Rights of Man; that bureaucrats equipped for international polity didn't encourage their wives' artistic bent in anemic, coloring-book pastels, hoard ten-year-old orange brandy on their sideboards until it had congealed to marmalade, or gather together like poorhouse gentility to tell each other ghost stories about flesh-eating crocodiles and man-eating termites in the expectation that, feeling their flesh crawl, they might know they were still alive.

"Oh, God!" Stone-Ashton cried out passionately, suddenly begging for deliverance. "Oh, God in heaven!" he entreated dizzily, spinning away from the porch steps toward the gate and the plane that had begun to crank its engines on the field beyond.

3

Good God! What happened!" Penny cried as she saw McDermott leave the front seat of the Land-Rover. He dropped the bag as she flung her arms around his neck, too surprised to do anything but hold her for a minute, his face against her blond head.

"Jesus, where'd you come from?" he asked quietly.

"Surprised you, didn't I?" She smiled, looking up at him. "But what happened to your face?"

His forehead was bandaged, one eye discolored, and his nose and jaw scabbed with cuts. "A little problem. An accident."

"What kind of accident?" She looked from McDermott to Roze-wicz who sat on the front seat of the Land-Rover, waiting. A second man she'd never seen before sat in the backseat.

"I lost the plane. When did you get in?"

"This morning. Lost the plane?"

"A little bad luck. I've got to go see Cohen. Stick my bag in the bedroom, will you."

"You're leaving right *now*? You just got home. Wait! Don't leave without me, okay?"

Rozewicz climbed into the rear seat when Penny reappeared, making way for her. Like McDermott, both he and the third Israeli were unshaven, their khaki shirts powdered with dust and smelling of woodsmoke.

"What do you mean, lost the plane?" she asked as they drove out the gate.

"Just that," McDermott said.

"Where—at Sudi?"

"Yeah—at Sudi." He was surprised she remembered.

"How'd you get back then?"

"We hitched a ride on a DC-3."

"You mean the plane crashed?" she asked, still trying to under-stand. "It just crashed?"

McDermott nodded, but didn't say anything more. *My God, here we go again*, she thought hopelessly. McDermott turned off the main road and drove back the rocky road to Cohen's villa.

"I'm confused," Penny persisted as McDermott honked at the gate. "The plane crashed with you in it or someone else?" The gates were heaved back and they drove forward as the Alsatians barked furiously. Three other vehicles were parked in the drive. On the porch above, Mrs. Cohen left her chair and walked to the railing, watching them leave the Land-Rover. Penny was closest to her. "It's just us," she called up, leaning over to stroke the brindled Alsatian that was sniffing her ankles. But Mrs. Cohen was looking at McDermott. She started to speak, stopped, looked helplessly at Rozewicz and the Israeli with the red beard, then back at McDermott, and disappeared from the railing. A moment later Cohen himself appeared, flanked by his two advisers. He stood silently at the railing, looking down at McDermott. Carefully he removed his dark glasses.

"What the hell's going on?" McDermott asked. Cohen looked at Rozewicz, his gray lips white, his mouth open—a thin, black line. Rozewicz had been puzzled, too, standing to one side, his brow furrowed, listening to the exchanges in Hebrew on the porch above. But then he had understood, shaking his head in resignation as he turned to McDermott.

"It's you," he muttered. "They're surprised to see you." The radio transmissions from Sudi had been garbled the first night and the error sustained in the transmissions that followed. The "accident" reported in cipher had been thought a euphemism. Cohen and the Israeli staff thought McDermott had been killed in the crash.

One of the officials from the Israeli embassy left the porch and hurried away. "How do such things happen?" Mrs. Cohen asked painfully, her dark eyes abashed. Her husband gestured expansively.

"Such things happen all the time." It didn't satisfy her; yet no one seemed to see the question repeat itself in her gaze except Penny, who waited for the answer. But Cohen had moved on, explaining his dilemma following the news of McDermott's death. He'd immediately requested instructions from Tel Aviv. The involvement of an American pilot in an Israeli operation targeted against an Arab country from the soil of a neutral Third World nation raised the most serious diplomatic and political problems. How was the matter to be handled? How could it best be explained to Israel's advantage? Were there any advantages? Tel Aviv had replied to Cohen's request with a request of its own: more facts.

Cohen lifted a telegram from the patio table and read it aloud. Rozewicz listened with growing morosity. McDermott sipped his second whiskey but said nothing, listening to Cohen explain the intricacies of his tactical problem. The other Israeli staff members sensed McDermott's indifference, Rozewicz's scorn, and grew uneasy. Mrs. Cohen was embarrassed and twice suggested that they discuss it another time. Cohen ignored her. McDermott's return had solved the problem, but hadn't released the mental energies Cohen had been devoting to the problem for almost twenty-four hours. He had prepared three drafts for Tel Aviv's consideration. The first suggested an official response if McDermott's activities had been linked in the press to the Sudanese operation; the second proposed language for raising it with Washington; the third, for discussions with the Ethiopian government.

The light faded from the porch. Two cars came into the drive. The Israeli embassy official who'd so quickly departed upon McDermott's arrival returned to the porch with the draft of a proposed cable to Tel Aviv. A third car entered the gates and the Alsatians had to be chained.

"Dr. Mulegeta is here," Cohen's secretary announced quietly, returning from the rail. "Shall I wait with him in the salon?"

"Yes. I'll be in in just a few minutes," Cohen said, scanning the telegram under the table lamp. Frowning, he inked in two sentences of his own language, altered a few words, and initialed the draft with a flourish. He pocketed his pen, looking first at McDermott and then at Rozewicz. "Deliverance and success," he said triumphantly. "In two months Sudi will be no more. Tel Aviv has agreed to give the Emperor three swift ships, to be based in Masawa. As a result, we've persuaded the Ethiopians to close down the Baro mission station and evacuate the village. In two months' time we'll begin flying weapons into Baro with a DC-3, to be taken across the border by porter. No flights into the Sudan, of course—we were unable to get them to agree to that— but in terms of total payload, we'll have a great advantage over the Sudi operation."

"Another two months!" Rozewicz bellowed. "Swift ships?"

"Shhhh," Cohen soothed. "Dr. Mulegeta is in the next room. We'll discuss the modalities. It wouldn't do for him to know our impatience."

"Two months!"

"What do you think?" Cohen asked McDermott. "The DC-3? No problem with that?"

"We'll talk about it later." He took Penny by the arm and left the porch.

"Am I going out of my mind or what?" Penny asked as the gates banged shut behind them. They were alone.

"I doubt it."

"What's wrong with that jerk, anyway?"

He didn't answer.

She waited, and then she said, "I know about Sudi. I guess you think all that back there didn't make much sense to me, but it did." She watched him as he drove, but he didn't turn. "I wasn't snooping or anything. I read a piece in *Newsweek* and I sort of put two and two together. You were flying into Sudan. I think that's pretty fantastic."

He looked at her face, and finally understood why she was back. "It wasn't fantastic. It was just a half-assed operation that wasn't going anyplace and wasn't helping anyone." His body still ached from the battering he'd taken in the crash, and he hadn't slept well in two nights.

"At least you were trying to do something."

In the darkness of the patio he nearly fell over the steps. She moved ahead of him, turning on the lights. He stood uncertainly in the living room, unbuttoning his shirt, but he couldn't pull it from his shoulder. He remembered the telephone call he wanted to make, found the telephone, and called the Moquo mission station representative in the capital. He asked him to tell Moquo to relay a message to Emily Farr at the Baro station the following day. He would be flying down within two days.

She watched him from the door. "In two days?"

"Maybe tomorrow." He went into the bedroom, still wearing the shirt over one shoulder and sat down on the bed. With great effort he took off one boot. He sat up and took a deep breath. "My goddamn ribs are killing me. My head hurts." He bent over and took off the other boot.

"Do you want me to fix you something?" she asked, watching him stretch out painfully on the bed.

"Maybe a drink."

"Don't you kind of think you've had enough?" He didn't answer and she went into the kitchen and fixed a whiskey. "Who mixed your drinks while I was gone? Who cooked your steaks?"

"I ate out." He took the glass and sat back. "Thanks."

"I'll bet. I said I got back today, but I didn't. I got back two days ago."

"Why'd you say that then?"

"I don't know. Maybe because I didn't want you to think I was anxious or anything." He didn't answer. "Tell me about the plane. It just burned, all of it? Burned up—totaled?"

"All of it."

"How'd you get out?"

"Climbed out. Jumped out. Blown out . . . I don't know."

She sat on the edge of the bed, studying his face. "You're not a born-again Jesus freak now, are you? Calling up those missionaries like that?"

McDermott laughed painfully, his ribs aching. "Not yet."

"Don't laugh," she said solemnly. "It happens."

"Not to me. I was raised in a Methodist orphanage."

She sat studying him silently, trying to imagine what had happened, how the plane had crashed, how he had gotten out, but she could visualize nothing. "Let's get out of here," she said suddenly. "Let's go away, far away. Montana maybe. Utah. Alaska. Anyplace."

"My contract's not up."

"Let's think about it, can't we? I hate it—you being stuck here the way you are. Sudi and everything else. It's not worth it. It just isn't."

"Why'd you come back then?"

"I don't know. Maybe I was stupid." She kicked off her sandals and lay down beside him on the bed. "It's hard to explain. It was just a feeling I had. It was just like this was the only place I wanted to be." Her head was against the pillow, her face toward him.

"Only it wasn't, was it? It was just someplace else."

She smiled for a moment. "No, not anymore. That morning after I came back from Athens, I went out to the airport to see if I could find your plane. I wanted to surprise you, but the only thing I saw was the Land-Rover. The next morning I went out again. The plane still wasn't there, and all I could think of was *Screw the blasted war, just screw it.* It wasn't any big deal anymore, not flying into the Sudan, not the rebels, not anything. I went up on the airport roof and had a cup of espresso. Then I caught a taxi back here and sacked out. It was raining and the house was dead. It was awful. I couldn't stand it. I couldn't relate to anything—not to anything else. It was like being dead. Only I couldn't leave. I just couldn't." She turned her head away and lay quietly, her blond hair twisted under her neck. "It's no good saying it doesn't happen. It does and people get wiped out and that's all there is. Maybe it's not idyllic, you and me—Alfred Lord Tennyson, or some perfect Camelot, the perfect fake romance, but it happens."

"You're just tired—tired of knocking around. Of living out of a backpack, being alone."

"Sure," she sighed, her head still on the pillow, her face still turned away. "Tired. Just freaked out, kid. Just screwed up, kid. Like always. Catch another plane, take Air France, see you around the campus, kid, the regs say no. I knew you'd say that. You think we couldn't make it together, just the two of us—that I'd get tired or you'd get tired, or I'd run off again." She sat up and wiped her eyes. "We could go to California or maybe Oregon. Just us. No one else. I've got a little money and that's all we'd need for starters. When two people are together, really together, that's all that matters. We could make it. I know we could."

"How do you know?" She seemed different to him, more relaxed, self-assured. Was the difference in him or in her?

"I just do," she said, leaning against his shoulder. She closed her eyes as she felt his arm around her waist and could feel his heart and smell his shirt.

"What would you do in California?" She didn't lift her head. "It rains there like everywhere else."

"If it rained, we'd do something else: watch the fishing boats come in, maybe drive up the coast and have a picnic in our rain gear. We could always do something. We'd make the world come to us. I know we could. There's one thing else, too." It was the secret she'd kept from him the longest.

"What's that?"

"You love me too," she said, her eyes still closed. "I wouldn't feel this way if you didn't. Why else would you put up with me? I know you do." She smiled, knowing he was watching her face. "So just don't give me any of this 'Goodnight, Irene' bull anymore." Her eyes were still closed. "You do."

It was late and he was tired. What could he tell her?

EIGHTEEN

1

Samuel Eko's son was born at six o'clock in the morning. An hour later one of the Nuer nurses carried the child out into the sunshine of the clinic enclosure, wrapped in a blue blanket. She let the father touch the face, the arms, and the tiny fingers. The wrinkled new face was contorted with rage, its body trembling as it howled the air from its lungs. The more the child screamed, the more pleased was the nurse, who rocked him in her arms.

Emily came into the enclosure from the mother's bedside and looked again at the child, whose tiny scarab face still held her transfixed, despite her weariness. Her face was moist and colorless, her hair bound in a midwife's scarf, but now she removed it, stepping away from the child. Samuel Eko stood studying his son, frightened by the infant's size and its incredible energy. He tried to still the howling lips with his fingers, but the nurse fended his hand away. Instead he lifted the edge of the blanket and peered at the tiny, crablike legs. "He's fine," Emily assured him, remembering his concern. The child had none of his mother's afflictions. Samuel Eko's sister-in-law came to look at the child, bringing their mother, too, and Emily moved aside. Beyond the enclosure opening William Latu and a few of the younger men waited, too, but they were dressed in olive-green fatigues, and on their collars was the brass emblem of the Anya-nya. She knew then that the rumors she had heard were true: none of the younger men of the village intended to be resettled to the east. They intended to go to the Sudan and fight.

Someone called to her from the door of the clinic and she turned away gratefully and went inside. An hour later she climbed the path to the cottage. As she turned through the gate, she suddenly realized that she had less than twenty-four hours left. The Ethiopian military trucks would transfer the villagers the following morning. She would leave after they did, taking Amina and the baby with her in the Land-Rover to Gambela and then Moquo. She stood at the gate, looking at the cottage and the garden beyond, where she hadn't had the courage to work since the news came. With Samuel Eko's baby here there was nothing left for her to do. She intended to spend only a few days at Moquo. Where would she go then—to Kenya, Uganda, back to the Congo? No, never. She was physically and mentally exhausted, perhaps morally too. Her time had come to an end, like most of the missionaries she knew, but their vocations had survived their calling. Yet they still clung to them, like Osgood—poor, frightened man—in grotesque parody of the duty that had brought them here. They had no place else to go. She would go back to Vermont. Perhaps she could work for a doctor in some rural village, find a small farm in the mountains. But she would never again find a wilderness so vast and so beautiful as this. She stood at the gate, motionless, looking west across the grasslands.

She wandered aimlessly through the house, collecting those few personal possessions not already packed. Little in the cottage belonged to her. The furniture was owned by Moquo—the crockery, the linen, even the chipped blue plates on the pantry shelf. The house was silent and the curtains stood away from the windows. She sat alone at the kitchen table, a cup of tea in her hands, staring out across the silent savannah as if waiting for the emptiness to claim her, and in the stillness it seemed to. Her body was drained, her mind empty.

She slept that afternoon, fully clothed, awoke in the late afternoon, and went to the clinic to see Amina and the baby. Samuel Eko wasn't there. She searched for him among the huts, but couldn't find him. As she entered the front gate again, she saw the Land-Rover parked in the side yard, the windows rolled up and the doors locked. The keys were on the kitchen table. Dusk fell and he still hadn't come. In the washhouse his *jalibiiya* and skullcap were hanging on the hook behind the door, his clay coffee bowl on the shelf together with the coffee beans, and the small harmonica. Old William was sharpening his sorghum knife on a whetstone in front of the fire. He refused her request to go to the village in search of Samuel Eko because Dr. Botewi might still be in the surrounding fields: he wouldn't leave Emily alone. The most he would do was lean over the front gate, asking the herdsmen passing in the dusk if they would deliver a message to Samuel Eko in the village.

But he finally came. At ten o'clock William rapped at the screen door. Standing on the front porch, she heard the chanting of the village children beyond the front gate:

"*Hajii Mazoot! Hajii Mazoot! Hajii Mazoot!*"

They were marching in place as they chanted, their feet drumming the dust from the track, their small, excited faces illuminated by the lanterns carried by a few of the villagers who had come to say farewell. The younger village men were also there, standing or resting in the grass before they began their long march. Some carried spears, others bows and arrows, but only a few, like William Latu, carried rifles. She studied each face in turn, all of them now soldiers in some ragged village militia, dressed unfamiliarly in tattered olive twill, on their way to join the Anya-nya in the Sudan. At last she found Samuel Eko, who sat in the grass at the end of the column, wearing a wrinkled uniform and holding an old Italian musket across his knees. She stood in front of him, tears suddenly in her eyes, but he didn't look up at her. A few voices called to him and he smiled self-consciously. A dark hand put a twill cap on his head, but he took it off in embarrassment.

"You too?" she asked, struggling to control her voice. But he didn't turn his head, and she kneeled in the dust, her arms around his shoulders, her wet face against his black cheek. "Samuel Eko," she pleaded, "the child—" She was crying.

William Latu moved to her side and kneeled beside her.

"I promised the child," Samuel Eko said, lifting her arms away and calling old William from the gate. Gently he tried to bring her to her feet, but she sat there, her head down, still crying. William the watchman crouched next to her, nodding to William Latu and then Samuel

Eko, and he watched them as they joined the others who were already moving forward in the darkness, their lanterns extinguished.

At noon the next day the villagers were still gathered in the meadow between the airstrip and the village, their belongings at their feet, waiting for the Ethiopian trucks that had been promised for ten o'clock. The cattle had left at dawn, driven eastward by the village cattle boys. By three o'clock the trucks still hadn't arrived. Neither had the UN observer team promised by Stone-Ashton. Emily told the village elders that the families could disperse for an hour. At four o'clock they gathered again, restless and uneasy. By six the trucks still hadn't come. Many of the villagers gathered up their possessions and returned to their abandoned huts to prepare their evening meals. With the younger and most vigorous men now gone to the bush to join the Anya-nya, the community was leaderless, apprehensive, and confused. A few of the old men, silent until then, began to complain bitterly about the evacuation. Some of the old women retired to their huts to sleep.

On orders of Ato Tefari the UN had removed Emily's sideband radio and left her with a UN portable unit provided its own technicians in the field, but it was inadequate. She'd called Gambela a dozen times without success; Moquo was beyond reach. As dusk fell, she was close to despair, knowing that the orderly evacuation she'd rehearsed with the villagers would be much more difficult at night. But then quite suddenly the trucks appeared, bouncing over the track in convoy, their lights gleaming ominously through the gathering dusk. They also came much too fast. As the young children waiting at the top of the meadow first spied them, they immediately fled for the safety of their empty huts, shouting, "*Galla! Galla! Galla!*"

She saw the lights from the radio room as the trucks circled in the meadow, the cloud of dust they stirred up already obscuring their headlights and their silhouettes as it blew down over the hillside, where other villagers began to take flight. She ran from the house and down the track, but before she could reach the meadow, two armed Ethiopian soldiers blocked the way. "I came to help," she said desperately. "We've been waiting since this morning. Everything is ready. They've rehearsed—"

"Back. Back," one soldier said emphatically, pointing toward the cottage. "Go."

"But I can help."

He took her arm and pulled her back up the track, stopped, and then shoved her forward.

"Officer! Officer. Please. Can you help me!" The Ethiopian officer who'd been talking to an NCO turned at the sound of her voice and crossed to the road, his flashlight held against her face. "My name is Farr. Please—I know these people. If you let me help, I'm sure we can manage it."

"Everything is taken care of," he told her. "There will be no problem. Is that your house? You should go there."

"But I can help."

"There is no need. What can you do?" He was a young officer wearing a brown beret, and a yellow scarf. His face was tired. He told her that the trucks had been on the road most of the day, had left without adequate rations, and had twice lost their way. He knew of no UN observer team. This was Ethiopian territory and he was carrying out his military orders. He turned and left her on the path.

"But I'm sure I can help!" He didn't turn. Along the edge of the village, she saw two Ethiopian soldiers dragging two young children from an empty hut. An old woman followed, shouting at them. A young mother tried to free the child from one of the soldiers, but another soldier took her from behind and dragged her up the hill, kicking and screaming. Frightened by the soldier's brutality, a few villagers who'd been assembling peacefully near the first truck began to slip away into the darkness.

"They're frightened!" Emily cried out. "Talk to them, please! Can't you speak to them?"

She attempted to slip by the soldier who still blocked her path, but he thrust his rifle against her. She refused to yield and he slammed it forward a second time, sending her reeling backward on the path. Regaining her feet, she ran back the track toward the cottage but veered off short of the fence and ran to the river, slipping down the hill to the bank which she followed, head down, until she was below the village.

She fell over a beached piroque, scraping her shin and knee, struggled to her feet, and ran up the path and into the village.

A few huts were in flames. An old woman near the center of the village had fallen trying to escape the soldiers and her lantern had spilled flaming kerosene across the wall of her hut. As Emily staggered into the clearing behind the clinic, the flames had spread, the villagers were in full flight, many running for the river, while the Ethiopian soldiers had made torches from the bundles of dried thorn and were pursuing them. In the light of a burning hut Emily found Amina Eko hiding inside the clinic enclosure, slumped against the ground, her withered leg twisted under her, the blanket-wrapped baby against her shoulder. Emily pulled her to her feet and they slipped out the gate, turning toward the river, drifting embers blown by the heat moving against their faces. Shots came from the meadow above, where the Ethiopian soldiers were trying to force the villagers they'd rounded up into the trucks. As they crossed the clearing, Emily saw an Ethiopian soldier's silhouette limned against a curtain of burning straw, his rifle raised toward an old man who was dragging a goat away into the shadows.

"*Stop it!*" she cried. "*Stop it!* Don't you understand!"

The soldier lowered his rifle and stared at her in astonishment. Ahead of her, Amina had fallen on the path, swept aside by two young mothers and their fleeing children. Emily snatched up the baby and was lifting Amina to her feet when a terrible, chilling pain slashed across her back and slammed her forward into the tangle of undergrowth above the ravine, still clutching the baby. She collapsed into the ravine, head back, her legs twisted under her, her back numb, lying amid the refuse from the huts nearby along the edge of the embankment. As she lay there in agony, the pain scalding her spine and neck, even her scalp, her mind seemed to drift at last, but each time the weight of the small infant against her shoulder fetched her back. She didn't know how long she lay there. At last she tried to change her position and sit up, but the pain forced her back. Above her she heard shots, feet thudding along the bare path, other voices, too, more deliberate now, speaking Amharic, not Nuer. The leaves from the trees still stirred in the wind sent up by the blazing huts. Far away she heard the sound of engines starting up. At last she found the will to lift herself, crying out at the pain, but forcing herself to her side. She slowly pushed her way up the bank with her legs, the child against her shoulder. When her eyes were level with the path, she twisted her head, searching for Amina Eko. She lay only a few feet away, lying where she had fallen. But dozens of villagers and soldiers had passed by then, and she lay to one side, her slight bulk no more recognizable than a few gouts of rag and bone now lying intermixed with the mud and dust in which they were embedded.

Emily slid down the bank in terror. *I'm dreaming. I'm dreaming, of course. Tomorrow it won't be this way at all.* She lowered herself to the bottom of the ravine and began her long, agonizing crawl up the far slope. By the time she reached the crest, most of the village behind her lay in ashes. She left the cool mud bank behind her and crawled through the wet grass, dragging herself only a few feet at a time before she was forced to rest. She couldn't look overhead. She heard no voices, saw no figures. When she finally reached the wire fence, midnight had long passed. Dawn was only a few hours away. "*William,*" she called weakly, barely able to speak. "William," she repeated, but her voice was only a husk, carried away by the night silence. Her fingers clutched the wire fence. She lifted herself and sat slumped forward, raising her eyes at last to the cottage.

Fresh flames flickered through the open windows. The interior was ablaze.

2

Reverend Osgood was worried. Three times he'd tried to raise the Baro station on the radio that evening and three times he'd failed. On the following morning the Swedish hospital reported to the UN that a group of wounded, panic-stricken villagers from the

Baro station had taken refuge in the hospital compound. A Swedish doctor fishing alone on the river had reported seeing smoke on the horizon at dawn. When Osgood learned that a chartered plane flown by a German pilot was en route to the Baro station from Addis, he asked if the pilot would stop and pick him up. Osgood was scheduled to accompany Stone-Ashton to Baro early in the afternoon, but the charter would put him there ahead of the UN group.

McDermott had hired the aircraft himself and was sitting in the copilot's seat, shoulder and arm still stiff, when the German pilot relayed Osgood's request. He reluctantly agreed.

As he climbed aboard, Osgood was flabbergasted to see McDermott sitting in the copilot's seat. "Land sakes alive, son! Everyone out this a-ways thought you were dead."

"So I heard," McDermott said. "What happened to Emily Farr's radio?"

"Radio?" Osgood blinked in recollection, fumbling with the seat belt. "Radio? I don't rightly know. It was all right last time I heard." He leaned forward from the seat behind and grasped McDermott's arm. "Thank the Lord you're all right, son. I know the folks out here will be happy to hear."

"Fasten your seat belt," the German pilot told him at the end of the grass strip.

"Sure will. How do you work this thing-a-ma-jig, anyway?"

McDermott leaned back and fastened it with a jolt. "Take it up," he said.

They flew southwest through scattered clouds, Osgood in the rear seat, the camera around his neck, jotting down idle notes for his monthly pastoral letter to church subscribers in the US. But a few details were still unclear in his mind. He leaned forward and tapped McDermott on the arm. "How come you were asking about the radio?" he asked.

"Because I've been trying to get a message to her for three days." He didn't turn.

Osgood studied McDermott's battered silhouette, looking at the cuts on his cheekbone and jaw. He made a few idle notations in his leather notebook, popped his ears, put a stick of chewing gum in his mouth, and worked it over vigorously as he gazed out the window.

A faint morning haze still drifted over the gorge of the Baro, mixed with the pall from the smoldering fires in the razed village and the burned-out shell of the mission house under the trees. Only the brick walls remained standing. McDermott's eyes traveled the lawn, the footpath to the clinic, and back along the track to the west toward the border.

"*Lord God almighty!*" Osgood gasped. "Looks like Satan himself has been here." He stopped chewing and unslung the camera from his neck, screwed himself around in his seat, and tried to take a picture, but he was too late. "Are you going to come around again?" he asked the pilot.

"Don't be a fool," the pilot said in accented German, dropping the landing gear.

McDermott was thrust forward in his seat, already unbuckling his seat belt as the pilot turned the plane toward the cottage. Osgood was slow leaving his seat and McDermott thrust past him, dropped to the ground, pulled the first-aid kit from the storage hold, and ran back the path toward the mission house. If there had been any survivors, he knew that she would have taken them to the river.

Osgood trotted through the front gate, the camera bouncing around his neck, but soon came to a halt in front of the burned-out cottage.

"Lord help us," he breathed, gazing through the charred door-frame and into the collapsed interior. "Lord help us all." He unslung the camera and peered into the range finder. But suddenly he heard a sound and lifted his head. The sound came again and he stepped lightly through the grass and up the tilting steps, identifying the sounds of boards being moved, the ring of collapsed roof tin, the fall of plaster rubble, and the bong of a piano string. In the corner of the gutted front room he saw a pall of plaster dust. "Praise the Lord," he whispered, "she's here." He stepped forward under the doorframe. "She's here," he whispered weakly. "She's here. Praise everyone."

The pall of dust and the fever of his excitement had left a damp mist on his spectacles and he slipped them off eagerly, retreating a half-step to wipe them on his handkerchief. As he moved his head, the black panga whistled like a guillotine blade just under his left ear and buried itself in the erect timber of the doorframe, quivering like a javelin. Osgood never identified the black arm that held it. The frame trembled convulsively and the parallel timber atop the frame dropped like a sash weight on his head and he collapsed backward, down the steps. Stunned, he crawled backward through the grass, his forehead bloody, holding the broken camera. Behind him in the house Dr. Botewi, mantled with plaster dust and black grime, set to work again prying away the fallen roof trusses, the heat-warped tin, and the smoldering two-by-fours from the old upright piano. The cracked varnish was blistered and peeled; a few tongues of flame still licked at its walnut skirt and charred legs.

McDermott searched the riverbank, the village, and the clinic. As he climbed back toward the cottage, the German pilot called to him from the kitchen window. "No one. She's not here. Just a madman in front." Osgood sat on the grass in the front lawn, dazedly holding his bloody head. McDermott circled the garden, went through the rows of beans and tomatoes, and finally climbed the fence and ran out on the track. Remembering Mustapha's launch, he moved on, taking the same path the Anya-nya took as they returned to the Sudan. Fifty yards beyond he stopped, turning to look back toward the cottage. *It's no good*, he thought. *She must be in the village somewhere, or with the refugees.* But the house would have been burning, the village too. Where else could she have gone? He turned back along the track, moving toward the border. Rounding a curve he saw her, a hundred feet ahead of him, lying facedown along the track, wearing her white shirt and khaki skirt. As he sprinted forward, he also saw the dark brown stain lying across her shoulders. Crouching down beside her, he saw where the blood had gathered, bright and red, along the waist of her blouse as she lay on the path, her body curved as if protecting something.

"It's all right," he whispered hoarsely, struggling to recover his breath, sweat burning his eyes. "It's all right now." But as he touched her unyielding shoulder, he knew it wasn't all right, but his voice continued painfully. "It'll be all right now—all right."

He took her wrist to find the pulse, and as he did he heard a small cry of life. Leaning forward, he saw the dusty, puckered face of the black baby lying under her, its shining eyes gazing up at him. The blouse was wet where the baby had tried to suckle from the loose drape of sleeve. Her body was still stiffly curved against the living form of the child lying in the blue blanket. McDermott touched her shoulders again. Although he wanted to believe that she had heard the sound of his voice or even the sound of the plane, he knew that she hadn't. He knew that even as they'd left Addis that morning, her mind was already gone and she was hovering over the trees the way the hawks were hovering, high on the morning wind, looking down and seeing her figure stretched out on the path, her bloodstained blouse and dark hair: seeing only herself and the small child lying together on the narrow path Samuel Eko had taken that night he had gone and left them there, abandoned at the edge of the grasslands on the banks of the Baro.

NINETEEN

McDermott didn't talk about it—not with Penny, not with Rozewicz, not with anyone else. Nothing had ever affected him that way. Penny knew something was wrong. She was hurt and confused. "Did you love her? I'd understand if you did. You know I will. Only you've got to talk about it. You've got to—for your own good. I won't get mad or anything."

But he didn't talk about it, and she had no time to draw him out. She'd received a telegram from her family in San Francisco telling her that her grandmother had suffered a stroke and was in serious condition. Although she'd bought a plane ticket the same day she'd received the telegram, she began to reconsider the same evening, unwilling to leave McDermott alone. He told her that she should go. As they drove to the airport the following morning, she changed her mind again, but McDermott drove on. At the ticket counter, her backpack only a few feet from the weigh-in scale, she changed her mind again, but McDermott lifted the backpack to the scale himself. "What if I told you I was pregnant?" she said suddenly.

"It's your grandmother, Penny. You'll regret it if you don't go. You know that."

"I know. Of course I know. That's the problem. But what if I told you I was pregnant?"

"What if I told you I had eight kids in the Kansas City orphanage."

"Maybe we could start our own orchard in Oregon—fruit pickers and everything."

As they waited for the flight to be called, she said that the trip would give her the chance to look at rural and mountain properties in northern California. "Don't you think that would be a good idea? That way we could see what we could afford."

"Sure. Go ahead."

But he didn't seem enthusiastic. "Don't think you're sending me on a wild-goose chase," she told him as the flight was called. "Because I'm coming back. If I don't hear from you in a month I'm coming back."

"You'll hear from me," he promised.

"You're sure?"

"I'm sure."

He kissed her. She turned away quickly and was gone through the gate.

He flew down through the rain clouds to the Moquo station for the burial service, delayed over a week because of the family's uncertainty as to whether to return her body to Vermont or have her buried in Africa. It was a bright, sunny day along the hills and savannahs below the escarpment. He flew a chartered Cessna and was alone. A few other aircraft were lined up along the strip, including the UN charter. He didn't go into the chapel for the services but waited outside in the grassy yard, standing far enough from the obsequies to escape Osgood's voice.

Emily was buried in the small, tree-shaded graveyard near the chapel. McDermott stood silently at the edge of the crowd, but as the plain wooden box was lowered into the ground and a few of the missionary women lost control of themselves, McDermott turned and went back out through the sunshine and stood near the plane, not wanting to be a part of their grief. He was standing on the field, still looking west as the services ended. As he opened the cabin door to return to Addis, a missionary wife came running across the field, calling his name, sent to summon him for the baptism of Samuel Eko's child in the chapel. The timing had been Reverend Osgood's, she explained: one life given for another—an end and a beginning. The young woman's words made no impression on McDermott. He didn't know her and her existence meant even less to him than that of the child, who no longer belonged to Samuel Eko, or even to Africa, but to the Moquo station and its missionaries.

He told her he wouldn't be attending. His plane lifted from the field at the same moment Samuel Eko's son was brought into the chapel for baptism in the arms of Bertha Ivy. Osgood paused until the sound of the plane's engines died away before he began the service.

McDermott flew another mission into the Sudan from Sudi, using a Beechcraft brought up from Nairobi. He flew it because there was no one else to fly. The Ethiopians had postponed use of the Baro strip by the DC-3 for another three months because of the burning of the village and the mission house. An inquiry was underway. Cohen had brought a German-born Israeli down from Tel Aviv to take over for McDermott during that time, but he'd taken one look at the Sudi strip from the air and decided he had better things to do.

Passing over the embers of the Baro station on that final flight, McDermott could hardly bring himself to look down over the moon-lit savannah at the wreckage lying under the trees. When he did, he discovered on the landscape below what was already in his mind and heart. Her death had robbed him of whatever reason he could find for still being in Africa. But before he left, he knew he must see the Baro mission once more in sunlight, with the savannah wind blowing and the leaves stirring their shadows across the lawn, if he was to find any relief at all from the poisonous root that had already begun to grow in her absence.

The Ethiopian military had stationed troops at Baro for a few weeks after the burning of the village, but had finally withdrawn them. The retreating soldiers had dug a few shallow trenches across the strip and left oil drums on the runway, but the trenches were poorly placed, and the wind and baboons had scattered the empty drums. On a warm, sunny afternoon with a light breeze blowing in from the northeast, McDermott descended to the Baro field for the last time.

He was alone, the Uzi and gun belt strapped in the seat next to him. The savannah wind blew through the sheltering trees along the fence and stirred the black dust under the charred timbers of the cottage. Blue and white anemones lifted their blossoms from the rubble of brick along the foundation wall. A dangling roof tin rattled against a collapsed sash. He moved from the yard to the garden, where the vines and stalks had been stripped of their fruit by the Ethiopian troops, who'd left tobacco papers, ration tins, and excrement among the tomato plants. The wind lifted the leaves overhead as he turned back, scattering broken sunlight across the shaggy, unmown lawn. Standing under the trees, he heard voices, saw faces, remembered silhouettes and shadows, sun soft against warm skin, conversations he had thought forgotten that now returned. When he could stand it no longer, he went blindly out the gate and along the path toward the open savannah, his back to the desolation of the station. He walked far out into the fields, looking at the sky and clouds. The grasses stirred as far as the eye could see. The white bone of moon was already visible in the sky.

He wanted to weep, the way others wept for their dead—for wives, husbands, children, mothers; for crew members dead in their bloody harness, for mothers and daughters bloody and broken in the rubble below. But he knew how cunning the mind was and how clumsy the body that nourished it. He knew how the brain transformed physical exhaustion and surrender into the blood and oxygen of biological reprieve—to persuade the body to weep so that the mind could live, if only to carry out the same acts after the body had recovered the strength to do so. If the mind couldn't rule by strength, it ruled by weakness. McDermott hadn't wept since he was a child. There was no reprieve. The mind had none but its own death; yet McDermott had never sought that. He knew what the others had believed of him—the pharisaical orphanage clerisy; the dull-witted schoolroom psychologists with Ph.D.'s in education; military clinicians and aerospace psychiatrists: that he was solitary, unfeeling, and proud; that he was death-seeking, as Rozewicz believed. They were all wrong.

Distinctly antisocial before Vietnam made him homicidal as well, an Air Force psychiatrist had written for the prosecution during his court-martial in Thailand, but which the board had suppressed. McDermott had read their eyes, guessed their thoughts, and heard their words long before Vietnam. He knew what they thought, but their thoughts didn't matter, just as their poisonous mediocrity didn't matter. Not until now. She had mattered, but now she was dead, as much a victim of their mindlessness as he had been, but without his defenses.

He stood looking out over the grasslands, looked toward the track where he had found her, and watched a bustard rise, following it with his eyes as it drifted out over the trees and soared higher on the currents rising from the river. He had forgotten the river. He went back along the fence and down the path and stood on the bank, watching the wide, swift current.

Far down the bank the old crocodile lay on the mud shoal, his ugly jaws open. "Old grandfather," McDermott said, but as he did he heard Emily's voice speaking the same words and his voice broke. He waited until he could say it easily—"old grandfather"—and stood afterward looking at the ancient reptile lying motionless against the rotting sorghum stalks. The flood of coffee-colored water carried his eyes away and he stood for one last time watching the Baro move past him on its great journey toward the Nile.

He walked down the bank and turned up the path toward the cottage.

Hey! What about me!

He heard the voice carry across the river, as clear as a bell, and turned and looked back. The wind had moved higher in the trees. There was no one. He turned back to the path.

Hey, wait for me, for God's sake, the voice came again. *This is the Planet of the Apes, man. What are you gonna do now, zap the universe?* He climbed up along the fence without turning back. In the weeds next to the fence he saw a small portable radio. It had been smashed. *So they're stupid and mediocre. So what else is new?* He stood looking at the broken radio. Lifting his eyes at last, he saw to the east the three rising columns of dust lifting in the wind as the trucks raced toward the Baro station. For an instant the wind carried the sound of their engines. *What about me. C'mon. Talk to me for a change. Just because you can fly five miles high doesn't mean I'm an ant or a bug too. What are you trying to do, anyway? Be some kind of space-age Johnny Appleseed, giving astronomy lessons to the stars?*

He walked back to the plane, climbed to the wing, and looked toward the three plumes of dust. The cabin door was open, the Uzi beyond, but he didn't move as he watched the approaching column, the canvas-covered frames visible above the grass, less than four miles away. This was the way the soldiers would have come that night—too fast, eager for a bloodletting, to reclaim a long resented sanctuary maintained by foreigners—*ferenji*. But darkness had fallen then; the cooking fires would have been lit, the light from the kitchen window showing through the dusk under the trees. He remembered without turning to look, the Uzi in his hands.

It was peaceful across the grasslands—the most beautiful time of day, she would have said. The rich afternoon light was translucent still, the way she would have remembered it, and he tried to think of what she would have wanted him to do, what he could still claim for her, his eyes narrowed against the sun as he still gazed westward, still holding the Uzi, remembering the light distilled to amber across her face and arms, her body stiff on the path, the small, dark eyes gazing up at him from the blue blanket. Puzzled, perplexed, he was no longer looking at the trucks at all.

The trucks caromed across the strip and banged over the shallow trenches, the dust lifting furiously in their wake. The Ethiopian soldiers spilled over the tailgates even before the wheels had stopped, rifles raised. The wind carried the dust back across their wet faces as they scattered blindly across the field, searching for what Ato Tefari and their officers had brought them here to find. A guinea fowl bolted from a small scrub; two grouse erupted from the edge of the field near Samuel Eko's abandoned burrow.

"*Ferenji?*" someone called in confusion.

The wind took the dust and carried it higher, obscuring still the small plane which stood at the edge of the airfield near the burned-out cottage, Ato Tefari's Jeep confronting the man who stood on the wing.

"This field is forbidden!" Ato Tefari called, standing in the rear seat, an officer in a yellow scarf rising with him.

"The plane is confiscated," the officer said.

"*Ferenji!*" an NCO called, summoning his soldiers from the far end of the field and beckoning his soldiers toward the distant plane. But as they jogged forward, a burst of gunfire smashed through the Jeep, ripping the standing figures backward into the dust and then shaking them convulsively afterward. The jerry can of petrol lashed to the rear bumper exploded, drenching them in fire.

It was peaceful out across the grasslands that evening. Along the border a few Nilotic herdsmen had been pursuing a dozen cows and steers which had been scattered from their kraal the night before during a raid on the village. During the late afternoon the first fusillade of distant gunfire from the burned-out mission station to the east rattled against their eardrums like dry sticks breaking, and then more fiercely, like the fury of a prairie fire driven by a hot wind, devouring everything in its path. They retreated to the west at first, forgetting their lost cattle. As they moved, they were followed by a few distant detonations that shook the afternoon sky as the plane exploded, wing tanks blowing flares of fire skyward, and igniting the dry grass nearby. They were still retreating as the dense smoke lifted over the trees. As silence returned to the savannah and dusk fell, the smoke continued to drift, but the moon came out, and afterward, looking back toward the Baro station, they saw nothing except the bright moon over the grasslands. No fires, no wind-lashed curtain of destruction. Nothing at all. But the explosions and the strange fires, now vanished, were far away in another country, and they knew they could never explain them or understand how they happened; so they put them out of their minds—banished them as quickly as the night sky banished a meteor falling across the arc of heavens. They made camp where they stood, gathering up dung chips, sticks, and grasses to heat their kettle, to guard their sleep, and to guide their lost cattle out of the darkness.

www.ingramcontent.com/pod-product-compliance
Lightning Source LLC
Chambersburg PA
CBHW030320200626
46816CB00006BA/1863